Island
SUMMER

Lori Hayes

Bling!
Romance
An imprint of Iron Stream Media

Bling! is an imprint of LPCBooks
a division of Iron Stream Media
100 Missionary Ridge, Birmingham, AL 35242
ShopLPC.com

Library of Congress Control Number: 2021934915

ISBN-13: 978-1-64526-323-4
Ebook ISBN: 978-1-64526-324-1

Praise for *Island Summer*

Lori Hayes' romantic novel *Island Summer* explores what it means to open up to love while letting go of the heartache and baggage of a narcissistic relationship. In her conversational style, internal fears and family drama unfold while readers are charmed with true romance, deepening friendships, and nursing home hijinks. Readers will be swept away with the beauty of the wild island ponies, and they'll want to settle down in Big Cat too, and have coffee with the endearing characters who live there.

~**Naomi Musch**
Author of *The Love Coward* and the *Empire in Pine* series

From page one, *Island Summer* pulls you into the coastal atmosphere. You can smell the salt, feel the wind, hear the calming ocean. And not only that, the flowing writing style will carry you right alongside the characters as they face real-life issues and heartbreak. If you're looking for a romantic beach read, look no further! Keith and Emily's story will certainly touch your heart!

~**Hannah Linder**
Selah Award Finalist and Regency Author

Island Summer by Lori Hayes is a refreshing jaunt to a lovely seaside setting where you can almost smell the salty air and feel the ocean breeze. A grandma's matchmaking skills launch this well-paced romance, providing an afternoon of relaxing reading with an added bonus of ponies! What more can you ask for?

~**Victoria Duerstock**
Award-winning author, speaker, and publisher

I highly recommend *Island Summer* that is intriguing from the beginning and delightful to the end. Lori Hayes blends an entertaining, meaningful story of adventure, and faith, and love

~**Yvonne Lehman**
Author of *Hearts that Survive*: A Novel of the Titanic

DEDICATION

*This book is dedicated to my mother, Marilyn.
She introduced me to writing and to the most
beautiful beaches ever.*

ACKNOWLEDGMENTS

Thank you to Sue Grimshaw for your tireless guidance with early edits on my manuscript. Without you, I wouldn't be where I am today, and for that I owe you a lot. I appreciate your advice and tough but wonderful edits, and for challenging me to rise up to the occasion. I am forever grateful.

Thank you, Del Duduit, for helping me take that big step into traditional publishing, and for encouraging me to be bold. I bet you won't do that again. Smiley face.

And special thanks to my editor, Jessica Nelson, at Iron Stream Media. Thank you for believing in me and taking a chance. You have taught me about refining my writing skills in ways I hadn't imagined, along with adding wonderful suggestions to the story line. I appreciate you and your positive editing style, and I look forward to working together in the future. Thank you for everything.

As always, I thank my mother, Marilyn, for always being willing to read and proofread my drafts before anyone else sees my stories. I love you beyond the moon and back.

Chapter One

This morning's meeting with the Cannon Island National Seashore was crucial. It was step one in laying the incremental foundation for the survival of Keith Stallings' ferry business. But for some reason he was calm, happy even.

Despite the uncertainty of the contract, he hummed to the tune playing on his car stereo as he drove to the meeting. He appreciated the glorious sun, reflecting off the water and enhancing the blue-green hue. Boats motored along with passengers sprawled out on the bows, wearing swimsuits, basking in the sunshine.

He chose a parking spot under a shady tree at the ranger station and strode inside. Meetings were his thing, and he was more than prepared to bid on the job. The park service planned to limit access to Pony Island in the future, and if he won the contract he would be the sole ferry provider to the most profitable island. Keith suspected there was some competition but had a feeling the park service preferred him. Although he knew better than to assume. But the biggest concern was if he could quickly acquire the larger boats needed for the job.

When the receptionist guided him back to a large corner office, he found himself shaking hands with the head honcho, Tony Campen, who stood near his desk. He waved for Keith to have a seat and followed suit.

"I understand you are the owner of *Sea Horse Ferry*?"

"Yes, sir," Keith said, spreading out documentation on the

desk between them. "I have an estimate on a new dock space that will hold more boats, am negotiating costs for two larger boats, and I'm working on acquiring financing from the bank."

Tony studied the material before him. "How fast can you be up and running?"

And there was the sticking point. Keith wasn't sure of an exact date until he knew the financing piece. "I will have an answer about the loan soon. Shouldn't be a problem because I also have an inheritance to use." It wasn't enough money but definitely helped.

"We are looking to move forward as soon as possible." Tony leaned back in his chair and crossed his arms. "I'll be honest, I have one other person bidding on this project in addition to you."

Keith suspected as much. There was a new man in town, Tim Cooper, who owned a large catamaran which provided entertainment cruises. But he didn't know the area or the islands as well as Keith did.

They talked back and forth longer than Keith anticipated, mostly turning the meeting into a tense conversation about tedious requirements. He rubbed the back of his neck to relieve a developing headache, without much luck.

By the time Keith left the building, he was exhausted and hungry. Fast food was a quick and easy option, not that a greasy hamburger sounded ideal. He could handle a fresh salad with grilled chicken, though. Due to the stress he'd been under the past year, what with his father's deadly battle with cancer and his grandma's health challenges, he had gained more than a few pounds. After seeing firsthand the debilitated patients in Gran's rehab center, he made a commitment to adopt a healthier lifestyle. More exercise and eating better were on his radar.

Poor Gran was probably the worst rehab patient ever. She was far too energetic and stubborn to hole up in some rehab center with a broken shoulder and sporting some nasty bruises on her face. By pure determination alone, she would heal faster than average. To her liking, she would be out of there in no time. Keith was in no such hurry. She was safe right where she was.

He drove past the exit to the rehab center while attempting to multitask by eating his salad, something he didn't do well. When he said goodbye to Gran this morning she had practically begged for him to bring her back home. She was independent, but the rehab center was the safest place for her right now. He just needed to convince her.

He pulled his truck into a tight spot across the street from the *Sea Horse Ferry*. The larger dock would require him to move his business to the opposite section of downtown, although relocating wasn't a huge deal, but still something to consider.

He made his way across the quiet road. Before long, Front Street would be crowded with shoppers and people strolling with no purpose other than to fill their souls with ambience and salty air. He wasn't complaining but simply enjoying the quiet life until tourist season picked up.

An attractive brunette caught his eye as she walked into his sister's coffee shop. She had quite a head of wild curls bouncing around. Keith liked curly hair, not that he was looking or anything. But there was something different about her.

She couldn't be local because people who lived here were more relaxed instead of bouncy. But she wore scrubs as if she were heading into work. Maybe she was helping out temporarily at the local hospital, a doctor's office, or the nursing home where Gran had been admitted for short-term rehab. The town of Big Cat seemed to always need medical assistance.

Well, it didn't matter. He had enough issues with the ferry, and since his last escapade with Vicki, dating was no longer his thing.

He waved to Kathy as he passed by the ticket booth. She was an energetic college kid out of school for a semester. She waved back as she attended to patrons paying for a day on Pony Island while they still had access.

Keith headed across the dock. There was almost nothing better than the sound of his shoes slapping against the wooden boards as he made his way to the ferry boat. He loved his job, loved living at the coast.

A squawk pierced the still day. A pelican Keith had named Sam, simply because he looked like a Sam, called out to him. The bird perched on his usual piling, awaiting a late breakfast. He watched closely as Keith stopped in front of him.

"How are you today, buddy?"

Sam stared at him. If a pelican could scrutinize, he was scrutinizing. How did he always know when something was on Keith's mind?

"Trust me, you don't want to hear all my problems."

Squawk.

"Okay, but remember ... you asked." He opened the cooler and pulled out a fish. Sam snapped his beak together in anticipation, and Keith tossed him the fish. It always amazed him how Sam swallowed it whole.

The bird stretched his wings out wide and flapped them several times as if to urge Keith to spill his troubles.

"Fine, but you're one nosy pelican. You don't need to worry yet, but if I don't get the contract, my sales will plummet. If that happens, I'll have to move to a big city to resume my career as an architect and leave the coast behind."

Sam didn't squawk this time, but his beady eyes drilled into Keith's.

"No more fish for you, and no more peaceful sea life for me. There aren't any architect jobs open here. Period." Keith couldn't take Sam's piercing glare any longer. "Well, a man has to make a living, ya know."

Squawk.

"I don't know why I'm talking to a pelican." Keith snapped the cooler closed to make it clear he'd had enough of the discussion. He wasn't used to sharing his thoughts in general, much less with a bird.

"Oh, trust me. You'll love her."

He was not interested in Gran's matchmaking schemes. "I need to run. It's time to take the ferry out." It was the truth but he couldn't wait to hang up the phone. By the time he returned to the rehab center tomorrow, he hoped she'd forget about fixing him up with the woman.

Nice or not, no thanks.

The larger of the two ferry boats he owned pulled into the slip with ease. Captain Bill was an expert, a stellar employee, and one of his father's lifelong friends.

They exchanged a wave.

When the passengers made their way off the dock, and before the next group approached, Captain Bill hopped back on the ferry. "What's on your mind, son?"

Surprised by his own transparency, Keith shrugged. "Just busy thinking, planning my strategy to win the ferry bid."

Captain Bill laughed, a deep rumble caused by years of smoking. He still smoked heavily but reasoned he might as well enjoy the remaining years of his life. You only live once, as he liked to say. He pointed to Sam. "You had a long conversation with our friend there."

He must have seen Keith chatting away with Sam when he pulled in. "So what? I like the bird." Keith's tone was defensive, even to his own ears.

Captain Bill raised his eyebrows. "Hit a nerve, huh?"

Before Keith fired back a witty answer, more passengers approached the boat. He helped an elderly couple step down onto the ferry, followed by a family of four. The man was probably their son, and the kids were likely grandkids. The terrain on the island was rough on seniors but Keith appreciated their interest in the island. A young couple boarded, a somewhat older couple next, and then a large group of friends.

Keith wondered when the park service took over, and the boats were large enough to accommodate more passengers, would more people flock to the quiet island as predicted? Wonderful from a business standpoint but Keith hated to see tourists take over the rustic paradise. More people meant more trash, more disrespect to the horses and nature, more crowded beaches.

After the last passenger boarded, Keith shot Captain Bill a wave as the older man pulled the boat out of the dock. Keith hopped onto the smaller craft he owned. He wiped off the morning dew from the seats and prepared for passengers wanting to tour the other islands in the area. There were several dredging islands scattered among the channel, a few of them only appearing during low tide. One of his favorites, not even close in comparison to Pony Island, was named Sand Dollar Island, another called Shark's Tooth Island. There was even Bear Island, because the shape of the island resembled a bear, as well as Goat Island, where someone had dropped off two goats some years ago and they still roamed the beaches.

He usually serviced the Pony Island route, but since he'd gotten a late start this morning, and because Pony Island was the busiest, Captain Bill had taken the run.

A loud squawk made Keith look up. Sam had flown to the nearest piling by the boat.

"What do you want? You already ate." Keith wished he had saved remnants from his salad to share with the bird as a treat. Sam made a noise again. "I didn't bring you anything. No more French fries, either. I'm not eating those anymore."

The bird studied him.

"Okay, you aren't begging for food. Did you want to continue to harass me?"

The bird squawked.

"Don't worry, I'm not planning to move anytime soon."

Squawk.

At least Captain Bill wasn't there to see him conversing with the bird. Keith gazed past Sam and out at the blue-green water. There was a unique, distorted reflection across the surface from the puffy white clouds overhead with a hint of Carolina blue sky, the ambience a strong reminder of how much he loved working the channel. How could he ever return to a desk job?

His cell phone rang. "Gran, what's wrong?"

"You need to get me out of this old folks' home."

Keith dragged in a long breath, trying to find solace from the peaceful view but no such luck. "I thought you liked it

there? The therapy is outstanding," he reminded her.

"Do you know why they call therapy PT?"

Keith glanced at Sam, who watched him closely from atop the piling, as if he understood the conversation. "Because it's physical therapy?"

"No. It's physical torture. Occupational therapy, OT, stands for 'other torture.' Come get me."

Keith burst out in laughter. "Gran, you need to behave for them."

"Nonsense," she said with determination in her voice. "I need to break out of here tonight. Come pick me up."

"I'll do no such thing," he said with patience in his voice. "It's in your best interest to stay there and receive therapy."

"Everyone is against me," Gran complained.

A change of subject was crucial. "Let's hope at your next ortho appointment your doctor gives you clearance to move your shoulder, so you can start exercises. The sooner that happens, the sooner you can return to your horses." He knew Gran well enough to know she wanted to get home to her animals.

Gran sighed loud enough Keith was sure Sam heard her.

There was no way she was ready. He worked long hou[rs] at the ferry and his sister worked even longer hours at Co[ffee] Break. How would they manage Gran if she returned h[ome] alone with her arm in a sling? Heck, they were barely d[ealing] with things as they were.

"Will you stop by my house and check on my hors[es and bring] the book sitting on my nightstand in the mornin[g? I need] something to do around here."

"Of course," he said. Passengers started mak[ing their way] down the dock toward the boat.

Before he excused himself from the conver[sation,] "By the way, I met the sweetest girl. I can't [wait to tell] you when you come see me."

Silence. "Gran ..." he warned.

Chapter Two

The smell of coffee permeated the quaint little shop and gnawed at my memories. There was nothing better than waking up to the delicious aroma of coffee and sizzling bacon at my grandmother's house when I was a child. I couldn't believe how much I missed her.

"I've seen you in here a couple of times now," the spunky redheaded woman behind the counter said with warmth as she placed a to-go cup of coffee on the counter. "I'm Jenni. Are you new to town?"

I had stopped by the shop yesterday before work, and again this morning.

"Yes, I'm Emily McMillan." I reached forward to shake hands before giving her my credit card. I knew all too well how gossip ran rampant in small towns and was hesitant to say too much. Sure, I wanted to make friends, but needed to heal from my trust issues first.

"Where did you move from?" Jenni asked, ringing up the sale and then handing back my card.

I swallowed hard. "Raleigh." I cringed and hoped the pain of the past would disappear soon.

Even though Raleigh was a good three hours away, it didn't seem far enough.

"Don't be a stranger. I own Coffee Break, so I'm here most of the time. If you ever have questions about the area, just ask. I'll be happy to help you."

"Thanks. I just might take you up on your offer." But no matter how much I wanted to, I knew I wouldn't. I glanced behind me and noticed the line for coffee growing longer. Stepping away from the counter, I said, "Nice meeting you."

More customers filed into the shop, causing the chimes above the door to tinkle almost continuously. Big Cat was a small beach town caught between the present and the past, and it seemed to be traditional, a bit old-fashioned, and filled with southern charm. So far I was in love with it. What a great place to hit the reset button on life.

I stepped outside and breathed in a soothing scent of salty air. A light breeze blew a set of curls around my face and I had to dodge yet another customer entering the popular coffee shop. I caught an earthy whiff of rosemary and thyme growing from several overstuffed clay pots placed along the sidewalk.

Heading toward my car I followed the boardwalk for a short distance, taking in the scenic view of the boats bobbing in the marina. Even the sounds were satisfying, like the flags flapping in the humid breeze, the seagulls singing in a voice, reminding me of only the beach. Perched on a nearby piling, a large pelican watched me. He was likely readying himself to fly off if I made the slightest move toward him.

This was why I retreated to the beach. It had a way of healing one's soul.

As I neared my car, I dodged around another set of clay pots, these filled with colorful petunias, and then climbed into my Camry. Starting the day off with a cup of good coffee, a chat with a friendly shop owner, and a serene view of marina life was far better than waking up to arguments and stress.

Before long I was at work, recalling room numbers and confusing hallways. It was always somewhat nerve-wracking to start a new job, but here I was, ready to work this morning with my physical therapy patients. I muddled along as I greeted other employees with a wave and a smile. One thing for sure, I loved helping the elderly. I assumed because I no longer had grandparents of my own, my job filled a void in my life.

In a hurry to start my day, I turned the hall corner and almost collided with an attractive man with messy sandy-colored hair. He stopped short, then, to my surprise, he reached out to steady me.

"Excuse me," he said, his southern accent thick, as though surprised by my presence.

It was obvious he worked outside, as he sported a golden tan and made me envious. It accentuated the most gorgeous light blue eyes I had ever seen. But temporary lines etched his forehead in a zigzag pattern as though he was concerned about something, or someone.

"Guess I need to slow down," he said with a sexy little half smile.

"No worries." Ugh, that came out like a squeak. Get a grip, Em. He might be handsome, but good looks didn't mean a thing.

I recognized his kind. He was the handsome type who stole a woman's heart. Well, I'd already been there, done that.

But I couldn't help but ask, "Can I help you with something?" I barely knew my way around the building, but the worry lines on his face made me want to at least try.

He shook his head, his eyes intense but kind. "Gran ..." He hesitated as if trying to regain his composure. "This time she broke her right shoulder. She needs more help with the horses but won't listen to reason."

"Horses?" I didn't understand what he was talking about, although the mention of horses grabbed my attention. As far back as my early childhood, I had always wanted one.

He shifted his weight to one side in a casual way, appearing to relax. "I know I'm rambling but my gran manages a dozen or so of the wild horses. They are rescues from Pony Island."

Printed on his t-shirt were the words *Sea Horse Ferry*. Not wanting to appear clueless, but curious about the area I'd just moved to, I said, "I don't know much about them." When his eyebrows arched, I felt the need to explain. "I moved here last weekend. But if you're looking for your grandmother's room I might be able to help you out."

"Thanks, but I definitely know where she is. Guess I have a lot on my mind and was distracted when I almost bumped into you." He fiddled in his pocket, pulled out a business card, and handed it to me. "There are close to 120 wild horses on a small, deserted island just off our coast, in case you're interested. When you've settled in, I'll take you to the island for a tour."

Was he asking me out on a date, or drumming up business?

It didn't really matter. I needed to concentrate on work. The last thing I wanted was to involve a man in my complicated life.

"I appreciate it." I reached out and took the card from him. A personal tour of the island did sound fun but then a wave of panic darted through me. I vacillated between the desire to run in the opposite direction, or to continue to stand there and talk to him. I reminded myself he was here to see his grandmother and I had a job to do, so I took a small step backward. To my surprise and relief, he did so as well.

"I hope to see you soon." He smiled and waved at me, no longer the preoccupied man who'd almost collided with me moments before.

Thank goodness we parted ways. As I headed down the hallway in the opposite direction, I managed to locate my first patient's room, but Ms. Daniel was still in bed eating breakfast.

"Hi, I'm Emily with physical therapy." I reached out to shake the older woman's hand and noted her kind eyes.

Ms. Daniel set down her fork, and with a grin, she shook hands with me. "Good morning. I should be dressed and ready to go in about an hour. I'm not going to shower today but just run a washcloth over myself. A bird bath, if you will."

I grinned, loving the way my patients had no problem telling me every detail. Sometimes it bordered on too much information. "All right. I'll see someone else first and I'll be back soon."

I reentered the quiet hallway, and found the next room number somewhat easily. Unfortunately for me, the man was in the shower with the assistance of his occupational therapist.

Glancing over my schedule, I retraced my steps in search of the next patient on my list. Thank heaven for the fancy plaques hanging on the walls of each hallway with the range of room numbers emblazoned in silver. Somehow I found myself back on the same hall where I had almost collided with the handsome man. I slipped his business card out of my pocket and for the first time I glanced at his name. *Keith Stallings, Sea Horse Ferry, Owner.*

I shoved the card back into my pocket. I had no time for ferry rides with men, business or not. One of the main reasons I moved here was to get away from my ex-fiancé, ex-pain-in-the-heart. Frank Coleman had been the love of my life and I had been crushed when he left me for my best friend. Along with my dad walking out on us when we were kids, it was a vast understatement to say I had abandonment issues. Was it too much to ask for the men I loved to treat me right and to stay around? Everyone I loved always left me.

I strolled down the hallway. Sighing, I stopped in front of my next patient's room. *Geraldine Stallings* was written in elegant script on the nameplate. Sure enough, Keith was relaxed in the recliner next to her bed with his ankle resting across the opposite knee. I tapped lightly on the door.

"Physical therapy," I announced as I entered the room.

"Emily, we meet again. And this is my grandson, Keith." Ms. Stallings glanced between us with a conniving grin on her face.

Oh, heck no. I wasn't about to have his grandmother set me up.

A pitiful purple bruise covered a large portion of her right eye, along with her right arm tucked away in an asymmetrical sling. She sported a colorful dress with bright fuchsia, yellow, and white oversized flowers, colors my own grandmother would have worn. My heart did a little squeeze.

"Nice to meet you again," I said to him, flashing a tiny wave. Suddenly I felt awkward and couldn't wait to leave.

"When are they going to learn how to cook real food?" Ms. Stallings asked, placing the lid back on the breakfast dish.

"Gran," Keith cautioned.

I couldn't help but smile, and even though she was ornery, I liked the spunky woman. From my peripheral vision I saw Keith studying me. Another day, another time, I might have been interested in him. Instead I focused on the intriguing woman sitting in front of me.

"Can you help me fix this blasted sling?" Ms. Stallings asked as she pulled against the misplaced material. She wore a mischievous grin, and I was sure she was up to no good. "You can't get help around here from the staff when you need it," she said. "I'd be better off at home."

"You need to stay here, Gran." Keith's voice sounded exasperated. More than likely he had experienced the conversation repeatedly with his grandmother. "You have no help at home."

I raised my eyebrows at Keith, who met my gaze, a small smile escaping his lips. He had to be around my age, I guessed, or at least he didn't look any older.

"I'll hire someone. I don't want to be in an old folks' home."

I cringed. "It's a rehab center, and your stay here is short-term." When she stared at me, I added, "The objective of skilled nursing rehab is to offer you more intensive rehabilitation, far more than you would receive at home." The rehab center was known for the best therapy in the area and had been my first choice of places to work. "My goal is to discharge you home safely as soon as possible." I wanted to offer her hope.

Ms. Stallings glared at her grandson. "Did you hear what she said? I'm here short-term." She pointed a crooked finger at him but glared at me. "I'll leave when you decide I'm ready, not when he thinks I am." She jabbed her finger toward him.

To Keith's credit, he remained calm and continued to lean back against the recliner. I had worked in therapy long enough to notice when someone was exhausted. I agreed with him about keeping his grandmother at the facility longer, but with the challenges ahead, she would likely need assistance at home until her shoulder was no longer immobilized.

"The sling, please," Ms. Stallings redirected the conversation back to the issue at hand.

When I removed the sling, I noticed the swollen arm was also splotchy with ugly purple bruises. The poor lady.

I tugged at the fabric to adjust the sling so it better supported her shoulder. I could only imagine how traumatic the fall was for her, not to mention for her family. According to the chart, she had tripped over a large tree root on her way to the barn. She had no cell phone in her pocket and had lain there for four hours until someone discovered her slumped body on the ground.

"Let's walk to one of the living rooms," I said to progress the therapy session.

Keith stood up. "Gran, I'm going to leave. I need to get back to the ferry."

"Fine, but hear me out first," Ms. Stallings said with her crooked finger pointed at him again. "Get the contract with the park service, so you are the one providing the ferry transportation."

Keith frowned. "It's not that simple."

Ms. Stallings grabbed her cane from the side of the bed and stood. "Figure out a way. If you don't, they'll run you out of business." She headed for the door and I stopped her long enough to wrap a gait belt around her waist for added security. I suspected her balance was fairly good with the cane, but until I knew for sure, I wanted the belt to hold onto.

Keith kissed the top of his grandmother's head. "Behave for Emily."

The gentle but sexy way he said my name, the tender way

he kissed his grandmother's head, made my cheeks burn hot. I turned away so no one would notice. Keith touched my arm for the second time this morning and thanked me for helping his grandmother. If he noticed my embarrassment he didn't let on, and within a moment he was out the door. I held onto Ms. Stallings' gait belt with one hand and slipped my free one into my pocket to finger the business card.

Ms. Stallings attempted to walk with the cane for a short distance but became frustrated. "I'm not using this blasted thing." She handed me the cane.

The device offered more support but I understood the difficulty in using a nondominant hand for the cane. Besides, she needed it free to tend to her animals.

"Let's try without." I carried the cane and continued to hold onto her in case she lost her balance.

She walked the short distance to a small living room across from the coffee bar. To my surprise, her balance was fairly good but I wanted to discover more about her recent falls.

"Would you like a cup of coffee?" I asked.

"It doesn't taste as delicious as mine at home, but I'd enjoy a cup," she said, eyeing the nearest bench. "Regular with two creams and a packet of real sugar. I don't use artificial crap." Ms. Stallings chose the padded bench near the glass birdcage. "You're drinking a cup too?"

I didn't know the rules of the rehab center but didn't want to offend Ms. Stallings, either. "A rest break sounds wonderful." I poured two cups and returned to her.

She took one from me and held it on her lap. "You probably don't know but my granddaughter owns Coffee Break."

"So it makes sense why you love quality coffee." No doubt the cozy shop served some of the best I'd ever tasted. It was fast becoming my favorite place to write.

And writing was my habit lately. My biggest dream was to obtain a literary agent, who would sell my love stories to one of the big publishers in New York—although I wasn't an authority on either subject.

Think like an eagle, my father always told me. *Don't compare yourself to others and be brave. Aim high, write the best stories you can, and you'll be successful.* Though good advice, overall I held a lot of unresolved anger toward him. It was an ongoing theme with my family in general, and why this beach town brought me some much needed solace. I loved the idea of living here alone and away from the drama.

"My grandson is a handful, but I think the two of you would be wonderful together," Ms. Stallings said before taking a small sip. "Wow, hot." She popped off the lid and blew on the caramel-colored liquid.

Did she really just say that about Keith and me? I didn't know how to answer the comment, so I chose the safer choice and remained quiet.

"He's an architect, you know. He lost his job and had trouble finding another high-paying one in this area. He didn't want to move from the beach, so he decided to buy the *Sea Horse Ferry* in the meantime." Ms. Stallings blew into the cup. "But if he doesn't win the ferry bid, he's going to have to move."

Heed her warning. I needed to avoid getting involved with anyone who'd move away and break my heart. Once was enough, thank you.

She held up her cup at me. "But will he listen to reason? The boy needs to date again."

Ms. Stallings was the handful, not her grandson. I hoped someday I held zip and zest like her. Actually, I needed those qualities back in my life now.

Two vibrant women strode toward us. Not knowing I'd already met Jenni, Ms. Stallings introduced us. I noticed how much she resembled her grandmother.

Ms. Stallings leaned forward to receive a kiss on the cheek, and then pulled away to look up at Jenni. "We were just talking about your delicious coffee."

Jenni smiled in answer but focused her attention on me.

"It's nice to see you again so soon. I'm on break and thought I'd come to see Gran." She opened her hand toward her friend standing nearby. "This is Claire Rhoades, our very own wildlife photographer. You might have seen her studio down the street from my coffee shop." Claire was possibly about my age as well.

Oh, I had seen her gorgeous pictures all right. I stretched out my arm and shook hands with her. As I had adored Ms. Stallings right away, I also liked both of these women. "I've been in your studio and your photographs are gorgeous." My words didn't begin to describe her work. Claire captured the most unique shots of wild horses. I assumed they were the ones from the island Keith mentioned earlier.

"Thank you," she said, smiling as though embarrassed. "Have you visited Pony Island yet?"

"No, but I plan to." My curiosity about the wild horses was growing.

"You need to go see my brother," Jenni said. "There is nothing quite like taking his small passenger ferry out to the deserted island. The scenic view is an experience alone." Jenni's facial features lit up with excitement when she talked about the horses. "There aren't a lot of people touring the island this time of year with school still in session. More importantly, you'll avoid the bugs since it isn't too hot yet."

Gran flashed her conniving grin again. There was absolutely no way I wanted to date anytime soon, especially not one of my patient's grandsons.

Claire added, "The island is rustic, pretty much desolate. The sand is white with water so green you'll think you're on a Caribbean island."

"Now I have to visit," I said, my curiosity piqued even more, despite the mention of Keith.

"When you're ready, we'll go with you," Claire offered. "I'm always looking for an excuse to take photographs of the horses. My husband, Jeff, is the ranger on the island."

I almost felt at home in Big Cat. The town was named after

a rampant rumor that flew through town about a big cougar running loose down Front Street. The more I heard about the area, the more I fell in love with its nuances.

"And I'll show you my rescue horses when you let me leave this place," Ms. Stallings said, bringing the attention back to her. "By the way, they are called Banker Ponies."

I smiled at the older woman. "I'll get you back home to your Banker Ponies as soon as possible."

"Is that a promise?" Ms. Stallings asked.

"Yes, ma'am." In the meantime, I needed to plan a day trip to Pony Island. But the question was who I would choose as my tour guide, if anyone.

Chapter Three

The next day I spent most of the morning avoiding Ms. Stallings and her family.

Instead, I worked with Mr. Hardy, a man with stark white hair, faded overalls and a pocket torn off. He worked his way back to his room in slow motion as I walked next to him. At least he was walking. He'd had a long stay at the hospital after a tractor accident, the machine actually falling on him. With everything he had lived through so far, he was a miracle.

"I can't wait to leave," he said to me.

"I'm happy for you. Even though you are going to an assisted living now, you know how I feel about leaving so soon." Despite my recommendation for him to stay at the rehab center longer, his daughter planned to pick him up first thing in the morning. He had his bags packed and waiting by his bed.

We turned left at the next hallway just as Keith entered his grandmother's room a few doors down. And Ms. Stallings was next on my schedule.

As I often said to myself, looks weren't everything. That was what got me into trouble before. My plan was to take the necessary time off from my past relationship to work on myself, to finish the book I was writing, to have the much-needed freedom I deserved. Relationships required time. Right now I wanted *Emily* time and was tired of expending effort on an unappreciative man. As my mother always said, "You get what you put into it." But her advice was contrary to my latest experience.

So why was my heart pounding? Well, I did have issues with anxiety. Yep, that was it.

"What are you thinking about?" Mr. Hardy asked, startling me out of my deep thoughts.

"Nothing at all." I concentrated on his gait and plastered the usual professional mask on my face.

"Ah, come on. Let me in on your secret," he said. "I recognize the thoughtful look. I've been married for forty years."

What look? I was horrified. "Forty years is a long time," I said, changing the subject with awe in my voice. "What's the secret to a happy marriage?"

"A man needs to say *yes ma'am* and do whatever his wife asks." His chuckle made me laugh with him.

"What's the real truth?"

"Never go to bed mad, always kiss before you fall asleep, no matter how mad you are. Loving someone and putting them first." He reached his doorway, directly across the hall from Ms. Stallings. I noticed Keith sitting in his grandmother's recliner and glanced away before our eyes met. Mr. Hardy rolled the walker into his room and plopped in the recliner.

"Let's try again," I corrected. "Keep inside your walker when you turn. And reach back for your chair so you know where it is, and it doesn't move." I had the same conversation countless times a day but I didn't mind. "I won't mention what could happen."

"You're right." He pulled the device in front of him, stood back up, and demonstrated the correct technique to sit down safely. "Happy now?"

"Much better." I glanced at my schedule to make sure Ms. Stallings was actually my next patient. And she was. I glanced back up at Mr. Hardy. "Good luck and be safe at your new assisted living. I enjoyed working with you, but I don't want to see you back here." I winked at him.

"Point taken." He hit the arrow on the controller and reclined the chair. "You excel at your job, Emily. You're a good girl. Hold out for the right man and don't *settle.*"

The wisdom hit a nerve. I forced myself to swallow and not react. No more thinking about the past. Cheers to a new future.

I squeezed his hand. "Best of luck. You'll do great."

I left the room and started across the hall but more anxiety danced through me from seeing Keith again. Before I knocked on the door I inhaled a long breath.

"Hi, Emily! Come in," Ms. Stallings exclaimed. "Perfect timing." She grinned at her grandson, who was sitting upright in the recliner.

"Good morning," I said with a lighthearted tone I didn't feel. The sweet, perky woman wore another wild, flowered outfit and was sitting on the edge of the bed. I risked a glance at Keith but before I could hide it, a small smile escaped my lips. "Hi there."

He wore a bright grin as he shot his hand upward in a half wave. No words were necessary.

I glanced back at Ms. Stallings. "How is my favorite patient today?"

She pointed a wrinkled finger at Keith. "Not so good. He won't help me break out of here. I've asked, threatened, and begged him but he's as stubborn as his father was."

Pain flashed across Keith's face so fast I almost missed it.

"And you, Gran, are my father's mother," he said. "So you are just as stubborn."

She cackled with laughter. "He's right, Emily. I'm stubborn."

I enjoyed the playful camaraderie between them. Not only did I miss my own grandma, I wished my family was as close as Keith's. My mother and sister lived in Mexico, a short-term plan and more of a hiatus than a living arrangement. Nevertheless, they were a lot alike and I didn't really get along well with my sister.

If anyone asked me about my father, that situation was even more complicated. Not only had he walked out on us when I was little, he moved a couple of states away and was remarried with two kids half my age.

Enough already. I redirected my attention back to Ms. Stallings, who had settled on the bed by sinking onto her left side and resting on her elbow. "Let's take your stubborn streak and put it to work," I suggested, playing off the words they used. "By climbing steps today."

Keith's laugh was a low, warm rumble.

Ms. Stallings stared at me. "Did you know PT stands for physical torture? I heard another patient say that."

I laughed, but I heard the comment so often I was no longer offended.

"Absolutely," I joked, going along with the charade. "While we're at it, we'll get down and do fifty pushups, one-handed, of course. If all goes well, we can try a few cartwheels."

Both Ms. Stallings and Keith laughed.

"This girl has spunk. I like her," she said, sending Keith a pointed look as if he needed assistance in noticing my humorous attributes.

I couldn't help but wonder if Ms. Stallings was further interviewing me as a potential match for Keith. The thought was rather horrifying.

Keith sat forward, looking like he was ready to spring from the chair to escape the room.

I shared his obvious desire to flee. The previous playful banter turned awkward. It was my job to fill the silence.

"Ready?" I asked.

"For the pushups or the cartwheels?" Ms. Stallings asked with exaggerated interest. She appeared to enjoy the interaction between us, unaware of the disturbing tension in the room.

"Let's start with walking down the hallway." I wrapped the gait belt around her and made a point to be extra gentle when placing it under the sling. "Then we'll work on steps." We had a makeshift staircase in the gym with a railing on each side. "Yours at home . . . how many do you have, and what side is the railing on?"

"I have four Keith rebuilt because they were rotting." Ms. Stallings flashed him a look of appreciation. "He's good at building things. Of course, he would be because he's an architect."

I ignored the reference to Keith and her matchmaking tactics. "Railings?"

"One on each side," Keith answered.

"Perfect." I waited close by as she stood. "By the way, I like your colorful outfit today. It's one of those feel-good dresses."

"It makes me think I'm forty-five years old." Ms. Stallings followed my lead and stepped forward without the cane as I held onto the belt to ensure she had good balance.

This morning Keith hung around while his grandmother participated in therapy. I was warming up slowly to his presence in the most disturbing way.

The three of us walked out the doorway and down the hall until Ms. Stallings had to stop for a sequence of standing rest breaks. I educated her again on breathing techniques to keep her from growing so fatigued.

When she caught her breath, she asked me, "When are you making a trip out to the island?"

"What island?" My attention was on therapy and I had no idea what she was asking.

"Pony Island. Remember the wild horses we talked about yesterday?"

"Oh, yes," I said, slightly amused she was correcting my memory. "Maybe I'll venture out there this weekend." After all, I needed to do something other than unpacking boxes and writing. I had boxed up my apartment in Raleigh quickly to move down here, but unpacking was going much slower.

"You have my card," Keith said. "I'll be working the ferry

Saturday."

Ms. Stallings snapped her fingers. "I forgot, Captain Bill is off because of his daughter's wedding. You do plan to go, don't you?" she asked Keith.

He shrugged.

She shot him a pointed look. "Yes, you do. It's important." Ms. Stallings stood taller as if she were going to start walking again but hesitated. "Take Emily with you, so you have a date. God only knows, it's past time."

My mouth dropped open. Take *me* to the wedding? What was she talking about? Another awkward moment passed between us.

Keith glanced at me, his gaze fixed on mine. "It's last minute, but will you accompany me Saturday night?"

The breath squeezed out of my lungs. I barely knew him, wasn't sure I was prepared to interact with him for an entire night. And I didn't know who Captain Bill was, or his daughter.

"Sure, I'll go." The words slipped out of my mouth before I could stop them. I resisted the urge to tell him I didn't want to date anyone, let alone my patient's grandson. Not that this was a date. I was simply helping Ms. Stallings and Keith out with a problem.

"Hot dang," Ms. Stallings exclaimed. She began walking again for another fifty feet until she became winded.

"Do you need to sit down?" I asked, pointing to a padded bench nestled in a small alcove.

"Yes," she said and headed toward the bench.

When she sat, I planted myself next to her, and Keith hovered nearby. I pretended not to notice his developed biceps, or his toned chest. It was too easy to see the fine definition through his shirt. And I tried to ignore his calves. I bet he was a runner, and if I wagered a bet, I would say he wore shorts year-round unless the temperature outside dropped to below freezing.

Not a date. But my mind argued not to be like my mother,

who was older and alone.

"I want a selfie," she demanded. "You know, to prove you went."

"Why wouldn't we go?" Keith asked, shaking his head.

Ms. Stallings rolled her eyes. "You just might be trying to make an old woman happy."

There was a lot of truth in her words. But still, she added a bunch of pressure to an already tense situation.

Keith studied me. "Want to meet somewhere first to get to know each other better?"

While I found his enthusiasm interesting, the conversation was more than uncomfortable. Especially in front of his grandmother.

"Sure," I said with feigned nonchalance and stood to encourage Ms. Stallings to continue walking to the rehab gym.

"Coffee on Thursday evening, or dinner Friday night?" he asked. He was direct, and it made me nervous.

"Both," Ms. Stallings answered for me.

"Both works," Keith said, grinning. "Let's start with coffee at my sister's shop on Thursday. It's the best around. Then, we can do dinner Friday night, or maybe a tour of Pony Island on Sunday."

And a wedding Saturday night? I tried to fight off a rising wave of panic.

Here I was trying to heal from a disastrous relationship, and yet I had agreed to a series of terrifying yet simple dates in order to pacify his grandmother.

I must be crazy to agree but replied, "Okay."

All I needed to do was focus on date number one. Coffee. If it didn't go well, I would be off the hook for the wedding.

Chapter Four

Keith was on uncomfortable ground. This was his first date in over a year with someone he had possible interest in.

The past year had been one of change. On a positive note, he had acquired the ferry, bought another service boat, and developed a closer bond with his sister, Jenni. And he was still working on his relationship with his mother.

Thinking about her, he made a mental note to stop by for a visit tonight after work. With all due respect, she had to overcome several huge adjustments over the past year in dealing with her husband's death. To Keith's surprise she was embracing her freedom, of which he had mixed feelings. He was happy she was thriving and becoming independent, but he wasn't ready to see her date again. Keith's loyalty belonged to his father.

He parked on the street and to his delight, a line was already forming at the ferry booth. Most customers wanted to spend the day on Pony Island as opposed to a smaller one, the horses a huge draw. As Gran had said, he had to find a way to win the bid.

Keith climbed from the truck and with a little extra vibrancy in his stride, he made his way to the dock. He waved to Kathy, who was working as fast as she could to sell tickets. Despite the hectic pace required at certain times of the day, she always smiled. Customer service was Keith's motto, and apparently hers as well. In his opinion, it could make or break a business.

He headed toward the ferry, the wooden planks of the dock

squeaking under his feet. Sam wasn't perched on his favorite piling yet for his morning snack, although Keith was a bit early.

Captain Bill was busy readying the smaller ferry for departure. People flocked to the islands first thing in the morning to fill their bags with big shells and random finds. Keith raised his index finger at him.

Captain Bill wagged the cloth at him that he was using to wipe off the seats. "Good mornin'."

"You too," Keith said, stepping onto the larger boat. He had about twenty-five minutes to ready the passenger ferry for the ride but they weren't running every half hour yet until tourist season picked up. Once it grew hotter outside, and when school let out for the summer, business would increase. The demand was heaviest on the weekends for now and Keith had another captain who helped out during the busier times, so he could have weekends off whenever possible. During the summer the ferry stayed busy daily.

Sam flew over the boat, squawked as he passed by, and landed on the nearest piling.

"I swear you know my schedule better than I do," Keith said to the pelican. He climbed off the boat and strolled over to the large white cooler. The bird hopped down onto the dock, pacing back and forth. "You're spoiled. Don't you know you're wild and not my pet?"

Squawk.

Keith pulled a fish from the cooler and tossed it to him. Sam caught it with his bill, tossed it into the air, and then swallowed it whole. Keith grinned. Another benefit to living on the coast was he had access to fresh fish, which he paid a local fisherman to provide for Sam. The habit was becoming expensive but Sam deserved the best. He was a loyal friend and a good listener.

Sam squawked repeatedly.

"Why are you making all that racket?" Keith leaned against the piling nearest the cooler. The bird wasn't interested in more fish but was interested in gossip. *His* gossip.

Squawk.

Keith swore Sam was smiling.

"What's so funny? Just because I'm in a good mood today is no reason to laugh."

The pelican continued to mock him.

"Okay, so I met this woman. She's new to town," Keith said. The pelican opened his beak wide and then snapped it shut. "What's so funny?" He glanced at Captain Bill, who was preoccupied behind the helm of the boat and out of earshot.

Squawk.

"You want to know about the girl?"

Sam cocked his head to the side as if listening.

"Okay, the truth," Keith said. "I asked her out. I probably overdid it, though."

Squawk.

"How? I asked her to be my date to a wedding Saturday night. But I didn't leave it there. I invited her for coffee and possibly dinner, and maybe a tour of the island. Heck, I don't have time to date, nor do I want to." He was just trying to appease Gran.

Sam flew from the dock back to the same piling he usually perched on.

"I don't need therapy when I have you to talk to," Keith said. Sam remained silent but continued to watch Keith. "Say something," Keith ordered.

"I say you're crazy talking to a bird," Captain Bill said from behind.

Keith turned around, startled. He had no idea Captain Bill had climbed onto the dock and was listening in on his private conversation. "I thought you were on your boat." Keith sounded grumpy and hoped the captain would back off. It was a game they often played back and forth.

"I was, but it's much more fun to listen to you talk to a bird." Captain Bill laughed in his deep, rumbly cough laugh.

"You were eavesdropping," Keith said in a defensive tone. He snapped the lid in place on the cooler. His feathered friend had eaten enough fish.

"So you're bringing a date to my daughter's wedding?"

Keith shrugged. Apparently Bill had overheard the entire conversation.

"Wonderful. About time you ask someone out." Bill strolled away toward the boat in anticipation of the crowd about to flock upon them. He called back over his shoulder. "And your pelican is right. Buck up and stop being afraid. Love is worth it." He hopped onto the awaiting ferry. The man always liked the last word.

Passengers flooded the dock and filled Captain Bill's boat. When he started the engine, bound for the little islands, Keith flagged his hand to send him off. Bill raised his arm in the air as he navigated away from the dock. The next group of tourists filled Keith's boat, their destination Pony Island.

The morning was sunny, sporting a bright blue, cloudless sky. Once the skiff started moving, though, the slight chill on the breeze made Keith zip up his lightweight jacket. Sam flew behind them for a short distance before he changed direction and disappeared into the channel.

Turning on the microphone Keith filled the tourists' ears with romantic legends of how the wild horses possibly swam ashore from sinking Spanish galleons after hitting hazardous shoals off the North Carolina coast. Locals called it *The Graveyard of the Atlantic*. One theory regarding the horses consisted of people using the island to allow their equines to graze and perhaps abandoning them on the land, but there was genetic testing linking the horses to an extinct Spanish breed. The horses had occupied the island for so many years, some locals even believed they were native to the area.

Pony Island itself was interesting. At one point English descendants settled there, and by the mid 1800s several hundred people took up residence and it became a whaling community.

Eventually they evacuated due to numerous hurricanes, one large debilitating storm, in particular. In Keith's opinion, the island was the best-kept secret of the North Carolina coast.

Keith preferred to keep it a secret as long as possible and resisted commercialism in general. At the same time he made a living off tourism. As far as Keith was concerned, there was a fine line between protecting the island with its horses and making a living, a line he preferred not to blur. The horses were always his priority.

He shifted the history lesson into an educational lecture about the rules and regulations governed by the park service. A few people asked questions, but most passengers stared out at the marsh, still golden from winter but turning greener by the day. Keith never took the view for granted. He loved the water. Peace filled his soul when he was on his boat.

A teenaged girl shrieked as they approached the island. She spotted a herd of eight wild horses gathered near a small tidal pond close to the point. A foal, about a month old, leaned her head underneath her mother's belly to nurse while the mare grazed next to another horse. Keith didn't know the herds well; from a distance it was difficult to differentiate between the stallions and the mares, and he didn't dare get closer to them.

It was low tide, so he navigated the ferry into a wide sandy cove and pulled as close to the shoreline as possible. Unfortunately, they'd have to wade knee-deep in water but sometimes it was unavoidable. No one complained and most were overjoyed to see the horses. Spotting them was a treat. Sometimes tourists spent the entire day on the island and never saw one.

"Mom, can we get closer and take pictures?" the girl asked.

Keith reminded the passengers to stay at least fifty feet away for everyone's safety. Countless times people broke the rules by trying to feed the horses grass, or trying to pet them. They were wild animals, after all, and would defend themselves if needed.

The day flew by, hardly feeling like work. It was early evening when he hopped into his truck and headed toward his mother's house. He had called earlier to make sure she would be home as her lifestyle was growing busier. She had been a housewife, doting over his father for years and even more so once he got sick. Her days had been spent at church and caring for her husband, but now his mom was getting involved in various community functions. Though lately it seemed she had no time for her family.

Once he made the mistake of mentioning it to Jenni. She got defensive, asking if he expected their mother to stay at home and mourn. Of course he didn't, but he couldn't put his finger on what bothered him other than it was likely he was just slow to adjust to change.

When he arrived, she was outside cleaning remnants of leaves from a rather harsh winter out of the flower beds. Despite their strained relationship, it was great to see her.

Maybe his fear was she'd start dating again and forget his father. Intellectually he knew that wasn't possible, but sometimes fears and emotions were irrational. Maybe everyone else was getting on with their lives and he was the one not moving forward.

Keith approached her and kissed the top of her head. To his relief, she glanced up and smiled.

"Hi, son." She peeled off her gardening gloves and tossed them onto the sidewalk next to her. She positioned herself onto all fours in attempt to stand but had trouble. Keith held out his hand to help her, surprised she was having such difficulty. He pulled her to her feet with ease.

"I'm glad to see you outside working, Mom. It's a gorgeous evening."

"It is." She dusted off her bright blue stretchy pants, another difference. His conservative mother, who usually wore dresses or slacks and a cross around her neck, was wearing stretchy neon clothes lately. A smaller cross still hung from around her neck but she'd changed clothing styles to the extreme. Maybe it was some kind of late midlife crisis.

Keith knew she was still adjusting to the change. Heck, maybe they all were. When the doctors had diagnosed his father with cancer, Keith had been in denial. It was amazing how fast his dad had declined and Keith had trouble accepting the inevitable.

His mother flashed him a knowing grin. "Gran called earlier. She said you've been visiting her at the nursing home."

He shrugged. No answer was the best choice if he wanted to avoid an inquisition about Emily.

"She mentioned you asked out her physical therapist."

He didn't bother to respond and was well aware of Gran's meddling ways, but he didn't think she'd call his mother so soon and drag her into the equation. Gran was always scheming and interfering in his life but Keith wouldn't have it any other way.

"How are things going at home?" he asked, wanting to change the subject to a safe topic.

"Oh, no, you don't," she said. "Spill it. Tell me about Emily."

He stifled a groan. The women in his family were relentless. His mother even knew Emily's name. "What about her?"

"I hear you invited her to the wedding Saturday night. And she said yes." His mom stood still, feet planted on the sidewalk, clearly waiting for an answer. She wouldn't dare move, or offer her usual hospitality of a glass of sweet tea, until she got an answer from him.

He might as well tell her something or they'd stand there all evening. "Yes, I asked Emily to the wedding. Gran suggested it." At the mention of Emily's name, he couldn't hold back a smile as it spread across his face.

His mother noticed, raising her eyebrows and grinning. "Interesting." She studied his face. "I've never seen such a soft look in your eyes before."

His mother had officially joined the dramatic, matchmaking

mission with Gran. "There is no look in my eye. And I smiled at you."

"No. You *smiled*."

"So what?"

"Your father used to look at me like that. I recognize the twinkle in your eye."

Keith fought the urge to roll his eyes. He couldn't disrespect his own mother, but he'd had enough of being center stage in their scheme. "She's attending the wedding as a favor to me. Gran invited her."

His mother laughed. "Right."

She strolled into the house and Keith followed. "Gran also mentioned a coffee date, a dinner date, and possibly a wild-horse date."

The depth of their interference amazed him.

His mother slapped her hands together in excitement and he realized he was smiling again. "I'd say this is a lot more than Gran trying to matchmake," she said.

He couldn't deny the truth. He was surprised at himself for the whimsical approach he had taken with Emily. He was unsure of what caused his momentary, delusional reasoning for asking her out on three dates but he was excited to see her beyond the perimeter of the rehab center.

"Keep me updated," she said, almost squealing with joy. She handed him a glass of southern sweet tea and he drank a long swallow, because his mom always made the best. After she topped it off once more, she followed him back outside.

"Can I help you with your flower beds?" Without waiting for an answer, and to move the focus off him, he dropped to his knees while setting the glass on the ground. He began raking leaves into a pile with his bare hands. He'd have the job done in no time, and then he'd head home before his mother pried more into his personal life. But one thing was certain: Emily was on his mind the entire time.

Chapter Five

What was I supposed to wear on my first coffee date ever? I rummaged through my closet for something casual but cute, something not too sexy but not baggy, either. These were the moments I wished I had my mother nearby, or one of my best friends, Kelly Adams, who I'd left behind in Raleigh.

If I'd had enough warning, and if a mall were close by, I would drive to a department store to purchase something. Between working a new job and unpacking my plethora of boxes, I had no choice but to settle for something in my closet.

After trying on several different shirts and tossing them aside, I pulled out a forgotten blue top I had worn only once. When I bought it last year while shopping with Kelly, she declared it was my color and admired how the vibrant top brought out the deep blue hue in my eyes. And I only hoped she was right. I chose a nice pair of white capris and matching sandals to go with the outfit and placed them on the wicker chair next to my bed. I wanted a second opinion to see if it was too much for a first get-together, so I grabbed my cell phone, snapped a photo, and sat on my comfy bed.

Kelly and I went back to the eighth grade. A true friend. We had been through thick and thin together, and she had encouraged me to make the move to Big Cat. I rolled onto my back and sent her a quick text, attaching the photo of the outfit. Immediately she texted back.

YES, THE TOP IS PERFECT. AND CONGRATS ABOUT THE DATE! I WANT TO

HEAR ALL THE DETAILS LATER.

A date. The word made my belly knot into a tight mess. I guess I thought of it more as friends getting together for coffee. Keith hadn't shown up this morning at the rehab center, and I assumed we were still on. A positive side to his absence was Ms. Stallings was more focused on therapy.

I did have his business card but felt uncomfortable texting him first. Call it ridiculous nowadays but I labeled it as a lesson learned from dating Frank Coleman. The mere thought of me taking the initiative drove home some annoying, deep-rooted fear. No more. We had agreed to meet at Coffee Break, so I planned to be there no matter what.

I realized a lot of old issues were resurfacing and I needed to relax and enjoy the process. Keith was probably nothing like the men of my past, so I needed to get a grip and stay calm, not overthink things.

It was only coffee.

If I wanted to be on time, I needed to hurry to take a shower, something I always did after working at the rehab center. Once finished, I dressed quickly and reapplied a light shade of makeup. My mother had always taught me to appreciate my smooth complexion, a genetic gift passed down from my grandmother. I realized I had somehow finished in record time and still had a half hour before I had to leave.

I sat on the couch and opened my laptop. I swore by the importance of writing whenever I had snippets of time, and my book in progress was begging for attention. I was usually a morning writer, but with the early hours of my new job, I found it difficult to write at 5:30 a.m.

Setting a timer so I wouldn't be late, I read over a few pages to refresh my mind. Something was wrong with the scene and it needed more clarification, more conflict. I reread it, determining the fix was a quick one. Once I placed my fingers on the keyboard, the words poured out onto the page as if the book were writing itself.

It was a love story and made my heart yearn for a man similar to the hero. The heroine had been verbally abused in the past, had been cheated on, and needed to heal in order to find love. This was what made fiction so wonderful. I created the man of her dreams by the click of the keys on my laptop, and to my surprise, I realized he was surprisingly similar to Keith.

When the timer went off, I jolted upright.

With reluctance I closed the computer and placed it on the coffee table, ready to embrace the evening. I plucked my purse and apartment key off the cluttered part of the countertop. Though I was a neat and tidy person in general, there was always one countertop that followed me from apartment to apartment.

I pulled the door closed behind me and was deep in thought. Was I supposed to buy my own cup of coffee, or wait for Keith to offer? Did we sit across from one other in a booth, or side by side? I needed to stop overthinking things.

When we were at the rehab center, talking to him came naturally but meeting him for coffee seemed forced. Was it too late to back out?

Just stop. Keith was an ordinary guy, one who looked sexy in shorts ... had nice legs and a handsome smile. No big deal. I didn't have to date him, it was just coffee.

As was my usual habit, I arrived five minutes early and was just about to go inside when I heard my name called from behind me. "Hi, Emily."

I turned around, surprised he was early too. He was so down-to-earth, so friendly. There was no way I should be nervous looking into those pale blue eyes.

"Hi, Keith," I managed to say. A trace of nervous energy still circulated through me but I assumed it was a normal reaction. My mother used to always say no one could tell when I was nervous unless I told them. I drew in a deep breath and glanced into his calming blue eyes again. They reminded me of refreshing pool water on a hot summer's day.

To my pleasant surprise, he opened the door for me. Jenni stood behind the counter and wore the same friendly smile and the same kind eyes of her brother. If she was surprised he brought a date, or a non-date as the case might be, into her coffee shop, she hid her reaction well.

"What would you like to drink?" he asked as we neared the counter.

I glanced over the menu even though I usually chose the same thing. Maybe today I needed to try something new. Despite the calories, I really wanted a cold decaf mocha frappe with chocolate chips to offset the warm evening. And when prompted, I agreed to a small dollop of whipped cream on top. Why not? In all truth, there was nothing blasé about tonight.

Keith ordered the same thing, except instead of a dollop he ordered extra whipped cream and caffeinated even though it was evening. If I had ordered anything with caffeine it would keep me awake most of the night.

With our drinks in hand Keith pointed to an available, overstuffed loveseat with two heart-shaped pillows in the corner of the room next to three matching chairs. "There?"

I nodded and drew in a long sip of the delicious frappe. It was so rich and I had to lick off a smudge of whipped cream from the corner of my mouth.

We made our way back to the little makeshift living room and my mind worked in overdrive again. Was I supposed to sit on the sofa with him, or in the chair?

The decision was taken away from me as he took the lead, planting himself in the chair, leaving the loveseat for me. One thing I found most attractive about a man was when he was confident and kind. Keith seemed both those things.

He leaned back and took a long swallow of his drink and I couldn't help but notice his strong square jaw and sandy stubble. He must not have shaved this morning or maybe it was a five o'clock shadow. Either way, he was handsome.

We chatted easily and discussed everything from my job,

to the ferry contract, to how we chose our career paths. And he actually took interest in my manuscript by asking several detailed questions about what I wrote and why. I never thought about why but guessed it was an escape of some sort. In exchange he told me about his father, his mom's road to redefining her life, and his sister's prior struggle to keeping the doors of Coffee Break open.

"What about your family?" he asked as he finished the last slurp of frappe in his cup.

I almost hated to admit the truth but it was what it was. "Well, my dad remarried, lives out of state and has younger kids, so he's busy. I'm close to my mom but she's a lot like my sister, who I don't get along with well." I hoped he didn't ask me to explain in too much detail. "And both my mom and sister live in Raleigh but are taking a hiatus in Mexico."

He raised his eyebrows at my answer. "Would you ever go back to Raleigh?"

I swallowed hard, surprised he thought to ask. "Never. That place can't be far enough away."

He looked puzzled. "Why?"

I wasn't sure I wanted to get into the specifics of my past but somehow the topic seemed important. "I was engaged and not long before the wedding, he left me for one of my best friends. But now I can almost say it was for the better because I ended up here." I held up my hands to include my surroundings.

Keith flinched. "What a rotten thing to do to someone you love."

"That's just it. I realize now he never loved me." The truth still stung. In all honesty, I had given the relationship everything because I had thought we were until death do us part. But Keith didn't need to know the specifics.

Maybe I had said too much, as he was being quiet, but at least I was honest.

"The good news is, I moved here to start over with my own life." For some reason I felt the need to explain.

He glanced down at his empty cup before he said, "I can understand being left right before your wedding because the same thing happened to me. It hurt more than anything I'd experienced until my dad died. And family tension . . . I've been there too. I used to resent my father. Well, my mother too, because she put up with him. But then one day he was diagnosed with cancer. Before I realized it, he was gone. If you ever have an opportunity to make up with your family, I would encourage it before it's too late."

I stared at him, knowing full well he was right.

He seemed to sense the topic was uncomfortable for me, so he changed the subject.

"Dinner tomorrow night?" he asked, standing up to collect my cup and toss them both into the nearest trash can.

"Yes," I said without hesitation, not realizing I was smiling until he grinned back.

We walked to the door and he shot a wave at his sister. She was busy with customers but waved back. "It was nice seeing you again, Emily," Jenni called out.

"You too." I looked forward to getting to know her better.

Once we were outside I inhaled the same whiff of rosemary and thyme I had noticed the other day. To my surprise Keith reached out and touched my elbow. "Did you drive or walk?"

"Walked. I figured the exercise was good for me." It seemed a pleasant idea at the time but now I was tired and it was still hot, so I wished I had driven. It was almost sunset, and I was surprised at how long we'd chatted in the coffee shop.

His smile was warm and infectious. "Can I walk you home?"

"Sounds great." At first I thought he was going to offer me a ride but a stroll together was much better as I wasn't quite ready to end our evening.

He reached down and took my hand, studying my reaction as if to make sure I was okay with the gesture. I wasn't sure why but I didn't pull away.

"I live in the apartment complex north of town."

"The Dolphin?"

"Yes." I hoped he didn't want to come inside, as the place was a mess with the stacks of boxes and I wasn't comfortable enough with him yet.

We strolled down the street in no hurry. The relaxing scent of the nearby water smelled of fresh salty air and I hoped my senses never grew accustomed to it. The ambience was quaint, the shops along the street were artsy, and small-town living was simple, delightful even, and better than a big city with honking horns and crime.

There was even an ice-cream shop with a crowd of people gathered outside, licking their cones. Vibrant colors painted the canvas of the sky. The mood was festive, everyone laughing, talking, and enjoying the evening. Once again, I felt a deep connection to the town of Big Cat, and sensed it was a healing place where I could belong.

We walked in comfortable silence, and as we left the buildings behind, we turned left onto my street. I was disappointed the evening had come to an end. "There, the last building on the right." I pointed to the second floor, overlooking a narrow canal. "That's mine."

He walked me to the entrance of the building. "I enjoyed tonight."

"Me too." An awkward silence fell between us.

"I almost forgot ... our selfie," he said, pulling out his cell phone and holding it in front of us.

I tried to smile but the whole thing seemed ridiculous. Why did his grandmother need proof we went out, anyway?

"Hmmmm. You look terrified." He held up the phone for me to view my wide eyes staring back at me.

I laughed, and it felt good to relax long enough to feel like my normal self. He snapped another picture, and this time I was smiling. Now his grandmother would think we were a perfect match. What a nightmare.

He must have misunderstood my laughter as well. He

leaned forward and brushed my cheek with his warm lips. I inhaled a long breath, my confused mind dancing in the breeze. I couldn't believe he did that. I should have run upstairs, right then, but instead I stood frozen in place.

He backed away slowly. "Good night and sweet dreams. I'll pick you up tomorrow at 6:00?"

For a writer who thrived on words, I was speechless. All I could do was nod.

He flashed an easy wave and left me standing there, contemplating my racing heartbeat.

Chapter Six

I have to say, after going out with Keith, it was somewhat easier to write about men in my manuscript. I wasn't a person who believed in instant relationships or soul mates meant for dreamers, but fictional love stories I could write.

Well, wait a darned minute. I *was* a dreamer, but in my own defense weren't all successful writers fantasists? And I wasn't technically successful yet but often imagined what it would feel like to be a multi-bestselling author. First things first, though. The reality was I needed an agent to help me find a publisher, although that was not as easy as it sounded.

The naysayers told me to be content with the mere blessing I had the gift to write, but I held onto my dad's words, even though we weren't close. He said I was a trailblazer because I was brave enough to try something new. He was right, and I had to hold onto the belief I'd make it in the publishing world no matter how long it took.

Before I sat down to write I shot off a text to Kelly.

Awesome coffee get-together. Handsome and a gentleman.

You deserve it girl.

After all I had been through with my ex, I agreed it was time to meet nice people in my life.

Pulling out my laptop, I folded myself into my favorite overstuffed chair. The porch door was open and the refreshing, salty air drifted in, feeding my soul for writing. The next hour the words spilled out onto the pages and my manuscript progressed nicely.

Once again I realized how my manuscript correlated with my life. The main character, Lizzy Lyons, had met this amazing man who worked with his hands as a construction worker. She didn't expect to like him but ... she did. A lot. Their first date was different from any she had before.

Similar to my experience, I hadn't suspected Keith and I had anything in common, yet his ex-fiancée had also dumped him right before the wedding. We appeared to be kindred spirits from that painful experience alone.

Surprised it was 9:15 p.m. when I folded up my laptop, my stomach grumbled and reminded me I had forgotten to eat dinner. I peeled myself from the chair, stiff from sitting in one position too long, and had to stop to shake out my leg to wake it up enough to walk. It didn't really work and I stumbled my way into the kitchen to search for a snack. It was too late to eat dinner, so I rummaged through the pantry and found a fruit cup and a package of crackers.

No sooner than I finished eating, the familiar upbeat ringtone of my phone sounded from the countertop next to me. I glanced at the number, not recognizing it. It was unusual for someone to call this late, so I hesitated for a moment before I clicked accept.

"Hi there. This is Jenni," the voice said in an apologetic tone. "Sorry to call after 9:00."

I grew silent, trying to figure out who Jenni was.

"From Coffee Break. I'm Keith's sister."

"Oh!" Confused by how she got my number but curious as to why she was calling, I decided to make a little bit of small talk first. "By the way, your coffee is delicious."

"Thanks, I appreciate it." She laughed, her voice rich and upbeat. "I'm heading out to Pony Island on Sunday with Claire and wanted to know if you'd like to join us?"

I was fairly certain Keith had invited me to go with him on Sunday too but guessed it depended on how our upcoming dinner and wedding event went. On the flip side, making new friends in the area was a good thing, but being introverted, this was a struggle for me. Maybe visiting the island with a small group was better than going alone with a man, though. I didn't want to give him the idea I was ready for anything other than friendship. It was important for me to take the appropriate amount of time to heal.

"Keith mentioned possibly venturing out there Sunday. Why don't we go together?" I hoped he wouldn't mind I took liberty inviting them along, but it was for the best.

"Sounds great, and speaking of Keith, I saw the way he looks at you," Jenni said, and I could hear her smile through the phone. "And just so you know, he's never brought a woman into my coffee shop before. Actually, it's been a while since he's even dated."

Despite my involuntary smile, my belly clenched. "Well, I wouldn't say we're dating, but he seems to be a great man."

"Of course he is. He's my brother, so I'm biased, but I can honestly say he is respectful and genuine." Jenni's voice changed to reflect her affection for Keith.

Sometimes I wished I had a brother, mostly because the sibling rivalry I had with my sister was disappointing. Terri had always done her own thing, just like she was doing now by living in Mexico with our mother. I wished the three of us were closer and got along well, but I was becoming almost immune to the situation. In all truth, I didn't even know why I didn't like her other than I was jealous of the time she spent with Mom. Mexico wasn't helping.

Jenni's voice penetrated my thoughts. "Why don't we meet at the ferry around noon?"

To my chagrin, I was nervous to accept. It had been a long while since I had to make a new friend group. Remembering the point of moving here was to develop community, an extended family, I accepted the invitation.

"I can't wait," I said, mostly true. "I used to ride one of my grandmother's horses as a child and had always admired them. The thought of seeing wild ones is intriguing." Again, I hoped Keith wouldn't mind all of us going together. I just needed to explain to him my thoughts on the subject of dating.

He was an easy person to be around. As Jenni said on the phone, he was respectful and genuine. From day one I sensed his kind heart, a rare treat nowadays. His gentle eyes said a lot. He was a good catch and some woman would snap him up in a hot minute, now that he seemed open to dating again.

The conversation waned and we ended the call. I wasn't tired and to distract myself I sat down to write.

It was midnight before I crawled into bed and the morning sun shone through the window way too early. I had tossed and turned most of the night with strange dreams about my mom and sister in Mexico. They were just too far away for comfort.

Often my dreams had meaning, or they answered questions I was pondering. One distinct message I woke up with was to submit my previous manuscript to agents. I had finished writing it about six months ago but it was buried within the files of my computer. Between the breakup and moving, I had pushed it aside. Although I had shopped it around briefly, the feedback had been encouraging. I was possibly the closest I'd been to finding my dream agent and publisher, so I needed to continue the submission process if I wanted to be successful. I set a goal to submit my manuscript to at least two agents tonight after work. *Be bold, girl* was my new motto.

Exhausted before the day began, I wished I had a dose of Jenni's delicious, caffeinated coffee this morning. Unfortunately, running late meant I didn't have time to stop to buy a cup, so I had to settle for the subpar coffee at work.

Once I saw my busy schedule, I groaned. I hoped someday all the late nights spent working on my manuscript would pay off in a big way and I would get paid to write full time. In the meantime, I settled for sipping bitter coffee to keep me awake. It was barely hot and I took a long sip and then pushed the full cup aside. No matter how tired I was, the awful coffee wasn't worth the suffering. Ready to get my day started, I dumped the contents down the sink and headed out to the floor.

As I passed by the elevator the silver door slid open to reveal an older, slender woman named Isabelle Snyder. She was standing inside the elevator with her walker and wearing a mismatched yellow housecoat with pink pajama pants. On the days when her dementia was worse, I heard she rode the elevator up and down, never stepping off. Eager to help, I spoke softly to her and held open the door.

"The coffee bar is this way," I suggested as a distraction, although it was difficult to recommend the coffee to anyone. I knew better than to ask Ms. Snyder any questions and risk agitating her.

"I love coffee," the woman said, stepping forward.

Thank goodness she was cooperative this morning, bless her heart.

"This way to the coffee bar," I repeated, so the woman remembered where we were walking. I touched her lightly on the elbow to show affection and to guide her, and thankfully she smiled. "I'll make a cup of coffee for you."

"You're a sweet dear." The woman allowed me to direct her to a table.

"Thank you." I pulled out a chair and she nestled into it. The alcove was set up to resemble an elegant coffee bar, offering two different insulated decanters of regular coffee plus a decaffeinated option, as well as one with hot water for tea.

I remembered from her daughter she liked her coffee with two creams and a packet of sugar. Ms. Snyder took the cup with a delighted smile as if I'd given her a gift.

A pang of longing ached in my heart for my grandmother. I considered all of the residents here makeshift grandparents, and I treated them as such.

Eager to start treating patients, I excused myself and

walked to the rehabilitation hallway. At Mr. Kane's room I knocked on the door, announcing who I was. He was sitting in a recliner with his feet elevated as I had recommended to decrease the swelling in his oversized ankles. He had his catheter bag attached to the side of the chair and his rolling walker pushed off to the side.

"Good morning," I said as I entered the room. "It's time for therapy."

He grinned big enough to show off his loose dentures. "I'm always ready to see you, dear." He lowered the foot rest to the recliner.

"I'm going to use my gait belt, so I have something to hold onto if needed." I waved the yellow belt with smiley faces in the air. "I call it my happy belt."

He nodded and I wrapped the belt around his waist. "Well, the 'happy belt' works," he said. "You're always happy and it rubs off on me."

If my patients were benefiting from my joy, makeshift or not, then so be it. It was a matter of time before it became real. Breakups were hard on a person but intellectually I knew Frank wasn't the only man in the world. True, I had thought he was *the one,* but the idea of only one soul mate was ridiculous. Not that he had been my soul mate, I corrected myself.

"What are you lost in thought about?" Mr. Kane asked.

I hadn't meant to bring my personal problems to work. "Oh, I was thinking about how complex men are." I laughed, trying to make a joke out of my deep thoughts.

"It's not men who are complicated, dear, it's women." His low rumble of laughter filled the room.

"I guess it depends on what gender you are. How long were you married?" I asked with curiosity. I loved knowing the details of my patients. It made therapy more individual, and in my experience, I found patients loved talking about their own lives. The result was they worked harder in rehab and seemed to enjoy the bond I tried to create on a professional yet personal level.

Before encouraging Mr. Kane to stand, I reached down and hung his catheter bag on the lower rung of the walker to allow gravity to work to our advantage.

"Been married forty-two years," he said. His smile grew even bigger than before as if he loved reminiscing about his deceased wife.

"What's the secret to a happy marriage?" I asked, fully aware the wisdom of the elderly population was immeasurable. I held onto him as he attempted to stand, pulling up on the walker. "Remember to push off from the recliner," I reminded. "It gives you more leverage and it's safer."

He placed his hands on the armrests of the chair and, without my help, pushed himself to a standing position.

"Easier?"

"Much. You're a smart woman, Emily."

"It's all about technique." I enjoyed working with him, as he was kind and gentle, a similar personality to Keith.

Mr. Kane rolled the walker toward the wheelchair awaiting him in the hallway outside the door. I strategically kept it there, so he'd have to walk farther.

He paused in the doorway. "The key to a happy marriage is loving each other, putting the other person first, and never going to bed angry." His advice was pretty much the same as Mr. Hardy's, so it must be true. Mr. Kane turned around with the walker and backed up to the wheelchair.

I watched to make sure he remembered the ideal hand placement but had to remind him.

"I don't know why I keep forgetting," he complained. "I can remember details of my past, mostly useless stuff, but sometimes I can't remember what just happened."

"That's normal," I explained with empathy. "I'm throwing a lot of new information at you and it's hard to remember everything. I bet not reaching back is a habit, and here I come along overwhelming you with suggestions."

"Yeah, it's an old habit," he said, more than ready to rationalize his short-term memory loss. After I moved the catheter bag underneath his wheelchair, hidden in a privacy bag, he said, "Are you getting married soon?"

I laughed harder than I meant to. "I'm nowhere near getting married, not even dating anyone."

"Not yet," he said. "But someone with your vibrant personality and good looks, it's a matter of time before you find a special man."

"Thank you." While I struggled with his compliment, I pushed him in the wheelchair to the rehab gym, so we could work on strengthening exercises and balance. I wanted him safe as possible when he discharged home.

Once I returned him back to his room, I headed to Ms. Stallings'. To my surprise, when I noticed Keith wasn't there, I felt conflicted between relief and disappointment. Even though I had enjoyed our coffee get-together, for some strange reason my belly grew anxious at the mere thought of meeting him tonight for dinner. Maybe I should cancel and only attend the wedding as I had promised.

I had no idea how to resolve my fear of relationships, or even if I wanted to.

I knocked on the door of Ms. Stallings' room. She glanced up from her book and said, "Come in, darling." She placed a multi-colored bookmark inside her romance novel and set it aside.

"Let's take a walk to the living room," I suggested. "They are passing out ice cream." I found the promise of a treat usually motivated my patients to walk farther.

"I knew I liked you." She stood, and unlike Mr. Kane, she remembered the correct technique for hand placement. She was a sharp, cognitively intact lady, but I imagined the same independence caused her to be a handful with her family at home.

"By the way," she said, heading toward the door. "I saw

the cute selfie from last night. The two of you were smiling as if you were enjoying every second."

I sighed. "Actually, the first photo wasn't great. The one you like was because I was laughing. It doesn't mean what you think it does." I wanted to leave the room and treat my next patient.

"Whatever you say but smiles don't lie."

I wanted to argue with her but the purpose of going out with him in the first place was to make her happy. Let her have her brief moment of joy.

Ms. Stallings had a tendency to walk too fast. She believed the quicker she moved, the sooner the physical therapy session ended, and the sooner the rehab center would discharge her home.

"Let's slow down a bit and focus on foot placement, cadence, and safety," I suggested. "Plus, I can't keep up with you." I laughed to soften the correction.

Ms. Stallings slowed down a bit. "Better?"

"Yes." Once again I wished I had grandparents and would love to adopt both Ms. Stallings and Mr. Kane.

When we reached the living room, Keith entered the rehab center with a big grin as if he owned the world. He didn't notice us sitting near the dining room and continued to walk through the lobby toward Ms. Stallings' room, until his grandmother whistled at him as if calling one of her horses at feeding time.

Keith and a handful of residents turned to stare at Ms. Stallings. I swore he recognized the whistle.

"Gran." He strode toward us as Ms. Stallings rested on a nearby couch.

"Emily is going to reward me with ice cream for good behavior," she said as she kissed him on the cheek. He hugged her and planted his usual kiss atop her head.

I couldn't help but notice how gentle and caring he was with his grandmother and tried to ignore the annoying swirl in my belly as the warmth worked its way throughout my limbs.

Only once had I felt this way about a man, and it hadn't ended well.

Somehow, I needed to usher Keith aside and let him know I wanted to back out of our dinner plans.

"Ice cream, huh? You must be on unusually good behavior then," he said with affection.

"Would you like some?" I asked.

His gaze met mine and lingered.

I noticed from the corner of my eye Ms. Stallings was watching us closely.

"I'd love some," Keith said, his gaze filled with gentle interest.

Ms. Stallings remained silent, clearly enjoying her grandson's interest in her physical therapist.

The scrutiny made me swallow hard. "Vanilla, chocolate, pistachio, strawberry?" Speaking was difficult with those blue eyes searching mine.

"Chocolate," he said in a low, hoarse voice.

The tension, similar to a tight rubber band, pulled at me and I prayed my nerves didn't snap. I risked a glance at my patient, who was grinning with delight. "What would you like?" I managed to ask her.

"You don't want me to answer," Ms. Stallings said.

"Gran," Keith warned, his low voice vibrating. "She's asking about ice cream."

Before I responded, Ms. Stallings said, "Strawberry, please."

Feeling a bit dizzy, I walked away as calmly as I could, knowing full well they were watching me.

I strolled into the sunroom where a group of residents sat around several tables covered in white linen. The facility was elegant yet cozy and welcoming. The sunlight gleamed through the glass, basking the tables in early summer warmth.

"Hi, Emily," the activity director called out. "Want some

ice cream?"

Everyone who worked here so far seemed friendly and approachable. "My patient and her grandson would love some." I gave them the ice cream order.

The older woman scooped it from the containers and filled two clear plastic bowls. "Don't you want any?" she asked, handing them to me with a plastic spoon stuck in each one.

I loved ice cream, mint chip especially, but it was the last thing on my mind. Summer meant swimsuits and shorts. "No, thank you," I said instead of acknowledging the craving.

If I had any common sense, I would abandon their ice cream bowls and head in the opposite direction, leaving Ms. Stallings and her handsome grandson to their own devices. Too bad it was unprofessional. Nope, I needed to suck it up and carry the bowls to them. Besides, I needed to talk to Keith about tonight.

When I returned with the ice cream, Ms. Stallings reached out for the bowl. I handed it to her and passed the other to Keith, not meeting his direct eye contact. I had no idea how I was supposed to tell him about tonight.

"Thank you, dear." Ms. Stallings didn't wait to spoon up a large bite. When she finished the mouthful she said, "Emily, I expect more pictures of the two of you having dinner, smiling and enjoying yourselves like last night."

My mouth dropped open. Keith was watching me closely, and I couldn't bring myself to tell them about wanting to cancel. I was unable to shake off my desire to please her, and all because she reminded me of my own grandmother.

What would it hurt to go to dinner with him?

Chapter Seven

Keith stared at the poor choice of clothes in his closet. He wanted to wear something a bit nicer than shorts and a t-shirt for a dinner date. If he planned to start going out again, he needed to upgrade his wardrobe.

There was one decent shirt hanging there. It was bright blue with a collar but his ex-fiancée, Vicki, had picked it out for him. It seemed strange to wear it on a date with another woman but what the heck. It was all he had. He thumbed through his clothes and found two pairs of khaki pants, one he was sure no longer fit him, the other a larger size he planned to wear to the wedding Saturday night. If he could get away with wearing shorts to both events, he would.

It was getting late fast. Although he had offered to pick up Emily tonight, she insisted on driving to the restaurant herself. She gave him mixed messages. One minute she acted as though she was into him, and at other times she behaved as though she was either nervous or not interested.

Since she was new to the area, the restaurant he chose was on Front Street. It was nestled between an art gallery and a boutique. Lucky for him most of the shops were closed already, so he managed to find a parking spot near the front door of the two-story restaurant. The building housed huge windows on both floors and the sign out front promised to offer a spectacular view of the water. He glanced around for her. Choosing to wait inside the restaurant, he climbed from the truck and the most mouthwatering aroma greeted him. The tantalizing smell was likely a combination of grilled steak and fresh seafood. The day had been too busy to eat much, so his stomach growled in anticipation.

He wouldn't admit it to anyone, but a swirl of excitement competed with a knot of apprehension at seeing her again. His nerves tossed around inside him like a mixed salad. It had been a long time since he'd gone out with someone other than Vicki, although it was obvious from the get-go Emily was a special lady.

He climbed the stairs to the side entrance where he greeted the hostess, dressed in a flowy summer dress. "Two for Stallings, please." Again, he was reminded of how he was supposed to be a party of two by marriage but he was thankful at the same time that Vicki had left him. It was bound to happen and best he hadn't married her.

"Outside or inside?" the woman asked.

He wasn't sure about Emily's preference but guessed she was an outdoor sort of lady. "Outside, please."

She wrote down his name. "It won't be long, maybe fifteen minutes."

"Thank you." He stepped off to the side and out of the way. Come midsummer when the tourist season was full throttle, the wait was usually over an hour.

As if he sensed her approach, he turned to see a gorgeous woman with curly brown hair and captivating blue eyes. She was dressed in a peach-colored dress and left him momentarily speechless.

He stepped forward to give her a gentle hug that lingered for longer than he anticipated. "You're stunning." She seemed surprised by his compliment but then a small smile crossed her lips. It couldn't be possible she wasn't used to praise, looking as gorgeous as she was.

He stood close enough to her to catch a light, clean whiff of her perfume and had to resist shaking his head to clear his mind. He needed to get a handle on things.

Her cheeks turned a slight shade of pink.

It was just the two of them, despite the buzz of the busy restaurant muted in the background.

"I've been looking forward to seeing you tonight," he said, making her blush even more.

"Follow me," the hostess said, interrupting Keith. As they worked their way around the bar and through the restaurant, he noted how she glanced around, taking in the scene.

Keith placed his hand on the small of her back as they followed the woman through a glass door and onto the deck. People were spread out among cozy tables adorned with lit white candles flickering in square glass containers. As luck would have it, she seated them at a four-top along the railing, overlooking the water with boats bobbing in their slips.

They sat at the table and she stared out at the water. "What ambience. Thank you."

Great, she approved of his choice. "You're more than welcome."

"Even the sky is gorgeous."

The sun looked like a broken egg yolk frying in a pan. Dark golden streaks spread throughout the burnt orange as it mixed with a pale yellow. Above, there was a layer of flat-bottomed darker clouds. Hints of bright light peered through here and there. A replica of neon color reflected off the water, wrapping around the silhouetted dock.

She pointed to several pelicans perched on nearby pilings. "Check out the bird. He's staring at us."

"That's Sam, my buddy." Sam recognized him and he had his wings spread wide, flapping them the way he did at times.

The server approached to ask for their drink order. They both requested water and declined alcoholic beverages. He wasn't a huge drinker and she appeared uninterested as well.

After the server left, Keith turned his attention to Emily. "So Sam likes to make a ruckus but he's my personal friend and confidante. He visits me daily and well, I just might admit to the fact he likes me because I feed him fish."

She chuckled and Keith laughed with her, guessing it did sound strange to have a pelican for a pet.

"Most people get a cat or dog, but a pelican is so cool."

The conversation was somewhat stilted but he figured she was nervous. "Not so sure cool is the right word. He's a demanding, fish-begging bird who squawks at me. Usually he wants me to feed him faster."

Emily laughed again, clearly enjoying the vision of him shoveling fish at Sam as fast as possible.

The bird was quickly stealing her attention, so Keith redirected her gaze back on him. "By the way, Gran adores you. You're very patient with her."

When the server set the water on the table Emily took a long drink. "She's wonderful. I enjoy her enthusiasm."

He chuckled. "What a polite way to describe her."

"My favorite patients are the frisky ones." She scanned the menu, likely taking the hint he had made his choice when he set his on the table. The server returned and asked for their order, and she chose stuffed grilled shrimp with a tossed salad, and Keith ordered grilled flounder, a twice-baked potato, and a vegetable medley.

"Oh, we promised Gran a photo of us together," he said, standing and walking over to her side of the table. He swore she wanted to avoid the whole selfie idea.

He wished she would relax. "What do you think?" When she nodded, he posed next to her and couldn't help but grin. He glanced at the photo but she appeared tense. "Try another one? We're supposed to be having fun."

"Sorry." She smiled bigger as he clicked another photo.

"Much better." But dang, he wasn't going to push her if she wasn't interested, although he did hope to convince her to change her mind about him.

As the horizon grew dark, various lights on the harbor

turned on, lining the shoreline with twinkles. Several dark figures on the water wore bright lights like shadows searching for lost love. "Those are shrimp boats trolling for fresh seafood."

"Mmmm. They probably caught my dinner tonight."

Jimmy Buffett played on the overhead speakers, a befitting choice for a beach lifestyle. More than anything he wanted to remain in Big Cat for the rest of his life, *if* the park service cooperated with his plan.

As dinner progressed, she leaned back and chatted more. She told him about her writing, her goals to obtain a literary agent and a publisher, as well as her goal to someday be a best-selling author. He talked about being an architect, designing houses, and getting laid off. Eventually the subject of the upcoming wedding came up and what time he would pick her up. He told her how Captain Bill had been his father's best friend, and how Keith used to sail as a kid with them to Pony Island.

She mentioned how she used to ride her grandmother's horse. The conversation led into a discussion about heading out to the island on Sunday with his sister and Claire. He had hoped to show her the horses himself, but if she felt more comfortable having Jenni and Claire around, so be it. Claire knew more interesting history about them anyway, so Emily would likely enjoy hearing her stories.

For some unknown reason Keith sensed her mood shift once again and was curious if the dinner was too much for her. Heck, it was almost too much for him.

"Is something wrong?" he asked.

"Nothing at all. Tonight is wonderful." She pushed her plate aside and seemed to shake off whatever she was dealing with internally. "And dinner was delicious although I can't eat another bite." She had finished most of the entrée but had left remnants of the salad behind.

He leaned back in his chair. "I hope you saved room for

dessert."

She shook her head. "No thanks. I'm as stuffed as my shrimp were." She glanced out at the dark water, the candlelight flickering across her face like one of the lights on a shrimp boat.

A light smell of fish and saltwater blew on the breeze and Sam was long gone. A bit distracted, Keith hadn't noticed when he'd flown away.

When the server approached, Keith paid the bill with cash. "Would you like to go for a stroll along the boardwalk?"

"Sounds wonderful."

He scooted his chair back and stood, but before they made their way inside through the barrage of tables, he reached for her hand. It was so soft against his callused one, like the smooth sea water after a rain.

They stepped outside the restaurant and he dropped her hand. "I apologize. I hope I wasn't being too forward. I thought it would be easier to move through the crowd."

"No worries at all."

He stepped closer to allow a couple to pass by, his arm brushing hers. She shivered.

"Are you chilly?" He started to wrap his arm around her to offer warmth but stopped.

He was trying to be a true gentleman like his dad taught him.

She pulled on the sweater she'd brought and he assisted her with the sleeve but noticed she had a strange faraway look in her eyes.

"Do you still want to walk?" This was one of those confusing moments where she gave off mixed signals. He needed to back off a bit. Besides, he was plenty busy between Gran and the ferry contract.

They strolled together down Front Street, along the boardwalk. Couples, families, teenagers, most of them locals, were mingling with each other. The glorious night was one to be enjoyed to the fullest.

A breeze blew her hair away from her face and one loose ringlet danced across her mouth. He turned his head, refusing to look.

He pointed to a nearby shop with a crowd of people socializing outside. "Are you too full to enjoy an ice-cream cone?"

She hesitated at first. "I'd love one. Somehow there is always room for ice cream."

He held open the door for her and they entered the General Store. The bell above dinged as if they stepped back in history.

"Wow." She pointed to the old-fashioned barrels loaded with colorfully wrapped candy. "This place is folksy and friendly."

"It is," Keith said as she picked up a rainbow-colored lollipop. He swore it was as big as her hand. Then she picked up a t-shirt with the town's name printed above an image of a wild horse and her face gleamed.

She glanced back over her shoulder. "Can't wait to see the horses."

"Me, either." They walked over to a display case along the wall with several tubs of different flavored ice cream and a chalkboard above with a handwritten menu with a choice of various sandwiches.

"Too many to choose from." She bit her lip as she studied each flavor and chose a waffle cone with one scoop of mint chip. She laughed in amazement when the girl handed her the overfilled cone. "If this is one scoop, I can't imagine how they'd fit two in this cone."

Keith had ordered the same size and flavor. "No kidding." He ran his tongue around the side of the ice cream to keep it from dripping. "Delicious."

She followed his lead and licked hers. When she noticed he was watching, her cheeks grew red.

"Do you want to sit outside or at one of the tables?" He nodded toward a set of tables in front of a stage. "They play beach music there on Friday nights when the tourist season picks up more."

"Sounds like a lot of fun." She licked her ice cream once more before saying, "Outside would be great."

The bell dinged above the door as they headed outside to a nearby bench. They sat down and he took a large bite out of the center of the scoop.

"Don't your teeth freeze?"

He laughed and did it again.

"Just curious, if you don't get the contract with the ferry service, what will you do?"

He sensed his answer was important but needed to be truthful.

"Well, I'll continue to look for work nearby as an architect, but there isn't any. If I lose the contract, I will have to move to a big city like Raleigh."

He saw her flinch.

Then she changed the subject although her body seemed tense. "What a gorgeous night."

Not sure if he should let it go or address her concerns, Keith sat in silence.

Heck, he didn't want to leave, to give up working on the water, the sunsets and salty air, or stop wearing shorts year round, but as he said to others, he needed to make a living.

He understood she had a problem with Raleigh but the past was the past, and she needed to let go of her baggage and start anew. Otherwise, there would be no room in her life for someone ever again. The same thing happened with his ex and yet here he was, ready to explore the possibility of entering a new relationship with a wonderful woman. But it was obvious she wasn't ready. He hoped when she was, he'd still be here.

He wanted to know more about her situation and had to ask. "What was so traumatizing about Raleigh and your ex?"

She popped the last bite of the cone into her mouth and chewed slowly before she answered.

Keith touched her knee. "You don't have to talk about it, although I'm a good listener." He hoped she wanted to share with him and trusted him enough to tell him what happened.

"Well, you should probably know ... basically the short version is I fell in love and he cheated on me, but the bigger issue was his verbal abuse and demeaning, secretive behavior."

He stopped eating his ice cream and met her gaze. "I'm sorry, Emily. I don't mean to sound insensitive but I have to ask, why were you with him then?" He never understood why people stayed in an abusive relationship.

She glanced away. "It's complicated. At first he showered me with love. Then he started withdrawing and refused to communicate. Then he love-bombed me again. It's very confusing when someone you love mistreats you."

"I'm sure. Why would he do that?"

"Because he is a very selfish man. He lied to hide his secret life from me, but when I found out, I was done with him. The worst part of it was I lost my best friend too." She swiveled on the bench to make direct eye contact. "He played mind games to gain power and it takes a while to learn what they are doing. In the meantime he cut me down, degraded me about my weight ..."

"Stop right there," he said, holding up his hand. "There is nothing wrong with your weight. Excuse me if I make you uncomfortable but you are gorgeous."

She blushed in the glow given off by the ornate lamp near them.

Keith shoved the last bite into his mouth, not waiting to speak. "The man is a fool. If he bothers you again let me know."

She stared at him and he wasn't sure if she liked seeing his protective side. But too bad. He was traditional and if she wanted to date him she needed to accept that fact.

"Do you ever hear from him?"

She remained silent.

"Emily?"

She shrugged. "Sometimes. He called me after I moved down here and threatened if I ever return to Raleigh he would know."

"What does he mean?"

"Either he wants to suck me back in so I'll go back to him, or he's irate and wants to intimidate me."

Now it made more sense why she despised Raleigh.

He closed his eyes for a moment and shook his head in slow motion. "Again, I'm sorry you had to deal with that." He squeezed her shoulder. "I won't lie or yell at you. I promise."

She nodded but he wasn't sure she believed him.

"What about you?" she asked. "What's more of your story?"

He glanced away. "The short story is when she broke things off, she left me devastated. Then my dad was diagnosed with cancer and I was in denial. I couldn't stand the thought of losing him and I resented him. I wasted a lot of time being angry."

"What's the long story? If you want to tell me."

He sighed but had asked her the same thing.

"Fair enough. I met her in college while I lived in Raleigh. She still lives there and I moved away when I graduated. The biggest mistake I made was asking her to move down here."

"Why? Was she a city girl and didn't like living in a small town?"

"Exactly right. I was selfish to ask and should never have asked her to marry me. She hated Big Cat and when she took a trip up to Raleigh to visit her family, she decided not to return."

He stood and offered his hand to help her up. "Ready to go home?"

"Okay." Once standing, she didn't let go of his hand.

The lights from the town reflected off the dark water as the street lamps lit the way along the boardwalk. He glanced down at her. "Do you still want to attend the wedding with me?"

She hesitated and then said, "Of course."

He held on a little tighter to her hand as the planks from the boardwalk creaked underneath them. When they reached the front of the restaurant, patrons were leaving and a man locked the door. Keith glanced at the time, seeing it was getting late but he didn't want to part with her company yet.

"Which car is yours?" he asked.

She pointed to a used but well-loved Toyota Camry.

He walked her to the driver's side and gently turned her toward him. "I had a wonderful night." His voice sounded unusually raspy.

Emily lifted her chin. "Me too."

He stepped closer to her, closing the space between them. "I'll pick you up for the wedding tomorrow night."

She nodded, appearing to freeze in place, and didn't speak.

He leaned away and whispered, "Good night, Em."

She inhaled a long breath. "Only my family and close friends call me Em."

"Sorry, won't happen again."

She chuckled and the soft breeze blew a long curl into her face. "I love the way you say it. Night."

He stepped away, too far away for his liking. "Text me when you get home, so I know you're safe."

She nodded and they needed no words to understand they both enjoyed each other's company tonight, even if it remained just friendship. Although, he wanted more.

They waved to each other and he made himself turn away as she backed out and drove off. He wasn't sure what he was thinking by pursuing a woman when they both hadn't fully recovered from their intense past relationships. But as he said before, the past was the past and the future looked promising.

Chapter Eight

Keith walked down the boat ramp. As usual, Sam was perched on his favorite piling, all smug and expecting his breakfast treat.

"I saw you spying on me last night," Keith accused.

Sam opened and snapped his bill shut.

"Yeah, isn't she pretty?"

Clank, snap, squawk.

"I agree. Yes, the date was good. Amazing, really."

Sam clapped his beak several times and then cocked his head as if he wanted to know more.

"Fine. It was the best date I've ever had." Keith opened the cooler on the dock and reached inside for a small fish. He tossed it at Sam, not taking time to make sure his aim was correct. Sam flew off the piling and caught the fish in his beak before he landed on the weathered dock.

"Good catch. Sorry, buddy." Keith reached inside the cooler for another fish and tossed it directly at Sam this time. The pelican caught it easily and swallowed it whole.

"Mornin'," Captain Bill said in his raspy voice as he made his way down the ramp toward them. The older man took a long sip from his paper coffee cup, most likely bought from Coffee Break. "Today looks to be a busy day."

Saturdays were always hectic during the season though it was still early, and Captain Shep, who worked during the summers only, started next weekend. "Bring it on," Keith said, distracted by trying to snap the cooler lid in place. He really needed to buy a new one but hadn't had time. "What are you doing here today? Thought you were taking off for your daughter's wedding."

"I am, but I needed to escape." Captain Bill hopped down onto the boat and sat on the bench behind the helm. "House is full of women running around."

Keith laughed. "I get it." He imagined the chaos that ensued before a wedding. No thanks.

Sam flew back to his perch on the piling and watched Keith's every move.

"Your bird is man's best friend."

"Better than a dog," Keith said as he hopped onto the boat. He had thirty minutes before Collin Davis, the boy who assisted him on the ferry, showed up.

While Captain Bill complained about the women taking over his home, Keith wiped overnight condensation off the seats with a dry cloth. He detested dirt and sand on his boat. Every square inch was clean, the life preservers stacked away neatly. His aim was customer service and providing the best experience possible.

His cell phone disrupted the peace. "Excuse me," he said to Captain Bill as he clicked to accept the call. He turned his head away for privacy. "Hey," he spoke into the phone to Scott Botticelli, his old childhood buddy and Jenni's husband, who was the vice president of the local bank.

"Thought you'd want to know some news." Scott's voice was gruff, too gruff. "Between us, Tim Cooper just talked to me about acquiring a loan to supply boats for the park service during the takeover. For the record, I'm not the one telling you this news."

Keith froze in place. "No." It couldn't be true. Up until now he hadn't fully considered the fact he might lose out to the catamaran owner.

"Afraid so, man." Silence. "Come in and see me. We'll figure out a plan."

Keith needed the contract. "I appreciate you." They ended the call and he sat down near Captain Bill, who pointed to Keith's phone.

"What's up?"

"I have steep competition bidding against me for the contract with the National Park Service." Tim Cooper was wealthy and would be difficult to beat. Did Keith really want to use his entire inheritance along with acquiring a significant loan to win the bid? But he detested the alternative of moving to the city if the ferry deal fell through.

He rolled his shoulders to release the developing tension. He was a small-town man. It was disturbing to think about replacing a salty lifestyle with concrete and buildings. The wild horses, the sea, the fresh breeze off the water were an integral part of his life.

How was he supposed to leave behind Jenni and his mom? Without his dad around, his mom needed help with the house along with added emotional support. Not that he was great at it but he was trying, and it wasn't fair to dump the entire responsibility of Gran's rehab on his sister. Of course, Gran wasn't a burden. She was a rock and he needed her chutzpah, but still ... They were taking turns feeding her horses, among other duties. Besides, Keith loved being close to his family and had wasted too much time pushing them away when his father died.

"It will work out, son." Captain Bill stood as a group of passengers made their way down the ramp toward them.

Collin hopped on board to begin his shift, smile and all. He extended his hand to help people onto the vessel, his positive professionalism something Keith appreciated.

"Look! A pelican." A lanky boy made a leap toward Sam, still perched on the piling.

The parents did nothing to stop the kid from trying to grab

poor Sam.

"Hey there," Keith said, stepping closer in case he needed to climb off the ferry in a hurry. "Sam's my friend, so just look at him and don't touch." What he really wanted to say was to respect nature and wild animals.

In general, he saw a lot of disrespect on Pony Island. People left trash behind, let their dogs loose off their leashes, tried to feed the wild horses. Once a boatload of men, who were drinking heavily, tried to capture a younger horse with a lasso and bring him aboard their skiff. During the struggle, one of the men had fallen into the water and hit his head on the side of the boat, nearly drowning. In addition to an expensive visit to the hospital he had to pay a hefty fine for disturbing the horses.

Captain Bill climbed from the boat, seemingly prepared to intervene on Sam's behalf if needed.

Thankfully the boy listened and backed away. His parents didn't correct him and they climbed aboard and chose a seat near the bow, though it appeared the kid intended to stand for the duration of the ride. Keith planned to pay close attention to him.

The ferry filled to capacity. He appreciated the busy weekend schedule to help cover the bills until the season picked up during the weekdays. He flipped on the switch to the overhead speaker. "As we pull away from the dock, please keep your arms in the boat and stay seated at all times. There are life jackets available overhead if needed." Collin pointed to a zipped blue tarp where they were stored.

Keith navigated the ferry with ease and backed out of the boat slip. Years of practice paid off, thanks to his father, who had owned a sailboat when Keith was too little to walk and had taught Keith most everything he knew about boating. The memories choked him up still.

The boy climbed on the bench and hung over the side of the boat to tap a piling. Collin stepped forward to redirect the kid, meeting Keith's glance in silent agreement to keep the boy under close watch.

As much as Keith wanted children, especially a house full of boys, he didn't look forward to raising a child in this world. Parenting was difficult and people didn't seem to discipline their kids anymore. Keith grew up in a military home where he and his sister hadn't dared talk back. He credited his father to his success in life and strong work ethic. Even though Keith still had some lingering issues with his mother, he appreciated her sweet nature and Christian values.

The ferry motored through the no-wake zone and the boy stood up on the seat but turned to assess Keith's reaction.

Collin was busy chatting with a customer, so Keith flagged the kid over in attempt to redirect him. He encouraged him to sit on the Captain's bench. "Go ahead, take the helm," Keith said as he tapped the cushion on the Captain's bench. Removing his own hands from the wheel he allowed the boy to take over. The kid's face lit up and Keith remembered the all-too-familiar exhilaration of those early days.

Keith leaned over so the boy could hear him over the roar of the engine. "What's your name?"

He glanced up with a huge grin, his curly hair blowing in the breeze. "Zack."

"How old are you?"

"Eight."

"Have you been on a boat before?" Keith found himself thinking about his dad a lot lately.

The boy shook his head.

"Well, you're doing an excellent job, Captain." Keith patted the boy on the back to encourage him. His mom was busy snapping pictures and his father sat back and watched. The scenic view of the lime-green marsh entertained the rest of the passengers and always marked the beginning of tourist season, transitioning from the winter straw color.

Keith turned on the overhead speaker and gave his familiar

history report on the area and the wild horses. The boy steered the skiff with Keith's hand still on the wheel as Keith talked to the crowd over the microphone briefly.

"All right, let me take over," he said to Zack. "Want to go faster?" The kid nodded and scooted over as the boat picked up speed. Water sprayed over the side from the choppy channel and doused the passengers sitting in the back.

As they neared the cove on the far end of Pony Island, he reversed the engine to slow down before banking the boat onto the sand. "Watch your return times and let us know if you want to come back earlier," Keith said as Collin helped passengers climb down the ladder and onto the shore. Keith assisted them with their folding chairs, coolers, and beach bags for a day of shelling, swimming, picnicking, and searching for the wild horses.

On the last ride of the day he beached the ferry close to the shore, waiting for one last couple.

"There they are!" a passenger yelled, pointing in the direction of a dune.

The couple strode toward the boat, a black stallion following behind them with his ears pinned back. Based on the horse's demeanor, it was clear something sketchy had transpired. The horses usually wanted nothing to do with humans.

The lady's straw hat flew off in the breeze but she was smart enough not to stop and fetch it, nor did her husband. They hurried in the direction of the boat with the stallion making strides to narrow the gap between them to protect his herd grazing off in the distance.

Due to the low tide, Keith wasn't able to ride the boat up onto the shore, so the couple had to wade into the water to climb aboard. The husband helped push his wife up the ladder while Collin pulled her arm. As she tumbled inside, her husband scrambled to climb in behind her. The stallion stopped about thirty feet away, his head held high in the air with his neck arched, as if glad to send the people off.

Keith shifted the boat into reverse and the engine roared. "I need everyone in the front to move to the back until we scoot off a shoal."

The stallion watched, his gaze trained on the couple. They needed to count their blessings the ferry had been waiting for them. Horses were able to swim, so the couple would have had no escape.

The engine rumbled a deep growl and with some struggle it freed itself from the sandy claws of the shore. Keith turned the skiff around against the current, irritated at the irresponsible couple, but was able to make up time by increasing the speed to Sand Dollar Island. When he slowed the boat to approach the beach, the engine was quiet enough for Keith to ask the couple, who were sitting close to him, about what happened to make the stallion mad.

Silence for a moment, and then the man spoke up. "My wife tried to feed him some grass. He ate it and then plowed her over."

The woman wiped sand and tears from her face. "We tried to get away but he followed us."

Keith exhaled. What did it take to teach people to respect the wild horses? "The law is to stay away at least fifty feet." He always stressed the rules before the passengers climbed from the boat, as the speech was part of his ritual. "There is a fine if you break the law," he reminded them. He planned to turn the couple's name into the ranger station and let them handle the situation.

Once he finished work, he texted Emily to let her know he would pick her up in an hour. His home was nearby and he rushed to shower and to dress in the same pair of khakis he wore the other night but with a nicer shirt.

As predicted, he pulled up in front of Emily's apartment with three minutes to spare. Usually he prided himself on being earlier but at least he wasn't late. When he climbed from the truck, Emily stepped out of her building to greet him.

She wore the prettiest smile he had ever seen. And her hair ... it was pinned back and had locks of long curls twirling around her face. There was something unique about her and it lit up his insides. Her flowered dress blew in the lazy breeze and he imagined her standing in a field of wild daisies on a sunny day.

Dang if he didn't have it crazy bad for her.

There was no one he'd rather show up to the wedding with. He hoped she didn't want to dance, though. He enjoyed watching other people scoot around the dance floor having fun but usually sat back and observed. Slow dancing was a possibility if she insisted.

"You look stunning," he said to her as he opened the passenger door, something his father always did for his mother.

"Thank you, and you look handsome." She flashed her bright smile at him.

The church was nearby and when they walked through the front door, people noticed. They weren't used to seeing him with a date and many turned to study Emily.

"Hi, Keith," Pamela said in a long southern drawl as she approached them. She was someone who had a longtime crush on him but he had never felt the same way toward her. For one reason, she came on too strong for his taste. And her smile was nowhere near close to Emily's natural one. She wore her hair in a tight bun at the top of her head, her lips painted on with a bright red.

"I was hoping to see you here." Pamela ignored Emily and locked her full attention on him.

Concerned Emily would get the wrong idea, he flashed her a reassuring smile with an added wink to convey the woman was a piece of work. But if Emily minded Pamela's presence, she showed no signs.

"This is Emily," he said, sure his affection for her was obvious. "And this is Pamela." His gaze remained on Emily.

"It's nice to meet you." Emily reached out to shake Pamela's hand, although the other woman was hesitant but returned the gesture.

Without another word they beelined inside the sanctuary. He chose to sit near the middle, and placing his hand on her lower back, he gently guided her into the pew. She gathered her dress like the lady she was and sat down with such feminine grace he stood there for a moment to marvel at her.

With those blue eyes she glanced up at him and he hurried to sit, hoping she had no clue how smitten he was. People continued to stare at them and he waved with a large grin.

The wedding began shortly after they sat, and when Captain Bill walked his daughter down the aisle, Keith almost failed to recognize him. Instead of faded shorts, a worn t-shirt, and a ball cap, he wore a tuxedo with a flower in the pocket. Keith cleared his vision to make sure the clean-cut man before him was the salty friend he worked with almost daily.

In all actuality, marriage wasn't on Keith's bucket list of things to accomplish. He was content running the ferry service and returning home. Sometimes, though, the quiet drove him batty. The home he built was perfect for a family, although his desire for kids wasn't a driving force behind why he designed the house the way he had. At least not consciously.

Uncomfortable, he shifted on the pew. He made a silent promise if he ever did say "I do" it wouldn't be a long, drawn-out ceremony. Why bore his friends and family? He'd prefer the outdoors, perhaps on his land. If his fiancée, of course, approved. Women had a way of changing your dreams, but then again, dreams should be shared.

Not that Keith wanted marriage anytime soon.

He glanced at Emily, who was watching the ceremony intently. Considering she didn't know anyone, she looked interested in the vow exchange. Women seemed to love romance. After all, she wrote love stories and enjoyed chick flicks. Truth be told, he could watch romantic movies as long as it was with her.

When the wedding ceremony was over, friends and family

packed into the reception hall at the local country club. Both Keith and Emily enjoyed one of the best dinners he remembered eating in a while. They chose the steak and shrimp option instead of the vegetarian choice and Keith mentally calculated the cost per plate for all the guests and cringed at the price.

He glanced at Emily again. Her eyes were warm and mushy as she watched the newlyweds engage in the first slow dance. Unusual for him, he actually wanted to slow dance with her, wanted to hold her in his arms and lose himself in another world.

To think Gran's fall was what introduced them. How ironic.

Thinking of her, he wondered how she managed all day. He hadn't been by the nursing home this morning to check on her since he had to work the ferry. But she hadn't missed a beat. She texted him, criticizing the selfie from last night.

Her response? She said Emily wasn't smiling enough and it was his job to fix it. She demanded a better photo tonight from the wedding. No pressure there.

He had no idea how he was supposed to ask Emily for another selfie for Gran. They were surrounded by a bunch of people and he didn't want to draw unnecessary attention to them. He solved the issue by requesting someone sitting near them to snap a quick photo but Emily was barely smiling in that one too. Gran was putting undue stress on him and he didn't appreciate the interference.

"Was that for Gran?" Emily asked.

He refrained from rolling his eyes. "Of course, but I'm glad we have it too."

She nodded but seemed tense about Gran's demands.

After several unfamiliar fast-paced dances vibrated the dance floor, they finally played a classic slow song. He noticed Pamela staring at him from the next table over. Turning away from her, he stood and held out his hand to Emily.

Although she appeared surprised, she pushed her chair back and stood slowly. Placing her hand in his, they glided out to the dance floor, but for some reason she seemed hesitant. "Are you okay?" he asked. "We don't have to dance."

Emily forced a smile, not the usual glowing one he had come to admire. "I'm fine. It's been a while since I've danced with someone."

Was she thinking about the dirtbag ex-boyfriend again? Keith was in no hurry to rush her, so he turned to head back to the table, but she tugged on his arm and stopped him.

"Really, I'm fine. I want to dance with you." Her sincerity convinced him.

His hand still in hers, he led her to the center of the floor to blend into the crowd. Dancing might not be his forte, but with Emily he was a natural.

He held her close. He must be doing something right because the steps worked themselves out. He lost himself in the scent of her hair, inhaling a whiff of fresh spring flowers. She had wrapped her arms around the backside of his neck, her face brushing his once, so softly that for a moment he imagined kissing her. But he knew better. He had to wonder if the budding romance was in his mind alone.

The world blurred around them, and if someone hadn't bumped into him, he wouldn't have realized the music had stopped. Reluctantly he pulled away, and within an unwanted moment, a faster song replaced the romantic one.

She bopped to the music. Again, without much thought, he found himself moving to the beat with her, and at this moment he wouldn't stop for anything.

He was certain he'd hear about this from Captain Bill tomorrow but right now he didn't care.

Chapter Nine

I woke up this morning, both excited to visit Pony Island and resistant at the same time. The excursion offered a mixed bag of feelings, for sure. Keith and I were spending a lot of hours together, maybe too many if I wanted to keep my emotions in check, which I did.

The excursion itself piqued my interest, and I looked forward to learning more about Claire and Jenni. Trying to make friends was high on my priority list despite my own issues with being shy.

To my credit, healing was a process, and I needed to be patient with myself. Frank had been harmful to my self-esteem, but sometimes I needed a swift kick to remember to live in the present. The pain, the hurt and embarrassment, the *how-could-I-have-been-so-naïve moments* were normal.

My plan was to grow my friend base to satisfy my desire to belong somewhere. Although I was having a harder time fitting in than I had anticipated, at least I was working on it, hence the reason I agreed to go to the island. And Big Cat checked off all the boxes; a quaint, friendly town, fulfilling my needs on a deeper level.

We weren't meeting until later, so I enjoyed the slow sunny morning lying in bed and staring out the window at the green tips of the marsh and the blue sky. The laughing gulls made their happy beach sound as they flew overhead. There was no comparison to living at the coast as opposed to stressful Raleigh.

Eventually I decided to roll off my bed and make a small pot of coffee. When it was finished I slid open the door and sat on the balcony to enjoy the view. A variety of different bird noises filled the sunny morning, and I realized my idea of heaven included a combination of coffee, spindly grass, and salty water. And wild horses, of course.

Several white egrets perched along the edge of the tidal marsh and one had a fish flapping from his beak. Once I unpacked my apartment more I planned to invest in quality binoculars to view the birds up close, as well as to purchase a book on waterfowl, so I knew what species I had the pleasure of viewing. I sipped my coffee in awe, studying the narrow canals cutting through the greenish-colored grass like a gray snake. The scenery wasn't only pretty, the estuary was an entire ecosystem in itself.

To add even more character to the salty life of coastal living, I enjoyed watching a lone fisherman anchored in a skiff at one of the canal openings, his line cast into the water. He had his feet kicked up on the bow of a colorful red boat, relaxed back in a chair attached on the front.

Knowing the wild horses were roaming out there on their private island offered me a strong sense of peace, as if they kept guard over Big Cat, over me. They added a flavor of romance to the already cozy small town.

Despite the mixed feelings about venturing out to the island, my belly started turning in a knot. The idea of spending the day with a group of people I barely knew was gnawing at my nerves. Boy, Frank's verbal abuse had taken more of a toll on my self-confidence than I thought.

I had to pull myself away from the view to shower and get ready. One good thing about anxiety was I finished in record time, but before I headed out the door my phone beeped. Thinking it was Keith, I glanced down at it, shocked when I saw Frank's name on the screen. Early on he had texted a couple of times, just saying hi and asking how I was doing, but I refused to respond back.

ARE YOU IGNORING MY TEXTS? I MIGHT HAVE TO DRIVE DOWN THERE TO FIND YOU.

I dragged in several breaths with great effort, and my adrenaline was soaring. The man scared me. In a weak moment I had told him where I was moving and now I regretted it.

Instead of walking out the door to meet Keith I had to sit for a short spell on the couch to calm my nerves. I wasn't sure if Frank was trying to frighten me, but knowing him, he usually followed through with his threats.

I didn't know how long I sat there before I remembered the time. If I hurried, I could still make the ferry and meet Keith. I shook off my unpleasant thoughts but knew Frank's text would haunt me.

Before long I parked in front of the *Sea Horse Ferry*. There was a young lady with spiked blonde hair standing in a small, rustic but classy ticket booth decorated with fishing nets, crab pots, and shells. Her face was tanned and somewhat windswept and I suspected she was a college student. As I waited, she was busy explaining to an older couple how there was only one primitive bathroom out there, no restaurants, and no cars. The couple appeared shocked. She continued to tell them it was a remote island with approximately 120 wild horses roaming free. "No," she said, "people can't ride them, pet them, or feed them. They are *wild*."

The couple purchased tickets anyway and sat down on a nearby park bench to wait for the next ferry to depart.

Just as I walked up to the window to buy my ticket, Keith approached me. "This ticket is on me," he said to the young ticket lady. His hair was still damp from showering and he smelled fresh, a combination of sea and spice. He ran his fingers through it while he studied me.

"Thank you," I said, accepting his offer.

The day was still a little chilly and we were both dressed in shorts and t-shirts. At least I thought to bring a lightweight jacket. He carried a backpack with water bottles in the pockets on each side and I wondered if I was supposed to have packed supplies. Honestly, the thought never occurred to me.

He took my hand, disregarding the obvious curiosity of the ticket lady. Hand in hand, we strolled down the ramp and to the ferry. No patrons were allowed on the dock until ten minutes before the scheduled departure, so I felt special.

The dock creaked under our feet as we walked to the far end where a pelican sat perched on a piling. It seemed likely it was the one Keith mentioned the other night and he watched us closely. Judging from all the curious interest we were getting, I had to assume Keith didn't bring women on his ferry often.

The pelican—for the life of me I couldn't remember what his name was—snapped his beak several times to communicate to Keith.

"Hungry this morning?" Keith let go of my hand and opened a white cooler sitting on the dock. He pulled out a much bigger fish than I expected and tossed it to the bird, who gulped it down. He then grabbed a smaller one and held it out to me.

I stared at it, unsure of what he wanted me to do.

"Take it," he said and pushed the fish closer to me. "Sam is waiting."

I scrunched my face and Keith laughed but continued to hold it out as an offering. Not a fisherman, I pinched the tail with as minimal contact as possible, and Keith laughed harder.

Impatient, Sam clanked his beak together as though he were starving and wanted me to pull myself together and toss the dang fish.

Fine, I could do this. I flung it toward Sam, and to my surprise, he swallowed it whole again. Grossed out I had fish yuck on my hand, I stared at it and grimaced.

"Here," he said chuckling as he opened a water bottle and ran it over my hands.

Content somewhat, and since I didn't want to seem too city-like, I wiped them dry on my shorts.

"All aboard," Captain Bill called out to us.

I hardly recognized him in this briny element without wearing his tux. Even though he was older and weathered from the sea, he was a handsome man.

Keith reached out for my elbow to help me onto the boat before he climbed on behind me. Captain Bill extended his hand to shake mine. "It's a pleasure to see you again."

"You too, and beautiful wedding." I was actually shocked by how much I had enjoyed last night.

"Thanks." Captain Bill stood tall and proud.

"I appreciate you working today after your daughter's wedding," Keith said as he offered me the bottle of water from the fish incident and took a long swig of his own.

"Are you kidding?" Captain Bill sat down on the captain's seat and winked at me. "My house is still full of women. When I left they were all talking at once in the kitchen."

The vision made me laugh. Captain Bill was a joy to know, and with Keith's father deceased, I could understand how the captain had possibly taken over the paternal role.

The dock creaked and I glanced up to see the crowd of passengers making their way to the ferry. I couldn't help but think how different my life was now than a few short months ago.

"Time to herd cattle," Captain Bill said with gruff laughter.

Even though today Keith was officially off work, he offered his hand to assist people onto the boat and helped them with coolers and chairs. Captain Bill hung back and stayed at the helm. He chatted easily with the customers and seemed to thoroughly enjoy his job.

Jenni and Claire were the last two people to step onto the vessel. There wasn't room by us, so they sat near the bow of the boat and we grinned and waved at each other. They each carried a lightweight backpack and I suspected Claire's included her camera. Once again I wished I had thought to pack a bag of snacks and such. Next time, for sure.

Captain Bill started the engine. "Hold your ears. You're about to hear a loud horn," he warned the passengers before he honked for three long bursts and shifted the boat into reverse. As Captain Bill maneuvered his way out of the boat slip, Sam watched from his perch on the piling.

The bird took off after us as the ferry coasted through the water. He flew near the boat for several minutes before he swerved toward a group of pelicans on another dock. Sam's bond with Keith amazed me.

The blue water sparkled from the sun and its beauty tried to break through my underlying tension caused by the text I received from Frank. There wasn't a cloud in the bright Carolina blue sky, and the sun warmed the morning with a promise to heat up the day and melt away my stress.

We navigated the water with ease as we passed several islands with sugar-white beaches. One beach in particular sported a dozen or so fisherman, wearing waders and standing in the water, hip deep with their reels in hand. Several boats were anchored on the shore with families already scattered on the sand. When I chose this area to relocate to I had no idea it was so beautiful. I was sold on Big Cat, North Carolina.

The thought reminded me of Raleigh, of Frank again, and I shuddered.

Keith watched me closely. "Are you cold?"

His perceptive nature surprised me. I wasn't sure how much to share with him, but my own intuition told me to be honest and tell him about the text. I retrieved my phone out of the pocket of my shorts, pulled up the text, and passed it to him.

He read it and glanced up at me, his eyebrows raised. "He sent this to you this morning?"

I nodded but words escaped me.

He passed the phone back to me and I tucked it away in my pocket.

"If he so much as sets foot in Big Cat, I want you to tell me."

I didn't answer, unsure of how to react. A traditional, protective man wasn't something I was used to. My guard went up as I wondered if he was controlling and possessive too, but deep in my soul I knew he cared about his friends, including me.

My fearful reaction was probably my old baggage rearing up in my mind but I wasn't sure.

As the ferry approached the end of the no-wake zone, Captain Bill announced to everyone to either remove their hats or to turn them backward on their heads. The boat sped up and the breeze was cooler, causing goose bumps to rise on my arms. I scooted closer to Keith and he looped his arm around my shoulders, warmth radiating from his body. Jenni and Claire were watching us but I didn't mind. Instead, I gazed at a flock of birds taking off in unison as the ferry neared them.

Keith leaned closer to my ear and pointed in the direction of a long narrow island off in the distance. "Pony Island," he said with unmistakable passion in his voice. He was working the perfect job for him and I hoped he won the bid. It was hard to imagine him working in an office or loving any job as much as owning the ferry.

As we neared the island, Captain Bill slowed the ferry and angled it toward a small cove. I marveled at how he reversed the engines to resist the strong current, and then steered expertly onto the sandy beach.

"Make sure you don't swim in this area," Captain Bill instructed the passengers. "The current is strong. After about ten feet, the sand drops off to a good forty feet."

Keith unwrapped his arm from around me and stood. People fiddled with their paraphernalia, much too abundant and cumbersome for a simple day on the island in my opinion. Both Keith and Captain Bill helped them maneuver their things off the boat.

Jenni and Claire waited for us on the beach until all of the passengers unloaded. Most of them made their way a short distance down the shoreline and dropped their belongings onto the sand to set up camp for the day. According to Keith, a few stragglers with shell bags in hand turned the opposite direction to venture out to the point of the island where the ocean met the Sound.

He pointed toward a faraway dock, extending like a long finger out over the water. "Just beyond the farthest bend on the horizon there is a large oak tree leaning over the beach, marking the entrance to the old graveyard."

"Graveyard?" I asked, shocked people were buried on a deserted island.

"This island was once a whaling community. Approximately 500 people lived here." He slid off his pack and pulled out two baseball hats. He handed one to me and placed the other on his head backward. "Protection," he said. "The sun is intense out here."

I noticed Jenni and Claire were now wearing hats too, so I placed it on my head and pulled my ponytail through the back.

"The terrain reminds me of photographs I've seen in magazines."

Keith nodded. "If you didn't know you were in North Carolina, you'd think you were on a deserted island in the Caribbean." The landscape consisted of sand dunes, increasing in size off in the distance. Beyond the wooden structure the terrain changed to woods. "The maritime forest."

"Gorgeous." And I meant it. This place was a drop of heaven. Scattered along the creamy beach were large pieces of washed-up boards along with oversized branches from previous storms. Such a peaceful but primitive place. If I hadn't traveled with a boat full of people to the island I would have thought no one else had ever laid foot here before.

Keith pointed to the right of the dock. "Over there is a path that leads to the ocean. And north of the path is the Marsh Pond and sometimes, especially on hot days, you'll see the wild horses drinking from the watering hole."

"Do you think we'll see them?"

"With Claire here, it's almost certain." He took a long drink from his water bottle before speaking and I followed suit. "People come out here with hope to see the horses and get frustrated when they don't. They have to remember they are wild, and sometimes it takes work to find them. The best way is to climb a tall dune and study the landscape closely. You'll often see the topline of the horses while they graze in the valleys."

My enthusiasm must have been obvious because he grinned. Claire unzipped her backpack and unloaded an impressive camera with a long lens. She placed the strap around her neck and supported the body of the camera with one hand.

"What do you want to see first?" he asked me.

I suspected Claire wanted to photograph the horses as much as I wanted to see them. "The horses, but whatever the group wants is fine with me."

"Horses," Claire answered.

"Horses," Jenni said, pointing at a trail of hoof prints heading into the dunes.

"Horses it is," I said, excited everyone chose the Banker Ponies over the graveyard.

Keith laughed. "Okay, okay."

Claire, the more seasoned one, led the way to the adventure I knew I'd never forget.

But when we approached the wet sand near the Sound, the footing was difficult and barely manageable. It swirled into a large tidewater pond where short Spartina grass grew near the water's edge.

Keith pointed toward a set of fresh, lone hoof prints in the sand. "Probably a bachelor stallion."

"A what?" I asked, unsure I had heard him right.

"A bachelor stallion," Claire explained. "When the young colts get older, the lead stallion kicks them out of the herd to fend for themselves. My husband Jeff oversees the horses, managing them with the assistance of the local veterinarian to administer birth control to a select number of horses he doesn't want reproducing. He keeps track of which mares are with what stallions, how many foals are born, and what area the bachelor stallions are roaming."

"I had no idea there was so much involved," I said in awe. "But it seems kind of cruel to kick a young horse out of the herd. I mean, why?" I was curious and wanted to learn everything possible.

"There is one stallion per harem," Claire said, walking alongside me to explain herd dynamics. "Once the colts are old enough, they leave to eventually create their own group. They fight, or threaten to fight other stallions to acquire mares. I've seen mares wander away willingly and join a new harem. When her stallion finds out one has defected, there is usually a scuttle if he wants her back."

"Horse dynamics are much more complicated than I realized."

"A true statement," Claire said, leading the way toward the nearest dune.

We hiked up and down the hills, some steep and deep with powdered white sand, and some flat with grassy valleys and random wild blue flowers. We hiked to the oceanside without seeing so much as one horse. I didn't mind the hike, although the terrain was more difficult than I imagined, but I really wanted to spot the horses.

We strolled down the rustic beach with the jagged edges of the dunes cut off by storm surges. More driftwood littered the beach and small shells covered the sand. Feeling young and free for the first time in over a year, I darted away from a crashing wave at my feet. I yearned to remove my shoes but then remembered I'd have to wear them with sandy feet to hike the rest of the day.

Up ahead there was a huge object lying in the shallow water. I jogged up to the lump and squealed with delight. It was the largest conch shell I had ever seen. It had a bluish tint and was the size of two of my hands together. When the wave retreated, I bent down to pick it up and studied the flawless curves.

I wished again I had thought to bring a backpack but didn't want to toss away the gorgeous shell. I'd carry it all over the island in order to bring it home to place on my nightstand near my bed. What a perfect spot, and the shell would remind me of today's precious memories.

Keith must have read my mind, or recognized a good find when he saw one. He slipped his backpack off his shoulders and held out his hand. "I'll carry it."

"But it's heavy."

"I don't mind in the least." He took the shell from me, gently stowed it away, and then repositioned the pack on his back. What had I done to deserve meeting such a kind man? Maybe I had paid the price by dating Frank, who was nowhere near half the man Keith was.

But the skeptic in me wondered if it would last. In my experience, the men in my life always stepped on me or left me behind like a chipped seashell.

Chapter Ten

Amazed by the size of the various dunes, I followed Claire as we explored the area she claimed the horses often grazed. The sun baked on the sand, making me question if we were in the desert instead of Pony Island.

As we reached the top of a sandy hill, I had to stop to catch my breath. I really needed to enroll in the local gym.

Jenni pointed to a grassy valley. "Emily," she said in almost a whisper. "The horses."

I screeched under my breath, pressing my hand against my mouth to muffle the noise to avoid frightening them. Sure enough, I spied a brown horse, barely visible between the dune and tall grass and wished I had a camera of my own.

"I love your enthusiasm," Claire said, likely ready to shoot photos if the horse stepped into full view. "It's nice when people appreciate the precious gift God has blessed us with. We are lucky to live near the wild horses."

I was excited all right. I had a sudden urge to buy one of Claire's photographs to hang on the many bare walls in my apartment. "I need to shop in your store. Your pictures will make my apartment homey, make me feel more connected to Big Cat."

Claire's expression brightened. "I'll give you a discount." The horse stepped forward, and Claire shifted into optimum position on the dune to better angle herself to snap unique pictures of her four-legged subject.

Later, when I looked at Claire's photos from today, I wanted to recall the story behind them, where they were taken, what the circumstances were to differentiate them.

I was beginning to like Claire and Jenni. They were impacting my life in a positive way already and lent me a sense of support. When I was younger my father's advice was to choose my friends well, to surround myself with people I admired. Quality friends added to the quality of life.

Advice I needed to apply to men today. I glanced at Keith, who seemed a good choice. Time would tell.

"The Marsh Pond is just beyond that dune." He pointed to the tallest hill I had seen so far. "The stallions take turns letting their herds drink from the pond, depending on their hierarchy."

I was finding the habits of the wild horses most interesting.

"If we climb the dune we shouldn't encroach on their natural habitat," Claire said to me. "We'll have a better view."

"Absolutely love the idea." I trailed behind her, huffing and puffing, and Keith and Jenni played follow-the-leader behind me while we climbed. My legs begged to fall off my body but I continued to trek through the deep sand and hoped the workout was well worth the view.

Jenni powered past me as if she were walking a flat beach. "How do you make this look so easy?" I asked in a breathy voice.

Keith answered for her. "She's a marathon runner. This is nothing for her."

Me, on the other hand ...

Claire slowed down too as we climbed, Jenni passing her with ease and reaching the crest first. "Look, Emily! There they are."

Despite the shortness of breath, I passed Claire, who was bogged down with a backpack full of equipment, and climbed the last fifteen feet with anticipation to see what awaited me. When I reached the top, I drew in a sharp inhale.

Grazing in the grass in the valley was a foal. *A foal!* I couldn't believe our good luck. "Nine horses."

"A fairly large herd," Claire said from behind me. I heard the click of her camera as it began a long sequence of shots.

I decided living near the coast I needed to buy a camera to capture its extravagant beauty. From now on I promised myself I would be better prepared for a visit.

From what seemed like a bottomless pack, Keith pulled out his own fairly impressive camera. I wondered what else he carried in his bag in addition to the camera, water, and the shell I found.

The horses were so breathtaking, I stared at them in awe. They looked magical against the white sand, blowing green grass, backdrop of emerald-colored trees, and neon blue sky. Golden reeds grew beyond a strip of trees with a hint of sparkling water shining through in the sunlight. It must be the watering hole Keith spoke of.

Keith pointed to the edge of the knobby trees outlining the marsh. "The Maritime Forest."

"Stunning," I said in awe. The blue water of the Sound contrasted with the marsh and the forest, creating a breathtaking combination of color.

Claire aimed her camera at the foal with the picturesque backdrop. "Jeff, my husband, said thirteen foals were born on the island this year. I've only seen four of them. This one makes five."

"I'd love a picture of the foal." A photo of the baby hanging on my bedroom wall would be a treat to wake up to each morning. Again, the sharp contrast of this colorful rustic island versus the stress of city life confirmed a salty lifestyle spoke to my soul.

"Sure thing. I can hook you up with as many photos as you want," Claire said.

Of course, I planned to buy them from her.

A brown horse, the stallion according to Claire, studied us closely as if he found interest in the group of humans observing his herd. His multi-colored mane, consisting of silver and brown with highlighted red tips, blew in the breeze.

Claire clicked her camera several times while the stallion posed for her with his ears forward, face turned toward us. "They're waiting their turn for the watering hole. If you notice, there's another herd drinking."

Sure enough, through a carved-out path among the spindly trees and thick bushes, I noticed four horses near the water's edge. When they finished drinking, one by one they filed down the short, narrow path and disappeared behind a dune near the Sound. But the stallion of the herd we had been watching continued to monitor us.

A twig snapped nearby. A horse I hadn't seen, a brown one with a tangled black mane and tail, strode in our direction.

We backed up, following Claire's lead. "Horses are prey animals," she explained. "And each animal has a job, so the scout's duty is to survey danger, meaning us."

The horse began to approach Jenni, who was standing on the dune closest to the watering hole. She was at least 150 feet from the harem, but the scout was apparently curious and cautious. She was making her concern known; she wanted Jenni to move out of the way. The mare folded her ears back and jutted her nose at Jenni, the intensity of her energy speaking volumes. She wanted her to move. Now.

Jenni diverted her eyes and backed farther away.

"The mare is driving her backward to widen the gap between the entrance to the Marsh Pond and us for the safety of the harem," Claire said, and I was grateful she was with us.

As soon as Jenni was an acceptable distance away, the horse stood guard while the rest of the herd strolled toward the pond. They took turns drinking from the water and then relieving the guard horse at the entrance. When they finished they headed toward us, a few of them stopping to graze.

I was nervous about the situation, but Claire seemed relaxed.

Courageous in my opinion, she dared to snap a few more pictures. "They usually don't pay much attention to people. But it's cooler today, so they are more active. Also they have a foal to protect." She stopped taking photographs as the mare with the tangled black mane began to climb the dune toward us. "Let's back away and climb the smaller hill to give them more space."

I had to fight the urge to get the heck out of there.

We backed away again. Even though the horses were still watching us, especially the aggressive one, at least they stood in place.

"We need to count our blessings they didn't trample us. Maybe we need to leave." I wasn't an expert on the subject but I valued my life.

"They are more relaxed now, grazing lazily, and moved us where they wanted, as they do to one of their own. I believe that was their goal all along," Claire said. "They are allowing us to observe them but from afar. You have to listen to their silent communication."

I took her word for it. She was the expert, but I kept back a safe distance so I could run if needed.

Keith held out his camera in my direction and temptation got the best of me. I reached for it, eager to snap a few photos of the baby nursing from his mother. Trying out Keith's camera would give me an idea if I wanted to buy one similar to his.

A couple of years ago I was into photography. Nothing even close to Claire's expertise, but despite my love for the hobby, I sold my equipment to help pay for a wedding that didn't happen. I needed to reclaim my identity by indulging in my prior hobbies. My move to Big Cat was all about reinventing myself along with developing new interests and friends.

I snapped several cute photos. As if posing, the foal turned his head away from nursing and looked straight at me. He lifted his back leg to scratch behind his ears, and being a physical therapist, I marveled at his balance. I happened to be at the perfect angle for the shot.

"Good one," Claire said. "I'm envious but I don't dare move closer."

While Claire continued to kneel and take pictures, the rest of us sat on the dune together and watched the horses for a bit. Keith's knee touched mine. I wished I were in a different place in my healing process but I wasn't. And in my experience, no man was as pleasurable to spend time with. He was confident, peaceful but yet fun, and although he was fast becoming a good friend, there was definitely chemistry between us.

Claire hopped to her feet. "Let's go. I'm eager to explore other sections of the island for photo ops."

We followed winding paths through the rough terrain, becoming hungry and hot by the time we reached the Sound. By my calculations, we had circled around to reach the only dock and bathroom facilities on the island. I had noticed the structures earlier from a distance.

"The graveyard is just up the beach," Keith said, glancing back at me as we walked along the water's edge.

I cleared my throat.

"What's wrong with graveyards?"

I decided to come clean with my strange experience. "I've been leery of them since my grandparents died."

He slowed down and fell into step next to me as Claire and Jenni walked up ahead. "Why?"

"I guess they remind me that my grandparents are no longer alive, but there is a bit more to the story."

"Now I'm curious."

I looked away and admired the different landscape than the ocean side and the dunes. Large branches littered the beach along with seaweed. It was rustic but rugged and beautiful. I inhaled a long breath of fresh air to prepare myself for sharing my disturbing experience for the first time with someone.

"Once we had gone to visit my grandparents' gravestones but Terri had forgotten something in the car. She was gone so long my mom went to check on her, leaving me standing alone."

I paused and Keith waited for more.

"I was talking to them, mostly to my deceased grandmother, and I heard a noise behind me. A twig had snapped. But when I turned around there was no one there, although I had a strong sense I wasn't alone." I stopped talking to catch my breath. It amazed me how the story made my heart race like I was standing there now. "I heard the snap again in front of me and I swear I heard someone say they loved me. I turned and ran to the car and refused to go back."

Keith didn't say anything and I couldn't read his reaction.

"I know, you think I'm crazy."

He shook his head. "No I don't, but I'm sure there was a logical explanation."

I looked up into his blue eyes. "I tell myself that but my irrational side doesn't want to listen."

"We don't have to go to the graveyard. It was just something to do." He grinned as if trying to reason with my nervous self.

I shook my head. "No, you are right. There is no time like now to get over the ridiculous fear. I want to go to the graveyard." He raised his eyebrows as if he didn't believe me. I didn't believe myself. "Really, let's go."

"Okay, but how about we eat lunch first? We can sit on the dock and have a picnic."

I chuckled. "What all do you have in your bottomless backpack?"

He wiggled his eyebrows. "For you to find out."

Jenni had apparently overheard the comment about stopping for lunch. I hoped she hadn't heard my confession to Keith.

"I'm hungry too." She headed toward the dock, and approaching it first, she planted her backpack near the steps.

Keith moved around her and chose to sit on the edge with his feet dangling above the water, and I joined him.

"Why doesn't the ferry drop people off here?" I asked, swinging my legs back and forth, carefree and playful once again.

Keith pulled out two wrapped sandwiches, bags of chips, and a container full of purple grapes. I wasn't sure why, but I was surprised he made lunch for us.

"I find it easier to pull the ferry onto the beach. Besides, the dock is reserved for the park service." He handed me the food and dove into his sandwich. His mouth half full, he said, "The current is stronger here and the ladder is difficult for people to navigate with all their belongings."

"Oh." I understood the dilemma, and as was true with horse dynamics, there was a lot to learn.

Jenni and Claire sat on the stairs and pulled food from their packs. Next time I would offer to make lunch and would bring supplies.

We ate, laughed, acted silly and had a plain-old-good time. Jenni and Claire made me feel like I had known them for years, and I had no idea being with a man could be so much fun. Claire stood and announced she was walking down the beach to photograph driftwood. Jenni joined her, leaving Keith and me alone.

He looked away at the horizon as though lost in thought. "There's something I want to tell you," he said, swinging his legs again.

I stiffened and knew whatever he wanted to say was important.

He continued to stare off at the horizon when he spoke. "You told me about your past. Now it's my turn to share more."

I listened, thankful he wanted to open up to me. Talking about personal experiences with someone safe was foreign to me.

"So I mentioned to you I was engaged to Vicki, and we dated for a couple of years. I thought I loved her but now I'm not so sure."

He looked to be busy watching a ski boat off in the distance, so I waited for him to continue with his story.

In the meantime, I focused my attention on the small fish moving about below us.

"I was angry, hurt. I didn't understand why she no longer loved me." His chest heaved as he paused.

I flinched, surprised at the pain his words caused me. I looked forward to the day I no longer cared about Frank and my former friend's betrayal. My best friend now, Kelly Adams, said it was about them and had nothing to do with me. I didn't fully understand what she meant but I was trying.

He began to swing his legs harder, faster. "My dad's diagnosis with cancer was one of the darkest moments of my life." He looked up as if staring at heaven.

I reached for his hand and held it tight.

"The other dark spot was when my sister died. It's a long story but there was a boating accident."

I covered my hand over my mouth to try to hide my shock. "Oh, my gosh. I'm so sorry."

He shrugged as if to dismiss the pain.

I learned it was the tough conversations we needed to talk about. "What happened?"

Keith swallowed hard. "When we were kids, Jenni and my sister went sailing on Scott's boat. His dad let him borrow it for the day."

I filled his pause with a nagging question. "Scott? Isn't that Jenni's husband?"

He nodded. "It took her years to forgive him but then they started dating and are now married. Scott blamed himself but it wasn't really his fault. A storm came up and my sister, Brittany, fell off the bow and they couldn't find her."

My mouth dropped open. "How tragic."

"Yeah. My sister was the oldest and Daddy's little girl. She had never done wrong in his eyes and she was a beautiful person inside and out." He leaned back on the dock, resting his arms behind him. "I tried for years to fill her shoes in my dad's eyes but was never successful. Even my failure to get married felt like another shortcoming where he was concerned. When he was diagnosed with cancer I was angry, resentful. As I said before and want to emphasize, instead of spending his last days loving him, I pushed him away emotionally. The guilt eats me up."

I sat in silence, his words hitting home with my own family dynamics. I barely talked to my dad and was in competition with my sister. My relationship with my mom was hit or miss. We were either close or on the outs with each other.

I leaned toward him and our lips touched in a soft embrace. It just felt right, the thing to do.

"Excuse me, love birds." Jenni stood at the base of the dock with her pack on her back. "Let's get a move on."

Keith and I stared at each other for a silent moment. The importance of what he shared passed between us and I realized we crossed over into a new level of trust.

In some ways we were both dealing with abandonment issues between our exes dumping us before the weddings and similar struggles with feeling like a failure in our parents' eyes.

Keith stood first, holding his hand out to me as I scrambled to stand. I was glad we had our moment of intimacy. Hand in hand, we joined Jenni and Claire as we strolled down the beach toward the graveyard.

Different from the rest of the island, dense woods lined one side of the rustic beach. Limbs and driftwood dotted the white sand, and thick marsh grew in the shallow alcoves. Several tidal pools hugged the shore with narrow canals connecting the alcoves to the Sound. If we wanted to explore the island farther, we needed to cross the canal.

"You'll have to carry your footwear and wade across the water," Keith said to me. He balanced himself with his backpack and removed his shoes. It was only seconds before he had his bare feet in the water. He reached out to steady me as I pulled off mine.

Claire kicked off her sandals and held her camera high as she stepped fearlessly into the water, Jenni following her lead.

After I scooped my shoes in my hand, I stepped into the cold water and the mucky sand sucked between my toes. We waded across the narrow stream and the current was a lot stronger than I anticipated. I lost my balance and grabbed for Keith. Thankfully, he held out his muscled arm to steady me. The last thing I wanted was to fall into the chilly water. Talk about a miserable ride back on the ferry.

We strolled about a mile down the beach. "It's almost as if we've been dropped back in time," I said, amazed by the large, overhanging branches of the trees, reaching out like knobby fingers and beckoning for visitors. The trees were almost spooky if they weren't so gorgeous with the Spanish moss dripping from their tips. "At every bend I expect to see an old ship in the water with pirates aboard."

"The island definitely has a mystical sense about it," Jenni said as she walked alongside me.

Our bare feet sank into the soggy sand, leaving a trail of deep footprints as I sauntered along the water's edge with barely a care in the world.

Keith pointed. "Up ahead. See the big oak tree leaning across the beach? It marks the entrance to the graveyard."

The graveyard.

Barefoot, with our shoestrings tied together and looped over our shoulders, we reached the bend where the huge ancient tree was almost falling over onto the sand. The low limbs beckoned us to step onto the narrow path leading into the mysterious Maritime Forest.

"Think about all the history the tree has witnessed," I said with awe.

Keith nodded. "Pirates, sinking ships, horses swimming ashore."

"People trying to survive on an island through hurricanes,"

Claire added.

The salty air blew against my face, blowing my ponytail around to whip my cheek. A handful of boats sprinkled the bright blue expanse of water. We stopped near the sandy dune at the base of the tree to wipe off our feet as best as possible. I pulled on my shoes for the upcoming adventure through the wooded area.

Keith asked, "Ready?"

I wasn't but didn't want to complain.

He climbed up the steep sandy slope and offered his hand to everyone. In a single line we pushed on and made way through the dense trees draped in moss. A musty earth smell made it difficult to breathe. The adventure reminded me of something we'd watch on TV, exploring the wild foreign tropical jungle.

The birds, hidden in the thick bush, sang their songs. They filled the forest with a friendly welcome.

I ducked under a low-hanging branch to find an overgrown clearing surrounded by encroaching trees. A thick rope marked off the boundary of a crumbling graveyard for approximately twenty headstones.

I tried to ignore the sense of someone watching us. No human was out there, I reasoned, but perhaps there was a wild animal observing us from the forest.

With the thigh-high rope keeping us at a distance, it was difficult to make out the faded dates on the mossy headstones. I had to admit I was curious. If I had a piece of paper I could color it with a pencil to see what dates the old carvings revealed.

Claire clicked several pictures, a few up close, several zoomed out.

We heard a loud snap of a branch in the woods and leaves crunching. I backed up, my arm touching Keith, and I let out a squeal.

"Let's get out of here," Jenni said. She spun on her heels and headed for the path and I gladly followed.

Chapter Eleven

A lmost a week had dragged by without word from Keith. Not trying to feel needy, but my feelings were hurt. And I'd had enough hurt to last a lifetime. I thought the adventure on Pony Island had gone well. Apparently, I was wrong.

I tried to reason it was possible he was busy with ferry negotiations and I attempted not to take it personally. But it was difficult. His silence tapped into my abandonment issues. My mother would say he was feeling vulnerable and it scared him, and I understood the emotion well.

Whatever the reason, I had no interest in playing mind games of any kind, intentional or not. No thank you.

But I had to remind myself the world wasn't meant for people to survive alone. Yet, before I moved here that was exactly what I had been, alone even though I was engaged.

Holidays were the hardest. Joyful people gathered in groups with friends and family for festive functions. The thought of spending a holiday without plans made my heart ache.

Society placed a lot of pressure on single people. If you weren't dating someone seriously, people assumed you had a problem.

And when people became involved in a serious relationship they seemed to put their friendships on the back burner. Well, not me. Making friends was my goal and balance was ideal. I wanted both at some point, a serious relationship and friends, all of which I might be cultivating now.

At least Fridays were busy at work and I had plenty to keep myself distracted. And tonight, I planned to submit my manuscript, not the one in progress, but the finished piece, to a small list of agents of my first choice.

I also signed up for a prestigious conference in New York City along with requesting a pitch appointment for an editor and an agent. I was allotted one ten-minute time slot for each, and what a fabulous opportunity. The conference was almost sold out and I secured a hotel room in the establishment. In my opinion, staying elsewhere detracted from the overall experience and decreased networking opportunities. The room was expensive, but if I wanted success, I needed to put myself out there.

Just thinking about the conference, my mood lifted. I was proud of myself for taking such a big step. In general, I wasn't one who liked large crowds, but when it involved my passion for writing, I almost forgot about my annoying fear of talking to a group of strangers. But when I thought back to the beginning of my writing pursuit, the level of commitment was overwhelming but rewarding. A proponent of positive thinking, I had learned to reframe my thoughts around reducing the individual tasks and goals into smaller segments, ones I could easily handle in an optimistic manner.

Stubborn, as my mother liked to say. She always blamed my perseverance on my astrological sign as a Taurus, not that I believe in such things. Besides, *determined* was a more accurate word. There was a huge difference between the two.

Once I returned home, exhausted from the long day, I showered as usual and then sat down to email proposals and queries to my list of agents. I had been rejected before, but I was again ready to put myself out there.

My father considered me a dreamer, and perhaps I was, but what was so wrong with dreaming big? Nothing at all.

Feeling invigorated now, I opened my laptop and pulled up the files I wanted. I sent out a query letter and the required documentation each agent required.

When I finished, joy filled me. Undoubtedly, writing was my passion.

I had the evening alone and began to write on my work in progress. Whatever the reason, my creative side blossomed here in Big Cat. With ease, words poured from my fingertips.

In general I was a plotter, someone who organized thoughts on a poster board with yellow stickies before I began writing a manuscript. Usually I figured out all the plot twists first along with the incremental scenes to meet the designated plot twists. But not for this book. Without the typical roadmap, as I called it, the words wrote themselves. Sure, in my mind I knew the usual happy ending, but as far as figuring out each scene? I was clueless.

As a result, the words were flowing like a waterfall. To my surprise, I was enjoying the love story, not only as a writer but as a reader.

My cell phone rang, jolting me from the delicious writers' high I was so enjoying. I normally didn't answer while writing but in case it was Keith, I grabbed the phone off the coffee table. It was Claire.

"Hi there," I said, surprised she was calling me. I enjoyed our day together on the island and was glad I had gotten to know her better.

"Would you like to join Jenni and me at Coffee Break tonight? We're going to view the photos from our day on Pony Island."

I was comfortable in my pajama pants and t-shirt and reluctant to leave the cozy nest I made on the couch. But then again, my reason for moving to a small town was to make new friends. Besides, I deserved a reward for sending out query letters.

"I'd love to. What time?"

Claire's voice sounded muffled and I could hear a child screaming in the background. "Jeff is watching our daughter, so I'm leaving in a few minutes."

"I'll meet you there." We hung up and I forced myself to crawl off the couch and change into decent clothes. Small town, new friends, and a spontaneous coffee outing were all wonderful things.

I hurried to pull on shorts and a nicer shirt, to apply a little makeup, and to attempt to control my curly brown hair. The joke in my family was I had been adopted, although at particular moments I didn't find their comments funny. Why everyone else had straight blonde hair was one of those odd genetic things. My facial features resembled my father's closely as well as those of my cousins, so I wasn't concerned.

Within twenty minutes, including the stroll down Front Street, I entered Coffee Break. There was nothing better right now than the delicious aroma of fresh coffee greeting me with a welcome.

"Emily, over here!" Claire called out and waved from the small makeshift living room in the back.

I headed in her direction and chose a soft chair with a heart-shaped pillow nestled in one corner. The decorations in the coffee shop consisted of several of Claire's framed photographs of the wild horses. Other pictures included boats, docks, fishermen in the water, and the *Sea Horse Ferry*, which made me think of Keith.

Claire noticed my interest in the ferry picture.

"Have you heard from Keith lately?" Claire wrapped her hands around the mug of coffee she held on her lap. An open photo album with pictures of the wild horses sat on the nearby coffee table and I couldn't wait to delve into them.

I shook my head, uncomfortable with the question. Normally I'd consider the conversation gossip, but I knew my new friends cared about me already and had true intentions. Also, they didn't strike me as gossips.

Claire's expression grew curious, her eyebrows rising. "Nothing?"

"Nothing." Not so much as a glance of him at the rehab

center, a phone call, a text. He had disappeared for five days now.

Claire shook her head and frowned. "I hate dating games."

"What dating games?" Jenni asked, approaching them while carrying two mugs of coffee.

I remained silent, so Claire answered for me. "Keith hasn't contacted Emily."

The way Claire described it made me sound needy, and I wasn't. I had survived much worse than a man not calling me.

"It's the stupid man code," Claire said. "They act all interested and then poof. They disappear. God help them if they show a woman they are interested."

Jenni handed me a mug. "I did my best to remember what you like in your coffee from the few times you've been here."

"Thanks," I said and took the mug. "I'm sure it's perfect." The warmth penetrated my hands, as suddenly I was cold.

"You know, Keith isn't a normal man," Jenni said.

I raised my eyebrows.

"I mean, he doesn't date much, if at all. He doesn't seem to play man games."

Claire chuckled. "You never really know someone until you date them."

"True," Jenni said. She relaxed back in her chair and crossed her legs. "It's possible he's busy with the contract for the ferry."

The specifics of why Keith hadn't called didn't matter and I pretended not to care.

Claire took a long drink from her mug. "What will he do if he loses the contract?"

Jenni shrugged.

"Will he return to being an architect and move?" Claire asked.

I sat taller, never having given it serious thought. Maybe it was best he hadn't called. I mean, why invest too much emotion into the budding relationship if he was going to leave? I relocated to a small town for a reason and had no plans to move again.

"I don't know," Jenni said, placing her empty mug on the wooden coffee table in front of them. "Let's just say the ferry contract needs to go through."

Chapter Twelve

Keith was so busy he barely thought about anything other than securing the ferry contract. He needed to reach out to Emily but his thoughts about her were complicated. He liked her a lot but also needed to focus on securing his future. Right now he was in survival mode.

In the parking lot of the park service, after another arduous meeting, Keith passed his opponent. The man, rather attractive and well-dressed if Keith had to admit, was walking toward the building. Apparently, he had a proposal meeting also scheduled. Keith, competitive but fair, nodded in greeting. Tim, successful and professional, nodded back.

The two of them kept a comfortable distance between them, no words exchanged, and Keith climbed into his truck. His thoughts were miles away and he reached the ferry without remembering the drive to the dock.

As he strode past the ticket booth, he paused long enough to greet an older retired couple who only worked the booth twice a week during the busy season.

Keith followed the small crowd of people making their way down the dock toward the boat. Running late today, he glanced around for Sam but he wasn't waiting for breakfast in his usual place on the piling. Sometimes during the busier hours and days he disappeared.

"Hey, Keith," Captain Bill called out. He was on the smaller boat helping visitors board the vessel.

Lost in thought and lacking the desire for conversation, Keith flicked a wave as he made his way around the people and onto the larger boat. His group would leave in a half hour, so he had plenty of time to tidy up and relax a bit. Dealing with the proposal from the park service was a major stressor point in his life. But he wasn't complaining.

As Captain Bill departed from the dock with a load of passengers, Keith stared out at the water, lost in thought. Each day the marsh grass turned greener and he loved this time of year. The water was so blue he could almost pretend he was on vacation in a tropical destination.

Honestly, he didn't know what kind of job he'd be willing to sacrifice this view for.

With all luck, he wouldn't need to find out.

Keith wiped off the benches surrounding the perimeter of the boat. Customers didn't want to sit on a damp seat from dew, but in all humor, they didn't seem to mind riding back on wet, sandy seats from bathing suits.

A group of customers thumped their way down the ramp and approached his boat. They were laughing, ready to enjoy their day of relaxation among the sand dunes. Keith reached out to help a family of four.

The last two women to climb aboard surprised Keith. Jenni and Claire held out their hands and he helped them aboard. Both women were dressed in t-shirts, ball caps—neon pink for Jenni and white for Claire—shorts and sneakers. Not their usual attire for a visit to the island. Of course, Claire wore her camera around her neck but wasn't wearing her usual backpack. While it was uncommon for the two of them to visit Pony Island during a weekday, the strange way they looked at him set off warning bells. They were up to something.

Once they were on the boat, Jenni glanced over the top of her sunglasses as if Keith were in trouble.

When he ignored the gesture, she crossed her arms and made a point to sit on the captain's bench. He positioned himself behind the helm next to her, started the boat and clicked on the overhead speaker. "Thank you for riding the *Sea Horse Ferry* today. Please keep your arms in the boat until we clear the dock, and stay seated for the duration of the trip."

He clicked off the microphone and set it down, sounding the horn three times before he motored the ferry in reverse out of the slip without bumping into the pilings. To relax he inhaled a long breath of salty sea air.

They moved at a slow speed through the no-wake zone. Customers turned in their seats and admired the islands for their sheer beauty, watching the choppy channel for a glimpse of waterfowl, dolphins, or just to zone out from the tranquility the water offered.

Jenni surprised him when she sidled up against him.

"So how's Emily?" she asked.

Keith shrugged. Not only hadn't he talked with Emily the past week, he had no clue how she was doing.

"Haven't you called her?" His sister enjoyed butting into his life and today was no different.

He shrugged again. Guilty. Why did she think it was her business?

"Don't you have a husband to nag?" he asked.

It was her turn to shrug. "She's going to think you aren't interested. Is that what you want?"

He didn't respond, just focused on the water ahead.

"Is it?"

"Is what?"

Jenni groaned. "Why are men so hardheaded? Are you interested in Emily?"

He reasoned if he didn't answer her, she would continue the scrutiny. "Of course I'm interested."

Jenni raised her eyebrows as if to ask what his problem was.

His nerves bristled. "Why do you care? What happens between Emily and me is between the two of us."

"Well, if you don't like her, then continue to ignore her."

He clicked on the microphone and spoke into it, giving a brief history of the island and the theories of how the horses ended up there. A couple of tourists had questions and he answered.

He told the story about how the woman fed the stallion some grass and he knocked her over before forcing her back to the boat. One of the women, who he assumed was dressed in designer swim gear, gasped.

"The moral of the story is the wild horses are wild. Don't go within fifty feet of them. Respect them, and they'll respect you."

Knowing the routine well, Jenni removed her ball cap and held it in her hand before he warned the customers about speeding up the boat and holding onto their belongings.

They motored through the water until they passed a nearby buoy. He throttled forward at a much faster speed, keeping in mind the water was rough today and wanting to assure his passengers had the smoothest ride possible. However, the boat hit a wave just right. It caused a stream of spray to shoot over the side, covering Ms. Designer. She screeched and flashed her partner a sour stare as if he were personally responsible for the incident.

Getting splashed was always a risk when riding the ferry.

They rode through a scenic marshy area. Up ahead and off to the right, a large pod of dolphins arched out of the water. He slowed the boat, so his passengers could enjoy the show.

Claire took off the lens cap from her camera and began clicking away at a baby dolphin swimming close to his mother. Their fins were out of the water for a moment then disappeared under the surface. They rounded out of the water in unison close to the boat.

A few girls sitting near the bow squealed with delight.

Keith was on schedule enough to remain there for a few more minutes. In general, he loved the ride through the marsh, and the dolphins were always a treat.

Before Keith sped up the ferry, Jenni started in on him again.

"Think about it. You had a wonderful date, and you were the happiest I've seen you in a long time." She stared at him without blinking. "And then you backed off. You're giving her the message you aren't interested."

Keith didn't appreciate Jenni's approach. His life was his business. But she had a point, although he refused to give her the satisfaction of knowing he understood.

"What makes you an expert on what Emily is thinking?" As far as he knew, she hadn't talked with her since the day they visited the island together. Then again, neither had he.

"I like Emily." Jenni stood and leaned into him. "Women stick together, and we are sick of men giving women mixed signals."

Keith knew she was right. He thought about Emily often but had pushed aside the distraction to focus on the business. He couldn't have met her at a worse time because his future had never been this uncertain.

"Let go of the past, Keith. All women aren't hurtful like Vicki was."

Vicki. He tried not to think of his failed relationship.

"Emily isn't Vicki."

A true statement, although he had serious trust issues regardless.

"Focus on Emily. Fix it," Jenni said, and then she slid away to sidle up next to Claire, who was still taking photographs of the dolphins. Jenni held onto the railing, leaning over to watch the entertainment.

Keith would fix things but it wasn't intentional he hadn't called. He had prayed to meet a sweet, down-to-earth woman, and now he needed to embrace this opportunity and have faith.

When his father died, Keith relied on work to help numb the pain. He refused to allow himself to continue the pattern. The contract was important, but so was Emily. When he thought of her, he saw a glimpse of their future together. His father had always told him when he met the right woman he would know right off. He only hoped he hadn't messed things up.

Jenni's words echoed in his mind.

Fix it.

Chapter Thirteen

I had enough of Keith's silence. Today I planned to do something about it. What exactly? I wasn't sure. I hadn't so much as seen him at the rehab center.

I was scheduled to work with Mr. Graham, a man who had a prosthetic leg. He was on the younger side compared to our usual geriatric population, and originally had a knee replacement. Infection had taken over and eventually he received a below-the-knee amputation.

Currently he was maneuvering his wheelchair down the hallway when I intercepted him.

"Good morning," I said and flashed him a southern grin.

He stopped wheeling. "Hi there, gorgeous."

The elevator opened in time for Ms. Isabelle Snyder, the sweet lady with dementia, to stare at us in confusion. Known for her unusual clothing choices, today she wore a pink flowered dress with purple pants and red sneakers.

In contrast, Mr. Graham was dressed in an ordinary t-shirt and khaki shorts with his prosthetic leg exposed. Her eyes wide open, Ms. Snyder studied his fake leg as if she knew something was wrong but didn't understand what. The elevator door closed without her stepping out. Evidently she was in one of her moods to ride up and down until someone distracted her.

"I'm going to get your walker from your room," I said to Mr. Graham and hoped someone intercepted Ms. Snyder on the lower floor before the door opened again. "Be right back."

I took off down the hall, walking quickly but being mindful of the residents ambulating around the facility. Whatever exercise I managed to participate in while at work helped with my new fitness goals and thank goodness I didn't work a desk job where I sat all day.

I scooted into Mr. Graham's room. The staff had pushed his walker against the wall near the bed, so I retrieved it and rolled it down the hallway back to where he was waiting.

I glanced down at his leg and was surprised I didn't notice it before but I must have been distracted by Ms. Snyder. "Your leg is on wrong. Isn't it uncomfortable?" His prosthetic foot was pointed at an odd angle.

"Yeah, the nursing assistants have no clue how to put it on right," he said, rolling his eyes.

"I need to teach you how to don it correctly." That way, when Mr. Graham returned home, he would know how.

The elevator door opened as Mr. Graham kicked his leg out with an exaggerated motion. Ms. Snyder stared at his leg as the prosthetic flew off and landed on the floor in front of him.

She yelled out, her face pale as if she might faint. Apparently, she thought his leg had really fallen off.

"Dang blasted!" Mr. Graham leaned forward to pluck the leg off the floor, oblivious to the startled woman standing near the entrance of the elevator.

The door slid closed and the woman disappeared into the abyss.

He stuck the leg back in place with only a cue from me about positioning it.

When he was finished, Mr. Graham stood with his walker placed in front of him. A woman approached the elevator and pressed the button. It opened and the woman squealed as she saw Ms. Snyder, who yelped when she noticed Mr. Graham's leg had returned. There was never a dull moment in the amusing land of skilled nursing.

As the day went on, I found myself delaying treatment

for Ms. Stallings. However, to reach my next patient, I had to bypass her hallway. As soon as I turned the corner, I noticed Keith heading into his grandmother's room. He stepped backward in his tracks and glanced directly at me.

I wanted to ignore him and keep walking, but it wasn't like me to be rude. Instead, I flashed a little wave in his direction.

His smile lit up the hallway.

Why did my heart have to practically flip in my chest? Because of the uncertainty of his job, I needed to safeguard it. Unfortunately my emotions had a different idea.

I picked up my pace and planned to see Ms. Stallings last. Hopefully Keith would leave by then. Avoidance was my new coping strategy.

"Emily," he called out.

I stopped in the middle of the atrium.

He hurried toward me, still smiling as if nothing had happened. "I'm glad to see you."

Funny. If that were true, why hadn't he called?

He stood with his fingertips tucked into the pockets of his khaki shorts, an awkward moment passing between us.

"Sorry for not calling." His gorgeous blue eyes stared through me. "But my proposal for the ferry contract was due yesterday and I've been focused on nothing else."

I understood all too well, as Frank's specialty was to hyper focus on work, but I was never on his priority list.

He glanced around as if making sure no one heard him. "Dinner tonight?"

The stubborn side of me wanted to refuse him. Then I remembered I had planned to reach out to him today anyway. "Sure. Dinner sounds good."

"There is a quaint little country kitchen outside of town." He was back to staring at me with his bright blue eyes. "It's nothing fancy but the food is excellent."

I loved exploring family-owned restaurants. Small places usually had the best food.

"Locals go there," he said as if he read my mind and then reached for my elbow. "I missed seeing you."

His words warmed me like a mugful of hot chocolate on an icy-cold day. I wanted to tell him I missed him too but the words made me too vulnerable—the last thing I wanted—so I smiled instead.

"Great. I'll pick you up at six?"

Still unable to speak I nodded, but we needed to have a talk. Setting boundaries was something I had to learn.

He bent forward and kissed me lightly on the cheek. The imprint tingled and the sensation found its way to the midsection of my chest.

A high-pitched squeal sounded from Ms. Stallings' room, and as we looked up in alarm, I saw her standing in the doorway, watching us.

From the delighted expression on her face, it had made her day to see her grandson kiss a woman, even if only on the cheek. I remembered Keith hadn't dated in a while and his family was thrilled about him pursuing someone. That someone was *me.*

He turned around and strode down the hallway toward his grandmother and I watched for a moment as he kissed the top of her head. To say the man swept me off my feet was an understatement.

In anticipation of tonight, the rest of the day at work dragged by in slow motion. When I clocked out, it was as if a week had gone by instead of a few hours. It seemed forever before I stepped outside and the temperature had dropped to sixty degrees. The ground was wet and fog swirled in low places among the trees and marsh.

I returned home and sorted through the pile of mail I had successfully ignored until now. I separated it into stacks according to statements, bills, junk mail, of which I filed in the trash can. Once finished, I glanced at the clock and had about an hour to write after showering and changing clothes for dinner.

Writing wasn't as solitary as one might imagine, thanks to

online writing groups. There was always someone interested in engaging in thirty-minute sprints, and when several other people agreed to join me, I set the timer and started typing. But for some reason, the words were harder to create tonight. It was too chilly and dreary to sit on the balcony to help the process, so I struggled to form complete sentences over the next half hour until I finally gave up.

The frogs were in full croaking mode and should have eased my mind but didn't, so I found a book in an unpacked box and snuggled into the corner of my couch to read. The remaining half hour flew by and before I realized it, a knock rapped on the door.

When I answered, I tried to act as nonchalant as possible, as the last thing I wanted was for him to know how much I cared about him. In my jaded experience, once a guy realized my feelings for him, he usually disappeared. Keith had already demonstrated that once.

He stood there, sexy in his khaki shorts and bright blue shirt. A musky, delicious aroma wafted into the living room, too delicious actually. If I had any sense, I would shut the door before he entered my apartment.

A stray cat I had seen a couple of times before and had named Tucker, trotted across the outside foyer to stand beside him. I had tried to pet him on numerous occasions but Tucker had refused to come near me. What was so special about Keith? Unfortunately, I knew the answer to my question.

Keith stepped inside, hesitating for only a moment before he gently wrapped me in his arms. His lips lightly touched me like a flutter of a butterfly. The warmth tingled on the surface of my mouth and I didn't want this level of attraction to him. It only meant hurt in the end.

He pulled away, his gentle eyes twinkling with delight. So he was feeling it too.

"Ready to go?" he asked, his voice husky.

I nodded and glanced away.

To my embarrassment I fumbled with the keychain in attempt to lock the apartment door. When unsuccessful, he reached out and took the keys from me to help, Tucker sitting near the door waiting for his attention.

As we walked down the steps Tucker trotted behind Keith, as if following him was an everyday occurrence, and across the parking lot to the truck. Perhaps he was a cat whisperer.

I chuckled and found the outward affection of Tucker toward Keith entertaining.

"What's so funny?"

I shook my head. "I've been trying to pet him since I moved here." In good humor I pointed an accusatory finger at Tucker, the traitor. "He runs off when I come near him."

He glanced down at the obedient cat next to his leg. "Unbelievable."

"It's the truth," I said laughing.

He opened the door for me, another luxury I wasn't used to. "The ride is about twenty minutes," he said, again ignoring Tucker, who was trying to climb into the truck. "But I think you'll enjoy the scenery." Gently he pushed the cat away.

Enjoy I did, as the view along the country roads stunned me with all the marsh and water, but when we passed by a lake with a mill, the fog swirled with mysterious beauty. I sat up straight. "Stop! Let's go back."

He hesitated at first and without asking why he turned around the truck and parked at the mill.

Cypress trees lined the edge of the silver pond. Several trees bathed in the still water with a layer of fog wrapped around the tree trunks, creating a magical ambience. My creative mind swirled with ideas of writing a suspense novel.

"Claire would love this," Keith said.

"Yes, she would. I wish I had my new camera about now." I had ordered one similar to Keith's and was still awaiting delivery. The view too good to waste, I pulled out my cell phone and tried to capture the depth of the thin layer of fog surrounding the trees. Its distorted reflection mirrored on the glass-like lake.

"Let's go check out the old mill house," I said, feeling a sense of joy I was beginning to embrace as normal. We strolled along the moist grass in the mist as I took several more photographs of the water spilling from the large wheel attached to the building. The spray of water bounced off the water's surface, mixing with the fog. It was simply breathtaking.

I captured more photos than I imagined I would, Keith staring at the view as if he enjoyed the picturesque scene too. After one last click, I turned around, only to bump into him. His chest was toned, broad, so ... nice. Was the word *nice* descriptive enough? Hardly.

I hadn't expected to warm up to him the way I was. Maybe I missed him when he was silent and it made me realize how I enjoyed him in my life. I wanted his lips on mine again, but instead of kissing me, he reached for my hand and we headed back to the truck.

Physical touch wasn't something I was used to experiencing. While I had enjoyed hugging or holding hands with Frank, he always projected an element of emotional distance. I despised feeling neglected, but my mother labeled the relationship emotionally abusive and it probably was.

Keith was different in many ways.

"Ready for dinner?" he asked, glancing at me with a boyish grin.

I swallowed hard. "Yes."

He closed my door and went around and sat in the driver's side. "You're about to experience the best cooking Down East has to offer. If you like southern BBQ and hush puppies, you'll be in heaven. They have the best Brunswick stew in town."

My stomach rumbled. After a short drive, we pulled into the gravel lot of a small, homey-looking restaurant, more of a ranch-style house than anything. The place was packed.

He took my hand, his grip firm but gentle, and we entered

the diner. It was small with thick wooden tables in the center and several booths lining the far wall. The hostess seated us in the corner by the window. Instead of sitting across from me, he slid on the bench beside me, our legs touching. And believe me, the contact was electric.

I picked up the menu and studied it but already knew what I wanted. The southern BBQ sounded delicious. I pushed aside the menu, my decision made the moment he had mentioned BBQ.

The server, wearing tight jeans and a low-cut top, approached. A hair clip barely contained the wild mane of thick curly hair. "What can I get y'all?" She drawled out the sentence in the southern Down-East way.

We both ordered water and the same entrée with a side of green beans and hush puppies. The server left to place the order and then set a basket of hushpuppies and little containers of butter in front of us. There was nothing better than steaming hot hush puppies dipped into cold butter.

"We are so much alike," he reflected as he blew on one to cool it.

I had to chuckle because I was doing the same thing, and then I remembered the stray cat, Tucker, following Keith around like a puppy and laughed.

"What's so funny?"

"Tucker."

His brows drew together in confusion.

"The cat." I kept laughing and had to set my hush puppy on the plate. "He followed you around like an obedient dog instead of the feral cat he is." My laugh grew harder and by accident I snorted. It had been a long time since I laughed like this and I realized joy had been contained in a tiny little compartment of my soul and had burst open. The image of the cat trotting behind him in the foyer of my apartment, down the steps, and across the parking lot without Keith so much as noticing, as if he were used to cats following him all the time. "You're the cat whisperer."

"The what?" He started to laugh too.

I snorted again, not even caring the diner was crowded or who heard me. When the urge to laugh hit me, I had to go with it. I hardly ever snorted, couldn't remember the last time, and it made me laugh more.

He joined in with my craziness and started laughing with me. "I don't know what got into him," he said in spurts when he caught his breath enough to speak.

We were interrupted by the server, who smiled at our silly behavior. She topped off the water glasses while she watched us with interest. "I have a question for you."

We glanced up and Keith said, "Sure."

The woman focused on me, though. "Are y'all married?"

I shook my head quickly and her question sobered me up. Keith didn't respond.

"I didn't think so," the woman said as she fiddled with the notepad in her hand. "But I'm enjoying your romance. You don't see it often."

Our romance.

Keith was relaxed next to me, his shoulder and leg touching mine, even though he didn't offer a response. Perhaps that was answer enough, and the woman's comment didn't seem to unravel him. Other than his disappearing act this past week, he didn't seem afraid of commitment, not that I wanted a relationship.

Having a man friend to laugh with was a new experience, and I had to admit, I was enjoying him.

All too fast dinner was over. I found myself wanting the night to continue, but he had already paid the check and the server had cleared our plates. It seemed we were both stalling to prolong our date.

"Do you want to go somewhere for ice cream?" Keith asked, pushing his wallet into the back pocket of his jeans as we stood.

Once in a while I could justify eating dessert but with my

fitness goals, it wasn't something I wanted to indulge in a lot. My plan was to fit into the bright blue bikini I bought on sale at the end of last summer.

"How about a walk instead?" I asked as we headed toward the front door.

"Great idea. A stroll or for exercise?" Keith waved to the server and thanked her as he opened the door for me. The sun was sinking behind a building and an array of orange color lit the sky on fire, surprising me, what with the fog earlier. Before long the temperature would drop more. I had forgotten a lightweight jacket, but so far I was comfortable.

"Exercise," I said. "I don't mean power walking but more than strolling." We walked across the parking lot and once again he opened the door for me. I was starting to love his traditional mindset.

"How about downtown Big Cat?" he asked as he slid into the driver's side.

"Sounds great." And there were always people around so it was fun. I loved to people watch and one of my favorite things was to eavesdrop and then concoct stories about them in my head. Walking with Keith was an added bonus and it would also be a good time to discuss my thoughts about the past week.

Before long he parked in a spot near the water. We walked hand in hand along the boardwalk until the path ended, and then we continued down the street at a moderate clip. I didn't know what I was thinking about seeing people because there wasn't a lot of action downtown to entertain me. After all, it was a weeknight and I was used to the city.

"Emily," he started to say.

There was something about the way he said my name that gave me pause.

"I apologize for not reaching out to you earlier." He gave my hand a quick squeeze. "I was focused on my proposal. You should know, though, my sister is your biggest advocate."

It was nice he apologized, but what was he talking about?

"Advocate?"

He chuckled under his breath. "She and Claire rode my ferry over to Pony Island today."

That wasn't unusual.

"During the middle of the day ... and Jenni gave me the riot act." He glanced down at me. "She said I was giving you the impression I wasn't interested in you."

So, he only asked me out tonight because his sister gave him a difficult time? Of course, I appreciated Jenni and Claire's support but wanted Keith to ask me out because he wanted to, not because his sister confronted him.

"Believe me, I'm interested in you," he said with such sweetness it made my heart soften. For once I ignored my logical mind and kicked to the curb my usual fight-or-flight response. Instead, I needed to face whatever was happening between us. The opening for my talk presented itself.

"I'm interested in you too, but you need to know something about me."

He watched me closely. "What's that?"

"I'm not one who tolerates being ignored when you're busy, and I'm not here for your convenience."

He looked down at the ground. "I'm sorry I made you feel disrespected."

"I'll be honest with you. My dad walked out the door when I was young as if we were unimportant and only saw us when it fit into his schedule." I swallowed hard. "Guess I have abandonment issues, but when someone shuts me out, it brings up my fears."

"Oh, Em. I'm so sorry." He pulled me into his arms and held tight. "I promise never to neglect you." He bent down and kissed me softly.

From then on he called at least once a day and we kept a slow-paced conversation circulating between us by text. It was casual and offered me a deep sense of peace.

But the peace didn't last long. Unfortunately, I received

another text from Frank.

As I said before, if you don't respond back I'm coming down there. I know this is your phone number because I can see you've read my texts.

I started shaking and fought the urge to respond but was afraid he'd show up here. Now I looked back I should never have told him where I was moving. But if I did answer it would only engage him in conversation. He'd start by saying how he missed me and then it would end in a verbal lashing. No longer would I tolerate his abusive behavior. Unfortunately it was long into the night before I got any sleep.

I didn't tell Keith about the text, nor anyone else except for my best friend, Kelly, the next morning.

You aren't thinking about going back to him, are you? Kelly texted.

No way. I'm not stupid.

Except I had gone back to him before, several times after arguments. He used to have a spell on me and I'd like to think I had grown well past him.

One night, rather late in the evening, my mom called from Cancún.

"Mom, are you and Terri having a good time?" I asked over the festive background music filling the air space from Cancún.

"We're having a blast. You should fly down here to see us." The phone muffled for a moment and it sounded as if my mom was talking to someone. "Terri says you'd like the men here."

I rolled my eyes. They acted like wild teenagers on spring break. Mom was always the impulsive one, opposite of me. "Mom, I have a job. I can't just take off and fly down there."

"Boring," my mother said.

Was I the only responsible one in my family?

Speaking of responsibility, I glanced around my small but cozy apartment. I wasn't one to judge, as I had yet to finish unpacking, but at least I was making slow progress. "I'm glad you are enjoying yourself. Are you safe?"

My mom laughed. "Are you sure you're my child? You've

always been so guarded. Be adventurous, impulsive."

The words stung.

I resisted the urge to defend myself. Perhaps I was so *guarded* because my mother was such a free spirit and lived in the moment, and my dad was emotionally unavailable. I craved security and learned to make my own.

"Listen, I've got to run," my mother said.

I heard people partying in the background. "Be safe. Tell Terri I said hi."

"Bye." The phone clicked.

I sat there with the phone still held to my ear. I had wanted to say "I love you." Anything besides a click and dead space.

Maybe my mom was right. Maybe impulsivity was the ingredient I was missing in my life.

Chapter Fourteen

Deep in thought, Keith strode toward Gran's room. According to Emily, she was making good progress in therapy. The plan was to discharge her in a few days, although she hadn't reached the level of independence he wanted.

In his opinion, she was nowhere near ready to perform such a hefty task of caring for her horses, but apparently that wasn't reason enough to keep her at the rehab center. Emily had recommended someone help her feed and care for the horses but Keith reasoned she needed to stay at the rehab facility longer. Unfortunately, the insurance company didn't see it the same way.

He entered Gran's room and stopped short. She walked out of the bathroom with Emily behind her and he wasn't looking forward to addressing his apprehensions about Gran leaving.

"Emily taught me how to get in and out of the shower again." Gran's grin warmed his heart as if she were happy to be returning home, but he had serious concerns.

"I'm glad, but didn't you know how to shower already?" Keith asked, confused.

"Not with my arm compromised. But I'm not allowed to take a real shower until the doctor says so. We were just practicing."

His gaze met Emily's and he couldn't help but notice she wore the prettiest smile on her face. "If she isn't allowed to shower yet, then why is she being discharged home?"

Emily's smile faded. "Because we can't keep her here until then. The insurance won't pay."

"By the way, good morning," Gran said, making him realize he was being rude.

"Sorry, guess I am uneasy. Good morning, ladies."

"Good morning," Emily said in a different, more professional voice than she used outside of the rehab center. But she wore a lopsided grin large enough to show off her pretty white teeth.

Keith tried to tone down his own smile but was fairly sure it lit up the room.

"I see we're making progress." Gran seemed to enjoy putting them on the spot.

"Excuse me?" Emily asked with feigned innocence.

"Oh, please." Ms. Stallings pointed at Keith. "Look at him. Whatever happened between the two of you is obvious to everyone."

Keith glanced at his grandmother. "Everyone? You're the only other person in this room."

Gran cackled. "And you didn't deny my statement. Gotcha!" She headed for the door. "I'm ready to walk. Let's get going." She turned back to him. "Well, come on. You don't have to wait in this room."

He scooted behind them so as not to rile up Gran. As they reached the elevator, they were just in time to see a woman wearing a mismatched orange pajama top and red sweat pants step from the elevator with her walker. The woman stopped in front of them and pointed an accusatory finger at Gran.

"You!" the woman growled. "I told you never to come in my room again. You stole my book."

Gran stopped with such sudden movement Emily bumped into her and Keith reached out to steady Gran.

"What are you talking about?" Gran said in a defensive tone.

The woman raised her voice an octave. "Give my book back

to me."

Keith stepped forward to intervene, unsure who this lady was or how Gran would know her. "Gran, did you take her book?"

Gran snapped her head toward Keith. "You think I'd take that old woman's book?"

Emily giggled, and Keith stifled his own. He had to admit, the expression on Gran's face was entertaining. "Well, you do enjoy reading," he said.

"Keith Randall Stallings, I don't steal." Gran was causing a ruckus in the hallway, even more so than the woman. "I'm telling you, I didn't steal the old lady's book."

"I believe you," Keith said to calm her down but Gran's stern expression didn't change.

A nurse intervened. "Ms. Snyder, is this the book you're looking for?" she asked and pulled a paperback from Ms. Snyder's walker basket.

"Yes." She pointed at Gran. "She stole it."

"No one took it. The book is right here in your basket," the nurse said. "Let's get some coffee." She was able to successfully convince Ms. Snyder to follow her to the coffee bar.

Gran glared at Keith. "Thanks for your confidence in me. I want out of this crazy house."

"A few more days, Gran." Keith crossed his arms in a defensive manner.

Emily spoke up. "Let's deviate from the normal route and head toward the front door."

Gran didn't comment but changed her direction and strolled down the hallway leading to the lobby. Keith flashed Emily a thankful grin for saving the moment and distracting Gran. Dang, he loved his grandmother to pieces but she was a handful. She was loveable in her own ornery way and made him think he needed to visit his own mother, who was sweet, but learning bad habits from Gran.

Gran stopped near the front door to sit on a flowered chair

to rest. As it opened, a wave of heat washed in with Jenni.

"Hi there!" Jenni said to Emily but acknowledged Gran and Keith with a flash of a wave. Her unwavering concentration usually meant one thing, that she was about to accost poor unsuspecting Emily. "I hear Gran is going home soon."

Gran pointed a knobby finger at Jenni. "Don't you dare change her mind about letting me go home."

Jenni ignored her threat. "Why so soon? She can't possibly handle all of her horses and everything else."

Emily didn't seem to falter. "The insurance company gave us a deadline and they don't take horses into account. She can do everything we are asking here and has maxed out on her progress."

"Keith and I are busting our butts helping her with chores," Jenni complained. "We can't continue the workload much longer. And she's not as agile as she was before."

"I know," Emily said with what sounded like heartfelt concern. "I ordered outpatient physical therapy to help, but I'm not sure she will be completely independent with those chores again. She will need continued help, for sure."

Like a summer storm brewing from nowhere, Jenni's complexion paled. "Excuse me." She powered off down the hallway to the nearest bathroom.

"She's taking your news hard," Keith said. "Or maybe she pushed herself too much with her run this morning."

"I hope that's all it is," Emily said when her phone rang. She glanced at it and an interesting expression crossed her face that Keith couldn't read.

"Something wrong?" he asked.

She shook her head. "Sorry. I usually have my phone muted when at work."

His intuition alerted him there was something wrong but with Gran there he didn't want to push the subject. He'd bet most anything it was a call from her ex-fiancé and wished he'd leave her alone.

She glanced at her phone again, biting her lip, but then turned her attention back to Gran and urged her to stand.

Jenni turned the corner, her face a pale shade of yellow with a hint of green.

"Are you okay?" Emily asked as Jenni approached them.

Keith scrutinized his sister. He didn't say anything and knew Emily was analyzing Jenni's appearance too.

Gran stopped dead in her tracks, Emily managing to stop short before bumping into her again.

"What in the blasted heck is wrong with you, child?" Gran asked. "You need to return to bed with a good book." Bringing up the book subject was a bad idea. Gran pointed at Keith. "Don't question me again about the book."

"What book?" Jenni asked.

"Never mind," they said at the same time.

Some topics were better off dropped.

"Oh, no, you don't. We aren't changing the subject. They accused me of stealing a book."

No one responded.

Gran started moving forward again. Without looking at Jenni, she asked, "Why do you look like that?"

Jenni paused before answering. "Gee, Gran. Thanks."

"You look horrible." Gran glanced slightly back at Emily. "Where are we going?"

Emily nodded toward the front door. "I'd like to take advantage of the nice day and see how you do walking down the handicap ramp and on the uneven surfaces of the grass. After all, horses live on grass."

Good idea. Keith knew without doubt Gran would be out in the pasture with her horses first thing when she returned home.

"A ramp? What for?" Gran continued to walk toward the front door but she slowed down. "In case you haven't noticed," she said, "I'm not handicapped. I don't need to use a ramp."

"Gran, be nice." Keith attempted to calm down his grandmother but his effort was futile.

"Do you think I need to use a ramp?"

"No, I don't. I suggested it because I wanted to see you walk in the grass." Emily sighed as though mentally exhausted and not used to dealing with such crazy family dynamics. Although, there was a tiny smile on her face, as if she were enjoying the interaction on some level.

Gran ambled in slow motion out the front door, Keith and Jenni following behind them. Several people sat on wicker chairs, a handful had guests visiting with them, and a few were eating bowls of ice cream.

"Do I get ice cream if I'm a good girl and do what Emily wants?" Gran asked Keith. She was dead set on trying to start an argument with him.

He wasn't playing into her mood. "Gran, if you want ice cream, I'll scoop it myself."

"Two scoops? One chocolate, one vanilla?"

Before Keith could answer, Jenni ran toward the bathroom.

"What's her problem?" Gran asked. When Keith didn't respond fast enough for her, she said, "Maybe she's pregnant."

Keith about choked when he swallowed.

"Well, she is a newlywed." Gran stopped in front of the ramp. "You want me to walk down that steep hill? You going to catch me if I lose my balance?"

Emily placed her hand on the gait belt. "You'll be fine. This is why we are practicing."

Keith smiled to say, "Told you she was a handful," but he refrained from expressing the words. To his surprise, Gran maneuvered the ramp and grass with slow and steady progress but he still didn't want to see her taking care of her horses with a compromised shoulder.

After they finished and returned inside, Gran headed down the hallway toward her room but reminded Keith about the ice cream. Keith turned on his heels and entered the dining room, noting Jenni still hadn't resurfaced from the bathroom.

When he returned to Gran's doorway, he overheard their conversation.

"The boy's got a thing for you," Gran said in a matter-of-fact voice.

"Think so?" Emily's voice held a lilt as if she were hiding that little smile of hers.

"I know so. And a warning to you to treat him right. He's a good one."

Emily didn't respond and Keith was surprised by Gran's words but appreciated how his family had each other's backs.

"Sorry for being so forward, but I love my grandkids." Gran's voice softened.

It seemed wrong to eavesdrop, so Keith entered the room as Emily said, "I understand." She then turned to leave, almost bumping into him as they had the first day they met.

"In a hurry?" he asked to instigate a reaction in her.

Her face turned pink and she adopted the Stallings' strategy of not answering. A simple wave of the hand and she was out the door.

"You ran her off," Gran accused.

No, Gran ran her off but he wasn't about to challenge her. His family was close and he was about to find out if Emily was able to handle small-town living and his overbearing family.

Chapter Fifteen

Rejection was always hard. It was also difficult to shake. A mild depression took root, a heavy feeling filling me with self-doubt about my writing skills. One of the emails I had sent out stared back at me with an accusatory finger. I couldn't help but think negative thoughts. You aren't good enough. Quit writing. You're wasting your time. My mind translated a polite rejection letter with words of insecurity. It was the main reason why I had stopped submitting previously.

At least the rejection letter wasn't from my favorite agent at my dream literary agency, but still, it hurt. But as they often said in the publishing world, a rejection meant I was one step closer to a yes.

The best advice I had received from a successful author was to keep writing, to never give up. The problem was, I lost my desire to write today.

Usually I allowed one day to mope around and to feel sorry for myself before I forced myself to shake it off. Tonight, though, I decided to make myself step up and pull out my laptop anyway. No words came to me, but so what if I sat there with my fingers poised on the keyboard, waiting for the words to flow. Eventually I typed one word, then a long pause, and another word. I almost folded up the blasted laptop and shoved it back into my bag when a vague scene developed in my mind.

One sentence, then another began to surface, and before long I was writing without much thought. When I finished the scene I yawned, realizing it was almost ten o'clock on a work night.

Listening to the frogs in the marsh, I climbed into bed but my thoughts vacillated between writing, rejections, Keith, failed relationships. Vulnerability had stung me before but I also understood if I wanted to be wildly successful in my writing career, as well as in my personal relationships, I needed to take risks.

The thought of being hurt by Keith caused almost a panic to set in. Hadn't I learned not to open up so quickly? The enjoyment and laughter we experienced about Tucker at the diner popped into my mind. What a perfect scene to write in a book but in real life those fun-loving scenes were temporary.

Depression stunk no matter how short-lived it was.

The next morning I stopped by Coffee Break to check on Jenni before heading into work. As always the aroma of freshly brewed coffee greeted me when I opened the door. There was nothing better. The place was surprisingly busier than usual for seven o'clock in the morning, with at least six people standing in line in front of me.

Alex was working the counter, so I glanced around the shop for Jenni but was out of luck.

The line moved quickly, so when it was my turn to order I asked if Jenni was working today.

"No, she's out sick." In a hurry Alex filled my order, and when she handed me my cup she said, "It's strange. She's never sick."

"I hope she's okay." If Jenni wasn't pregnant, I hoped it was nothing serious.

"I'll tell her you stopped by." Alex waved me off and I left the shop, pondering the different causes of why Jenni might be sick.

On the way toward my car I passed by the ferry and tried not to look, but it was difficult not to notice Keith on the dock below, having a full-blown conversation with his pelican friend, Sam. I tried to squelch down the warm, fuzzy feeling bubbling up inside me. Avoiding Keith would be difficult. I passed the ferry dock and unlocked my car parked in a diagonal space on the street.

"Emily."

I turned around to face the man I was trying so hard to evade. It didn't matter if his scent was a combination of sun and salt, didn't matter if he looked handsome in his orange t-shirt and khaki shorts, or his muscular tanned legs begging for attention.

He bent down and pressed his lips onto mine. "Dinner tonight? I want to discuss something with you."

More rejection? Here it was, as predicted.

When I didn't answer, he kissed me again, his lips warm and gentle but yet eager for more. If he planned to rebuff me, then why was he kissing me?

Against my better sense, I agreed to dinner. After all, he was persistent and I found myself caving in to his touch.

"Why don't I pick you up around six tonight?" he asked, glancing over his shoulder at the passengers lined up, waiting to stroll down the dock to board his boat.

"Okay," I said with little enthusiasm thanks to my situational depressive state. "Lucky you for being able to spend the day on Pony Island." A get-away from my troubles was exactly what I needed.

He leaned toward me, his hand on my arm, lending me a false sense of security.

"One day you'll be able to visit Pony Island whenever you want, Ms. Bestselling Author."

I must have looked surprised and confused because he pulled me into a bear hug.

"You're going to sell your book. Many books. You'll be able to take a vacation anytime you want." He let go of me and his gaze met mine.

How had he known what I needed? His words uplifted

my spirit a notch and I only hoped his insight was correct. Tomorrow was another day and my confidence in my writing would return. It always did.

"Don't lose hope." He backed away. "Gotta run." He turned around and jogged toward his awaiting customers, who were now making their way down the dock toward the ferry.

I replayed my conversation with Keith on the way to work. One thing I needed to learn was how to allow my life to unfold the way it was meant to without the need to control every aspect. Life wasn't outlined like one of the books I was writing.

I parked under a shade tree at work and entered the building. The hallways were quiet except for the sound of forks dinging against plates as the residents ate their breakfast. I walked into the gym and set my lunch bag and purse inside a small cubby marked with my name, cringing as it reminded me of a kindergarten classroom. As a person who paved my own path, the marked-off space felt constraining and my mood didn't help. I chose an available computer.

"Emily, I saw you at dinner the other night with a man." Stacey, the OT, sat next to me.

I shrugged, unwilling to divulge my personal life.

Another coworker joined the conversation. "You've met someone already? I've lived in Big Cat for a year and haven't found anyone worthwhile to date."

Yet another coworker asked, "Who is he? Big Cat is small. I bet we know him and can tell you his childhood history and more."

All faces turned toward me and I felt my cheeks grow hot.

Steve, a physical therapist, chimed in. "Quite frankly, it's not our business."

Thank you, Steve! To my relief, the subject was dropped.

All day I tossed around different scenarios of what Keith wanted to discuss tonight. My thoughts drifted back to the conversation this morning with my coworkers. Not only did most of them know him from Ms. Stallings, but if they lived here for any length of time, there was a good chance they knew his life story too. But I wanted to learn his history on my own.

I headed down the hall with the plan of seeing Ms. Stallings while Keith was at work. Dressed already, she was standing near the closet reaching off-center and fiddling around with hangers.

"Ms. Stallings, make sure you stand closer."

She continued to try to maneuver a sweater off the hanger. "Why? I'm fine."

I helped her. "Because reaching challenges your balance and changes your center of gravity." Teaching patients to work inside their base of support was one of the most challenging exercises I faced.

"And call me Gran if you will."

"Thank you, Gran," I said, trying out the name, as it made me feel like family.

Gran's face lit up. "Come visit me at home after I leave. Keith will show you where I live."

Keith ... everything always circled back to him.

Why was everyone trying to push the two of us together? If it wasn't meant to be, then no matter the pushing, it wouldn't be. I hated depression, as it made me focus on the negative.

Gran plucked another shirt off a hanger. "Let me tell you something." She fixed her gaze on me as if to emphasize her point. "I was married for fifty years before my husband died. Sometimes you have to let your guard down and let a man be a man."

What did she mean?

"Men get quiet when they think." Gran tossed an unfolded shirt and the sweater into an open suitcase on the center of the bed, already packing for her discharge tomorrow. "Men are supposed to emotionally support you, to love and protect you, and you return the same level of commitment. It's simple."

My eyes just about crossed in disbelief. "You make relationships sound easy. It's difficult to find a man who is capable of such devotion."

"That's where you're wrong."

I planned to perform my own casual survey among the married patients on my caseload to see how they stayed married so long.

"Keep believing," Gran said. "Trust me, you found a good one. And not because he's my grandson."

The next several patients on my caseload had been married for close to fifty years. The men had drastically different advice than women on the subject of what it took for a happy marriage.

All of the men voiced they needed to agree with whatever their wives said. I wasn't sure if they were joking, or if they were serious. When prompted for more details some men elaborated and said never to go to bed mad. It was far better to sleep if you at least agreed to disagree. The women, however, suggested to talk until the issue was resolved, or at the very least to kiss goodnight and to discuss the disagreement the following day when well rested.

The common theme was respect, love, communication as well as to trust in a higher power. Interesting. Of course, I believed in a higher power but didn't practice my belief to the extent Keith did, but it wouldn't hurt for me to consider becoming more spiritual.

After I returned home, my mild depression subsided and I was excited to write for an hour before I finished getting ready to see Keith. The conversation with Gran inspired a new scene between the heroine and hero in my book, where the hero's grandmother emotionally adopted the heroine in the story. In this case the hero had broken up with her before this happened and resented the budding relationship between them. I hoped there wasn't a similar correlation between what I was writing and my own life but I continued to develop the story line.

The words poured onto the page like a waterfall. When my cell phone alarm went off to warn me it was time to set my laptop aside to dress for dinner, I had written nine hundred words. This morning when I tried to write, I struggled to create one measly paragraph.

I had just finished applying a subtle shade of pink lipstick when the doorbell rang. As usual, he was early.

The unknown topic of tonight's dinner lingered in my mind as an unwanted aftertaste of bitter coffee. Anxiety and maybe a hint of excitement swirled in my belly. I wasn't sure if he wanted to move the relationship to the next level, or end our friendship. What I did know was I needed to chill out and let the night happen on its own.

I opened the door and stood still, frozen almost, unsure if I should frown or smile.

He didn't give me long to think about it and wrapped me in the sweetest kiss of my life. It was masculine but gentle, filled with urgency but patience.

It wasn't a breakup kiss.

"Ready to go?" he asked, his voice deeper.

He had a habit of stealing my words, so I blinked and nodded. I stepped past him, our bodies touching, and he pulled the door closed. Instead of waiting for me, he took the door key from my hand and locked the apartment. Was this what Gran was calling leadership? If so, I rather enjoyed it.

He took hold of my hand and we walked together down the steps. "I thought we'd dine somewhere a little nicer tonight."

First a passionate kiss, then holding hands and the mention of a nicer restaurant.

To my surprise, we walked through the doors of a cozy but fancy Italian restaurant just outside of town. Elegant Italian music wafted through the open space. A decorating genius had painted the walls with vibrant scenes from a vineyard and had sectioned off individual tables with partitions covered in faux ivy. Small white decorative lights sparkled from deep inside large plants to add romantic atmosphere and privacy.

"Nice," I said with awe. "Whoever decorated this place did a fantastic job."

Keith's face radiated from my approval of the restaurant.

We were seated right away at a table surrounded by tall tropical plants with red tips and glittering white lights. Italian music wafted through the restaurant to create elegance. The hostess handed us colorful laminated menus and took our drink orders.

Glancing over the menu, I had no idea how I was going to decide which delicious entrée to order. After a few minutes, the server approached and introduced herself, setting a long basket on the table loaded with of a variety of different breads before she left us alone. On a small plate was a dipping bowl of olive oil with what looked like rosemary and diced garlic layering the bottom. To satisfy my craving, despite my diet goals, I dipped a chunk of bread into the oil placed on the table between us. It was the most mouthwatering bread I had ever tasted.

"Have you decided what you'd like to order?" Keith asked. Our chairs were so close our legs touched.

"Chicken Griglia." At his raised eyebrows I read off the description from the menu. "It's a boneless chicken breast marinated in balsamic vinegar, olive oil, and rosemary." My mouth watered just saying the words. "I love rosemary. The entrée is served with grilled vegetables and Asiago cheese, another one of my favorites, and a fried panzerotti. I wonder what a panzerotti is."

"I think it's similar to a calzone but fried. It's probably a pocket filled with cheese and some other goodies."

"Sounds delicious." My decision was an excellent choice. "How about you?"

He closed his menu. "Linguine Con Frutti Di Mare. Basically it's shrimp, clams, mussels, and calamari in a marinara sauce."

When the server returned she took our order, and after she left, Keith's expression turned serious.

He took my hand. "Emily ..."

I swallowed hard, nervous all of a sudden.

"I want you to know I really like you." He paused.

The tension was thick enough to make me want to crawl under the table.

He must have noticed my hesitation. Turning up my chin, he studied my eyes. "I like you a lot. I don't know if people do this anymore, but I do. I want us to be a couple."

I inhaled long breaths. He wanted us to be a couple. This was *the talk.*

"Are you okay?" he asked.

What a complicated question. "Yes, I want to be a couple too." Where did those words come from? My mind screamed, *No! Stay safe, and don't be vulnerable again. It hurt too much the first time.*

He leaned forward, wrapping an arm around me to pull me closer, and pressed his lips into mine.

The server tried not to interrupt us when she approached with a tray of food but I found her presence a relief. While I was excited at the idea of being exclusive with Keith, it half scared me.

"Thanks," Keith said as the server placed a picture-perfect plate in front of me, and his entrée was just as photogenic.

I picked up my fork but Keith stopped me. He took my hand and blessed our new relationship and the delicious food.

Who knew what the future held, but I was willing to find out.

Chapter Sixteen

As I sat at the computer at work, Stacey said, "Emily, you look different today."

I had to wonder if my change in relationship status was obvious. If that were the case, I needed to work on disguising my transparent emotions.

"Yeah, she does look different," another coworker said. "Did you highlight your hair, or cut it?"

I laughed. "No. Besides, I have no idea what you're talking about." I was the same person, I think, although I had to admit there was a lighter spring to my step.

"You even look younger," Stacey said.

"Um, thank you?" Had I looked older before?

"I recognize her expression," a third coworker commented. "She's either glowing from pregnancy, or she's falling in love."

"Pregnancy?" Stacey asked with alarm.

"No," I clarified. "I'm not pregnant." But maybe someday.

"Ah, but she didn't deny the falling in love part," Stacey said with her eyebrows raised.

My coworkers turned to study me.

I focused my attention on the computer screen, hoping if I ignored the comments maybe they'd go away.

"That's it," Stacey said, taunting me. "Emily's in love."

"Who is he?" the second coworker asked.

Steve walked up and sat down with us to pull up his

schedule. "Stop badgering the girl."

The last time I glanced into the mirror I was a woman, not a girl, but I appreciated him standing up for me.

"Oh, what fun are you, Steve?" Stacey asked. "And I noticed you were apprehensive to open your cabinet."

A tiny grin formed on his lips. "Not apprehensive. I work with people who think it's funny to hide tennis balls in my personal work space."

Stacey laughed. "But it was funny when you opened the cabinet and they all came bouncing out."

I had to admit, I loved my job. Despite all the teasing, or maybe because of it, this job was fun. Even though I wasn't ready to share my commitment to Keith with them, I was starting to think of my coworkers as my work family. Besides, they'd find out soon enough if they noticed my interaction with Keith in the hallway.

Throughout the day the peace from earlier began to turn into my annoying fight-or-flight pattern. Was I really ready to commit to a man who I barely knew?

The shortness of breath and underlying anxiety was all too familiar. I hadn't been like this until I experienced my heartbreaking relationship with Frank, and I had to learn to let go of my fear.

When I reached home, I tried to lose myself in my writing but to no avail. There was a favorite writing exercise I used during times of temporary writer's block, but in this case the problem was my phobia of commitment more than writing.

But all I really wanted was to commit with peace. Keith was a good man, so why continue to let my past haunt me?

I needed to make myself sit down and write, so I engaged in the writing exercise, which consisted of jotting down whatever words popped into my mind in a twenty-minute period. The object was not to think or to edit but to write with fluidity to free my resistance. If only the technique worked with commitment-phobic women such as myself.

I placed my fingertips on the keys of the laptop and waited for a few moments before a scene unfolded with ease.

The family sat down to eat pizza for dinner, except her father was missing as usual. Mom said he worked late nights to put food on the table. Mom was always home. Without a second car, there weren't many places to visit.

Not having eaten much for lunch other than peanut butter sandwiches, no jelly, both girls dug into the pizza with fervor. Her belly knotted in hunger from anticipation of gooey cheese pizza, not the frozen kind from the oven but the kind where the man delivered it in a box at the door.

She sank her teeth into the first bite, a bite she'd always remember. Her father chose that moment to burst through the door. Without so much as a hello, Princess, he made his way to their parents' bedroom.

The closet door opened with a thud, heavy items removed, drawers opened and slammed shut. All kinds of deafening noises escaped the room like a wild animal attempting to break free of a cage.

Alarmed, Mom followed Dad into the bedroom to check on things. His voice loud, her voice hushed. What were they fighting about?

Without comment, he made his way to the door, dragging overstuffed suitcases, with Mom following behind him. Why was she crying? She tugged on his shirt, trying to prevent him from leaving. But he left, without a goodbye, Princess.

Mom spent the evening crying on the phone about not having a job or a car.

What about Thanksgiving, or Christmas? Would Santa still come?

Even though that one bite of pizza had tasted so delicious, it now tasted like paper. Despite wondering if they'd ever eat again, she pushed away the pizza.

Unnerved, I set my laptop down and began to pace the living room to wear off a surge of panic. Why was a pizza scene bothering me so much? Somehow it seemed all too familiar.

To distract myself, I strode into the kitchen and began scouring the sink in an attempt to decrease the jittery, caffeinated feeling of my racing heart.

I had no idea what was wrong with me, or why such a short but touching scene disturbed me like this.

○

Keith made his way down the dock, whistling a carefree Jimmy Buffett song. It had been two long years since the painful breakup with Vicki, but right now life was more fulfilling than he imagined possible. Not only did Emily and he enjoy dinner last night, they were now a couple, a dream come true, really. What a surprise, but until now he hadn't realized how much he yearned for a healthy relationship with her. After Vicki, he had never thought he'd date again.

With a watchful stare, Sam sat on the familiar piling waiting for his fish.

"Good morning," Keith said to him, whistling as he opened the white cooler and tossed a small fish to his bird friend.

"Aren't we in a good mood today?" Captain Bill asked, his weathered ball cap placed backward on his head. He paused from wiping the dew off the passenger seats of the smaller ferry. "I can't say I've ever heard you whistle."

"Now you have." Keith pulled out another fish. "Sam, this is your last one in the cooler. I'll buy you more later."

The bird snapped his beak together, and then opened it

wide with anticipation.

Keith tossed him the fish before closing the lid. "Enjoy, buddy." There was an older fisherman at the end of the wharf who supplied enough fish to keep Sam happy, and Keith planned to stop by after work to replenish his stock. He glanced at his wrist for the time and hopped onto Captain Bill's boat for a short visit.

"What has you all fired up?" Captain Bill continued to wipe off the seats as he chatted. "Oh, wait! It's your woman ... what's her name?"

"Emily."

"Ha! Man, you have it bad." Captain Bill turned his gaze on the bird. "Did you hear that, Sam? Keith's in love."

The bird made a strange noise.

"I'm not sure he's happy for you, Keith. Maybe he's jealous." Captain Bill finished wiping off the last bench before he made his way around Keith, who took a seat on the bow of the boat with his feet resting on the passenger seat. Bill lifted up the captain's bench and tossed the towel inside.

"Of course, Sam's happy." Keith leaned forward to rest his arms on his knees but kept his gaze on Sam. "As long as I feed him, he's thrilled."

The dock squeaked as Scott Botticelli, Keith's brother-in-law, strode down the wooden planks. He was usually too busy at the bank to stop by the ferry on a workday.

"What's happening, bro?" Keith jumped up to greet him. "What brings you here?"

Scott hopped onto the ferry in his carefree style, demonstrating his lifelong ease with boats and the water. "We need a guy's night out. Your sister is driving me nuts."

Keith smiled. "Nothing unusual. Jenni has been driving me nuts all my life."

"This is serious stuff," Scott explained. "She's been crying all the time and snapping at me. I can't seem to do anything right."

"That's a woman for you." Captain Bill barked a deep laugh. "Mark my words, she's pregnant."

Scott froze in place.

Keith whistled. After Gran mentioned the possibility the other day, Keith thought it was a high probability. "If she is pregnant, her mad rush to the bathroom explains a lot."

Scott stared at him. When he recovered, he said, "How did that happen?"

Captain Bill slapped Scott on the back. "Buddy, if you don't know the answer to that question, we can't help you."

Scott's mouth hung open.

"Traumatized?" Keith asked him.

Scott slowly nodded. "I had no idea. Never crossed my mind."

The dock squeaked and numerous footsteps slapped against the boards. Sam didn't like crowds, so he left his perch. He flew in a circle around the boat as if to say goodbye to Keith, and then soared off into the blue sky.

"Guys night tonight?" Scott asked as he stepped from the boat. "Shoot some pool?"

Keith stood to help people onto the boat. "Sure thing, *Daddy*. See you then."

Scott's mouth dropped open again and Keith laughed. Teasing him for nine months sounded fun.

The morning floated along as Keith dropped off one group after another onto the wild shores of Pony Island. Captain Bill was navigating the shorter trips to the smaller islands. All of them were special to Keith, but he preferred Pony Island by far. He loved the history behind it.

When his dad passed away, Jenni used her inheritance to save Coffee Break from financial distress, and if the coffee shop proved profitable in the future, she planned to expand along the coast. Keith put significant thought into the decision of using his money to purchase the other boats if he won the contract. The problem was, his number one competitor was also trying to secure the same bigger dock space.

If the contract didn't work out, there was a local architectural company in Mooresboro one town over. He also had connections at a rather large company in Raleigh, although he didn't want to leave his hometown, or Emily, but some things were out of his control. What would it hurt to at least send out resumes?

As he cruised along in the boat, the passengers were happy to gaze at the gorgeous marsh. A great white egret with long, spindly legs stood still as a statue in the now green grass. Keith slowed the ferry for the passengers to snap pictures and to admire the bird while his mind drifted to Emily.

She seemed surprised he wanted a relationship with her. Why wouldn't he? She was the sweetest, smartest woman he had ever met, along with her natural beauty. When he allowed his mind to imagine the future, he saw her there, etched in great detail like a fine, finished charcoal drawing.

But if he had to relocate for work, how would the move impact their relationship?

One of his biggest fears was falling in love with her and having their relationship fall apart. He wondered if Emily would relocate with him. It wasn't fair for him to ask, but long-distance relationships were difficult, and he had an overwhelming sense they wouldn't make it. Although, as Gran said, it was better to find out the truth beforehand instead of after the proverbial words *I do.*

Up ahead, dolphins jumped out of the water, so Keith kept the slower pace to give the passengers a better view. He pointed them out to the few unaware people staring off in a different direction.

One of his most memorable ferry rides was watching a herd of horses wade through the water to reach a grassy shoal accessible only during low tide. Claire had been aboard the ferry and had taken several spectacular photos. She blew up one of his favorites and it was hanging above his fireplace.

His thoughts shifted to Gran. Once she was discharged home, a whole new set of problems would ensue. She would engage in risky activities such as working in the barn alone. Keith and Jenni agreed to a schedule consisting of them taking turns spending the night with her and performing the barn chores until Gran allowed them to hire extra help.

Keith wanted to improve her entire dysfunctional layout of the barn and install outdoor runs off the stalls to decrease the daily turnout requirements. If he redesigned the pastures by creating a path between them, the change would allow her to drive her cart between the fences and feed the horses without ever leaving the golf cart. But stubborn as she was, she refused to allow him to use his skills to make her job easier. Until he convinced her, they would need extra help.

When the luxury of watching the dolphins wore off, he throttled the boat faster to continue the journey to the island. Before long, they approached the cove on the far end of Pony Island where a small herd of horses and a foal grazed near a tidewater pool.

One little girl squealed as she pointed to the baby.

Keith maneuvered the boat as close to the shore as possible but it was low tide. "Please remain seated until the boat stops. The tide is low, so you'll have to wade. Expect the water to be about a foot and a half deep." He heard a few groans but there was no way to pull in closer.

Once everyone was unloaded, a returning group waded to the boat and climbed aboard.

A moment of nostalgia kicked in. If he didn't get the contract, he'd really miss this island, and this job.

Chapter Seventeen

There were two important emails in my inbox, both from agents I had submitted my manuscript to. And I was climbing the walls, excited to read them. I saw them pop up on my phone earlier but promised to make myself wait until I returned home for the evening in case I was devastated once again. And if I had good news, I wanted to be able to yell out with joy and do a happy dance.

I had one more patient to see and scanned Pastor Ralph Conway's chart. Unfortunately, he had three different kinds of cancer and I understood why he declined additional medical treatment except therapy. My job was to teach him and his caregivers safety training during general care and while using a walker for short distances. The option of utilizing a bedside commode was preferable but Pastor Conway refused, stating he still had some dignity left. As long as he was able, he wanted to walk into the bathroom and I admired his tenacity.

I knocked on his door but he didn't respond, his faraway expression a concern to me. "Mr. Conway?"

Slowly he turned his head in my direction, and although he looked at me, his eyes were vacant.

"I'm Emily." I stepped inside the room and lightly touched his hand with mine. "I'm here for physical therapy."

He was a shrunken, thin man engulfed by an oversized recliner. He had two blankets wrapped around him to keep warm. Who was I to disturb this man's dying process?

"Emily," he repeated in a murmur and stared at me in an unnerving manner as if he saw straight into my soul.

"Always stay sweet." He patted my arm. "You will be rewarded."

Shocked by his words, I said, "Thank you." I hated to make him move from his cozy nest but it wasn't therapeutic to let him sit there. Unfortunately, I had a job to perform. "Mr. Conway? I'm here to help you walk to the bathroom."

He blinked. To my surprise he moved the covers aside and slowly scooted to the edge of the chair to stand up. "Hold onto me. I don't want to fall."

"I promise." I placed the walker in front of him to offer support. I wrapped my happy belt around him, the yellow smiley faces bringing a ray of sunshine to the decrepit man's room.

Then I had him stand for a moment to find his equilibrium, and also to allow me to assess his strength and static standing balance. To my surprise, he needed no assistance other than for me to hold onto the belt for safety.

"Very nice," I encouraged. "Let's take a couple of steps."

He took three steps, rested, and repeated the process. When I first saw him bundled in the chair, I'd had concerns about walking.

"Honey," he said, "listen carefully. When you've praised the man upstairs all your life, you realize how to allow God to control your circumstances. You have to let go and stop paddling in your own direction, and allow your path to unfold the way He wants."

Wise words, indeed, and ones I needed to hear.

He stepped into the bathroom and backed up to the commode, pushing his hospital gown aside with one hand and holding onto the grab bar with the other as he lowered himself onto the commode. "I've been a preacher for as long as I can remember. It's my passion."

He sat there for several minutes. I wanted to leave the room to give him privacy but also wanted to ensure his safety.

"What's your passion?" he asked.

"Physical therapy." I loved helping people. Sometimes they fought the process, but most people wanted to achieve their own personal goals, and I simply assisted in the process.

He shook his head. "No. I feel something more in you. What's your real passion?"

How did the man read me so well?

"Writing ... writing is my passion."

His face lit up. "And you're going to be a writer. Really big." He performed his hygiene and stood. "The sink ..." He gasped for breath from the effort involved.

"Breathe slowly, as if you're smelling a rose and blowing out a candle."

He washed his hands and then stood there while he studied himself in the mirror.

"That's not me. I look like an old man."

What a profound thought. Apparently in his heart, he was still the young man he knew.

He turned to stare at me. "Name three wishes you have."

Taken aback, I took a moment to think. "I want to have a career as a full-time professional writer, to be a multi-bestselling author, and to get paid accordingly. I want to make a difference in my readers' lives."

"What's stopping you?"

A loaded question and I didn't have an answer.

I shrugged for lack of better words. "I write the stories and now I'm waiting for an agent to represent me, and for a publisher to buy my work."

He shook his head. "Those goals are said with the tone of the future. Take the lid off your restraints. You are bigger than your limitations."

I gasped.

He started picking his way back toward his recliner. "You see, dreams are in the future." He paused to catch his breath.

"You have to feel the success now. Claim your triumph, child."

He sat down in the recliner and it almost swallowed him whole, so tiny and frail compared to the enormous chair.

A mere thank you for his words weren't enough. "I will pray for you," I offered, on uncharted ground to say the least, all professionalism aside, but he seemed to need as many prayers as possible. Usually I made a point never to discuss politics or religion at work.

"Pray for me now." He closed his eyes, waiting.

I didn't know where to start. "I'm sorry, but I've never prayed out loud in front of someone before."

The man kept his eyes closed as if waiting for me. Praying for him now was far outside my comfort zone and I thought about Keith. He didn't seem to have a problem with it.

"I meant I'd pray tonight for you. When I get home." Certainly, he would understand how uncomfortable I was.

He grabbed hold of my hand so tight it hurt. "It's a good time to start. Remove the walls you've created for yourself."

I closed my eyes, unsure how but I managed to stumble my way through an awkward but heartfelt prayer. I was surprised the words came to me, and he added words where he felt necessary, a few amens along the way, and then he prayed out loud for me.

When he finished he opened his eyes. "We'll both write two hundred and fifty words about how we impacted each other's lives today. Bring it to me Monday." He closed his eyes, dismissing me from the room.

Unsure of what I had done to receive such a blessing from a broken, humble man, I left the room in amazement. I'd had the intention of helping him, and here he was giving me a gift.

Little did I know how much I needed his uplifting words when I returned home to check the two emails awaiting my attention.

Which letter to read first? I chose the least important one to me but really, even though neither was my favorite choice of agents, both of them mattered. But as I read through the words, my heart sank. It was polite but stated how the agent didn't believe she was the right one to represent my work and thought the story was too niche and didn't know how to sell it in today's market.

The next email was from an agent at a small to middle-sized agency. The agent said she enjoyed the characterization and the storyline and requested the full manuscript. *The full manuscript!*

I jumped up and danced around the living room, pumping my hands in the air. Then it dawned on me I had no one to call to share the good news. My dad was busy and had no clue what I was trying to accomplish with my writing. My mom and sister were in Mexico with limited cell phone coverage, and my best friend, Kelly, was likely making dinner for her family, so instead of calling I sent her a text. But it wasn't satisfying enough.

I couldn't call Keith since I just started dating him and hadn't shared much with him about my writing dream—or career, I corrected.

Lift the lid off your restraints. My new friends, including co-workers, didn't know I wrote, either.

Whose fault was it but my own?

The thought made me nervous. Here I was a trailblazer, independent, one who persevered, yet I needed to open up and allow people to become my friends. That was the entire reason for moving to a small town. Pastor Ralph Conway's advice was true with friendships as well as with writing.

Being free spirited was something I secretly admired about my mother and sister. Look at them. They were living in Cancún and I only imagined the freedom of embracing life in a tropical setting. If I became a multi-bestselling author, I could reside anywhere in the world I wanted and write. Was I the big dreamer my father accused me of? Absolutely. As an author, dreaming was what I did best.

I spent the next hour glancing over my manuscript, and then with trepidation, I emailed it to the agent.

The need to share my big news refused to disappear, so I decided to reach out and contact Keith. Despite my shortcomings, I did yearn for a long-standing relationship.

Not wanting to minimize my excitement by texting, and before I overanalyzed my decision, I called him.

And to my surprise, he answered on the first ring. A relationship without games ... what a novel concept.

"Emily," he said when I didn't respond to his greeting.

"Um, hi." What a stupid thing to say. "I have some awesome news and wanted to share it with someone." With him. I wanted to share the good news with him.

"Wonderful." He waited a moment for me to continue before he asked what my news was. His voice was kind, curious.

"I submitted my query and sample pages from one of my recently completed manuscripts to an agent and she requested to read my full manuscript." I didn't mention the disheartening rejections I also received and preferred to focus on the positive.

He remained silent for a moment, most likely to grasp all I said. "Wow, congratulations! Your news is cause for a special treat. Let's walk downtown and eat an ice cream."

His reply surprised me. I wasn't sure why, other than I half-expected him to barely listen, or to reply without enthusiasm. "Okay, let's do ice cream." A surge of excitement overcame me. The request really was a big deal, and it was nice to be with someone who supported me.

"I'll change clothes and come over," he suggested. "If you want, we can pop into Coffee Break to see if Jenni is working, so you can share your good news."

I felt important, acknowledged. "All right. And Keith," I said, "thanks."

"Hmm," he said. "Emily, you don't have to thank me."

My chest filled with a swirly warmth.

When we hung up, I scurried around to fix my make-up

and to slip on a pair of cut-off shorts, a casual but cute top, and sandals, and within twenty minutes the doorbell rang.

I opened the door to see Keith standing there smelling delicious and dressed in nice khaki shorts and a pullover shirt. Suddenly I felt self-conscious about my casual choice in clothes, my usual go-to attire for a stroll downtown.

"Let me change first," I said.

He reached out and held my wrist with a light touch. "Why? You're beautiful. And the shorts show off your legs." He grinned at me as if I were the most gorgeous woman in the world.

After a verbally abusive relationship, one where my clothing choices and body were under constant attack, I was still working on improving my own perception of myself. Keith was right, I was beautiful, and that was progress. As a person who enjoyed wearing comfortable clothes in general and being true to myself, I stepped through the door and locked it with finesse. He was sweet, smart, sexy, and I was surprised by my burst in confidence.

Tucker appeared from around the corner. I hadn't seen the furry creature in days. He strode up to Keith and began rubbing against his legs as if they were best friends.

"How is it you're so good with him?" Animals never lied, so Tucker's behavior meant Keith was a good man.

The cat meowed in agreement.

"He keeps a wide berth from me," I said, as I watched in disbelief.

Keith bent down and ran his large hand across the cat's spine. "He's skinny and hungry, and just wants me to feed him." The cat arched his back to encourage Keith to rub him more. "We'll bring some cat food back for you," he said to the cat. Tucker meowed again.

While I didn't want the cat to go hungry, I also didn't want to own a cat. "They say once you feed a stray, they are yours."

Keith shrugged. "So be it."

What a sweet gesture but I needed more details. "Will you

take him home with you, or leave him here?"

Keith shrugged again. "Not sure. For now I'll provide food for him here."

The cat followed him down the steps and across the parking lot, where he planted himself at the edge, never taking his eyes off Keith. We rounded the corner and Keith took my hand.

The night was mild, high seventies, I guessed, and I chastised myself for not bringing along a light jacket for later. We strolled into town and crossed the street to the General Store. The crowd outside was confirmation itself on how delicious the homemade ice cream was along with the extra-large servings for a reasonable price.

We climbed the few wooden steps and he opened the old-fashioned heavy door, with its long pane of thick wavy glass. The tinkling bell welcomed us as well as live beach music radiating from the stage at the far end of the store. People sat with friends to enjoy the music or joined the crowd on the dance floor.

Keith and I waited in line, hand in hand, in comfortable silence with each other. When we reached the counter, I peered into the glass case to view at least eight tubs of different flavors. One of my favorite games to play with my sister as kids was to imagine each flavor on our tongues to help decide which to order. I tried the technique and this time I chose peach instead of my usual mint chip. I had them scoop it into a bowl to reduce calories.

After he paid for the ice cream, we sauntered outside to join a group of people standing on the sidewalk and sitting on benches. I watched one adorable little girl wrap her little tongue all the way around the cone to keep it from dripping. It was a social gathering and Keith introduced me to several people.

"Tell me about the manuscript you sent out. What's it called?" Keith asked with interest when it was our turn to sit on a bench.

"*Changing Seasons* is the manuscript that's finished, and

my newest work in progress is called *Changing Tides*."

He nodded with approval. "When will you hear back from the agent?" He took a bite of his ice cream.

I winced, feeling the cold pain in my front teeth just watching him but scraped my own bowl clean with the spoon. "The email said approximately eight to twelve weeks, which sounds forever away."

"I don't fully understand the process of submitting your work, but I know you'll do well."

He was supportive and I hoped he was right. "Obtaining an agent is harder than acquiring a publisher. The competition is steep."

He crunched his cone into his mouth, chewed, and spoke with it half full. "If you don't get this agent, you'll find the one who's meant for you."

I stared at him in disbelief.

We stood and tossed our trash in the nearby can and strolled down the street. Next on the agenda was visiting Jenni at Coffee Break and I was eager to find out how she was feeling.

Keith held the door open and I walked through, the delicious aroma of coffee greeting us along with the cozy jingle of chimes announcing our arrival. I loved this town and all the old-fashioned chimes above the doorways.

The coffee aroma provoked a distant memory of my father cooking waffles and bacon, of mouthwatering smells of mushrooms and onions sautéing in a pan on the gas stove. The once familiar smells of home before the divorce. A moment of nostalgia captured me and the emotional piece I wrote about the little girl eating pizza popped into my mind. I needed to understand that little girl more.

I smiled as a vision of Keith cooking in an apron held a lot of sex appeal.

He wrapped his arm around me and pulled me in close to him as we waited in line to order coffee. He whispered in my ear, "What are you smiling about?"

I giggled, feeling younger and freer than I had felt in years. "An image of you in an apron, cooking."

He pulled his head away from me in feigned shock, his eyes wide.

I laughed at his reaction. "That came out wrong. The homey smell of coffee reminded me of when my father used to fill the house with delicious smells of food cooking." I yearned for the familiar sense of security again and realized I could create it on my own.

"Wouldn't it be fun to take a cooking class together for date night?" I asked, knowing that learning to cook required instruction, and I didn't inherit the gene from my father.

He stared at me as though wondering what my sudden interest in cooking was. After a long moment he asked, "Are we going to bake or cook? There is a difference, ya know."

It was my turn to stare at him. "I guess we should start with cooking."

He laughed. "Cooking it is." We stood in silence until the coffee line advanced and he turned to me. "What do you want to cook together?"

He was taking my suggestion seriously. "I don't know. How about Japanese food?"

"Why don't we start with something difficult then?"

I nudged him playfully. "The hardest part is cutting up everything."

"Yeah, and then we have to eat the vegetables," he said, groaning. "But I'm getting better about it."

My cell phone rang and surprised me. I dug it out of my purse and swallowed hard at Frank's name as it flashed across the screen. I glanced up to see Keith watching me.

"He's still bothering you?"

I nodded without answering and it became difficult to swallow.

Keith held out his hand. "Want me to take care of it?"

Yes, no ... I didn't know. Without thinking, I handed him

the phone.

He clicked on the button. "Keith here. How can I help you?"

My knees grew weak, and not understanding why Frank's call had such a nauseating effect on me, I wanted to crawl underneath one of the tables and disappear.

Keith pulled the phone away from his ear and stared at it. "He hung up on me."

Maybe he would get the hint I had moved on from him and was seeing someone new.

He handed the phone back to me and with shaking hands, I placed it back inside my purse and zipped it closed to bury my turmoil. I looked forward to the day that man no longer disturbed me.

The line advanced and it was our turn to order.

"Hey, kids," Alex said, leaning on the countertop toward us in warm greeting. "What are you doing tonight?"

"Hi, Alex. We wanted to order coffee and to check up on Jenni," Keith explained. "Is she around?"

Alex leaned back. "She's in the office. Want me to get her?"

Keith reached for his wallet in his back pocket. "Sure, but we'd like to order first."

"Of course." Alex obliged by taking our order and pouring it into mugs.

Usually I preferred not to drink coffee in the evening but ordered decaf. Worst case scenario, if it kept me awake tonight, I would write. It wasn't likely I'd get much sleep anyway after Frank's call.

Keith leaned onto the counter and lowered his voice. "How's Jenni doing?"

Alex's face resembled a deer caught in headlights. "Fine?"

"The truth?" he pressed.

Alex inhaled a long breath and let it out slowly. "She's been quiet, to herself. I don't think she's feeling well."

Keith straightened. "That's what I thought." He took the

mugs off the countertop. "Thanks. Would you let her know we are here?" He stepped back to allow the next customer access to the counter.

"Will do," Alex said. She took the next order and then disappeared into the office.

We searched for a table, and I was amazed at how busy the shop was in the evening. There was a small table for two against a wall, or a loveseat available in the corner.

Unlike our first coffee date, we chose the cozy loveseat, although it was small and Keith was a stocky man. I didn't mind our bodies touching from our shoulders to knees.

We were halfway through sipping our coffee when Jenni approached. Keith lifted his mug to her as if to say cheers.

The comfortable chair next to us opened up and Jenni sat on the wide armrest. "What brings y'all here tonight?"

Keith spoke up. "An agent requested Emily's full manuscript and we are celebrating."

Jenni turned toward me. "Congratulations. I didn't realize you are a writer."

"Thanks, and yes I am." It was far past time to let my friends know the real me. I took a sip from the mug and placed it on the table. Being myself felt good.

"How long have you been writing?" Jenni asked.

The focus on me was uncomfortable and something I needed to get used to. "About four years, but I don't have anything published yet."

"She's about to," Keith said, pride in his voice.

No pressure there but I appreciated his steadfast confidence in me. Keith and everyone else, including me, would be disappointed if the agent rejected it. No wonder I hadn't shared my goals with anyone up to this point. But I needed to believe in myself.

"I agree with Keith," Jenni said. "It's a matter of time, so never give up." She lifted her open hand to include the coffee shop. "There was a time I almost quit, but I didn't. Look what I have to be thankful for every day."

"And my ferry service." Keith's expression turned slightly dark. "I have to remember the same advice, not to give up."

Jenni leaned forward and touched him on the shoulder. "You'll be fine, one way or the other. If it's meant to be, you'll win the contract."

"And if not," I said, trying to be uplifting despite the knot in my belly, "you'll find another job you equally love."

Keith shrugged off our comments but I knew him well enough to know he took our advice to heart.

"And how are you feeling?" he asked his sister, changing the subject.

Jenni glanced away.

"Are you okay?" I asked, concerned maybe it wasn't pregnancy after all. "The last time I saw you, you weren't feeling so hot."

Jenni stood up from the awkward position on the armrest and settled deep into the chair as if preparing to have a longer discussion and fixed her gaze on Keith. "I was going to initiate a family get-together but I may as well tell you now."

Keith leaned back in the chair and crossed his legs. "Sounds serious."

She grinned and her entire face lit up. "I'm pregnant."

He smiled, and I figured he didn't want to admit we all suspected as much. "Pregnant?"

"With twins."

"Twins?" Keith asked, his eyebrows arched. The news got us both.

Jenni laughed with such a light spirit I got a glimpse of what she might have looked like as a child. "Yep. I've always wanted twins. Well, here they are."

I jumped up to pull her into a hug and we both squealed in excitement. Keith took longer to process the information. "I'm so happy for you and Scott," I said, although I barely knew her husband and wanted to get to know him better.

Several questions raced through my mind, such as I wondered about her training for the marathon, and if it had impacted her pregnancy.

"Congratulations are in order, my dear sister." Keith stood and squeezed us into a group hug. "Boys? Girls? One of each?" The smile on his face said all I needed to know. He was thrilled.

She shook her head. "I don't know yet, Uncle Keith." She chuckled at the name, and I had to admit it sounded wonderful. "I'll find out at my next ultrasound appointment."

"Amazing," he said as he shook his head and sat back down. "I'm going to be an uncle. And you're going to be a mother of twins." Awe and disbelief showed on his face. "What about training for the marathon? Are the babies okay?"

Keith had read my mind.

Jenni shrugged. "Babies are worth giving up a race, and I switched to walking as soon as I found out, so all is good."

"I'm so happy for you, and twins will be fun," I said in disbelief. But to be honest, for a moment I had a flash of jealousy before I pulled myself together and mentally kicked myself. Someday I would have my own family, when the timing was right.

I risked a glance at Keith and noticed he was studying me with interest. The last thing I wanted was for him to think I was wanting kids with him at some point. Any man would likely run away as fast as he could. Believe me, I had enough of men kicking me aside as if I didn't matter.

Chapter Eighteen

I had to believe Ms. Stallings was going to be safe returning home. She had to be.

Her insurance wasn't going to allow her to stay any longer. I voiced my usual concerns to Jenni and Keith, as in my recommendation for additional help, but didn't dare tell them I was anxious.

And to my surprise, I was going to miss her. It amazed me how I was already starting to think of her as extended family. I would also miss seeing Keith daily at the rehab center.

I made my way down the hallway to her room to say good-bye before she left this morning. When I tapped on the door, Jenni and Keith both turned toward me as Jenni zipped up the overstuffed suitcase on the bed.

"Emily! I'm going to miss you!" Ms. Stallings stood and reached out for a hug.

I dodged around a bag of toiletries sitting on the floor and wrapped my arms around her. "I'm going to miss you too, Gran," I said with ease—a milestone for me—and no one else seemed to notice except Gran. I usually didn't allow myself to get attached to patients and discharge was part of the process, but I'd let down my guard enough to think of Gran as more than a patient.

"Thank you for all your help, sweetheart." She planted a shaky kiss on my cheek. "Please visit me at home, and I'll give you a tour of my barn and introduce you to my horses."

"I'd love to," I promised and reasoned it would have to be a casual visit with Keith.

"Oh! Did you hear?" Gran grinned at me as if she had eaten her favorite flavor of ice cream. "We're having twins."

It was my understanding Jenni had planned to have a family get-together to announce the pregnancy but apparently not.

"There is no 'we' in this. I'm the one throwing up," Jenni said as she placed a sweatsuit and a shirt into a smaller bag at the foot of the bed.

Gran patted her on the back. "You'll survive. Think of the journey as a blessing."

Jenni rolled her eyes. "I know you're right, but when I'm bent over the toilet it's hard to remember."

Gran sat down to rest, looking a bit worn out by everything. "The first thing I'm going to do at home is to groom my horses."

Keith snapped his head upward to meet his grandmother's stare. "With your arm in a sling?"

Gran glared at him. "Let's get one thing straight. You aren't going to tell me how to live my life."

"Gran, we aren't going to argue with you on every point," Jenni said, clearly frustrated. "The horses are off limits right now, and Keith and I will take care of them."

I chimed in. "While your balance has improved since you've been here, you did have two falls at home. Please let them help you however possible."

Her glare softened a bit when she looked at me. "Then I'll drive down to the barn," she said with her good hand on her hip, accentuating her stubborn streak.

"Absolutely not," Keith said. "As I mentioned before, why don't you let me redesign your pastures and barn to ease your workload? You'll never have to carry buckets of feed again."

She shook her head. "I like carrying buckets. And I don't want tire tracks on my grass."

"It's better than broken bones," Jenni added.

Gran sighed with exaggeration. "Please." She dragged out

the word for dramatic effect.

Both kids refused to budge on the topic and I didn't blame them.

"Fine. Do the repairs." Gran scowled.

The room was silent.

Without further confrontation, Jenni packed the last of Gran's clothes into the bag and pulled the drawstring. "Finished. Let's check out and get you home."

I leaned forward and kissed Gran again on the cheek. "I enjoyed working with you, and our talks." I even appreciated her obstinate resistance to change and my job wouldn't be quite the same without her here.

She sniffled, touching a warm place in my heart and making me think of my grandmother once again.

My last patient of the day was Pastor Ralph Conway. I was ready to read my 250 words to him and folded the paper into a tiny square, shoving it into my pocket. I tapped on his doorway to announce my arrival, and again the recliner engulfed him as it had yesterday. His feet were elevated and buried under a pile of blankets, his eyes holding a faraway stare.

An attractive lady, impeccably dressed with her hair fixed in an elegant pile atop her head, sat perched at the foot of his bed. She was younger than he was, but not enough to be his daughter, yet she exuded confidence and familiarity toward him. She held his hand as only a wife could.

I reached forward and shook the woman's free one. "I'm Emily with physical therapy."

Her lips parted into a partial smile. "Thank you for helping my husband. He needs all the assistance you can provide."

I loved when family members appreciated my job. Usually they had complaints about staff, food, care, or whatever the case might be but compliments were always nice.

"You're very welcome," I said and touched Mr. Conway. When he didn't respond, I called out his name but his empty gaze stared back at me. Then he smiled slightly as if he might recognize me. "I brought what I was supposed to write for you."

"Good," he managed to say with a breathy voice.

His wife wore a confused look on her face, so I explained our pact from the day before.

"Were you able to write yours?" I asked but immediately regretted the question. Of course he hadn't written anything, as he was in no shape to hold a pen against a piece of paper.

His stare was blank. Mr. Conway didn't remember our talk yesterday, nor did he remember me. I pulled out the neatly folded paper, thinking even if he didn't recall the conversation, he would appreciate the writing on some level. Or at least his wife would.

I unfolded it, choking down a wave of unexpected emotion from a place deep inside my soul, the place where dreams and hope existed. I cleared my throat and began to read.

Today I Met an Angel

My job is to help others, all day, every day, even when I'm feeling down. Sometimes it seems as if there is no one to help me. I pray and know God is there. But what do you do when you aren't hearing answers? What do you do when you feel you can't go on another day, another moment? Perhaps life has pushed you one step too close to the edge and you don't see tomorrow.

That's when God sends you an angel.

The angel isn't wearing wings and a white robe. He is a thin man who quietly sits in his recliner in a skilled nursing facility. He has a windy road ahead of him but he never loses faith. He is faith.

I offered to pray for him, and that is the moment that changed my life. He accepted my offer, held my hand so tight it hurt, and closed his eyes. I meant I'd pray for him at home, not out loud, here, in his room. I told him I've never prayed aloud before other than saying grace at the table at Thanksgiving. He shocked me by saying now was a good time to start. I didn't want to pray out loud, but God led this man to push me out of my safe boundaries and to pray for someone who needed God's prayer. I closed my eyes and prayed out loud for him. Sure, I stumbled, hesitated at times, but the words came to me. He added words where they were necessary, a few amens, and then prayed out loud for me. What had I done to receive such a blessed gift from a man whom I was supposed to help? The gift was given to me.

I told him my goals. He told me to take off the limitations, the roof on my dreams. Claim it and say my dreams are the next logical step. You see, dreams are far away, but the next step is right there around the corner.

He asked me to write 250 words, and he would as well, as to how we impacted each other's lives in the hour we spent together. But it wasn't just an hour, it was a lifetime. He looked into my eyes and saw my soul, my heartbreak, my life and I knew God had already healed me. I am not the person of walls and restrictions; I am the person of belief, of faith. It took a stranger of God to light the path of freedom from myself.

Tears gathered in his eyes. He let go of his wife's hand and gently took mine. "Beautifully written, my dear." A tear zigzagged down his cheek, his eyes red.

I hadn't intended to make him cry and regretted reading it to him.

"I love it." He reassured me as if he understood my hesitance. "You will be blessed, child."

His wife blew her nose on a tissue as she embraced her own set of emotions. I had created nothing but chaos.

Chaos they seemed to appreciate on a deeper level.

I handed the poem to his wife. "It's yours to keep."

The woman dabbed the corner of her eye with another

tissue. "He's right, you know. You will be blessed." She tucked the folded paper into her purse and without explanation, I knew when the man lost his battle with cancer, my words were sure to be read at his eulogy.

I was exhausted by the time I returned home. Despite my desire to crawl into bed and call it an early night, there was no better activity than to take a long walk. Then, once I returned home for the night, I planned to write away the stress and fatigue of the day.

In the silence of my apartment, my cell phone rang. I swallowed hard and prepared myself for the possibility it was Frank, but when I glanced at the screen, it was my father calling. While hearing from him was far better than Frank, my belly still knotted into a tight ball. For some reason the scene with the girl eating pizza popped into my mind and I let the call go into voicemail.

Instead of listening to his message, I pulled on exercise pants and a sporty dry shirt to whisk away any sweat. Who was I kidding? I usually didn't walk fast enough to sweat. Maybe I needed to change my philosophy and work out harder, so I tightened my shoelaces for extra support and then left the apartment.

Waiting in the breezeway was Tucker. He meowed but didn't approach me even though I knelt down to pet him.

"If Keith were here, you'd be all over him," I accused, but he ignored me.

"Come here, kitty kitty," I said, determined to encourage Tucker to approach me. This was crazy, to feel rejected because a cat was dissing me. Then I noticed a bowl of cat food and water near the door and my respect for Keith deepened.

No wonder Tucker wasn't interested in approaching me, as he was no longer hungry and had no need for me. It wasn't until I stood and headed down the flight of steps that he followed from a distance and trotted across the parking lot behind me.

I turned back. "He doesn't live here, you know."

Meow. He stopped at the edge of the asphalt and sat on his haunches.

"Okay. See you later." I waved to him as if he understood and hoped no one saw me chatting up the cat, but then again, I was getting to the point I no longer cared about people's criticism.

I walked at a good clip and turned right at the corner of Front Street. Facing me was a book shop begging for me to pause at the bay window to ogle several books showcased in a beachy theme. One novel was written by a local author from a nearby town, and I yearned to pick it up, to read the back, to thumb through the pages. I made a mental note to return to the shop another day to study the book further.

I visualized my own book on display in this very window, even imagined conducting a book signing in the far corner of the shop. If I were lucky, people might show up to buy my book. The thought of talking to strangers and conversing with them not only scared me but excited me as well. *Take the lid off my self-inflicted restrictions.*

With some reluctance, I pulled myself away from the shop window to continue on my walk. Not only was I engaging in physical exercise, the salty breeze blew away the stress of the day.

Before long I passed by the *Sea Horse Ferry* as it glided into the slip with expert ease. I tried to determine who the captain was, but between the amber remnants of the sunset glittering on the water and a couple of passengers blocking a portion of the helm, visibility was difficult. I did recognize the silhouetted pelican waiting on a piling to greet the boat.

The old familiar, nagging question was never far from the choppy surface of my mind. It was difficult to bear the thought of Keith leaving if the ferry contract fell through, and with stunning honesty, I realized the small town felt cozy and safe knowing he lived here.

I passed by Coffee Break and pushed aside the desire to stop in and ask how Gran was managing at home. I reminded myself to maintain a professional barrier with patients, and Gran wasn't my business. Besides, I needed to get home to write if I planned to someday see my book in the bookstore window.

When I climbed the steps to my apartment Tucker was nowhere to be seen. The cat bowl had been licked clean, the water dish empty, and I realized if Keith did move, I now owned a cat.

Compared to the fresh air outside, my apartment was stuffy. I cracked open the deck door, and then returned to the kitchen to pull a premade salad from the refrigerator. I dumped it onto one of my colorful Mexican plates, compliments of my mother, and grabbed a fork from the drawer. I set the items on the coffee table and opened my laptop.

This part of the story was my favorite. The heroine and hero were together, things were going fairly well despite the risk of him leaving her behind, and she was falling in love with him. They went on dreamy adventures together, talked about plans for a possible future, but that was where the problem was. Either the heroine would have to relocate from the sweet life she had built for herself, or face her fear and return to the dreaded city where her life had been utter agony. The heroine hadn't realized how bad her situation had been until she escaped the claws of abuse.

Tonight the words spilled onto the page with ease, and there was a high probability this manuscript was shaping into one of my favorite stories, filled with a special romantic, breezy flair. It was different on many levels, mostly because it was an emotional journey of the characters.

I climbed into bed, and late as it was, sleep seemed inevitable. But it wasn't the case.

Half lost in dreamland, half buried deep in the creative dimension of my writer's mind, I envisioned a couple walking on the beach, exercising, riding bicycles. They were traveling on an unknown journey together, maybe a path to their own happy ending. People weren't meant to live life alone.

The man was trustworthy, secure ... safe. I had never trusted a man so much as him. The man was Keith.

But the possibility of a move. Inevitable pain. I was in too deep to save myself.

Chapter Nineteen

The week flew by, between working the ferry and taking care of Gran's horses early in the morning. The workload was taking a toll on Keith, but well worth the effort if it meant keeping Gran safe. The last time she was in this predicament they paid Alex, who worked at Coffee Break, to help out. He had already placed a phone call to her.

However, a disturbing thought continued to gnaw at him as he dumped feed into the bucket of one of Gran's rescue horses. He didn't know how to handle the situation with Gran if he had to move out of town for a job. Family came first. *She* came first.

After he fed the horses in their stalls, he led the mares outside individually. Thankfully the floodlights were on and highlighted the path.

His phone buzzed in his pocket. "Hey, Mom."

"How's Gran doing, Keith? Do you need help with the horses?"

His mother knew next to nothing about horses but at least she was offering to help. "I appreciate it but things are under control. I plan to start the barn-renovation process this weekend." He was going to have to farm out most of the labor but he would oversee the project.

She whistled under her breath. "How's Gran handling the change?"

He locked the gate behind him as the horses grazed in the pasture. The rising sun peeked through the trees, turning the sky a deep shade of streaked peach. "She's less than thrilled but the renovation will save her at least an hour each feeding."

He heard the familiar sound of his mother sipping from her mug of hot coffee and for a moment he missed seeing her.

She sipped and swallowed in the earpiece. "What about the ferry contract? Have you heard anything?"

He shook his head and opened the stall to the newest horse residing on the farm. The Wild Horse Foundation pulled the foal off the island because they no longer wanted his bloodline reproduced at such a rapid pace. "Nothing. The silence is killing me."

"Isn't Scott helping you with a loan?"

Scott was doing everything in his power to assist with financial matters, but it wasn't enough. "There is only so much he can do."

Whoever won the contract would have to follow the list of restrictions, including a strict departure and arrival schedule. Off-season hours would decrease to a few rides back and forth to the island, weather permitting, of course. The ferry would operate consistently in the summer, the hours of operation more frequent and longer.

Right now he was in charge of his own schedule and able to make his own weather decisions.

"Will you move if you don't get the contract?" Her voice was sad and made him flinch.

She had lost so much in the past year with his father's death.

"I won't have a choice." He didn't want to break her heart, so the less he told her the more he could spare her feelings.

"Have you applied for jobs, and if so, where?" The sound of her taking a long sip from her mug filled the air space between them once again.

Keith shouldered his cell phone to let the foal loose in a small turnout with another horse. He planned to build lean-to sheds in each paddock to allow the horses to stay outside as much as possible. Not only would the change reduce the amount of stall work daily, but altering the layout of the space between the pastures would save tons of time when feeding.

"Mom, it's not as if I want to move." He figured he owed her a general explanation, and although his voice was compassionate, he had to fight the defensive tone from creeping in. He was independent and resisted his mother wanting to keep him close to the nest. "I've sent out resumes within a 300-mile radius." The lack of response from the companies was difficult to handle. Sometimes he wondered if his email program and phone were working. When he called them to follow-up, he received the runaround.

She inhaled a sharp breath. "What about Jeff? Can he help?"

His childhood buddy, who was Claire's husband and the wildlife biologist on Pony Island, kept him abreast of the contract situation as much as possible. "Even Jeff is unsure of the ferry's future." The good news was, Jeff's family owned a construction company. The bad news? The company wasn't hiring architects.

His mother set her coffee mug down hard enough on the table Keith heard it through the phone.

"Have faith," she said in a quiet voice.

Keith understood what she was saying but he was a proactive man, and it was hard to sit back and wait. He slapped dust off his hands and opened the door of the truck. Not looking forward to checking on Gran, knowing full well she would lecture him about the horses and the building project, he chose to sit in the truck to finish the call with his mom.

When he didn't respond quickly enough, she filled the silence. "I learned the hard way about having patience by seeing your dad die. I think the lesson here is for you to be patient and not feel you have to run off in search of something else."

Keith doubted her logic. Life was life. Things happened to people and forced them to adapt and move on. "I know Dad's death was painful. I wish I could do more."

"Stay in Big Cat, if you can."

Keith despised feeling guilty. He shook it off, and when they finished the call, he pulled up in front of Gran's house. Old memories jabbed at his heart when he saw the glow of the light in the kitchen window. When he was a kid, he often stayed overnight and helped her in the mornings by feeding the horses and mucking out stalls, only to find a pancake and sausage breakfast waiting for him in the big country kitchen. Today there would be no cooked breakfast, as age was claiming his grandmother.

He climbed the steps onto the old porch, surprised to see her waiting for him outside. She was wrapped in a blue and white crocheted blanket and sitting in a wicker chair overlooking the paddocks. Without a doubt, she was supervising his efforts from afar.

"Thanks," she said but her voice held an edge. "I can feed my own horses, you know." It wasn't a question and fell just short of an accusation.

He kissed the top of her head. "I know, Gran. Let us help you."

She sighed loud enough to make him wince.

It was too early in the morning to argue with her; besides he needed to get to the ferry. Captain Bill was able to handle the first run alone before the crowd picked up. "Jenni will be here this afternoon."

He backed up, edging toward the steps.

"Go to work," she commanded. "I'll be fine here."

"I have a call into Alex," he said, pausing.

Gran shook her finger at him. "I like Alex but she's busy too. Between college and the coffee shop, she doesn't have time to help an old lady."

Keith hated when she referred to herself as old. More attempt at guilt. "Gran, we love you. We'll figure it out." He worked his way to the bottom step, never taking his eyes off his grandmother. She had wrapped a blanket around her shoulders and looked aged, shrunken even, since the last unfortunate fall.

"Behave and don't do anything you aren't supposed to do," he warned.

She sighed again.

The thought of leaving her alone today, as well as in the future if he had to move, disturbed him. How was he supposed to abandon his family, the life he loved?

Then there was Emily. His feelings were growing for her despite the walls he tried to erect between them. He had been hurt before. The plan wasn't to allow himself to experience the same level of pain again, nor to break Emily's heart.

He wasn't sure how she felt about him, but he knew his feelings toward her were intensifying, and he had never met anyone like her. But what kind of man was he if he weren't able to provide? He needed to establish his career before he allowed his feelings to deepen. He heard his father's advice: *Don't allow your emotions to rule over common sense.* If Keith needed to move elsewhere in order to make a career change, then so be it. Guilt aside.

There was a time and place for love, marriage, kids.

Now wasn't it.

Keith's mom was an optimist. Even when her husband was dying of cancer, she had maintained a positive outlook. She demonstrated with devotion how she loved his father to the bitter end. Keith was thankful for her influence and she was a champ. Even now. He was thankful for the church members helping her and friends and family were the secret to life.

Friends and family.

Despite what happened with his job, he needed to figure out a way to stay in Big Cat.

Chapter Twenty

As I was lost in my typing, an email alert pinged. I chose to ignore it, and the words poured onto the page. Unlike the last manuscript, this one practically wrote itself instead of the usual need to pause and contemplate what to type. As if it were its own identity, the story developed itself beyond the brief outline I had at first made.

The love story between the heroine and hero was developing nicely. As he leaned in for a gentle kiss, I closed my eyes for a moment, remembering the first kiss Keith gave me. The memories flooded onto the screen in the way of words, his warm, masculine but gentle lips touching hers. Emotion stirred deep inside me as I translated the feelings onto the page.

In all truth, Keith was my real-life, romantic hero.

Another email alert sounded. At first I ignored it but something inspired me to glance at the incoming folder. One of the emails was junk mail but the other was a name I recognized all too well. I stared at the name on the computer screen, my first choice of agents.

My mind raced.

I contemplated reading it later to maintain the flow of my writing in case it was a rejection, in which case the words would come to a sudden stop. I placed my fingers on the keyboard but nothing. Instead, my mind kept returning to the unopened email, so I inhaled a long deep breath to calm my nerves and stared at the agent's name again. Whatever the outcome, I had to remain positive and trust my writing career was moving forward in a positive, bigger way than I imagined.

Read it. Push fear aside and be brave.

My mind soared as I read the words. *Dear Ms. Emily McMillan ... I find your premise intriguing ... Please attach the full manuscript...*

Another request for a full manuscript! And from my first choice of agents!

My pulse raced as if I had sprinted down the street. What an enormous accomplishment to receive such a request from an agent with such good standing. As I did before, I jumped up and did the happy dance, thrusting my arms upward, pumping my fists high above my head as I bounced around. I just might have squealed too.

I stayed up late to email the first agent despite the early morning wake-up call. Before sending, I read it several times over for accuracy. The thought of two agents wanting to read my story was confirmation I was on the right path with my writing.

When I finished, I glanced at the time, eager to call Keith and share my good news but it was eleven o'clock, far too late. Unable to resist, I texted instead that I had good news.

He replied back immediately. *Can I call you?*

Yes!

Within moments my cell phone rang.

"What's the good news?" he asked with genuine excitement in his voice.

I swear my belly swirled with overactive butterflies like a high school girl with a crush. "I received another email requesting my full manuscript." My voice raised an octave or two, maybe three. "So I have two requests." Never mind the rejections. I decided to focus on the positive.

He gasped. "Congratulations, Ms. Bestselling Author."

I loved the sound of his words. "I'm not a bestselling author yet," I reminded him. *Lift the lid off my restraints.*

He laughed. "Oh, my dear, you will be."

An adrenaline rush soared through me like I was riding an exciting, steep rollercoaster.

"I hope you're right." I didn't want to sound too eager, pompous or arrogant, so I refrained from saying what I was thinking. But one of my dreams was to see my books on shelves in stores, to see people reading them on the beach, to help them or at least to entertain them.

"Emily, you have what it takes. I believe in you."

I caught my breath.

"Thank you, Keith." My chest did some unfamiliar warm thing, a sensation filling me from the inside out. "I read an article once about surrounding yourself with a team of people who root for you, who believe in you."

"I'm here for you, Emily." His voice was deep and sexy. He was probably snuggled deep in his bed while talking to me.

Support was something almost foreign to me. "For the most part, my family doesn't understand my passion for writing and feels the copious amount of effort I spend on my hobby is a waste of time." I wasn't sure why I was getting so real with him, but like my writing, the words spilled out. When, or if, my success arrived—and I hoped it would—I owed everything to answered prayers.

"Your writing isn't a hobby, but a calling, so never let anyone tell you otherwise."

With humbleness and vulnerability, it was past time I let go of caring what everyone else thought about me. I just needed to be myself. According to the self-help books I read when I had occasional downtime, it was what they called self-love, confidence ... joy.

How people treated me, such as Frank, was a direct reflection on how they felt about themselves, not about me.

If I reduced the watery mixture of reasons for moving to the coast down to a rich sauce, I realized I relocated not to run away, but to discover myself.

"This time we need to celebrate with more than ice cream." He changed the subject. "I have some news to tell you too."

News? "What kind of news?"

"I'll tell you in person," he said.

He was going to make me wait? I despised waiting. "Are you kidding?"

He chuckled, clearly enjoying taunting me. "How about dinner at my place tomorrow night?"

Dinner at his house sounded dreamy, though I wasn't sure I could wait until then. As I was learning, things happened at their own pace, and patience was a valuable lesson I was trying to learn through the art of publishing. "Dinner sounds wonderful."

Morning came too early, and after my snooze alarm went off three times, I dragged myself out of bed, showered, and pulled on a pair of mandatory blue scrubs with the company's name inscribed on the front.

Once at work, I sat at one of the computers and pulled up my schedule, the heavy caseload surprising me. If I practiced excellent time-management skills and cut my lunch break short, I might be able to still meet Keith on time for dinner. After all, he was a priority.

Before I set out to see my first patient, my phone rang. Frank's name flashed across the screen and my hand began to shake.

Unsure of what it was going to take to get him to leave me alone, I stepped outside and clicked to answer. Despite my flat voice, inside I was quaking. There was no time like the present to head this off.

"Why haven't you returned my texts or phone call?" His voice held an angry edge I knew too well.

The answer was obvious: I didn't want to talk to him. But I didn't dare say the truth, knowing full well the verbal backlash that would follow. "Frank, I'm at work and can't talk but a second."

He ignored my comment and dove into his rant. "You're ungrateful for everything I've done for you. If it weren't for me, you wouldn't be living it up at the beach."

I swallowed hard to gather my nerves. "If it weren't for you, I wouldn't have moved to the beach." Don't play his blame game, I reminded myself.

"It's obvious you don't appreciate anyone but yourself. But I do kind of miss you."

I shook my head hard. "Well, you should have thought about the consequences before you cheated on me with my best friend."

He sighed hard. "Come on, baby. We've been through this before. It wasn't planned and she has nothing on you. Ya gotta believe me."

No, no, no. "You're right, she has nothing on me. I have morals and integrity, unlike the two of you." It was difficult to breathe as I dragged air into my lungs. Two employees walked past me and stared, and I bet I looked like a bedraggled mess. Just hang up the dang phone, I scolded myself.

"I'm going to come down there and we are going to talk this out." His voice was scratchy as if he'd been drinking all night and had just woken up.

"There is nothing to work out and I won't be home." I was grateful I had plans at Keith's house and wouldn't be around if Frank showed up.

"Already gotta boyfriend, I hear. Well, he's a temporary fling and won't last because you still love me."

Did I still love him? I wasn't one to give my love away easily and for a crazy moment my heart skipped a beat. How could I love someone who was abusive? What a horrible repetitive cycle I, as a victim, was going through. Everything he said was nothing but lies and manipulation. My mind knew this intellectually but my heart didn't seem to listen to reason.

Well, not this time. I would not, could not, go back to him. Manipulators don't change and he was trying to win me over like some cheap prize at an amusement park.

"No, I'm not interested and I need to get back to work. Goodbye." Without waiting for his reply, I clicked the phone off, proud of myself for resisting his dysfunctional games.

The day dragged by, my mind heavy with worry that Frank would show up unplanned at my house.

My last patient of the day was Pastor Conway, and I was looking forward to talking with him again. I hoped my writing had touched their hearts. Instead of taking the elevator, I opened the heavy door to the stairwell and jogged upstairs to the second floor. Every little bit of exercise helped throughout the day. With a long stride, I headed toward his room.

The first thing I noticed was his nameplate missing from the wall near the door. Not a good sign. I peeked in his room. The bed was made along with the bedside table pulled midway across in effort to welcome newcomers. His oversized recliner was empty.

I spun around in the doorway and about bumped into the nurse in the hallway.

"Where's Mr. Conway?"

She shrugged as she continued typing on the computer placed on her cart. "We discharged him to the hospital," she said in a flat tone as if he were just a name.

Did she not understand what a special man he was? Did she not see him as a person, with a family and a wife? He was a pastor, a man of the light, full of wisdom. The short session I had with him had forever changed my life, changed my way of thinking. Of course, the nurse was busy and cared for numerous people daily, sent them out when necessary, maintained the required superficial rapport with patients to minimize the risk of emotional involvement. But Pastor Conway was different.

"What happened to him?" I asked in fear of hearing the answer.

The nurse shrugged again. "He was having difficulty breathing and most likely won't return."

I was astonished by how the news bothered me, especially since I made a point not to get attached to patients. It required a learned skill set but made me wonder if I made it a general habit with people. Had I gotten so practiced I pushed everyone away? The reality hit me hard.

I looked up to notice the nurse staring at me.

"Honey, you can't allow yourself to get too close to your patients. It will tear you up inside."

I exhaled a long breath. "Actually, life is about caring for people, not keeping a wall up with everyone. Caring not only for their needs but for them as a true person." I wasn't the ideal one to teach a nurse about humanity, but I wasn't able to stop myself.

The nurse glanced away, ignoring my speech, and pushed her cart in front of the next door to continue passing out medication.

On the way back to the therapy gym, I saw Stacey and shared the story about my written piece for Pastor Conway. She offered compassion and a hug when I mentioned he was admitted to the hospital.

As we entered the rehab gym and sat next to each other at the computers, I was reminded once again why friends and coworkers were important in life. The amount of support given to each other at this job was truly an act of teamwork. Without people, life was dull.

A bent-over, little woman with stark white hair stood on command from Steve, the physical therapist working with her. Her pants started to drop but Steve grabbed hold of the backside and held them up instead of using the gait belt around the woman's midsection. The woman took several slow steps, hunched over. Steve cued her to correct her posture by not leaning on the walker, but if the woman tried to fix the situation, it was unseen by my eyes.

A succession of gassy wind passed from their direction in the gym.

I focused on the computer screen, pretending not to hear anything.

"Mike, the bathroom is down the hall," Kevin, another occupational therapist, mumbled out of earshot of the older woman as he typed on a nearby computer.

"I know. It's a common problem of mine," Mike said. He was one of the younger physical therapists and was so tall he almost had to duck when walking through doorways.

Stacey chuckled, and I managed to fight off a giggle of my own.

"You really need to get your situation checked out," Kevin said in a casual tone. "It could mean a more serious health condition." He pecked on the computer as if their conversation was an everyday occurrence. In all reality, their sense of humor was an ongoing competition between the men in the rehab department, and I found the lighthearted banter a welcomed release from the tension of our jobs. Between the level of responsibility managing patient safety, decision making, problem solving, physical requirements of lifting patients and teaching them how to walk again, I welcomed their bathroom humor.

Mike turned to look in Kevin's direction. Deadpan, he said, "Right. I'll make an appointment first thing tomorrow."

"You do that."

Another choppy sequence of wind flooded the far section of the gym. Everyone buried their attention into their computers without reaction. Kevin pushed his desk chair back and stood to pull out his belongings to return home for the afternoon. "I expect a full report from the doctor on my desk tomorrow."

"Got it."

I realized in the moment how much I cared for my coworkers. They were almost family too.

A strong, unpleasant odor wafted toward us but I zeroed in on typing my notes so I could leave for the day. Two of my patients had been cancelled, one of them Pastor Conway, so I had plenty of time to make it to Keith's house for dinner.

When I arrived home, the inspiration to write was overpowering and I glanced at the clock. It was tight but I had a little time before driving to his house.

First I rinsed off in the shower and changed clothes, and then carried my laptop onto the balcony to write. The frogs were already vocal, as one of them started singing and the rest chimed in as the voice of a chorus. To my usual amazement, they stopped in unison until a single frog started the music again. The dynamic puzzled me but I enjoyed the soothing interaction from nature.

I shifted my thoughts from last night's worries about visiting Keith's house, to Frank possibly showing up here, to the laptop in front of me. But the words refused to surface. I was able to peck a word here and there, enough to write a few sentences, but nothing like the experience of when the words filled the pages as fast as I could type them.

I hoped someday my dedication to writing paid off in a big way, that I wasn't wasting my effort and valuable time as my family suggested.

If it weren't for the vision I held for myself, I would have stopped the writing process a long time ago. Most of my writer friends had already found success and ensured me I had talent, but truth be told, sometimes I thought about quitting. Thankfully, my passion for writing never allowed me to give up.

Lift the lid off my restraints. Pastor Conway's words were now my motto.

Disappointed, I closed my laptop. Not only did I experience fear in writing but in dating Keith. It took a brave soul to become vulnerable in a relationship and to share thoughts and dreams. After all I had been through, I had to wonder if I was capable.

Come on, I needed to give myself some credit. I was beginning to open up emotionally, proof in itself my heart wasn't closed off forever. And if I needed more evidence, I was beginning to have strong feelings for him, feelings I hadn't felt in a long while.

I thought back to Pastor Conway. Vulnerable and shrunken in his chair, dying of cancer, yet I was blessed he had touched a piece of my soul. I had said it perfectly earlier today. Life was better when you cared about people and it was time to love again. Just because I feared being emotionally hurt, I had to step out of my comfort zone and take a chance.

Tonight, at Keith's house, I planned to make an effort to let my protective walls down more. Bravery was the key to life.

Chapter Twenty-One

Keith tried to recall the last time he'd invited a woman over for dinner. Honestly, it had been too long to remember. And tonight he had a special surprise for Emily in addition to creating a nice meal.

He held a secret obsession for cooking. Of course, his family knew he was a closet chef, waiting to impress his skills on someone special, and he owed his passion to his father, who had owned one of the best restaurants in town.

When he was a kid, he resisted working summers at Stallings, but his father always claimed he was a natural.

Keith used his chef's knife to finish dicing the organic vegetables as his father had taught him. He had chosen a selection of homegrown sweet potatoes, the freshest green beans he could find, bella mushrooms, and a bunch of scallions. Then he scooped the firmer produce into peanut oil in the hot wok first. One by one he added more vegetables, depending on the required length to cook them thoroughly. He used his favorite bamboo spatula to push the finished ones higher up on the wok to keep them warm, and the breaded chicken breasts were almost finished baking in the oven.

The doorbell rang and snapped him back to reality. He was guilty of enjoying the process of creating a fine meal so much he almost forgot he was nervous about having Emily over. He had been taught men were supposed to bury their tender feelings for women and hide their vulnerability, but after all he'd been through with losing his sister and his father, he had since learned the logic was old-fashioned.

He turned off the burner, wiped his hands on the dishtowel hanging from the oven, and made his way to the front door. Emily stood in front of the glass, looking beautiful in a simple but classy black dress, a bottle of Sauvignon Blanc in her hands. The wine was an excellent choice for the baking chicken breasts.

He took the bottle from her, stepped back and invited her into his house.

She glanced around as if she were in awe. The soft piano music playing from the strategically placed speakers, along with a warm embrace, was his way to offer his welcome.

He tried to see his home from her point of view. The angles were sharp, high, and the floor plan open. Her gaze stopped to take in the stone fireplace. It was vast, dominating at least half the wall space with a wide hearth. He designed it with the idea of being the focal point of the room.

She pointed to the picture above the mantel. "One of Claire's?"

He nodded. "I didn't have my camera and wished I did, so she snapped the photo for me. It's one of my favorites."

He motioned her into the kitchen.

"Your house ... it's gorgeous. Did you design this?"

He nodded as he set the bottle on the granite countertop. He removed two dark blue, tinted glasses from the cupboard and placed them next to the wine, and pulled a corkscrew from the drawer and opened the bottle.

"Your kitchen is huge. It reminds me of a chef's kitchen." Her expression was one of amazement.

"Thank you." Never before had he thought of his kitchen as a chef's kitchen, and he rather enjoyed the thought.

"Have you designed other houses like this one?"

He shrugged with indifference. It always made him uncomfortable when people complimented his designs.

"You have a lot of talent." She sat on a barstool and he had to admit, she added a sense of class and style to his kitchen. "Keith, you need to be sharing this gift with others."

"Thank you," he repeated but wasn't sure how to respond. His father had always echoed his talent as a chef, rightly so since he owned a restaurant, but never praised him as an architect. Then again, his father's plan was to pass Stallings on to one of his kids. It about killed him when he had to sell the business. At least Jenni owned Coffee Break, and that was as close to a restaurant as either one of them wanted.

He poured the wine to take the attention off of him.

In all honesty, he had built the house with plans to marry Vicki. It was smaller than she wanted but appropriate to start a family. Designing a larger house wasn't a problem as much as the role finances had played in the decision, in addition to paying for a large portion of the wedding because he hadn't wanted to strap his parents or Vicki's with the cost.

It was far smarter to build a house he could afford, to live well within his means and save money in the bank each month. His parents had taught him to provide stability, and a provider he was, for the family that never happened.

When his fiancée backed out before the wedding, his dreams were dashed and he almost sold the home. His father condemned him for keeping it, stating a bachelor didn't need a family house to maintain, but Keith enjoyed yard work and landscaping. Cleaning was a different story, so he hired a company once a month. Problem solved.

"Whatever you are cooking smells divine." She licked her lips, as if wanting to taste the aroma itself. She picked up the wine glass and sipped.

He stepped forward, sweeping a long curl over her shoulder. When she set the glass down, he pressed his mouth lightly onto hers. She tasted of delicious wine. While he kissed her softly, he couldn't hide the passion behind it. Never before had he met anyone who felt so right, so warm, so delicious.

He deepened the kiss enough to keep it gentle and sweet,

and to demonstrate his respect for her. But dang, what was this woman doing to him?

The timer on the stove buzzed, a perfect opportunity to offer him a distraction from her. He wanted to kiss her for hours but didn't want to give her the wrong impression, so he welcomed the intrusion of the chicken requiring his attention. After all, he wanted to serve her the most delicious dinner possible. The soft music continued to fill the room with light romance.

Opening the oven door, a wave of heat and a mouthwatering fragrance of baked chicken poured out.

"Oh my gosh, I think I died and went to heaven," she said, inhaling long, exaggerated breaths.

He laughed as he pulled out the baking dish and set it atop the stove and closed the oven door with his hip. It was interesting to note she was watching his every move and stirred up emotions he had no idea how to handle.

"Can I help with something?" She leaned against the counter. The long curl had fallen forward across her shoulder again.

"Bring the wine to the table?" He dumped the contents of the wok into a bright, blue-colored ceramic bowl and placed a large spoon inside. "If you want water, would you pour two?"

She opened the correct cabinet as if knowing where he kept the glasses.

With care, he scooped the chicken off the baking dish with a spatula, placing the breasts on a matching bright blue plate. One of his favorite kitchen stores was in Raleigh, and he took pride in the colorful collection of the dishes he bought.

He placed the items on the farmer's table, which was next to a wide window displaying a thin row of trees outlined by a magnificent view of the marsh water. From the refrigerator, he retrieved a large bowl of salad made from fresh greens, a variety of organic vegetables, crumbled bacon, cut-up strawberries, and topped with feta cheese. He set the bowl and homemade dressing on the table next to the plate of chicken.

They sat down catty-corner from each other and he took her hand and lifted his wine glass to toast. "To us, and to success in our budding relationship, along with good health, growing careers, and may we be blessed with abundance, love, and protection." They clanked their glasses together and took long sips.

He waited for her to gather food onto her plate and then he cut off a chunk of chicken for her. When she placed a forkful into her mouth, she closed her eyes and didn't speak, but from the dreamy expression on her face, she was savoring the bite.

"Fantastic." She speared another piece and closed her eyes again as she chewed slowly.

He watched her. She was the most feminine, sensual woman he ever met.

He realized he was in love with her and wanted her in his life for many years to come.

Dinner was a slow process between eating, enjoying the food, chatting, the soft music. Life was remarkable, especially with her beside him to share the journey. He never thought his heart would open up again, love again. While the experience in the past had left him hurting in ways he never wanted to revisit, he was willing to take a chance on love once more.

He excused himself from the table and walked into his room. From the top drawer of the dresser he pulled out a petite box. He had seen the gift in the shop window the other day when he was visiting Raleigh for a job interview. He planned to tell her about the opportunity but didn't want to ruin the moment. The news had to wait.

Carrying the little, dark blue velvet box with a tiny white silk bow on top, he paused before setting it on the table in front of her.

Her eyes widened in surprise, and she glanced up at him as if questioning if the gift was for her.

He offered a small smile. What if she didn't like his choice of jewelry, or maybe it was too soon to give her a fine gift?

She lifted the lid and gasped, glancing at him again, as if unsure of why he had bought her a silver heart with small diamonds.

"I thought about you when I saw it." He inhaled a slow breath to calm himself. He wasn't sure if she appreciated the beauty of the gift as he had. "You have my heart."

Her mouth dropped open. "It's beautiful. Thank you." She leaned forward, placed her hand on his, and planted a passionate kiss on his lips. He took her reaction as a sign of approval. It was true, she had his heart.

He wanted her to know his news had nothing to do with buying her the necklace and planned to enlighten her later.

"Also, the necklace is to celebrate the interest you've had with agents," he said in earnest.

She stood, closing the space between them, and offered him more passionate kisses. Of course, he loved the affection. Was it true diamonds were a way to a woman's heart? He mentally shook his head. The way to a woman's heart was to love her with all your soul. Gifts were an added bonus.

She lifted her sexy curly hair into a makeshift ponytail with her hands and he placed the necklace around her bare neck. Man, he loved her.

But he had to tell her about the interview.

Later came too soon. They moved out to the deck, overlooking the marsh and water but half covered by the trees he planned to trim back to enhance the view.

"Didn't you say you had news to share with me?" she asked, her shoes kicked off and her legs drawn up underneath her in the overstuffed garden chair. He turned on the fire pit and paced back and forth, unable to look at her. The words he had practiced disappeared.

Start with the truth.

He sat down in the chair next to hers and her bare foot touched his leg, making concentration difficult. "I went to

Raleigh the other day," he said, studying the marsh as if it provided answers. "I'm searching for an option if I lose the ferry contract."

She listened, but despite her relaxed position in the chair, he noticed her fingers squeezed tight around the glass of sweet tea she was holding.

"I'm not expecting to lose the contract, but I need a backup plan." He was trying his best to explain his situation without alarming her. "I don't anticipate moving, or at least not selling my home, but I need to be proactive."

Nothing. She sat there in silence but fingered the heart necklace he placed around her neck less than an hour ago.

"I ... care for you." He wasn't about to confess his love for her yet and had no idea if she felt the same way.

"I care for you too." She turned her gaze away from him as if searching for solace in the peaceful marsh.

He had spent hundreds of hours lost in that view, trying to resolve his pain from the past. The whys, the hows, of his failed relationship and the death of his father. But no longer did the marsh remind him of his history, and he wanted to share the view with her. As far as he was concerned, their future was bright, except for the lingering stress about the contract and the uncertainty of his job.

"The interview was at an architecture firm in Raleigh." He inhaled a deep breath to stay grounded. He wanted to explain things so there were no surprises later. "I would be designing houses like mine."

"You are gifted." She continued to stare at the marsh as if he were breaking her heart. "Isn't there an opportunity to work here?" she asked without looking at him.

"Work here is limited," he explained. He had reached out to all his contacts, had received several compliments on his skill level and the desire to have him on their team, but right now there were no openings. He shrugged, although the topic was anything but casual. "I don't want to move." At least he was being honest by telling her.

She crossed her arms. "I know."

If he did move would their budding relationship continue to thrive? He had to find employment, had to make a living. Then again, one thing he learned when his dad died was how important relationships were. He wanted to marry, wanted kids. If he got a job offer in Raleigh, he wondered once again if Emily would consider relocating. From what he understood about her, she retreated to Big Cat to escape bad memories of the city.

It was too soon to discuss the situation in more detail. He didn't want to spook her, and unless they were engaged or married, he wouldn't dream of asking her to move. That was what caused his failed relation with Vicki.

"Are you ready for dessert?" He hoped she left enough room for homemade strawberry shortcake.

She groaned. "No, but yes." Her laughter filled the intimate space between them.

He stood and held out his hand to help her up. She felt warm, soft, loving. He wasn't asking anything of her yet, but at some point they would likely have a decision to make.

Together they worked side by side as he made the homemade whipped cream and she sliced the ripe strawberries. There was a relaxed camaraderie between them despite the tense conversation moments ago. She moved about the kitchen as if she belonged, making herself at home.

When they finished they made their way back outside carrying dessert plates and mugs of coffee, but this time they sat together on the comfortable love seat his mother helped him choose. Their bare legs touched and he loved the physical connection between them.

He wasn't sure how long they sat together but the sun had long set. When she got up to leave, he walked her to her car, not wanting to say goodbye but they both had work tomorrow.

Locks of curls dangled over her shoulder and he swept back

one and embraced her again. He kissed her lips, and then her cheek as he whispered in her ear. "See you Saturday? A picnic on Pony Island? I'll pack you the best lunch you've ever had."

"Yes, but no one has ever packed me a lunch until you."

He kissed her and then opened the car door. One more ... kiss.

Before he caught himself, he whispered, "I love you."

Chapter Twenty-Two

I climbed into the car almost dazed. Did I hear Keith correctly? I swore he whispered he loved me.

Did I love him? At first my body buzzed with a warm excitement, but the closer I drove to my apartment, the more tense I grew. My bad habit of overthinking was taking over. But I was confused as to whether my intensifying discomfort was because of what Keith said, or because I was nearing home alone.

I glanced around to make sure Frank wasn't waiting in the dark of the parking lot for me. I kept alert but on my way upstairs, my cell phone rang and startled me.

I was relieved to see it was Jenni calling and glanced around once more before answering. Still on alert, I opened the front door and flipped on the lights. Thankfully he hadn't shown up, at least not yet.

"I hope I'm not bothering you." Jenni sounded happy, and it was easy to imagine the baby glow and smile on her face.

Except for the morning sickness, pregnancy suited my friend well.

I headed into the living room and curled deep into the couch to chat with her. I had to wonder, though, why she was calling, as we didn't normally talk on the phone. It was possible she had heard about the evening I spent with Keith, and small towns were notorious for knowing everyone's business, especially Keith's loving but meddling family and friends.

As one who wished my family was emotionally closer, I almost didn't mind.

"I called to invite you to a reveal party, where we announce the sex of the babies." She squealed with excitement. "Keith will be there, as well as Claire and Jeff. The party will give you a chance to meet a lot of people our age."

I was starting to feel as though I fit into Big Cat and it was fast becoming home. I jotted down the date on a pad of paper sitting on the coffee table. "I'd love to come. What should I bring?"

"Just yourself." Jenni's voice sounded lighter than usual. "Also, Claire and I are having a girls' night at my house Friday night, if you're interested."

"I'd love to." My social life was starting to pick up pace. I glanced around the apartment at the unpacked boxes still stacked against the walls and it made sense to work on those before my social calendar grew busier.

"We plan to watch movies, order Chinese food, and make margaritas. Virgin ones for me, of course."

"Sounds fun and I look forward to it." I was thankful to Gran for introducing us outside of Coffee Break. "By the way, how is Gran?" It no longer felt awkward calling Ms. Stallings by the nickname.

"Oh, Emily. She's driving Keith and me nuts." Jenni exhaled a long breath into the phone. "I mean, she's doing too much around the house and won't let anyone help her."

Gran was an independent, stubborn woman. "As much as I like her, I don't want to see her get hurt again and get readmitted."

"Exactly!" Jenni said, her voice intense. "And she wants to see you. She talks about you a lot."

Jenni and Keith had no idea how lucky they were. "I want to see her too."

"You're welcome to visit her at home, but she'll be at the reveal party."

I wanted to keep my professional life separate from my personal life, unless Keith and I became more serious. If I heard him right, that was what he was saying. Love implied serious.

But about Gran ... the ideal choice was to see her at Jenni's. Although I craved long talks with her on the front porch, drinking sweet tea, and hearing stories about her past. But if I got too personal with her, she would involve herself in my relationship with Keith. She had proven that back when she was matchmaking. I wasn't sure how much information I wanted to share with her, and right now I wanted to savor every private thought about Keith.

"Just a warning," Jenni said as if reading my mind. "Gran's nosey. Believe me, she'll butt into your business when you prefer to keep it private."

I chuckled. "I can handle her." But I wasn't sure it was a true statement, and I wasn't used to anyone meddling in my business. It was possible I'd resent the intrusion, but also likely I'd love it. Time would tell.

"Consider yourself warned," Jenni said with lighthearted laughter. "If you do visit her at home, she will consider you family. Family is fair game."

Family. What a cozy, heartwarming thought.

When we hung up, I pulled out my laptop. There were no new messages from agents today, so I relaxed into my writing space. Originally, I set out to write contemporary women's fiction, but the story had turned into a cozy, small-town romance. I had a real hero to write about now instead of the less-than-ideal men I had experienced before. At least my life was improving.

No sooner than I began to type, my mother called from Cancún. I set my laptop aside to give her my full attention. "How is Mexico?" I pulled my legs underneath me and leaned against an overstuffed pillow the color of the deep sea.

"Hot but lovely," she responded as if she were out of breath. Was she crying?

"Is something wrong?" I sat taller as if it would help.

My mom gasped as if choking down tears. "I had a little incident today, but I'm okay." She paused, knowing I needed a moment to process what she was saying.

"Incident?" If anything happened to my mother I didn't know what I would do. I had lost far too much already, and lately I was learning just how important friends and family were.

"Well, your sister and I took a tour outside Cancún." She started sniffling. "The sidewalk was rough and I tripped over the uneven payment when I climbed off the bus."

My belly clinched into a tight knot. "Mom! Are you okay? You fell?" Horrible visions took over my creative mind, and I imagined my mom with her arm in a cast from shoulder to wrist, or worse yet, one of her legs immobilized along with her arm.

More sniffling.

"It's okay, Mom." Pushing aside my anxiety, I tried to console her over the phone. I wished I was down there, so I could wrap my arms around her and offer comfort, even though we weren't a touchy-feely family. More progress, as I was fast becoming a hugger since I met Keith.

My text beeped.

"Look at the picture I just sent." Mom blew her nose into the phone.

I pulled the cell phone away from my ear and saw a sullen photo of my mom with a swollen and badly bruised nose, a splotchy black eye, and four upper teeth missing.

"Oh, my gosh!" I blurted out before I was able to filter my response. Actually, maybe filtering reactions to my own family members was part of the problem, making me emotionally unavailable. Through Keith I was learning to embrace the genuine person I was without holding back. It was more than okay not to hide my emotions.

Mom cried harder.

"I'm so sorry!" I exclaimed, my level of concern for her was almost unbearable. I was helpless while she was out of the country. "What can I do?"

Mom blew her nose again, and I could easily imagine her wiping her tearful eyes with the back of her hand, a habit of hers when she was upset. My heart was breaking in two.

"Do you need me to fly down there?" I suspected my boss would agree to give me time off in case of an emergency.

"No, honey. I'm flying home to have my dentist fix my teeth." She breathed heavily into the phone as if taking several deep breaths to calm herself down.

"When?"

"We're flying out tomorrow." Her voice sounded muffled as she moved about. "They will need to make molds for new teeth. The process takes a while."

I hadn't realized until now how much I missed them. "How long will you stay?"

"We enjoyed ourselves but have had our fill. We are coming home to stay."

I had to fight to contain my excitement and then remembered my new pact with myself to no longer suppress my emotions. "Yay!!!! What time does your plane land?" I wanted to meet them at the airport but had existing plans for girls' night, plus work, and a picnic on Pony Island scheduled on Saturday. How was I supposed to juggle all these responsibilities, albeit fun ones? I reminded myself family and friends weren't responsibilities but blessings.

"Four o'clock."

I could pull it off if my boss agreed to give me a half day of work tomorrow. To my surprise I wanted to greet them with balloons, offer plenty of hugs, check on Mom and hear their stories, and I might still have time to make it back to Big Cat for girls' night. It was essential to keep the movie date, as making friends was important to me too. But if I had to miss girls' night, so be it. My mom came first.

"The hospital visit was a nightmare. Remind me to fill you in later," Mom said, her voice sounding tense.

The hospital? I quivered at the thought. My poor mom.

When we disconnected the call, I texted my boss. It was late but I didn't want to wait until morning to ask for time off, knowing full well she had the schedule finished already.

Having not heard an answer from my boss by morning, I arrived at work early. Even if I didn't have a half day today, I planned to start the day earlier and work through my lunch to make it in time to greet them at the airport baggage return.

Such as luck was, I pulled up my schedule to see my boss granted me a half day. I'd now have plenty of time to stop by Mom's house to make sure it was tidy, and I didn't want them to worry about anything once they returned home. As usual I was trying to please them, to get their approval and I needed to stop. No, I wanted to greet them with balloons because it was who I was, and I was enough just being me. I had come a long way toward healing.

Before setting out to treat patients, I texted Kelly to see if she had time for a brief visit while I was in Raleigh. She was about the only person I missed there. But when my phone beeped, her text said both kids were sick and she wasn't feeling well. We texted back and forth a few times to catch up on each other's lives and promised to get together soon.

I had my three favorite patients today, so I headed down the hall to get my day started, but I had to admit returning to Raleigh dredged up all kinds of deep, dark thoughts.

In order to love a man, Keith specifically, my emotional protective wall needed to break away. Love was about trusting your significant other and being vulnerable enough to trust and have faith in him.

Of course, my emotional barrier hadn't been built in one day. It had taken most of my life to form and it was unfair to expect it to collapse overnight. And I didn't want it to. Vulnerability was scary.

My phone beeped and I stepped aside in the hallway to check to see if it was my mom, but it was from Keith. He must have known I was thinking about him. Strange how intuition worked.

GOOD MORNING, SUNSHINE. LOOKING FORWARD TO TOMORROW. THE WILD HORSES AWAIT.

I realized I hadn't told him I was leaving town. I typed back.

LOOKING FORWARD TO SPENDING TIME TOGETHER BUT I MIGHT HAVE A GLITCH. HEADED TO RALEIGH TO PICK UP MY MOM AND SISTER FROM THE AIRPORT DUE TO AN UNPLANNED INCIDENT. WILL FILL YOU IN LATER BUT I STILL PLAN TO GO TOMORROW. CAN I BRING SOMETHING FOR LUNCH?

JUST YOUR BIKINI.

I gulped. While I had been somewhat successful at losing weight, I wasn't ready to wear a bikini in public, much less in front of a man I liked. No, *loved*. I swore he whispered he loved me the other night but I wasn't certain. And was it even possible to fall in love with someone so quickly?

Bikini aside, the thought of swimming with him in the ocean, playing in the waves, laughing, splashing, was romantic. It was time I accepted my body for what it was. Self-confidence was where it started.

I knocked on the door to Ms. Andrews' room, a lady with a broken femur. "Good morning," I said.

Ms. Andrews flagged me inside. "It's good to see you, honey."

The next few hours breezed by, and after I finished typing my notes into the computer, I made my way to my car. I was eager to get on the road except for one brief stop for helium balloons to welcome them at the airport.

On the drive to Raleigh, I couldn't help but think about Frank, so to distract myself I listened to one of my favorite inspirational speakers. The topic of the day was about love and relationships. Interesting. My first response was to turn it off, normally ignoring any topic discussing romantic relationships, thanks to Frank, but now I listened with fresh ears.

But how was I supposed to embrace joy when I lived in fear of Frank showing up?

The balloons in the backseat floated between the seats and made me jump. I pushed them aside but had to laugh. It was as if Keith were in the car telling me to relax, not to overthink, as was my dreadful habit. Smiling, I fingered the heart necklace hanging around my neck.

I realized the inspirational message was important on another level too. Not only was the message about romantic relationships, it was about relationships in general. I came away with a better understanding of releasing judgment toward the people I loved. Of course, it was easier said than done. My father popped into my mind first, then my mother. Judgment had been the center of most of my family relationships. Well, boyfriends too.

Driving to Raleigh stirred up unbelievable fears in me.

Lift the lid off your restraints. I was ready for love, ready for mending the holes in the well-worn garment of my family. I could do this. How was it small-town living was helping me to grow in areas I hadn't realized needed such extensive work? The important takeaway here was the wounds of the past were healing.

But as I neared Raleigh, the feeling of entrapment overcame me and made me want to run, to escape. At the beach I was free.

Already I missed the fresh sea air. Breathing was easier at the coast.

As I reached the outskirts of Raleigh, the traffic picked up. Yet another reason to stay away from the city. The stop-and-go congestion lasted for ten minutes, and I considered myself lucky. It was usually worse.

The drive to Mom's house was shorter than I remembered. Unfortunately, Frank lived a couple of streets over, in the house we were supposed to share together. I dismissed the thought as fast as it popped into my mind.

I parked next to her car in the small, paved alcove below her house. An abundance of colorful, blooming flowers surrounded the stone steps as if welcoming me home, although I never actually lived in this house. The front porch was made from larger stones, the house painted a silver blue with white trim. If I hadn't known I was in Raleigh, I would have mistaken the house for a little beach cottage in Big Cat.

I climbed the steps and opened the door to a sunny foyer. The aroma of cinnamon welcomed me, and next to the door a dried flower arrangement sprang from an oversized neutral pot sitting on the polished hardwood floor. I was crazy to think I needed to tidy up my mother's house. The place was photo worthy of a magazine spotlight.

The focal point of the living room was a large stone fireplace, with more ceramic pots on the hearth, and photos, candles, and a collection of blue and white flowers on the mantle. I wished I had inherited my mother's sense of style but at least I was creative with writing.

When I straightened a pile of mail on the table, one envelope popped out at me. It was handwritten from a man, and the postmark was from Big Cat and addressed directly to my mother, Nancy McMillan. I couldn't help but wonder who Clark Randolph was.

I set the letter on top of the stack as a reminder to ask about it later.

Then a thought occurred to me. I pulled out my cell phone and snapped a picture of the man's name and return address. The least I could do was research him. After all, he lived near me. I placed the cell phone back into my pocket and headed down the hall.

The bedrooms were all tidy to a fault. My favorite guest bedroom had a blue and white quilt on the bed with large, overstuffed white decorative pillows lining the wooden headboard. The bed begged for me to crawl on top to take a nap. Too bad I had to leave soon for the airport.

One thing I never noticed before was her house oddly felt

like home, as it did hold memories. Not all good ones, such as tense Christmas get-togethers and birthday parties, but I planned to change my attitude by recreating new associations with my family.

When my mom and sister left for Mexico, the parting was awkward and I had been in a bad place emotionally with the situation with Frank.

If I found the nerve, I planned to do a quick drive past his house before I left town. Not so much for reliving life with him, but more as closure.

This trip provided clarity on one thing, for certain. I never wanted to live in Raleigh again.

I hoped Keith stayed near Big Cat. Otherwise, I was unsure of what our future held.

Chapter Twenty-Three

I paced the floor near the luggage return at the RDU airport. Whether I was ready to face my family, my past, the time was here. Waiting wasn't my strong suit and I had a bad habit of showing up too early. Usually I packed a book to read, or brought along my e-reader to work on an editing project. But today my hands were full of *Welcome Home* and *I Love You* balloons. Four to be exact.

I glanced at the time on my cell phone. The plane was due to land in five minutes.

A nearby family stood to greet their friends, hugs abounding, and they walked away still hugging and kissing. I sat down in their spot on a bench but continued to watch them until they walked through the doorway leading outside. More than anything I wanted a warm reunion with my own family.

No walls. Be myself. No holding back.

But anxiety continued to swirl around my belly while I awaited their arrival. Being at the airport was step one.

I stood and paced the area near the wall, the balloons bouncing back and forth into each other, making noises as they hit together. I must resemble a comedy act, but no one seemed to mind my nervous walking.

According to the monitor hanging up on the wall their plane had landed.

Within fifteen minutes, two familiar faces appeared as they rode down the escalator to the baggage return.

I gasped when I saw my mother's bruised face. It was one thing to view a picture, another to experience her condition in person. Terri, wearing a backpack, held onto Mom's arm, either for emotional support or for balance. I wasn't sure.

I stepped toward them, balloons in hand.

Terri spotted me first and waved, pointing me out to our mother, whose closed-lipped smile made her face look faded, aged even, but she smiled nonetheless.

I met them as they stepped off the escalator. Love. Be myself. I closed the distance between them, hugging my sister first, somewhat briefly, and then pulled my mother into a longer hug with my free arm. She seemed frail, beat up.

"It's so good to see you," I said while I had my arm still wrapped around my mom. "I missed you both." It was okay to admit the truth. No walls.

"It's good to be back. We didn't expect you to be here, so thanks," Mom said to me, pulling away and apparently uncomfortable with my affection. My sister stared up at the balloons.

There wasn't any mention of missing me, but all was okay. The hug was a start.

Thankfully, I ignored the brief pang of hurt and focused on the positive. Don't have expectations. Be myself and remain joyful and lighthearted despite the actions of other people.

I handed two of the balloons to Mom, and the other two to Terri. Luckily the I love you ones went to my mother. Stop.

Of course, I loved my sister too. Sure, jealousy existed between us, but those thoughts didn't belong in the present or the future. Start fresh. Their hiatus to Mexico offered us a new beginning.

"Thank you," Terri said, a small smile on her lips. She was tanned with sun-kissed cheeks, and Cancún had been nice to her. I could honestly say she was a pretty woman with straight silky blonde hair and fit from hours spent at the gym. Secretly, I wished I had my sister's body, especially since I needed to wear my bikini tomorrow.

I grabbed hold of my mother's arm, once again surprised at how loving I'd become thanks to Keith, and guided them to the luggage return to await their bags. The truth was, I didn't want to stop touching her, as my mother's vulnerable state disturbed me. "I can't believe how good it is to have you both home."

She smiled at me with closed lips, possibly to avoid revealing her missing teeth, and stifled a long yawn, hiding her mouth with her hands.

"Mom, don't worry about it," I said, wanting to make her feel less self-conscious. Then I realized I needed to practice the same sentiment with wearing a bikini.

My mother's eyes widened. "I'm not about to let anyone see me without teeth."

"You don't know anyone here," I reasoned, but then noticed several people studying her because of the bruises on her face. I needed to be more empathetic toward her.

Mom shook her head. "Well, I don't want you to see me like this."

Despite her earlier reaction from my touch, I pulled her into another hug anyway, and to my surprise, she didn't pull away. "I love you for who you are, Mom, and I'm glad you both returned safely."

Terri stared at me. I was sure she noticed how I was changing.

The moment was interrupted by the sound of the carousel turning on. Everyone seemed to claim their luggage, but after a few remaining pieces circled twice, my mother seemed to melt in defeat before my eyes.

"Your luggage is coming," I reassured her and hoped I was right.

"Just my luck they lost it." She touched the side of her bruised nose and winced.

My heart went out to them, as I was sure they were exhausted. The last two pieces of luggage spilled out onto the conveyor belt and Terri perked up. "There they are."

I grabbed Mom's and Terri reached for her own.

When we left the terminal and headed outside, the balloons whipped around in the breeze, and as Mom tried to contain hers, I swear I saw her glance up at them with a closed-lipped smile. Regardless if she acknowledged the truth or not, she enjoyed the balloons almost as much as having me greet them at the airport.

"Are you hungry?" I asked and tried not to glance at the time. I would return to Big Cat whenever I arrived, and meanwhile, my plan was to enjoy my family. At least Jenni was abreast of the situation about my unexpected trip to Raleigh and understood the possibility of my later arrival to her house.

"Food sounds tempting," Mom said, but her hand subconsciously covered her mouth again.

"Want to do Mexican? I need an authentic margarita," Terri said, and without explanation, I understood she probably needed something to knock the edge off her nerves.

"Margarita it is." I knew Raleigh too well and headed toward a restaurant I used to frequent.

I glanced in the rearview mirror at my sister, who was staring out the window, and suspected Mom's fall traumatized her.

We pulled into the parking lot of the best Mexican restaurant in Raleigh. When a man placed the chips and salsa in front of us, I forgot all about wearing the bikini and pigged out.

When the server arrived, my mother chose a margarita, refried beans, and rice, and Terri and I chose chicken fajitas. It wasn't until after we ordered and settled in that the tooth story surfaced. In great detail, Mom explained how they were exploring the ruins and the bus dropped them off at a stop in town to shop.

"The concrete sidewalk was cracked in several places," she said, and placed her hand over her mouth for a moment. "My sandal caught in the crack, and when I landed with a scream, a kind woman and a man ran over to help me. He picked me up and assisted me to a nearby hospital."

Terri remained quiet and I couldn't imagine what she had gone through.

"It was a small hospital, really just a clinic, and they were so busy it was like herding cattle," Mom said.

The server brought our drinks and placed them in front of us.

"They wouldn't let me inside with her," Terri said. It was the first she had spoken since the airport. "They took her away, speaking Spanish. I could barely understand it."

Neither of them spoke much Spanish, so I could only imagine the scene.

"I waited outside for four hours in the heat," Terri said, her face distraught. "I found a spot against the building and waited as it turned dark and we missed our bus back to the hotel. The police showed up with a dead man on a gurney, but I didn't ask them for help."

Mom nodded, her gaze distant.

"The doors opened and the police wheeled the body inside." Terri shuddered. "He had been shot and they didn't have the body covered up with a sheet or anything." She rubbed her face as if to wash away the memory. "I snuck inside before the door closed."

I stared at my sister in disbelief. "Wow, you're gutsy."

"Well, I got worried about her and she was in there forever." Terri took a long sip of her drink as if she fully appreciated the alcohol. "When I was inside, I found her sitting at a desk. They tried to escort me out, but Mom was finished anyway, so they let her leave with me."

Mom chuckled, although the laughter was stiff from stress. "You know how much the clinic visit cost me?"

I shrugged.

"Fourteen dollars and it was a good thing I had cash." Mom took a drink of her fresh mango margarita and I hoped she wasn't on medication. The glass was large, the contents filled with frozen, slushy goodness, the cold probably good for her gums.

"The bill at an American emergency department or urgent care would cost a lot more," Terri said. "In that respect, we got off easy."

"Glad you are back safely," I added. "What a nightmare."

"No kidding." Terri drank more of the margarita and appeared to relax as she leaned back against the back of the booth. "I've had enough of Mexico for a while."

"I'm sure," I said and turned toward Mom. "Please see a doctor as well as the dentist." The swelling of Mom's nose and the black eye concerned me, but then again, Terri was a nurse at a nearby hospital, so I'm sure my sister took excellent care of her.

"I already have an appointment set up." She pushed her drink aside and stood. "Bathroom break."

When she left to find the restroom, Terri confided in me. "We've been fighting long before the tooth incident."

I thought they never fought. "About what?"

Terri glanced toward the bathroom. "She's been dating a man for several months and he lives down by you somewhere."

That explained the card on the kitchen table.

"What about him?"

"It was a surprise to me." Terri took a long drink. "She wanted him to come down to visit us in Cancún for a month. A month!"

I raised my eyebrows. "Why?"

"I don't know. At first I thought he was after her money."

"What money?" I knew she was financially comfortable but didn't think she was wealthy by any means.

"To some people, just the fact you own a house makes them think you are rich," Terri explained. "But as it turns out, it seems he is the one who is wealthy."

I smiled. "Well, good for mom."

Terri's facial expression hardened. "Would you want some man to intrude on your hiatus for an entire month?"

I realized she was stressed and didn't react. "Not really." I took a long drink of water. No margaritas for me with the long drive ahead.

"He would have gotten his own hotel room, but that's not the point," Terri said with a sigh.

I wondered if she was jealous and resented sharing our mother with a man. "What is the concern?"

Terri scrunched her face and rolled her eyes. "I don't even know him."

"You would after he visited for a month." I wasn't trying to be sarcastic but it was the truth.

"Seems drastic not to introduce me to him beforehand."

Mom approached the table and sat but shifted her gaze between us. "You've been discussing me, haven't you?"

Neither of us answered.

"Thought so." She lifted her glass and savored a long sip. "What a dang good margarita. Better than the ones at the resort."

"They probably have less alcohol in them," I said, suspecting an all-inclusive resort might cut down on the liquor to save money.

"For sure," Terri confirmed, popping a nacho chip loaded with salsa into her mouth. "And the cups there are little. But at least the drinks were free."

The server brought our food and set the dishes in front of us, Terri's and mine sizzling. I tried not to watch Mom eat her refried beans but noticed she was having difficulty. I hadn't noticed any missing teeth yet, and other than trouble eating and covering up her mouth, I wouldn't have known.

After dinner I dropped them off at Mom's house and helped them carry their luggage inside. Well aware of my long drive home, I hugged them goodbye and promised to see them soon.

Even though I was in a hurry, I found myself driving by Frank's house two blocks over. His car was parked out front, the lights on inside, and my pulse started to pound. My reaction surprised me, and I didn't understand why since I was over him. Truly I believed it was the right choice to move to Big Cat.

Still, I had loved him and suspected his hold on me had to do with narcissistic abuse, although it was just a guess, as I wasn't in the mental health field.

I drove away, and with each mile I left behind I felt more lighthearted and knew living at the beach was for me.

When I reached Jenni's house, there were no cars parked out front but the living room lights were on. More introverted by nature, hence the reason I loved the solitude of writing, I found walking into group settings difficult. At least there were only two people attending tonight, or so I hoped.

I reminded myself meeting new people was a prerequisite to making friends. I had to embrace the situation, walk up to the front door, and knock. The rest would take care of itself.

That was exactly what I forced myself to do. Jenni answered the door barefoot with a bowl of popcorn in her hands. All was casual, all was good. She handed the overfilled bowl to me and I felt welcomed.

I followed her into the kitchen and Claire looked up from the sink as she finished washing the blender. "Perfect timing. We are ready to start watching the movie. Grab yourself a frozen margarita."

I had made special friends and felt at home. I took the margarita from Jenni and followed them into the living room. Another woman walked out of the bathroom and Claire introduced me to Gabbi, who I suspected was close to my age. She was more of the artsy type. A portion of her blonde flowing curls swept across her shoulders, a section of it pulled up in a colorful clip. She was dressed in stylish jeans and a long, slender top. As well as Jenni, she was barefoot and a deep sense of peace encircled Gabbi, and I liked her immediately.

I hadn't realized how much I missed girl time. Before Frank, I had a group of friends who would get together, but they didn't support my relationship with him—except Julie, the ex-friend who slept with him—and one by one they faded away, all except Kelly.

But the fun thing about this new friend group was they were an extension of Keith.

We sprawled out around the living room, Jenni lying across the floor with a light throw blanket on her legs. Claire was camped out in a comfy deep chair, Gabbi leaning against the couch with her legs crossed, and I was curled in a ball on the sofa. We started the chick flick while munching on popcorn and drinking mango margaritas. Life didn't get much better than this.

The margaritas reminded me of my sister and mother. The mysterious man came to mind, and when the chance presented itself, I would inquire to see if the other women knew him. As authors were known for, I planned to do extensive research into Clark Randolph.

Chapter Twenty-Four

Saturday morning arrived with a burst of sunshine. He had a hunch today's trip to the island would be full of adventure, though good or bad was yet to be determined. As long as it was with Emily, they could endure most anything. He had woken up early and was in the kitchen making a special picnic lunch for them.

Once he finished, he placed it along with cold packs into his bag and hoped she enjoyed a homemade smorgasbord.

When he was certain she was awake, he pulled out his phone to text her.

Our picnic lunch is made. Pick you up in an hour?

Her response was almost instant.

I'll be ready and looking forward to it.

Me too.

In all truth, he was ready to show up at her doorstep now but didn't want to seem too eager. Slow and steady was his way.

So he cleaned the kitchen, giving the sink a thorough scrubbing, and then packed the supplies in his truck. Once he arrived in the parking lot of her apartment he grabbed a bag of cat food and headed upstairs, taking a moment to glance around for Tucker.

She pulled open the door without him knocking. They stared at each other in silence, neither of them moving away, both seeming to enjoy gazing into each other's eyes. It was probably cheesy but he didn't care.

"I missed you, Em," he said, and as she stepped back, he set the cat food on the counter and then scooped her into a hug, pressing his lips against her warm ones.

They lingered long enough to muddle his mind. "Are you ready for an adventure you won't forget?" he asked.

She nodded but when her phone beeped, she glanced at her text. He swore her face turned pale.

"Something wrong?" he asked.

She shook her head but said nothing. Dang, he knew something was off, but didn't understand why she wouldn't tell him. "Emily?"

Still not answering, she looked up at him. "Everything's okay."

He decided not to press the issue for now and reached for her pack, knowing full well she was capable of carrying her own, but at the same time wanting to be chivalrous.

"Thank you. I can't remember the last time someone has carried my backpack ... well, I take that back. In the third grade there was a boy named Henry who always insisted on hauling around my school bag. But no one as an adult." She laughed and tossed her curls back in the particular way she did, and as if nothing was wrong.

"It's my pleasure, ma'am." The emphasis was on ma'am, to show he was a southern gentleman.

She pulled the door shut to lock it and Tucker appeared from nowhere, begging for Keith's attention. "Mysterious cat. He was waiting for you to show up."

"Can I have your keys?" When she handed them to him, he opened the apartment door and stepped inside to scoop a handful of cat food into Tucker's bowl. The cat, clearly in heaven, meowed as he dove headfirst into the food.

Emily knelt down but Tucker ignored her.

"You spoil him," Emily accused as if she were offended. "He clearly loves the man who feeds him."

Keith grinned. He dusted off his hands and then took Emily's to lead the way down the steps. As always, he opened the truck door for her as his granddaddy taught him, putting her backpack in the backseat of the truck next to his.

The short ride to the ferry dock was filled with an electric energy pulsating between them. Eager to start their day together, he parked the car, but before he had an opportunity to walk around to open her door, she climbed from it. A diva, she wasn't.

When he retrieved the backpacks, they headed toward the ferry, due to depart within ten minutes. Kathy was in the ferry booth and waved to them as they strolled down the creaky ramp ahead of the crowd. When they reached the end, Captain Bill winked at Emily and reached out his hand to help her climb aboard the ferry. Keith knew he approved of her, as did the rest of his family and friends.

Sam waited on his usual piling for his fishy breakfast. He snapped his beak closed repeatedly, making a ruckus to hurry Keith along. Before hopping on the boat to join Emily, he opened the cooler and tossed him a small fish. As usual, he caught it in his mouth and swallowed it whole. After another fish, Keith snapped the cooler lid closed and hopped onto the boat as passengers made their way down the dock. Together Keith and Captain Bill helped people on board as well as their paraphernalia.

Captain Bill removed the microphone and reminded the passengers to keep their body parts inside the skiff as he eased the ferry out of the boat slip. Sam flew behind the boat for a short time and then flew in the opposite direction toward a little island to join other pelicans skimming a line above the bright blue water covered with sun diamonds. What a splendid day for a picnic on Pony Island.

At about the halfway mark, the ferry passed the smaller one with Captain Shep at the helm and they waved at each other. They were well into the busy season, and Shep was helping out every weekend.

The early, cool breeze from the boat's movement caused Emily to close the slight gap between them and snuggle in close. Not that he minded one bit. They stared out at the waves as they splashed against the white sandy beaches of desolate, random islands. It didn't get much better than this.

Before long Captain Bill pulled into the cove, reversing the engines to slow the skiff from climbing the beach. Keith stood to help him offload the passengers and their plethora of belongings. When they were the last ones left, they chatted with Captain Bill for a few minutes.

"Watch the weather," Captain Bill warned. "There are thunderstorms expected later."

"I noticed the radar had a few scattered storms but they seemed far off," Keith said, pulling on his backpack. "We appreciate the heads-up."

Emily glanced at the sky. "It's hard to imagine the possibility of rain with the sky so blue."

"Don't be fooled," Captain Bill said. "And you, Ms. Emily, make sure he behaves. He's a wild one." Captain Bill laughed in his scratchy, smoky way and shook a long finger at Keith as if he were protecting his own daughter.

Not only was Captain Bill rough like the sea, he was genuine and a great friend. If Keith had to move, he'd miss the old man.

"Promise," Emily said and winked at Keith. "He'll behave."

"Go have fun, kids. Enjoy your picnic."

Keith climbed off the boat first and helped steady her. Once they were on the beach, he dug the obligatory ball caps out of his bag and handed her one.

Their gaze lingered. "Today it's your choice as to where we explore." The tour guide in him came forth. "From here we can walk around to the point for shelling, or we can stay on the Sound side and follow it to the dock. From there we can take a trail through the dunes to the ocean, similar to what we did before, and you might enjoy the lighthouse in the distance.

Or we can stay on the Sound side and follow the beach to the graveyard again."

She looked undecided at first. "Why don't we take the trail to the ocean toward the lighthouse?"

"Great choice." Together they skirted the lapping water along the jagged beach. One cove was so tight between the water and a sandy cliff they had to remove their shoes and wade through the lukewarm water. "The tide is still somewhat high but receding, so the shore is harder to navigate than usual. But during high tide it's impassable. You have to take the long way around on a trail through the dunes, so we got lucky."

"I don't mind at all. This is a memory I never want to forget."

There were several other spots where they waded across long ditches filled with deeper, slightly cooler water. Some of the currents almost knocked Emily over but she clung to his arm, and of course he didn't mind one bit.

Smooth rocks littered the shore along with old pieces of dock boards, black stringy seaweed, and the occasional broken bottle. But he noticed the sky was no longer a solid, neon blue but a sporadic collection of white fluffy clouds. Gorgeous, except a few had flat, darker bottoms holding the promise of rain.

"As you might have noticed, the beach and landscape are always different." He watched her, feeling his expression go soft. She was so dang beautiful from the inside out.

"I can tell Pony Island is your passion, a way of life."

He nodded but fought off telling her his soft look was because of his passion for her, not the island.

"How will you survive living in a city?"

He shook his head. "I dunno."

"Look!" She pointed to several horse tracks in the wet sand. Some prints were deep and larger, some tiny. A set of them entered the water, but most trailed along the shore from where the receding tide had left behind evidence. "I can't wait to find the horses again."

"I'm glad you like it out here." Loving this island was a prerequisite for anyone he dated, even if he moved to Raleigh temporarily.

They reached the dock where the only bathroom on the island was.

She pointed to a trail with more horse tracks.

"That's the trail we want. It leads to the ocean."

They trudged through the deeper sand and eventually the dunes became taller. "It's easy to imagine we're exploring the desert," she commented.

"Although I've never been to the desert, I would agree." He wiped sweat off his forehead. "Whew, the sun is hot with all this sand and no shade."

"How long is the trail?" she asked, finishing off her bottled water.

"A good mile or so." He stopped to pull out two more bottles, and then shoved the empty ones into his bag.

"I need to increase my cardio workouts if we're going to hike like this."

"You're fine just as you are," he said, swallowing a large gulp of water. He passed her a small bag of peanuts for a snack and they rested.

"By chance, do you know a man named Clark Randolph?"

"Of course. Everyone knows him." He began walking again, and Emily stayed close as they hiked along the sandy trail at the edge of a valley.

"Tell me about him."

He shrugged and kept his gaze fixed on the trail. "What do you want to know?"

She didn't answer but studied the valley. He had to admit the landscape through her eyes was gorgeous.

"Why?" he asked, prompting her to answer.

"Just wanting to know." Her raised eyebrows made him

think it was the first response she had come up with. "I mean, is he a good man? Does he have his act together?"

Keith had to chuckle. "Absolutely. He's well respected." He wasn't sure why she was asking but thankfully she dropped the subject.

He swallowed a gulp of water, twisted the cap back on the bottle, and shoved it into the side pocket of his pack. "The beach isn't much farther." They hiked until the dunes opened up and the trail spilled out onto the beach. "We're here," he said, planting his pack in the sand at the base of a dune, far enough away from the incoming waves. She set her pack beside his.

They pulled off their outer clothes to reveal their swimsuits, and she crossed her arms in front of her. Boy, her ex-fiancé did a number on her self-esteem but she was improving. He could see it, as she laughed more and shared more of her personal life with him.

"You look great," he said, trying to help her relax. "See, you worried for nothing. Your body is perfect exactly the way it is."

Her mouth popped open. "Um, thanks." She dropped her hands from her midsection and challenged him to a race to the water. It reminded him of children seeing the beach for the first time.

He dipped down to splash a cool spray of water on her side. His boyish grin made her smile, and she kicked her foot sideways, retaliating.

They waded for a good while in the crashing waves, rode them to their hearts' content, and then rejoiced sitting in the shallow water with their feet touching. They chatted easily about nothing really, their conversation light.

And then her phone rang. They ignored it, although she became tense. He wondered again who had sent her the disturbing text earlier.

Eventually, albeit reluctantly, they emerged from the water

but he noticed she didn't check her phone for a voicemail. Either she hadn't heard the phone ring or she was ignoring it.

Hands together they strolled along the beach in the direction of the lighthouse. He wasn't about to complain as she meandered along the beach with her backpack in place while wearing her bikini. He had the same idea, leaving his shirt off until his skin dried in the warm sun, and he enjoyed every minute of watching her.

"Whenever I venture this far down the beach, I appreciate the quiet ruggedness and lack of tourists." He also appreciated the boats sprinkled in the water as they motored along the waves.

She squeezed his hand. "You're right. It's a drop of heaven."

Man, he loved her. If love had hurt before, then it hadn't been real because the experience he was having at the present moment was delicious.

They rounded a sandy bend and he pointed out the lighthouse perched on a long, narrow island. It blinked at them every seven seconds from across the water.

"Oh! What a picturesque scene, a perfect view to enhance my writing." She snapped a photo with her new camera. "What island is the lighthouse on?"

"Cannon Island. Interesting story there," he said. "It was once connected to Pony Island but during a hurricane the raging water carved away the thin bight of land."

"The name Cannon Island drums up images of pirates and Spanish Galleons."

"Exactly." He slowed his pace. "That's where Brittany died." The mention of his sister brought him deep pain.

Emily squeezed his hand again. "I'm sorry. No wonder this place means so much to you."

He stared out at the lighthouse. "They were out for a day on the sailboat. I knew it was supposed to storm that day and wish I had stopped them from going."

"But you were only a kid, right?"

He glanced down at the sand in front of him and kicked a wet pile of seaweed. It rolled once and dared him to kick it again.

"Keith, it wasn't your fault."

He swallowed hard. "I know. Are you hungry?" The view of the lighthouse offered a serene place to eat lunch and he always felt Brittany's presence here.

"Ravenous." Emily's belly growled on cue and they both laughed.

They dropped their backpacks near a large jagged dune split by a narrow trail at the lowest section.

"Where does the path lead, and why is it in the middle of a desolate beach?"

"The graveyard. The horses go into the forest to get away from the bugs, heat, and hurricanes," he said as the sun disappeared behind a cloud. He noticed her pink shoulders as she pulled on her shirt. Sunburn was one thing he rarely experienced with his year-round tan.

"Not the graveyard again."

Keith studied the sky. "We need to eat quickly. I don't like those clouds."

They had grown more abundant, and random ones were flat and dark at the bottom.

He shoved his phone back into the pocket of his backpack and unloaded several containers, aligning them in a row on the sand.

"Did you make all this?"

"Of course," he laughed. There was homemade chicken salad consisting of real chicken, halved red grapes and chopped pecans, along with small pieces of toasted bread, a container of fresh salad, and another one filled with small chunks of watermelon.

"You're amazing." She leaned into him and kissed his cheek.

He couldn't help but grin wide like a boy wanting to impress his girl.

Her cell phone rang again, interrupting them.

She hesitated as if not wanting to answer it and instead glanced at the caller I.D. "It's Jenni," she said, sounding puzzled.

"Strange. Maybe you should answer it."

She clicked on the phone. "Hey Jenni. What's up?" Emily listened and then said, "It's okay, no worries. What's on your mind?"

She paused for a moment and then her eyes widened. "Oh, no! What did he look like?" Her face paled and she looked as though she might get sick to her stomach.

Keith raised his eyebrows but she turned the other way. He knew without doubt something was wrong.

"Don't give him any information." Visibly she started shaking and ended the call.

"What's the matter?"

She turned slowly to look at him, her expression serious. "Frank is in town asking questions about me. He stopped in to get coffee and Jenni didn't tell him anything, but he's here looking for me."

Keith started to pack up the lunch but she placed her hand on his. "There is no reason to hurry back home where he is waiting. I'm in the safest place, on this island with you."

He let out a long sigh. "I didn't think he was serious enough to drive to the coast."

She watched him. "Actually, he sent me a text earlier. He said he saw me drive by his house last night when I was in Raleigh. He followed me for a distance until he knew I was heading back to the beach. Guess he decided to drive to Big Cat today."

Keith stared at her. "You drove by his house yesterday when you were visiting your mother?"

She glanced down at the sand. "Yes, I did."

"Why? Do you still have a thing for him?"

"Heck, no!" She paused too long. "He lives a couple of

streets over from my mom and I was just curious. That's all."

He didn't speak.

"I'd have to be crazy to still be interested in him."

Keith wanted to believe her. "How does he know you live in Big Cat?"

She glanced down at a shell near her feet and began pushing it around with her toe. "I wanted to get back at him, like I was moving on. Literally. So I told him I was moving."

He sat quietly, and she started unpacking the rest of the food. He no longer had an appetite but he didn't stop her from eating.

"The chicken salad is the best I've ever had." She scooped another bite onto the toasted bread and placed it into her mouth.

He had been crazy to believe she was over her engagement so fast.

She held a piece of bread loaded with chicken salad up to his mouth. He turned away. Food was the last thing he wanted right now.

"Keith, I love you ... not Frank."

He glanced up, locking gazes. "You mean that?"

She nodded. "Yes, I do. Promise."

Instead of eating the bite she offered him, he kissed her hard.

When he pulled back, he glanced up at the sky again. "Let's finish up." The last thing he wanted was to get stuck out here without cover during a storm. Captain Bill had been right.

They finished eating and repacked his bag.

He glanced at the sky again. "We can hike back the way we came, or cut through the Maritime Forest, but you'll have to see the graveyard again. Those are the only two paths connecting the two sides of the island."

She shrugged. "It makes more sense to take the path right here, although I didn't enjoy the last experience with the spooky graveyard. Maybe this time will prove to be different."

"Okay, let's do it then." He stood, dusted off the back of his swim shorts, and hoisted his pack on his back and helped with hers.

The terrain was difficult due to brush, undergrowth, low-hanging trees, and roots but it wasn't nearly as hot as trudging through the sand dunes without shade. He was glad they chose this path.

The trail spilled into a small clearing covered by trees, the graveyard. She surprised him by walking away to view the old headstones from across the fence.

"They are difficult to read and most are crumbling."

A branch snapped behind them and Emily yelped. She whipped around as she faced a wild stallion. The steed was muscular, his long tangled mane knotted, adding to the wildness.

"Back away slowly and don't make eye contact," Keith warned. He learned a lot from his adventures with Claire. "Move along the fence line as far as you can. But it ends in a tangle of bushes. When you get there, you're going to have to step over the wooden fence and into the graveyard."

"Step into the graveyard," she repeated but did as he suggested.

Keith climbed over first and held out his hand for her.

With great reluctance, she grabbed hold of his arm and stepped over the fence slowly while the stallion scrutinized her. When they moved deeper into the graveyard, he tried to avoid walking on the old graves surrounding them, as he had no intention of waking up an old spirit. Trespassing on their sacred ground wasn't his idea of a fun adventure.

Removing the threat of the stallion attacking them was his immediate concern. He didn't know near as much about the horses as Claire or Jenni but it was amazing what he remembered from them. Emily seemed to trust him and that was what mattered.

He steered her sideways around a small grave.

"Oscar something, I can't read the last name," she said in almost a whisper, staring down at the headstone. "I don't want to think about the details of how the child died so young."

"Me, either."

They continued to move away slowly and he kept the stallion in his peripheral vision. It wasn't easy to make their way through the vines and undergrowth toward the other side. To his chagrin the stallion followed them down the fence line. The horse could easily step over the wooden structure, but he was respecting the man-made boundary.

"Why is he following us?" Emily asked, her voice sounding stressed.

"My guess is this is his territory and he has mares nearby, possibly a foal." Keith changed directions and they picked their way over the tree roots. "We need to make him understand we aren't a threat."

"We're hardly the threat, but he is," she said, tripping over a moss-covered log. "He's the island's version of *King of the Jungle*. No one dares to cross him, not even the other stallions. Until now. Two clueless humans encounter him deep in the woods of the Maritime Forest. No other humans are around to hear their call for help."

Keith chuckled. "I can tell you're a writer."

She glanced up at him and laughed. "For sure."

They worked their way around a large tree in the center of the graveyard, draped in Spanish moss. Emily was so busy watching the stallion instead of where she was going, she stumbled over a root. If it hadn't been for holding Keith's hand and his assistance, she would have fallen at the base of the largest headstone. *Harry Wade, 1835–1895.*

"I bet he was a whaler trying to make a living to support his family. He lost a son due to illness and lack of ability to seek immediate medical attention."

"I can't wait to read your novel."

She looked up at him, a surprised expression on her face.

"You mean no one has read your work before?"

She shook her head. "There are firsts for everything. You can read it if we get out of here alive."

"Rewrite our own plot."

She giggled, although he still heard tension. "Certainly, he'll grow bored of us and return to his herd."

"Keep walking," Keith encouraged with an added tug from his hand.

"He's still following us, and I've had enough." She pulled her hand away from Keith's and headed toward the bush-free corner farthest from the stallion and the trail they needed to find their way out of the forest.

"Emily ..."

Walking, she kept her gaze lowered and headed toward the far corner. Keith supposed she had also learned from Jenni and Claire.

The stallion stopped but watched her with interest, his head high and ears pointed.

The steed lowered his head and walked away. All be darned, her carefree tactic worked miracles because the horse wouldn't have moved away if he thought she was a threat. Keith, still watching the stallion, stepped around logs and gravestones to catch up with Emily, who continued on her quest to scurry from the graveyard.

Irritated she took a risk by paving her own path, he had to admire her gumption too. Her confidence was no longer an issue.

The stallion nosed the bushes nearest him, and three mares and a foal emerged from their hiding spot. He jutted his nose toward the haunches of the last mare in line and directed them toward the only path—the path Keith and Emily needed to take—but thankfully in the opposite direction.

"That's why he was being protective," Keith explained to Emily, who wasn't too far away from him now. "I bet the foal is close to three months old." The baby's short brown mane stuck straight up and his forelock was a fuzzy little wisp. Adorable.

"Makes sense now." Emily let out a long sigh and watched the baby as the herd moved down the trail away from them. "It was rather an intense moment I don't care to repeat."

Keith laughed. "He had me concerned too, as well as you heading out on your own."

She shook her head and tossed up her hands. "Yeah, it was probably dangerous but patience isn't my specialty."

Oh, he disagreed. "You're patient with your writing."

She laughed. "If I want to be successful, I have no choice."

They picked their way back to the path and had to duck underneath several low branches covered in Spanish moss. "We need to hurry," he said.

When the path revealed the remote, rustic beach on the Sound, they climbed over a small dune and set foot on the driftwood-littered sand. Black seaweed zigzagged along the water's edge in inky patterns.

Keith studied the sky. While they were detained in the dense forest, the clouds had grown heavy with rain. He pulled out his cell phone to scan the radar on the weather app. "Looks like a thunderstorm is moving in fast. According to the radar, we have about thirty minutes before it hits. I'm not thrilled with being stranded on an island during a thunderstorm with the nearest shelter at least a forty-five minute hustle." Nothing but a long beach stretched before them.

"What are we going to do?" she asked, looking over his shoulder at the radar.

"We need to hurry toward the dock where the bathrooms are. Let's hope we make it before this monster storm hits."

Chapter Twenty-Five

Dark shadows moved in and hovered over the beach like a menacing predator in a widespread black cloak. I expected the rain to begin at any moment but I wasn't able to keep up with Keith's pace.

"We have to walk faster," he said, holding my hand to encourage me to hurry.

By Keith's calculations, the shelter was at least a forty-five-minute walk. Judging by the thick clouds rolling in, it seemed likely the storm would hit long before we reached safety.

We approached a wide crossover, the water deep and snail-infested, and without complaint I yanked off my sneakers and socks. Sure, I cringed as I stepped on the masses of small, black mollusks underneath my bare feet. They were by far the grossest part of today's adventure.

Suck it up, Buttercup. Words from my father echoed in my mind as I stepped into the water.

The wet sand and round snails squished between my toes. In all reality, every drop of adventure with Keith was fun but wading through snails and getting pounded by a storm on Pony Island wasn't exactly ideal.

We reached the other side and I made my way to a washed-up log at the base of a barrier dune. In a futile attempt to wipe off my feet with my sock, but conscientious of the time, I ended up slipping my dirty feet back into my sneakers. In comparison to the snails, sand in my shoes was a small price to pay.

While waiting for Keith to finish battling with his shoes, I took a long drink of water from my bottle, guessing I wouldn't get another opportunity for a long while. At least the heat was letting up as the storm moved in and the temperature had dropped probably five degrees.

He finished and his jaw grew rigid when he glanced at the sky again. I was clueless about how to ride out a storm on an island, knew the bathroom shelter was still not in sight, and the clouds were rolling in faster than expected.

"Let's go," he said, hitting the sand at a power walk, and I did my best to keep up with him. As we scooted down the beach and rounded a sharp bend, I had never been happier to see a primitive bathroom far off in the distance.

"Are we going to make it?" I asked, wanting to stop to catch my breath but didn't dare. Once again I made a mental note to exercise more frequently, as Keith wasn't even short-winded.

He glanced up and frowned. "Not sure."

He was a man of the sea and knew what he was doing, and I had to admit, trust was coming a lot easier for me lately.

On the horizon, where the dark sky met the choppy silver water, a streak of lightning shot out like a bolt of warning from the angry hand of a Greek god.

In succession and without conversation, and despite my gnawing fatigue, we both picked up our pace to a jog.

The dock was within a thousand feet or so.

A breeze kicked up and blew off the water, causing my curly hair to whip around my face, stinging my cheeks. While I jogged, I tried to secure my thick blowing hair in a handheld ponytail, but it was no use. It blew like the thick mane of a wild horse running, almost blocking my vision.

We picked up our speed to a run now. The packed, wet sand squished underneath my sneakers as we dodged the incoming tide.

Another streak of lightning zigzagged in contrast across the darkened sky, only closer. The air cooled at least fifteen degrees against my sunburned shoulders and caused me to shiver.

A dark shadow passed overhead as if someone had adjusted a switch.

The fresh but threatening aroma of rain blew in on the sea air.

Safety was still too far away and I had to fight off the fear of getting hit by lightning. I risked a glance at the Sound and saw the rain moving in a sheet toward us. It was plausible we were about to get soaked, and with the temperature dropping, staying warm seemed unlikely.

Another flash of lightning lit up the sky off the shore. Too close for comfort. One Mississippi, two Mississippi, three Mississippi. A loud crack of thunder pounded almost above us.

Keith tugged on my hand. We were almost to the dock, to the shelter.

A chill straddled the breeze as it blew in with the storm. An even blacker turbulent sky promised no chance of letting up. I jumped when thunder boomed behind us, urging us to seek cover in a hurry. Keith held onto my hand with a firm grip.

Our surroundings grew dark enough I wished we had a flashlight. We braced against the strong wind, and I'd love to be anywhere else besides the island to ride out the storm. The safety of my couch in my apartment sounded fantastic. A swirl of fog rolled in off the water, creating a mystical atmosphere. Drizzle rode on the fog like a surfboard, spraying a light coat of mist on my curly hair, whipping it into my eyes and sticking to the corners of my mouth. The taste of sea salt warned the storm was a real threat.

The downpour was coming. It was a matter of moments.

As we ran, I risked glancing back. The bottom of the dark clouds was fuzzy as rain poured down onto the water in the near distance. The water was choppy from the wind and the rain pounded on the water's surface as it edged in a solid wall toward us. The scent was threatening, the sound vicious, as it blew toward the shore.

Keith's firm hand was protective, safe. A gnawing cramp plagued my side while I fought to breathe. There was no way to stop and rest. He tugged at me. We continued to fight the wind, making our way through the deep sand at the base of the dunes where the tide hadn't yet beaten it into a wet, flattened patty, as we ran toward the lone shelter, barely visible in the fog.

"Run!" he commanded. The rain was blowing in fast.

We were so close to the shelter but not near enough. Large, cold rain drops splattered against my arms, the wind picking up and blowing a cold spray of water onto my backside. Goosebumps rose on my skin. Our shirts were wet and stuck to our backs.

The shelter, at last. We darted underneath as the wind howled. The worst of the storm was yet to come.

With urgency, Keith tried to yank open the bathroom door but it refused to budge. He tried the other door. Locked.

Rain blew underneath the wooden overhang. Little shards of blowing sand stung his face like needles. He stepped in front of Emily as he pushed her against the wall, scooting her away from the overhang. Never before had he possessed such a strong urge to protect anyone. The back of his bare legs stung from sand pellets as if an army of fire ants were having a competition to see who could burn the heck out of him more.

He had seen many storms before while on his father's sailboat. It would blow over soon.

In the meantime, they needed protection. He wished the bathroom doors were unlocked, despite the inevitable stench certain to accompany the small confined space. He'd gladly endure the smell to ensure Emily's safety.

She shuddered against him. The air had cooled more. Keith pushed into her closer, and despite her slight shiver, her body felt warm pressed against his as he tried to chase away her chill. They went from a hot summer sun to a cold raging thunderstorm. Thankfully they had shelter, minimal as it was.

The sky grew so black it dared him to think it was nighttime. The ferry was scheduled to arrive at any moment, but they wouldn't be on the water in a lightning storm, and Keith and Emily were nowhere near the pickup spot in the cove anyway.

They snuggled close to each other under the overhang of the building.

He inhaled a whiff of light flowers from her hair mixed with the fresh ocean scent. His common sense and restraint blew away on the breeze. He buried his face into the windblown, wet curls of her hair and inhaled. His lips were so close to her neck, buried slightly underneath her hair. What was this woman doing to him?

His arms were chilled from the rain. If he was cold, she was too. He pulled her even closer to his chest and felt her shiver, although he was unsure if her reaction was caused by the drop in temperature, or if she was attracted to him as much as he was to her.

Her curls stuck against his wet cheek. The scene unfolding was romantic, despite the overhead raging storm.

Gran would say he had it bad for this cute little filly. She was right. He was smitten.

The rain pounded on the tin roof above them. A waterfall poured from a corner section of the roof and created a hole in the saturated sand.

They had this section of island to themselves, in a rainstorm, under an outcropping of the only building on the island. If he had to choose one person to be caught out here with, it would be her.

With reluctance, he pulled away from the delicious scent of her hair to glance back and assess the situation. The fog was thick and swirling in mystical circles over the Sound, covering the dock so it was barely visible, and snaking around the bathroom structure. The sand no longer held evidence of their footprints, washed away in the rain as if there were no trace of human life on the island. Knowing the wild horses roamed off in the distance added to the dreamy world he was caught up in.

The worst of the storm was almost overhead. Jagged lightning streaked across the sky with a boom of thunder so loud they both jumped.

He turned back to her. She was shaking.

He pressed his body against her more to offer warmth. Unable to resist any longer, his lips touched the heat of her neck. She twitched but he was certain this time it was from pleasure, not resistance. He hesitated for a moment, wondering if he should press his luck and kiss her again.

Unsure, he gently pressed his lips against her neck just under her ear.

She tilted her head to allow him easier access. He whispered so faintly he hoped she didn't hear. He wasn't used to saying the words. "I love you, Emily."

Not that he expected an answer, especially with his face buried into her, but he swore he heard her whisper the sentiment back. Maybe he was just hopeful she felt the same way about him. She'd said so earlier.

She turned and her lips met his. They were wet but warm. A little drip of water from a curl stuck to her forehead, dropped onto his cheek. It felt as though an angel kissed him.

Their mouths greeted each other, tenderly at first, and then increasing with gentle passion. Their tongues touched lightly. She was driving him mad.

He wanted this relationship to start off right. He wasn't about to mess up another loving connection. He wanted a future with this woman.

When they kissed, he lost all concept of time. An hour might have slipped by, perhaps a day. He didn't care. They wrapped their arms around each other and rejoiced in their first real kiss.

The storm raged overhead, the rain blowing in under the overhang protecting them. They pressed closer to the wall.

Again, he wished the bathrooms were unlocked. The fresh coastal air held the scent of salty rain. It was imperative to remain as dry as possible.

Once the storm moved off, he noticed Emily still shivering against him. He backed away from her and opened his pack, as he always carried an extra shirt. It wasn't a super warm one, but at least it was an added layer. Then it dawned on him. She needed to change out of her wet shirt and use it to towel dry her hair. He pulled the dry one out of his bag and offered it to her.

"I'll turn my back while you change."

"Thank you! What about you?" She pushed off the wall and was visibly quivering.

"I'm fine." So he told a small white lie, something he preferred not to do, but under the circumstances, she needed the shirt.

He turned his back to give her privacy and glanced at the time. With the inclement weather, those people left behind on the island would flock to the ferry pick-up spot in the cove to return inland early. The ride was guaranteed to be a cold one.

Emily stood next to him, looking sexy wearing his shirt. "Maybe the walk will warm me up." She glanced at him. "Well, you warmed me up too, but shedding the wet clothes helped."

"I hear you." The back of his shirt was clinging to him for dear life. He was slightly chilled too, but nowhere near as cold as Emily appeared. He wrapped an arm around her as they climbed down the steps, thankful they had been near the building when the storm hit.

Even with his embrace, she crossed her arms and rubbed them to warm up.

The sky was steel gray, and the water encroached on the beach. They didn't have time to waste. Soon the easy path back would be impassable due to the incoming tide, requiring a long, out-of-the-way hike through the deep and wet sand dunes.

Off in the distance the approaching ferry dotted the water. Keith and Emily walked as quickly as possible but the sand was difficult to navigate along the narrow strip of the beach. Unfortunately, they had to remove their shoes to cross a rising stream of cool water, once warmed by the sun. There wasn't a bird around, or horses, or even humans other than them. The beach was deserted at this end of the island, but up ahead, where the ferry-landing sign was posted on a metal stake, there were numerous people waiting. Most had their arms crossed around their chests to stay warm.

"Will there be enough room?" Emily asked.

"I hope so." The ferry would be crowded and Emily needed warmth. If they made it aboard the boat in time, a slim chance due to the slow progress they were making, the ride home promised misery.

Even if he called Captain Bill to give him a heads-up they were coming, there was no way for him to answer a cell phone while he was busy navigating the boat into the cove. They needed to hurry, otherwise they would have to wait for the next ride.

"We need to run," he suggested. He knew she was tired, but they didn't have a choice.

She groaned but began jogging. Together they ran at an even pace, although somewhat slow due to the terrain and bouncing backpacks.

In the distance the ferry pulled into the cove, and the captain's young assistant stood at the bow, ready to assist passengers. The crowd scrambled onboard. The boat appeared full but Keith refused to give up. As long as they were in compliance and under capacity for passengers, they would squeeze in between people for a place to sit. If anything, the close quarters would keep everyone warmer.

The young assistant waited at the bow after the last passenger boarded. Keith and Emily were still a fair distance away and Keith only hoped they noticed them running toward the ferry. He needed to conduct more training to make sure the captain and assistant scanned the area for latecomers trying to catch the boat. The schedule was tight and would be less flexible once the park service took over, but they usually had wiggle room to wait a few minutes longer if needed before departure.

The boy held up his hand to acknowledge them. Keith kept hold of Emily without taking the moment to wave back, as he didn't want to lose momentum. She was fading fast.

When they reached the ferry, both of them gasped for breath.

He thought he had a reasonable exercise routine at the gym, but his shortness of breath disappointed him. He planned to increase his fitness program in the future. As for Emily, he noticed she was panting harder. Next time he went to the gym, he would invite her to join him.

Captain Bill raised his hand in greeting when they climbed on board. "Glad you made it. Got wet, huh? I warned you about the weather."

Keith grumbled but was grateful they had made the ferry.

As he thought, the ride was chilly despite their shoulders being pressed into the people sitting next to them. He wrapped Emily in his arms and tried to keep her warm. What would he do without her if he had to move?

They didn't talk on the ride back, but the intimacy between them was touching. Enduring the storm had brought them closer together.

The marsh view he normally enjoyed was almost a blur in the fog. His arms encircled her, and she had stopped shivering, although goose bumps covered her chilled arms and legs. He wanted the woman sitting next to him to be in his life for a long time. He wanted to provide for her, for their eventual family. On Monday he needed to increase his efforts in finding a well-paying job to support her and their dreams. Even if he had to move to Raleigh.

Chapter Twenty-Six

The ferry ride about chilled me to the bone. That combined with the thought of Frank's unplanned visit to Big Cat, I wasn't sure which made me colder—my lower body temperature or knowing I had to deal with him.

"I appreciate you cranking up the heat," I said as Keith drove me to my apartment. I snuggled under a spare blanket he kept stashed in his truck.

"No worries, but you need to know something." He turned onto my street and then into the parking lot of my building, scanning it with intensity. "With crazy man driving down here and asking questions about you, I'm not okay with you staying here alone."

Was he asking if he could spend the night? I fought off a wave of rising panic.

"I'd like you to pack up an overnight bag and stay with me."

I grew rigid. "Keith ..." His suggestion stunned me.

He parked the truck and swiveled around in his seat. "I'm not suggesting anything inappropriate. I want you to spend the night at my house so I can protect you, and I have a guest bedroom. That's all."

I sighed and the tension drained out of me.

"Frankie boy might do anything if he's crazy enough to drive down here." He opened his door and stepped out. "Do you see his vehicle anywhere?"

I shook my head, knowing full well Frank wasn't about to park out in the open.

"Let's go pack your things and get out of here." He took my hand and, eager to change out of my damp clothes, we headed upstairs. Tucker was nowhere to be found. Maybe he knew Frank was around and chose to hide. Oh, having the gift to craft stories in my head was a hindrance at times. Frank didn't even know where I lived.

There was no sign of him but I packed an overnight bag and left food for Tucker. On the way downstairs, as we passed a set of bushes, I jumped as a dark shadow stepped forward. Keith pushed me behind him.

"Emily!" The deep voice I knew too well rang through the still night.

My heart about stopped beating. Fear overtook me and my feet wouldn't move.

"She doesn't want to see you, Frank. Head on out of here," Keith said, his voice calm and confident.

"She's my fiancée, so mind your own business." As usual Frank raised his voice because he always bullied people to get his way. His chin had overgrown black whiskers growing on it and his clothes were hanging off him as if he'd lost weight. He wobbled and I smelled a stench permeating from him.

My fear turned to anger and I stepped out from behind Keith. "Excuse me? I am definitely not your fiancée. You ruined that. Get out of here now."

Frank swayed closer. "Oh, come on, baby. You're just upset, so let's go somewhere and talk."

Baby. The use of the pet name boiled my nerves. "How dare you. Leave."

Laughing, Frank stepped a few feet forward and Keith protected me again with his body. Under his breath he said to me, "Emily, run to my truck and lock the door."

Run away from my problems again? No thanks.

I dialed 911 and spoke to the woman who answered, giving

her a brief synopsis of the situation.

Frank wasn't easy to scare. He grabbed at me but Keith blocked him with his arm.

"Emily, go to my truck," Keith commanded with such authority I took notice.

He was probably right not to provoke Frank, especially if he had been drinking. "Okay," I said and took off running. It wasn't a failure, was smart even, to leave the scene. As I got closer to the truck the doors beeped and unlocked. I climbed in and locked it, fearful for Keith but also knowing he could take care of himself. I hoped the cops arrived soon.

Pressing close to the window, I strained to hear what they were saying to each other but their words were muffled. Frank took a swing at Keith and he blocked it, but my heroic man didn't punch back.

To my delight, flashing lights streamed in from the back window of the truck as the police pulled into the parking lot.

○

The next morning, I had never been so happy to head to the rehab center. What a relief after the night I'd had.

At least I had felt safe enough to sleep well at Keith's house, knowing Frank had been charged with assault and battery. Apparently, provoking a fight in public was a misdemeanor offense. Due to Frank's prior convictions—something I found out after we had broken up—he had earned himself a short-term sentence in the slammer.

Nevertheless, I was happy to lose myself in my work. Mr. Graham watched himself in the gym mirror to assess his progress and posture.

"You're doing well," I encouraged. Wanting to someday specialize in outpatient rehab, I enjoyed the higher-level orthopedic patients. But for now, skilled nursing rehab was my heart.

While reading Mr. Graham's new orthopedic orders, his

surgeon's name, Dr. Clark Randolph, caught my attention. The same name as my mom's new boyfriend. Keith had said he was well respected but never mentioned he was a surgeon.

Mr. Graham was my last patient of the day, so once I clocked out and was sitting in the privacy of my car, I searched for him on the internet with my cell phone. An attractive, distinguished photo of him popped up on the screen along with the address of his office. One could never be too protective of one's own mother, now could they?

I still wondered why she hadn't mentioned him before but we mostly talked about her Mexico trip and her doctor's appointment. The doctor said there was nothing medically needed to fix her nose, other than to monitor the healing process for any complications. As far as my mom's teeth were concerned, she needed implants and had temporary ones for now.

I was curious as to how serious their relationship was. After all, it couldn't be too involved if she left the country to live in Mexico for several months. Then again, he had wanted to fly down to see her and implied a certain level of commitment.

I clicked on the map app on my phone and followed the directions to Dr. Clark Randolph's office, a large building with several other orthopedic specialists including an outpatient rehab center and an urgent care. The grounds were well kept with black mulch mounded around the base of the trees and shrubs curved to perfection. Huge clay pots filled with flowers and greenery welcomed patients. This late in the afternoon there weren't many cars left in the parking lot, so I tried to go undetected and not stalk his office for too long.

If it weren't so late, I'd drive by his house, having seen his return address on the envelope, but I still needed to run by the grocery store and make dinner. I did plan to have a long conversation with Mom today before Keith picked me up for our walk on the beach to watch the sunset and to stargaze.

I darted into the store to buy enough food for the rest of

the week. Actually, I didn't eat much in general, so it wouldn't take long.

I chose a few fresh fruits and vegetables and set them in the cart, or as they often said in this small southern town, a buggy. Not originally from the South, the word always made me giggle. The first time a woman asked me to move my buggy, I glanced around for a baby stroller.

When I returned to the apartment, I cooked a light dinner consisting of baked chicken, steamed broccoli, and a few strawberries. Eating healthy was difficult at first, having decided to limit carbohydrates, but I was enjoying the delicious food. My mother was the queen of mindful eating, so somewhere buried deep in my subconscious mind, I knew the benefits. I had tried to ignore the knowledge for the past several years, but between the desire to fit happily into my bikini along with dating Keith, I changed my mind.

After I ate and the dishes were finished, I embraced the opportunity to call her. I settled onto the overstuffed couch and dialed her number. When she answered, we engaged in the usual chitchat about the weather, upcoming doctors' appointments, and in general, anything new.

When the conversation stalled, I attempted to casually bring up the delicate subject. She had no idea Terri had told me about him, so I chose my words with care. "Hey mom, when I was at your house, before I picked you up from the airport, I saw an envelope from someone who lives in Big Cat. I believe his name is Clark Randolph."

The phone space grew silent.

I decided not to fill the quiet with chatter, a skill I learned when dating Frank. His favorite answer to questions he didn't like me asking was to remain still. I always grew uncomfortable and filled the space with talk, and later I figured out it was his technique to derail me, so he wouldn't have to answer. Instead, he always commented on my prattle, leaving the question unanswered. I decided to remain quiet to see if the method worked for me too.

To my surprise, she answered. "I met him at a friend's party."

"You go to parties?"

"Sure, I'm not dull you know. It wasn't long after I walked in and he started a casual conversation with me." She paused as if to recall the timeline of events. "He went on his way, chatting with several other people he knew. I did the same thing. He waited until I was ready to leave before he made his way back around to me."

"And you stayed longer." I laughed, knowing her all too well, as she had this innate skill for attracting a man's attention. The problem was, she kept them at arm's length and then lost interest in them before a true romance started, so it surprised me to hear she wanted him to visit her in Mexico. I suspected men fell in love with her because they had to work hard to keep her interested.

"How long have you known him?" I knew there was more to the story than she was telling me, and I shifted on the couch with impatience.

Another pause. "Eight months."

"What? Eight months and you haven't mentioned him?" Why did that hurt so much? I wished we were closer, wished she trusted me enough to share the personal details of her life.

"His wife died and I was allowing him grieving time."

Unsettled, I folded my legs underneath me. It was an old habit I developed when I needed to protect myself from hurt, and if I had to guess, I'd bet it started right after my dad walked out on us. "I'm sorry to hear about his loss. How long ago did she die?"

"A year. He had only been a widow a few months at the time of the party." Mom held the phone away, coughing. Or was she crying?

I wanted to ask but didn't want to intrude. If she wanted to share, then she would open up. If not, all was okay. It wasn't about me and I needed to stop taking things so personally.

At least I was making progress with personal relationships and recognized my own insecurities and reactions to my mother. To my family, actually. I was no longer the victim and needed to remember that.

Mom cleared her throat and continued to speak in such a tender voice it touched me. "I felt Clark needed time to grieve, and I didn't want to be a rebound."

I enjoyed the lighter tone my mother used when she mentioned his name. "I agree. Smart on your part."

There was her cough again but his time I refused to ignore it. "Mom, are you okay?"

She sniffled in the phone. "His wife died from cancer. It was pretty horrific for everyone."

"Did you know her?" Hadn't my mother had a friend who had died in the same time frame?

Another sniffle. "Yes, she was my friend from college. Dorothy was her name."

More questions surfaced but was it safe to ask? No more burying my own personality to keep people from getting uncomfortable. I needed to be myself. "Why were you at a party?"

She inhaled a long, deep breath as if to calm herself. "One of my classmates had a high school reunion party at her house. Even though Dorothy had died, Clark wanted to pay his respects by attending."

And he was hitting on my mother?

"I know what you're thinking. He wasn't coming on to me, just being friendly to everyone." Her tone sounded somewhat defensive. "If anything, I was interested in him."

I didn't know what to say.

"I know. It sounds bad." More awkward silence between us but at least she was opening up to me. "There aren't many quality men my age, and you have to grab them when you see them."

"I understand, Mom." I mean, who was I to judge? "I just wished you had mentioned him to me." The hurt was still there but again, I needed not to take it personally.

"Sorry. Before I mentioned him to anyone, I had to give him time to heal." She blew her nose into the phone. "Although I hadn't seen Dorothy in years, I had to deal with the loss of my friend too. At least you know about Clark now."

"I'm glad you met someone." I was shocked by the whole situation, but happy for her.

"How about you? Are you dating anyone special?"

Well, okay. I was guilty of the same thing I just mentally accused her of. After all, I had never mentioned Keith to anyone in my family. In my own defense, I hadn't had the opportunity since they had been in Mexico. Then there was the whole teeth fiasco, although not an excuse.

"I am, Mom. Keith's a wonderful man."

Mom screeched with joy. "How long have you known him?"

"I met him when I moved down here. His grandmother was my patient." My voice was quiet, and in all honesty, I found him difficult to share with my mother. I wondered why. I guessed I was afraid of being judged, the same thing I had done to her, and that made me a hypocrite. To my credit, at least I was aware of it now, and acknowledgement was the first step to changing.

I did want to be emotionally closer to my mom, to my sister as well, and was willing to work on myself to allow growth.

"I'd like to meet him when I visit," she said in a casual voice, but I could tell she was happy for me. "We got invited to a reveal party."

I couldn't help but yelp in surprise. "Whose?"

"Jenni and Scott. Clark was friends with his dad before he passed away."

I laughed. "Unbelievable. Jenni is Keith's sister, and I plan to attend the party too." Funny how things often worked themselves out because now I would get my chance after all to meet Dr. Clark Randolph.

"By the way, how is your writing?"

My mother always asked about my writing and it always made me happy. "It's going well," I said, remembering what I wrote about the pizza and the two little girls. "I need to ask you about an interesting piece I wrote when I was engaging in a writing exercise."

She hesitated but there was no way she knew what I was going to ask.

"What's that?"

As if I knew the answer wasn't going to be a good one, I curled my legs tighter underneath me. "I was randomly writing whatever came to mind and this scene unfolded about two sisters enjoying pizza when their father thundered into the house and made his way to the bedroom. He began to slam drawers and to shove clothes into suitcases. The woman was hushed but the man was louder, arguing."

Silence.

"The piece disturbed me on a deep level and I don't know why."

She sighed. "Honey, you're remembering the day your father left."

The day my daddy abandoned us. As if magic, a more detailed scene unfolded and I remembered. Mom spent hours with a girlfriend on the phone, crying, reaching out for a friend to listen. Yes, I remembered.

For emotional support, I rubbed the silver heart hanging around my neck. Would Keith abandon me too?

My mom changed the subject again and this time I was fine with sweeping the unwanted memories away. When we finished talking, I stared at a bare wall in my apartment, as if it held answers to the past. Suddenly chilled, I pulled a blanket across my legs and wondered if there was a deeper reason for moving to Big Cat other than dealing with the breakup with Frank. I believed I had more healing to do than I at first thought, and spreading my wings at the coast was healthy for me.

I was unsure how long I sat in the silence. Eventually I glanced at the time and sighed when I realized Keith would be here soon. I no longer wanted to head to the beach, but I couldn't back out at the last minute. It required great effort, but I forced myself to move from the couch, forced the heavy blanket of stress off me. Never before had I gone on a date on the beach and I needed to enjoy the outing.

As I slipped on my favorite pair of white sandals, the doorbell rang. In a daze, I walked back into the living room and saw my forgotten laptop half hidden under a decorative pillow on the couch. Before the conversation with my mom I had planned to write but the urge had disappeared. One thing was certain, my own painful experiences deepened the inner conflict with my characters, and strangely enough, the heroine in my story was in the middle of discovering her dad was cheating on her mother. I couldn't help but wonder if I discovered the reason my dad left. My gut instinct told me he had cheated, and odd how I remembered how he introduced us to a woman not long after he left. I was too young to understand then, but boy, I understood now.

The doorbell rang again. When I opened the door, Keith stood there with a bouquet of yellow and white daisies, my favorite.

I fingered the necklace he gave me. Keith wasn't the men of my past.

"Those are beautiful. Thank you." I leaned into him, and lingering, I pressed my lips onto his warm mouth and breathed in his fresh scent of sea air.

He was the most romantic man I had ever dated. When I pulled away, he handed me the flowers and followed me into the kitchen to watch me unwrap the cellophane and place them in a tall cobalt blue vase my mother had given me for my birthday last year. She loved flowers too, although at least she had skill in growing them. But it was past time to make my apartment homey, past time to cultivate my own flowers.

I set the vase in the center of the coffee table, so I could see them and think of Keith when I wrote. The fresh bouquet filled my apartment with a surprising warmth.

He wrapped me in another sexy embrace, kissed me until my toes practically curled, and then pulled away. "Ready?"

Ready for what? It took a moment for my mind to recalibrate. Oh, yeah ... the sunset and star date.

"Yes," I said in a whisper. The man darn near stole my breath.

We closed the door behind us and I glanced around for Tucker. I hadn't seen him in several days and the food dish remained full at my doorstep.

"Wonder if Tucker is coming back," I said, concerned. I was growing to like the cat—okay, adore the cat.

Keith watched me closely. "Emily, outside cats run around. He's not abandoning us."

I glanced up at him with trepidation. He was right, I supposed, as my mind went directly to my abandonment issues again.

Once we reached Main Street one town over, parking was a nightmare. Keith had to circle around twice before we were lucky enough to spot someone backing out of their space. Even though he had a big truck, he parallel parked with ease. For a weeknight, downtown was booming.

He retrieved an insulated beach bag from the back, hauled it over his shoulder, and then shoved a thick blue-and-white-striped towel under his arm.

"Let me help," I said, removing it from his awkward grip.

With his free hand, he took mine. It was warm and calloused but I loved how gentle his touch was. We headed across the road, over the wooden platform of the public access to the beach, and onto the sand.

I hoped to never overlook the blessing of being only ten minutes by vehicle from the beach.

The tide was high, with kids chasing the surf back to

shore, and the sun was low enough to cast an orange glow on everything. If there was one thing I loved about the North Carolina sunsets, it was the vivid colors. High in the sky, a streak of dark clouds blended into a bright blue, but the horizon was layered with vibrant shades of tangerine and burnt sienna. We didn't have long before the sun vanished.

Keith was lighthearted, energetic, playful and again reminded me of the dreamy fairytale romance in my manuscript. I wondered if it were possible for a couple to continue this delicious love for years to come, unless it was a fantasy, the proverbial honeymoon phase.

Enjoy the moment, Emily. Why did I always have to overthink things?

Whatever the reason, at least I was happy.

We kicked off our sandals, set down our belongings in a pile on the sand near the sea grass by a dune, and then walked hand in hand along the beach. An assembly of seagulls gathered along the edge of the shore but flew away in a flock as we neared. They swirled around us as a fluttering mass before landing farther up the beach. One of my favorite sights was watching a line of pelicans skimming the water in search of dinner.

Nature was stunning. We strolled along the beach for at least a mile with the fabulous view of the golden sunset leading our way.

When the beach began to darken, we turned around to head back to where our sandals and paraphernalia waited. The dark sky fell fast and it was difficult to make out any details of our belongings other than the shape of the pile and where we were stepping.

Keith pulled a small flashlight from the pocket of his shorts and shined it on the ground in front of us. Little crabs scooted across the sand and I was grateful I hadn't stepped on one. One crab froze in place and stared up at us, and then dodged into a dark hole in the sand.

Once we returned to our pile, Keith said, "I brought snacks."

"I love the way you spoil me." It was a first and I could easily get used to it. I spread out the large towel by the glow of the flashlight and I sat down next to him as he pulled the insulated bag onto his lap.

Curious as to what he brought, I tried to peek but he had taken the flashlight and it was aimed at the sand. The hint of light from a nearby floodlight from a hotel wasn't enough.

"Patience, my dear." He pulled out a bottle of pinot noir, two plastic wine glasses, containers of grapes, crackers, salami, and dip.

Excited to sample the food, I opened the containers and arranged them between us as he poured the wine.

"Try this. It's a new recipe." He topped a cracker with dip.

"You made this from scratch?" At his nod, I took a bite and groaned with pleasure as my mouth watered from the taste of crab meat, cream cheese, and onion. The pleasant memory of the dinner he had cooked for me lived in my mind. "That's the best dip I've ever eaten. Without doubt."

Between the spray of overhead light and the flashlight on the towel, I saw him smile.

"Thanks. I'm glad you like it." He shoved an entire cracker into his mouth and chewed with the smile still on his face.

An idea popped into my head. "Have you thought about opening a restaurant in Big Cat?" That just might be the simple solution he was looking for.

He finished chewing before he answered. "No way." He shook his head, outlined by the narrow speckling of light. The backdrop of highlighted sea grass blew in the breeze behind him as the full moon inched over the darkened water. "My dad pushed himself hard to develop Stallings, but he worked day and night, seven days a week, sometimes. No thanks."

I shrugged, understanding what he was saying but disappointed by his reaction. I thought I had found the ideal way to keep him employed near home. "Well, you have a gift, and I'm glad I'm the recipient of your delicious cooking."

He leaned forward and picked up the flashlight to aim it at a crab scurrying across the sand toward us. I squealed and tucked my legs underneath me. When it noticed us, it darted to the safety of a deep footprint and stared into the beam of light with big eyes. Then the crab grew brave, left the safety of the footprint, and scurried back from the direction it had travelled.

Once the crab was gone, I was again able to enjoy the sound of the black waves as they rolled with rhythm, almost lulling me into a meditative state.

The evening was perfect, better than any dinner date at a restaurant.

We continued to nibble the treats he brought. He scooped some dip onto a cracker and held it to my lips, and I took a bite, and then another. If I were an outsider watching us, I would relish the romance.

He retrieved a small speaker from the outside pocket of the insulated bag, and it took him only seconds to connect to his phone. A woman's voice filled the evening with an upbeat, romantic song. Relaxed, I leaned back next to him and rested my elbows on the sand, allowing the music to sweep me away.

The night drew darker and if I squinted I could see hints of stars begging to twinkle for us. It wouldn't be long now.

With the sides of our bodies pressed together and knees bent, I studied the moon.

"What planet do you think that is?" I asked. There was a solid bright circle below and off to the right side of the moon.

"Venus or Mercury. I'm not sure." He fiddled with an astronomy app on his phone, and together we tried to figure out the night sky, but it was no use.

Like teenagers in love, we stared upward and marveled at how the stars came into focus slowly, became brighter, as the sky grew blacker.

I pointed to another bright light bigger than the twinkling stars. "It has to be a planet too," I said in a breezy voice as though I were a carefree child, a sensation I hadn't felt since

I was young, before my dad left us. Reflections from the moon highlighted the inky black water. I closed my eyes, wishing I could fall asleep at night to the peaceful sound of waves crashing onto the shore, the soft air kissing my face, the smell of brine.

When I opened my eyes, a shooting star darted across the blanket of black velvet. I closed my eyes again but this time I made a wish too personal to share with the man lounging next to me.

"Did you see that?" Keith asked with a light tone.

"I did." My voice was husky and low from emotion.

His voice was almost a whisper. "I made a wish."

I didn't dare ask what his wish was, and they weren't meant to be shared anyway. It was safer to change the subject. "I could camp right here on the beach."

"Or on Pony Island, or on the boat." He was gazing at me, but I pretended not to notice as I lost myself in the night sky, identifying the Big Dipper and the little one.

When I turned back to him, our lips met, his mouth incredibly gentle but oh, so masculine. He was the best kisser ever. We kissed for what seemed forever, but not near long enough.

When we pulled away, our bodies still touching, I pointed at an orange flicker of lightning as it flashed on the horizon.

"Looks like a storm is rolling in," he said, his voice raspy. Between the waves crashing against the shore and the music playing on the speaker, he was difficult to hear.

"A Fourth of July show, just for us." Last year's holiday had been a nightmare, filled with arguing and a shove from Frank, who'd drank too much alcohol.

There weren't many people walking the beach tonight, but there was a group of kids, maybe around the age of ten to fourteen, searching the ground for something with a flashlight.

"What are they doing?"

"Crabbing."

Sure enough they carried little buckets. The poor crabs. Not far behind them were four adults chatting and laughing, clearly enjoying their stroll on the beach.

As the storm moved in closer, the orange flicker intensified on the horizon and we were blessed with streaks of gold lightning. The storm was still far enough off that we were able to safely sit on the sand and watch.

If I thought about Keith too much, my mind became dizzy with a set of my own fireworks flickering in my body.

Enjoy the moment. Enjoy the feeling.

I tried not to worry about what the future held. There wasn't a thing I could do to change the outcome, but with Keith's career uncertain, I knew somehow our lives were about to change. I just didn't know to what extent.

Chapter Twenty-Seven

The summer was zipping by at a fast pace. Until the dreaded phone call came, the one bound to change the path of Keith's life. Possibly Emily's too.

When he disconnected the call, he sat there in stunned silence.

He lost the ferry contract.

He'd had such certainty he was going to win it. What happened? He had a solid proposal and a real chance, or so he'd thought.

Disappointed, he rubbed his face with his hands. What was he going to do now? He stared out the kitchen window at the distant marsh as if the view provided the answer. At least he had a promising lead in Raleigh. The interview had gone well.

While he loved living in Big Cat, loved owning and running the ferry, if he was being completely honest he would admit he missed being an architect. Life always had a way of uprooting a person and forcing them to take scary but necessary steps, ones he wouldn't take on his own accord but incremental in the development of his career.

If he wanted a future with Emily, he needed to have a solid job. But would she join him in Raleigh? In all honesty, why would she? She loved Big Cat as much as he did. And she just moved here not long ago.

Was it fair to expect their relationship to thrive if he moved away? After all, he needed to have a steady income before he was able to provide for her. He didn't have a choice. If he received a job offer, he had to move.

To burn off some stress, he went for a long walk to the ferry. It wasn't his shift to work but nothing calmed him like the water. When he passed by the ticket booth, Kathy waved to him. She didn't question why he was there, although it wasn't unusual for him to pop in to check on things. Today was no different.

As he headed down the walkway to the dock his thoughts drifted to how well Gran was improving, and she was quite wicked on the ATV now since all of the renovations to the barn and fields had been made.

Sam was a refreshing sight as he awaited Keith from his perch on his favorite piling.

Squawk.

"Hey there, buddy." Keith swore the bird knew he was upset by the tilt of his feathered friend's head. He opened the cooler and tossed him a fish. "There you go."

Sam flew onto the dock to catch it, backed up a few steps and shook his head. He extended his neck and swallowed.

"I'm glad people don't eat the food I cook whole." Keith laughed.

Sam had a large lump in his throat pouch and wasn't able to squawk, but he was watching Keith's every move.

"Stop staring at me like that." Keith sat on the bench next to the empty boat slip. Captain Bill was taking a group of passengers to the island and wouldn't return for a short while.

Sam tossed his head.

"Fine. I'll tell you what's going on." Sam always knew when he needed to talk and was better than a psychologist. "I lost the ferry contract." The words stuck in his throat, and he was having his own difficulty in swallowing.

Sam cocked his head to the side.

"I thought I had a solid proposal." Keith rubbed his face with his hands. Unbelievable. "I don't understand how I lost out."

Was it money, personality, politics? He was trying to make sense of the decision, trying not to take it personally.

"Be glad you're a bird."

The pelican watched him, pushing his head forward as if to show he was listening.

"All you have to do is fly around, visit with other birds, and eat fish." Keith shook his head. "I want to be on my boat, be on the water, smell the salty air ..."

"Can't you have the same experience with a private boat?" A man's voice broke through the peaceful ambience.

Keith jerked his chin up. Jeff, the wildlife biologist on Pony Island and Claire's husband, leaned against a piling.

"How long have you been standing there?" Keith had no idea he had been sharing his soul to anyone other than Sam.

"Long enough." Jeff pushed off the piling and stepped toward Keith. "Maybe something bigger is calling you."

Keith shrugged, not sure he wanted to hear what Jeff was saying.

"The ferry is wonderful, don't get me wrong. But hiding behind the boat isn't going to bring your father back."

Keith winced. "Who said I'm hiding?"

"It's obvious."

Keith respected Jeff, but right now he didn't appreciate his interference.

"Your dad was a boater," Jeff reasoned, as if everything made sense. "When he got sick, passed away, God bless his soul, you were in a funk. You bought the ferry business and absorbed yourself mostly in work."

Part of what he was saying was true, but since he'd met Emily, he took more time off work.

"I'm being blunt. Friends do that." Jeff placed his foot on an upturned bucket and rested his arm on his knee. "What's up with the bird?"

"We have long chats." Keith laughed but the sound fell flat, his dark mood difficult to shake.

"You're a fantastic architect. Return to life. It's time."

Jeff's words stung.

"If you want to be on the water, buy a personal boat." Jeff squinted against the sun as he stared out at the water.

If he turned his ball cap around the correct way, the bill would actually keep the sun off his face. All in fun, Keith was always picking at him about wearing his hat backward.

Jeff had a good point, though. *Buy a personal boat.*

But he wasn't ready to sell the ferry and let go of his dreams. Were they really dreams, or was Jeff right? Was he holding onto his father by working on the water? Most of his good memories of his dad were of them sailing together. And boating was how his sister lost her life.

"I'll think about what you said." Keith was a natural overthinker. "The problem is, there is no architect work near Big Cat."

Jeff shrugged. "Then move to Raleigh."

Easy for Jeff to say. He lived here, not in Raleigh, and was married with a kid.

"I get it," Jeff said. "Emily lives here. But you have to make a living, dude."

"Yeah, I know." In all reality, Raleigh seemed the obvious answer. If he and Emily were meant to be, nothing would keep them apart. If they weren't, it was better to know now. But he was already knee-deep in love.

Jeff leaned toward Keith and whispered, as if to keep a secret from Sam. "Is she, you know, *the one?*"

Keith nodded.

Jeff sighed. "Then you have a dilemma."

I sensed something was wrong with Keith. He hadn't called nor texted as he usually did each morning, but maybe he was busy. Everything was okay … it had to be.

I carried on throughout my day, trying not to think about Keith, or our budding romance.

As if the morning couldn't get worse, I walked past the elevator when the doors opened to reveal Ms. Snyder, stark naked. A visitor walked past at the same moment and screeched. Before I was able to react, the elevator door closed.

"What's wrong with her?" the woman asked, her eyes wide.

I pushed the elevator button with hope the door would spring open and I could rescue her, but the task of guiding Ms. Snyder back to her room to put on clothes was a daunting thought. If she was already in one of her moods, it was unlikely she'd allow someone to help her dress. But I had to try. The woman need not be riding the elevators naked.

Of course, the door didn't open. It would be too easy. Through the open atrium, a screech echoed from upstairs as Ms. Snyder made her presence known.

I jogged up the stairs with the intention to intercept Ms. Snyder. No such luck. The elevator door closed with Ms. Snyder inside. I jogged back downstairs in time for the door to slide open and expose the naked woman standing there with a confused expression on her face and her jaw set in defiance.

With caution, I stepped closer and held the door open but kept outside her striking range. "Good morning, Ms. Snyder."

With fire in her eyes, she shrank against the wall and crossed her arms.

"Let's get a cup of coffee," I suggested in a soft, noncombative voice, knowing full well if I mentioned putting on clothes, the woman would likely become violent. I stepped next to her but not at her. "Let's get some coffee," I repeated due to her short-term memory deficit.

Ms. Snyder stepped toward me.

I reached out slowly for her hand. "The coffee is delicious."

"I don't want coffee." She raised her voice.

"Okay," I said in a calm voice. Somehow I needed to retrieve a sheet from the linen closet, but the problem was convincing

Ms. Snyder to come with me.

She flexed her fingers to make a claw and grabbed hold of my arm. The pain from the woman's sharp nails stung.

"Ms. Snyder, you're hurting me. Please hold my hand instead."

She lightened her grip.

"Thank you." With patience, I waited. "I'd love to get you a cup of coffee."

The woman nodded and took hold of my hand instead of my poor clawed arm.

The trick was to somehow redirect Ms. Snyder into her room. Several patients were staring, and a nurse, whose mouth dropped open as she turned the corner, offered to help.

"Can you grab a sheet for me?" I asked. It was easier than trying to convince Ms. Snyder to follow me.

"Absolutely," the nurse said as she scurried toward the closet and then rushed toward us. She raised her eyebrows in question.

I shrugged, not having an answer as to how the woman made it out of her room, down the hallway, and onto the elevator without anyone noticing.

The nurse tried to wrap the sheet around her but the older woman swatted at her and made a sound resembling a low-pitched growl.

I was still holding her hand. "I'm sure you're cold. This blanket will help keep you warm, so I'm going to wrap it around you."

Ms. Snyder stared with wide eyes.

"This sheet is warm. Let me wrap it around you to warm you up." When the woman's face relaxed somewhat, I made sure she saw the sheet before I placed it around her shoulders. It wasn't long enough to cover everything but the most important parts were now hidden.

"Okay. Let's go this way," I suggested, heading down the hallway.

"No!" Ms. Snyder was determined to turn toward the coffee bar despite her earlier resistance.

My text dinged in my pocket but I wasn't able to see who it was from.

"Okay," I said to pacify her but eager to return the woman to her room. "Let's go this way first. It will be warm."

Finally, the word "warm" seemed to do the trick, and thankfully I was able to encourage her to enter her room. A nursing assistant named Misty took over from there.

"Where was she?" Misty asked, clearly perplexed.

"Riding the elevator."

"Unreal," she said, already pulling clothes out of the closet. "Thanks for your help."

"No worries." I left the room as my phone dinged again. The text was from Keith.

EMILY, I NEED TO TALK TO YOU. CAN WE MEET FOR DINNER?

My belly clenched into several tight knots. I wasn't sure why, but the tone of the text was unlike his usual lighthearted messages.

SURE, I responded.

Tonight was the evening Keith usually worked late at the ferry.

Something had to be important enough to cause him to leave early. Several scenarios twirled around in my annoying writer's mind. Was Gran okay?

Or maybe there was something wrong with Jenni's pregnancy. I prayed for the babies, for Jenni, for their family.

I hoped nothing was wrong with Keith.

Stop. All the different scenarios would drive me batty if I allowed them to.

The rest of the day seemed to last forever. I had to wait for a patient to return from a doctor's appointment, wait for the occupational therapist to finish with our patient, wait for another patient to finish eating lunch.

By the time I pulled into the parking lot of my apartment, my nerves were sharp and raw like a strand of barbed-wire fencing.

I made my way upstairs and glanced into Tucker's bowl, but there were ants crawling on his uneaten food. Daily I changed the contents of the bowl and watched out for him. Where was he? Once again different scenarios popped into my mind.

Enough already! It wasn't as though agonizing over all the unknowns made the outcome change.

I stepped into the bathroom to take a quick shower and to wash off the day. When I finished, I had time enough to write, but sat with my fingers perched on the keys without typing anything. The timing was perfect to write the black moment in my manuscript, the point where all was lost and the hero and heroine broke up, but I was far too concerned about the upcoming conversation with Keith to type a single word.

Instead, I paced the living room floor. He needed to hurry up and knock on the door before I wore a hole in the carpet. When pacing did nothing to ease my mind, I opened the sliding door and stepped onto the deck. The peaceful view of the estuary and the birds' sweet songs always helped to soothe my soul, but not today. He had bad news to deliver.

Chapter Twenty-Eight

Without much success, Keith had spent a large portion of the day on the phone. His first call was to the park service, but they refused to divulge the reason as to why he lost the contract except they had a better offer. He assumed he lost to his archrival, but the park service also refused to tell him who won.

Frustration was an understatement.

The next call he placed was to the architectural company in Raleigh. At first they played phone tag, but once he reached the man who had interviewed him, they engaged in a long conversation, ultimately requiring an in-house discussion involving negotiations. The end result? The pay range was on the lower end of the spectrum, and he would be working as a consultant until a permanent job became available. But what choice did he have? He needed to secure a job while the offer was on the table.

But first, he wanted to talk to Emily.

If he held out for a higher paying or a local job, there was no guarantee he would find one. An offer was better than a ferry business with limited income potential. He loved the laidback job of the ferry and its awesome view, despite the long hours, but architecture was his dream. As Jeff had said, maybe it was time to embrace the gift God blessed him with instead of hiding behind the ferry business after his father died. All he knew for certain was he enjoyed designing houses.

Thanks to his father, Keith had a considerable amount of inheritance money in the bank and invested, but he believed in keeping his savings intact instead of relying on the money for living expenses, another essential trait he learned from his financially secure father.

The hardest part of making a decision was telling Emily the options, not that there were many to choose from.

Doubts played with his mind. Was he a failure for losing the contract?

In all fairness, the ferry business was still operable. They were able to run tourists out to the different islands, just not Pony Island, the bulk of the profit.

He finished showering, dressing in nicer clothes than usual and upgrading today's wardrobe to khaki shorts and a polo. He ran a minimal amount of product through his wet hair to add a slight spike, brushed his teeth, and added a hint of cologne.

He despised conflict but wanted to include Emily in the decision-making process as much as possible. If he wanted a future with her, she needed to help define what their future looked like. Would they be able to sustain a healthy relationship with the distance between them? Traveling several hours roundtrip to see each other was less than ideal.

He arrived at her apartment complex later than planned. He hurried upstairs to knock on the door when Tucker meowed and rubbed on Keith's bare leg.

"Hey there, boy." He bent down to rub Tucker, who meowed.

Emily opened the door. "He hasn't been around since the last time you saw him."

Keith glanced up with his hand still on Tucker's back. "His food is untouched." Strange for a cat not to eat. He guessed it was likely someone else had claimed him and was feeding him too.

As if Tucker read his mind, he dove nose first into the bowl and ate every scrap of food.

"He's hungry, although not skinny," Emily said, watching Tucker with interest. "I can't believe he knows when you visit."

Keith grinned. He had been notorious for feeding the feral cats in the neighborhood when he was a kid. His mother always claimed he had a way with them. Although he loved animals, his main interest when he was younger was sports. Football, basketball, skateboarding, surfing, and sailing were just a few of his favorites.

The thought of his mom made him wonder how she was doing. The last he heard she was heavily involved in church, and for that Keith was grateful. She seemed to be dealing with his father's death in a healthy way, and Keith was starting to adjust to the idea of her moving on with her life. Of course, she had to, as Jenni pointed out.

Keith closed the distance between them and pulled Emily into a hug. She felt so dang sweet, like a southern girl offering him a glass of sweet tea. He pressed his mouth against her soft lips. Heck, she even tasted sweet.

Dang, he loved this woman. How was he supposed to leave her?

When they pulled apart, she closed the door behind her and together they walked downstairs with Tucker following behind them.

Emily turned back to watch the cat. "I swear he's been missing since the last time you saw him."

"Wonder where he's been." The only thing that made sense was what he previously thought. Tucker had another family feeding him. When Emily climbed into the truck, he closed her door. As he started the engine, he asked where she wanted to eat. He had a few ideas but had no preference. Being with her was the highlight of the night.

"Not sure." She took in his nicer clothes, a look of uncertainty crossing her face. "You choose. Seems you have a place in mind."

"Not really. How about something on the water?" The

weather was about as pleasant as a person could ask for. Hints of peach and neon orange lined the horizon.

"Perfect."

She was perfect. Perfect for him. If that were the case then why was he accepting a job out of town?

He pulled into the parking lot of one of his favorite waterfront restaurant, Wharfs, different than the place he had taken her before. When they entered the front door, surprisingly the hostess was able to seat them outside without waiting. Maybe the talk with Emily would go well. Everything else was falling into place.

After they glanced over the menus and ordered, she asked with apprehension, "So, what's on your mind?"

"What makes you think it's a serious discussion?" He was surprised she had read him so easily.

"I have come to know you fairly well." She drew a long drink from a glass of sweet tea.

Really, they hadn't been dating long. They had spent a lot of time together lately, talking on the phone every night before bedtime, and texting throughout the day. He suspected she did know him pretty well.

"What's on your mind?" she repeated.

Keith set his glass of sweet tea on the table and leaned back in his chair. Despite the tension in his gut, the seagulls laughed off in the distance as they flew over the dark water topped with a peach hue from the remnants of the sunset.

Her face was void of her usual smile. She knew the discussion was important.

"I heard back from the park service."

Silence.

He had to tell her and inhaled a long breath before he spoke. "Emily, I lost the contract."

She gasped and reached across the table to grab hold of his hand. "I'm sorry!"

She wasn't making the conversation any easier. Guilt was

eating him alive.

Tell her all of it.

"Em ..." He stopped midsentence, unable to say the words but her raised eyebrows forced him to continue. "I need to find employment elsewhere. The ferry can continue to service the other islands, but it's not profitable enough to sustain a living."

There, he said the news. At least some of it.

She looked away, studying a boat passing by. "What will you do?"

He squeezed her hand to regain her full attention. "I want to discuss the options with you first."

"What options?"

"I got an offer in Raleigh. Remember the company I told you about?" He waited for her response but there was none. "The company I interviewed with?"

She nodded.

"They made me an offer."

Silence.

"It's less money than I hoped for, but at least it's a decent job." He wished she'd say something, anything. "I know this is difficult, but I need a steady income."

"Sounds like your mind is already made up." She returned to staring at the water.

The sky was now turning dark.

He was unsure of how much to say. He didn't want to frighten her by admitting he wanted to spend the rest of his life with her. They weren't quite at that stage yet.

"Why ask me? You don't seem to have a choice." She was still staring out at the water.

The evening reminded him of the other night when they walked in the sunset, picnicking by flashlight by the dunes and counting the stars. It was the most romantic night he had ever experienced.

"I also received an offer as a chef at Stallings, but when

my father owned it, I swore I'd never work there again." The memories were far from good ones. As he told her before, he had no desire to endure the long, crazy hours again.

She turned toward him but remained silent. The tension between them made his nerves twitch.

"I can no longer imagine you working in a restaurant."

"True."

She closed her eyes for a moment as if to ward off the reality. "There are no architectural jobs here?"

He shook his head. "If there were, I'd snap them up."

The server approached, his arms full of plates laden with a colorful array of aromatic food. He set the roasted chicken in front of Emily, along with a heaping spoonful of mashed potatoes and steamed broccoli with melting butter. Then he set down a plate of golden baked fish in front of Keith. Whoever the chef was, he knew about food presentation.

They ate their dinner in deafening silence. From the tense expression on her face, she was pondering his announcement. And she didn't appear happy about his news. Although he wasn't, either.

The entrée was so mouthwatering, Keith devoured his food despite the stress at their table. Unlike Emily, who pushed hers around the plate.

"You okay?" he asked. He didn't know what to say to lessen the strain between them.

Not looking up, she shrugged.

"Em, I'm sorry." Her disappointment was so strong, he felt her pain. "I don't want to leave but I'm not sure what the answer is."

Silence.

"Come with me." He had to ask, knowing his offer was a long shot.

She glanced up, setting her fork on her plate. "Keith, I'd love to but I can't. My new home is here."

"Why?" He valued her new life, her job, but she hadn't lived in Big Cat long. If she loved him, wouldn't she at least entertain the idea of moving to the city with him?

"I left Raleigh for a reason ..." He watched her hesitancy and it frustrated him.

It was his turn to set down his fork, although he was almost finished eating. "Is it Frank? Haven't you moved past him yet?"

A wave of anger flashed in her eyes. "I love you, but I have bad memories of Raleigh. For a lot of reasons, it's not somewhere I want to live." She pushed her untouched plate aside. "I'm sorry but I have no desire to return."

Why was she so stubborn?

How was it possible she loved him but still harbored good or bad feelings for Frank, keeping them apart?

"So we can't come up with a plan together? Em, you know I don't want to leave, right?" Keith accepted the check from the server and asked for a box, but maintained eye contact with her.

She frowned. "You don't have an option. The ferry can't support both you and Captain Bill, there is no available work in Big Cat as an architect, and you have a job offer in Raleigh. I can't imagine us being apart, either, but I don't see what other choices we have right now."

"I'm not sure I can go, Em." A surge of grief weighed his heart down to the point he thought it would break in two.

She glanced away. "And I don't want you to."

They sat at the table, neither of them talking, as there wasn't much to say. She was right. He had no choice.

"I don't want to date someone who lives hours away. What about impromptu dinners like we enjoy? What about ice cream, exercising, just being together? I don't want to walk by the ferry and not see you." She closed her eyes and then reopened them. "A long-distance relationship isn't what I want."

He nodded to show he understood but wondered if this was her abandonment issues rearing up. "Move with me, then."

She pulled in a long breath. "I love the beach, the salty air, the way I can write so easily down here."

It was his turn to remain silent. Did she love the beach more than him?

"If you accept the job, when do you start?" Her eyebrows were drawn in a straight line as if she feared to hear the answer.

It was difficult to talk, his throat thick with emotion. He took a sip of water before he attempted to speak. "As soon as possible."

She stared down at the box the server brought. He wondered if she was disappointed in him, in their relationship.

The sad expression on her face was almost more than he could tolerate. He reached out for her hand resting on the table and held it. She didn't pull away but also didn't exhibit any reaction whatsoever, disturbing him more than if she had become angry.

"I'm sorry." He said the words not only for her but for himself. "We can make it through this. Long distance relationships do work. We can see each other on weekends, and as soon as a job becomes available here, I'll apply."

She sat there with more silence, scraping her food into the box. He was unable to break through her intensity.

"I do wish you'd share with me why Raleigh is so repulsive. I know the reason but not the why." He hoped she would explain but she didn't respond.

After he paid the bill, he stood, ready to leave. For a moment he thought she was refusing to move, but then she pushed away her chair and stood. He placed his hand on the small of her back and guided her through the crowded restaurant. The ride home was silent.

When he parked, she climbed from the truck. He had planned to hug her, to kiss her, to talk more with her, but she didn't allow him the opportunity.

He climbed down from the driver's seat.

"I'm fine. You don't need to walk me to the door."

"I want to." Besides, he wanted to see her safely to her doorstep.

Somehow, he needed to fix things between them. She was putting up an emotional wall as if he'd moved already and her reaction bothered him.

She didn't comment, didn't resist his effort, so he took hold of her hand and they headed upstairs. When they were at the doorstep, she didn't linger but unlocked the door.

He swallowed hard. "Can I come in? I'd like to talk more about our plans for our future."

She shook her head. "There is nothing to discuss." She stepped inside, hesitated, then closed the door. The sudden dismissal startled him.

It made no sense to him why they weren't they able to continue their relationship long distance. She didn't have to shut him out, but apparently she didn't love him the same as he did her. It was best he found out now.

Sorrow weighed heavy on his heart as he left her apartment. He had imagined the night differently, had wanted a proactive conversation to develop a plan together.

Once he reached his bed, his thoughts turned for the worst. If this was how they worked together to decide their fate, they flunked. He was a fool to fall in love so fast. From past experience, he knew better and he had a sudden urge to start the new job quickly. Why stay in town with painful memories of Emily around every corner? The agony was too much.

Chapter Twenty-Nine

Tears covered my face. Even the frogs croaking in the night didn't ease the pain as I sat on the balcony. Already I missed him.

Vivid memories flashed in my mind's eye, a sad but romantic relationship ending in heartbreak. I saw us holding hands on the beach at sunset, the picnic under the stars by flashlight, the confrontation with the stallion in the graveyard. The ferry rides.

More tears.

My heart ached so much it was practically ripping out of my chest.

He was leaving, moving to Raleigh. A long-distance romance wasn't what I envisioned when I fell in love. With him gone, we would be limited to weekends at most, text messages and phone calls. I had pretty much experienced this with Frank because he travelled all the time, and look how that ended. He cheated on me. Hardly the romance of my dreams.

But dreams were just dreams, nothing more, nothing less.

I grew up with my father living far away and that was no life. This situation stirred up my abandonment issues, and if he didn't understand ...

Too bothered to sleep and with the night still young, I decided to embrace my emotional state and dump my painful feelings into my manuscript. Unlike my stories, though, the inevitable happy ending wasn't real life.

Barefoot, I padded inside and retrieved my lonely laptop resting in a rejected state on the couch. I set it on the countertop, heated a mug of decaffeinated green tea with a hint of mango, my go-to choice when I was sad or in need of nurturing myself, and returned to the balcony. The tree frogs serenaded me in their rich tone and then stopped at once. One alto frog began the song again and the others joined in, then they stopped suddenly in unison. Strange how they coordinated the timing.

I opened my laptop, the dismal breakup scene vivid in my mind. Taking a deep breath, I placed my fingertips on the keyboard, the frogs singing a bleak song, and words flowed from my mind faster than my fingertips could keep up.

The scene was dark, heavy, intense, all aligning with my current mood.

When I finished writing, the night had grown late but I didn't care. What was time anyway? It was the weekend and I no longer had plans. The last thing I wanted was to see Keith before he left town because the pain was too great.

I knew how I planned to resolve the couple's conflict in my love story. They always talked out their problems well, and I pondered how I'd resolve the situation if I were writing about us. I wanted the happily ever after too.

When I climbed in bed and snuggled under the sheets, I cried myself to sleep.

The next morning I woke up later than usual and had no desire to pull back the covers and start the day. What did it matter if I stayed in my cozy bed for hours? Sadly, I had no one to answer to.

It wasn't until my full bladder and growling belly beckoned me to roll out of bed that I got up. It was ten o'clock already but maybe my body was trying to tell me I needed a recuperation day.

After returning from the bathroom, I cooked a vegetable omelet and then sat in my favorite wicker chair on the back porch among my flourishing flowers. Thanks to my mom's influence, I had decided to try my skill at gardening in pots and had researched and learned, and so far I was rewarded with success.

Plants were easier to learn than men.

Having little to no appetite, I forced the omelet down. More than anything I needed to keep up my energy and not to allow stress to deplete my body. Of course, following my own medical advice wasn't easy. I set the empty plate on the nearby wicker-and-glass table.

For the twentieth time, I glanced at my phone but there was no good morning text. The gaping hole in my heart ached as it grew bigger. Really, it was my fault, but I couldn't bring myself to text him first. Ridiculous I know, but my fear of failure took over. Because of what I had been through with Frank cheating on business trips and then some, I was afraid of a long-distance romance.

I hadn't read my email in two days and silently scolded myself. Professionalism was important, especially with publishing inquiries out there.

Clicking on the program, I winced when a succession of emails dinged in my inbox. My eyes stopped on a message from my first choice of agents, dated yesterday about the time Keith made his announcement.

Did I dare open it when I was already overwhelmed and distraught? If the email was a rejection letter, I would be devastated. I didn't think it was possible for me to handle it right now. But if it was an offer of representation ... that was a different story.

With shaking hands, I clicked open the email.

As I read the letter, my heart practically sank to the bottom of the Atlantic Ocean. *I'm sorry to inform you that your project is not the right match for me.* The email encouraged me to continue submitting to other agents.

More tears fell from my face. I don't know why I tried so hard to write when all I received were rejections. Writing absorbed most of my free time, most of my vacation days. Maybe I needed to reconsider.

Prior to reading the email, my plan was to sit on the porch and edit the scene I wrote last night. But I was no longer interested in reading my own depressing words. I pushed aside my laptop to wallow in misery.

Returning to bed was an inviting thought. If I slept the day away, maybe my pain would disappear, even if only temporarily.

Oh, come on. I'd survived breakups with men and rejections from agents before.

Girl, get up and get your groove back. I would excel again.

Wasn't I allowed time to grieve, to feel sorry for myself? Of course I was, but I didn't have to hide under the safety of the covers of my bed.

Exercise. I needed to shower, get dressed, go for a walk.

And that was exactly what I did. Not up to my usual pace, I strolled until I found myself walking past the ferry and staring at the dock to see if Keith was working. Captain Bill was near the boat but there was no sign of Keith. I forced myself to continue on, but my feet led me to Coffee Break. The last thing I wanted was to talk to Keith's sister.

I ignored all common sense and opened the door to the coffee shop. The inviting jingle from above welcomed me, and I found myself in line behind a handful of people. Jenni and Alex were hustling behind the counter and hadn't noticed me standing there, lost. When the line advanced and it was my turn to order, I stood there clueless.

Jenni scooted from around the countertop and pulled me into a hug.

My throat tightened from Jenni's unexpected display of affection. I attempted to fight off tears but they dripped down my face.

"Everything will work out one way or the other," Jenni said, squeezing me tight.

Jenni's baby bump pushed against me, and while I was

happy for them, it made me think about the babies I wanted with Keith. Well, my dream was shot dead.

"I love you like a sister," Jenni said, pulling away but still holding onto my shoulders.

Another wave of tears threatened to spill from my eyes. I needed to get it together.

"A delicious mug of coffee will help. What would you like?" she asked, changing the subject.

I stood there speechless with more salty tears dripping down my cheeks.

"Oh, honey." Jenni hugged me again. "I'll make a special blend for you. Don't worry, I've got you covered." She scooted around the counter and busied herself by making me a fix-all potion of goodness.

When she returned with the drink, I handed her cash.

"This one's on me." She passed me a large mug, the coffee smelling divine and soothing my insides without even a sip.

Friendships warmed a person too.

"Thanks, Jenni." In a dull semi-trance, I carried the mug to a cozy corner to sit. The sense of family was so strong here in Big Cat, I never wanted to move and leave all this behind.

"Tell me what my brother did?"

I jumped, not realizing Jenni had followed me. While I wasn't one to share my innermost feelings with even my family, I decided to open up to her. After all, I just showed my vulnerable side to her by crying.

"I know he accepted a job in Raleigh," Jenni continued, not seeming to notice my hesitation. "He's crazy to move to the city, to leave you, but he has to work."

I remained silent but when she said the words it made me feel as though I was being selfish. I was acting like a spoiled, frightened little girl.

"I know," I managed to say.

Claire entered the coffee shop. Jenni flagged her over and scooted to the far side of the booth, and Claire sat next to her. I had the best friend group a woman could ask for.

"We were just talking about my brother," Jenni said, filling Claire in on our conversation.

Claire frowned and crossed her arms.

I wondered if she knew Keith accepted a job in Raleigh. Who was I kidding? Of course she knew, this was small-town living. Gossip ran rampant through small towns faster than cell phone service. Maybe I was just gossip.

That was unfair. These women had shown me nothing but kindness from day one. When had I become so cynical? It probably started when my abandonment issues had.

Jenni turned to Claire. "My brother accepted a job in Raleigh."

"I know. My husband told me." Claire gave me an empathetic frown. "I'm sorry." She tilted her head and said, "He asked Jeff if there were any local jobs for an architect in this area. Jeff's brothers come from a line of builders."

"At least he tried to stay in Big Cat," Jenni offered.

Their words validated what Keith had tried to say at dinner.

Claire leaned in and touched my hand resting near my mug on the table. "When I first met Jeff, I knew he was the perfect man for me. Then I found out he had a fiancée. Let me tell you, I was crushed. Never did I believe he would dump her and marry me." Claire smiled, her face lighting up. "Lynette Cooper is the queen of divas. She is rich and spoiled, and basically tried to bully me out of the town."

"I can relate," Jenni said. "I almost lost my coffee shop because there was another woman after Scott, and he was the decision maker about my loan."

I swallowed a lump in my throat almost the size of Sam's throat pouch when he swallowed a fish. "Are you saying Keith has another woman after him?"

"No!" both women cried out.

"We were just trying to say love isn't always easy." Claire pulled her hand away from mine and flashed me a nostalgic smile. "I never thought I was going to marry him, or have his kids, but here I am. The best advice I can give you is to have patience. What is meant for you, no one else can take away."

I wasn't sure I believed Claire's words, but who was I to argue?

"What about your writing?" Jenni asked. "Have you heard back from anyone?"

I turned away. No tears allowed. Usually I wasn't one to let my raw emotions hang out on the line to publicly dry, so I swallowed hard around the lump in my throat. I could do this, and I would do this.

"I got another rejection letter," I managed to say.

Both women sighed.

"But I have high hopes," I said, mostly to ease the concern of my friends. "I'm waiting to hear from one more agent who is reading the full manuscript." If I didn't hold onto the belief my book was well written and creative, that it would sell to a publishing house, then I was afraid I'd be all too willing to give up the game.

"Great!" Jenni said. "You have another opportunity. Are there more agents you can send to?"

I nodded, not feeling excited about pursuing agents right now. "Yes, but I don't have it in me, plus I want to wait to hear from the one agent who is still reading my manuscript. She is my second choice. No, I thought the other agent was my first choice but she wasn't a match."

"There you go," Claire chimed in. "There is someone better for you."

"Yeah." Jenni leaned toward me. "Remember to have faith in the process and to keep reaching for your dreams. *Believing* seems the lesson you are supposed to learn right now, between Keith and your book."

I stared at Jenni. She was right, and look how far I had come. My new friends were sisterhood, and they offered me an honest opinion of my situation.

The week dragged by in slow motion, and neither Keith nor I had reached out to each other. No calls, no texts. Even though I missed him, it didn't change the fact I didn't want a long-distance relationship.

Sorrow filled my soul as I realized how much I'd fallen in love with him. Keith was gone. The urge to call him was foremost on my mind but it wouldn't change the situation.

Once again, I glanced at the darkened screen on my cell phone. His frequent good morning texts had become familiar, his random playful comments, his goodnight calls. The cell phone stared back at me in deafening silence.

I should call to offer him well wishes on his new job, but I wasn't mentally in a good place yet. The unfortunate pity party I was attending alone wasn't over. I needed time to contemplate, to consider quite possibly he hadn't left me behind. That was an old way of thinking. Maybe Jenni and Claire were right, it wasn't about me but about financial responsibility.

When my cell phone rang, it startled me. It wasn't Keith but my father calling.

Haunted by my memory from my writing exercise with the little girl eating the pizza—*correction*—about my sister and me eating pizza the day he walked out on us, I fantasized about letting the call go into voicemail. I hadn't been able to talk to him since I remembered what happened, but today I was in a confrontational mood and clicked to answer the phone.

"Hi, Princess."

I fought off a growl. How dare he use my pet name. "Dad."

"Is something wrong?"

Oh, there was something wrong, all right. "We need to talk."

Needless to say, the discussion didn't go well. I had questions, a lot of them, and he had no answers. I asked why he left, how he thought his actions wouldn't affect his family for a lifetime.

Basically, he became defensive and dismissed the

conversation. It shouldn't have surprised me, as that was typical behavior for him. When things grew tough, he ran, or in this case, he said goodbye and hung up the phone. His lack of acknowledgement or ability to care for *Daddy's little princess* hurt.

I paced the floor, scrubbed the sink, disinfected the counter.

When the apartment was clean, I wished it were larger. What was I supposed to do with the anger, the adrenaline? I needed to distract myself.

So I sat on the couch with my feet tucked in a ball underneath me.

The thought of food made me want to vomit. I needed to force myself to exercise, despite the unappealing thought of moving off the couch, so instead I opened my laptop and stared at the screen.

Writing was less than desirable. Why bother?

I closed my laptop, having not written a single word yet again. How was I supposed to meet my self-imposed word count if I was unable to concentrate?

Mustering up enough energy to stand, I walked out to the sanctuary of my balcony. Reflecting my dismal mood, fog swirled off the water, creating a mystic ambience, and despite the warmer night, the breeze was slightly cool and danced in my hair. The curls I deemed obnoxious on more than one occasion blew around my face. I sat down and closed my eyes, breathing in slowly, allowing my soul to heal.

The fog carried a light mist, making my skin damp and causing streaks of hair to stick to my face. The layer of fog wrapped me in a protective cocoon and brought me a sense of comfort.

I imagined myself on Pony Island, standing on a dune with the salty breeze blowing in my hair and something lighthearted and spiritual cleansing my soul.

Time stood still. The only things in existence were the fresh air, the song of a chirping bird nearby, and the most incredible feeling of love I had ever experienced. The light breeze made one side of my face cool and was as refreshing as drinking a cold glass of lemonade on a hot summer's day.

The longer I sat on the balcony the more difficult it was to remember where I was, what all I had to accomplish today. My muscles were weak, relaxed, as I slumped against the back of the chair.

Thoughts of Keith surfaced but I pushed them away like a passing storm cloud.

A message popped into my mind, so loud and clear I chose to listen. *Have faith. Whatever is meant to be will be. Believe, trust, and most of all ... forgive.*

Forgiveness. How in the world was I supposed to forgive all that happened in my life? Like my father, my family in general, Frank.

Words began to flood my mind and a strong inspiration to write overcame me.

I went inside to retrieve my poor laptop and with excitement I brought it back outside to the porch. To clear my mind from obligations, I pulled up my email program. Staring at me was an email from the last agent reading my full manuscript.

If it were another rejection, now wasn't a good time to read it, as I had just recovered from the previous one and was finally excited to write. I minimized the screen and pulled up my work in progress. I tried to write but the nagging unopened email stole the earlier words that had flooded my mind.

Fine. If I read the email, I had to promise myself I would write no matter what the news was.

I inhaled a long breath and released it.

I opened the email and began to read. *I am pleased to have read your manuscript. I would like to extend a formal offer of representation. If you would please call me at a convenient time for you, or respond to this email to set up an appointment to discuss the details, I will be looking forward to hearing from you.*

A gasp and then a squeal bubbled up inside of me as I

leaned over and reread the letter again and again to make sure I understood it correctly. Each time I read it, my excitement grew.

When I stopped shaking enough to type, I wrote back and thanked her for reading my material and for the offer. As much as I wanted to call her now, it was the weekend and I was in no shape to talk anyway. I suggested we set up a phone appointment after work on Monday, and in the meantime, I planned to enjoy the news.

As usual, I reread my response several times over to double check my grammar and to make sure my words sounded somewhat intelligent. After I hit send, I pounced off my chair and jumped up and down, performing the happy dance in the middle of the deck with the fog swirling around me.

I wanted to call someone. Keith, to be exact.

Longing overwhelmed me. I pushed away the negative feeling, not allowing thoughts about him to impact my good news, but they did. I had long awaited, years anticipated, an offer of representation.

I dialed my mother, only to get her voicemail. I left a brief message asking her to return my call, and I had some good news to share. My voice was at such an elevated octave I was unsure she would recognize me had I not identified myself.

All the excitement and no one to share it with made me pace back and forth.

To my pleasant surprise, my cell phone rang and it was my best friend Kelly, who must have read my mind and called.

"How is everyone feeling?" I asked, remembering they had all been sick when I went up to Raleigh to pick up my mom and sister from the airport.

"All back to normal. How's the man thing going?"

Keith. "Not so good." I hesitated, unsure of how much detail I wanted to share. The breakup was too painful to talk about. "He moved to Raleigh for work." There, straight to the point.

"Oh, no! How often do you get to see him?"

"Well," I said as I moved into the living room to sit on the couch and curl into a pillow. "I decided not to keep dating. A long-distance relationship isn't what I want." Keith probably despised me right about now.

Kelly exhaled into the phone. Not one to sit still for long she was probably multitasking and exercising while talking on the phone. "Em, what's a few hours' drive? You seem to really like him."

No, I loved him.

"If you think he's the right one, I hope you go after him." She breathed heavily into the phone again, and I was certain she was exercising while talking to me. "Don't miss out on this opportunity."

She was right. "I was foolish and now I'm trying to figure out what to do about it."

"Call him."

"Hmmm," was all I could say. "Oh my gosh, Kelly! I got an email from an agent and she made me an offer of representation. I'm supposed to talk with her Monday after work." My mind spun as I talked.

"Wow, awesome! No one deserves it more than you."

"I'm not sure about all that but thanks." We chatted a bit longer, delving into each other's lives deeper, and when we hung up, I missed her. I needed to exercise to burn off a combination of excess stress and exhilaration.

I changed into workout clothes, pulled my curls into a ponytail, and left the apartment.

This time Tucker was waiting by his food dish. He meowed at me, and I reasoned he must know Keith was no longer around, and I was his second choice.

"Be right back. Don't go anywhere." I picked up his bowls and filled them with food and water. When I returned, Tucker meowed again, and I took advantage of him eating to kneel down beside him. He moved away to the opposite side of the bowl to put distance between us. "I need to tell someone my news." Tucker watched in silence and continued to eat. "I received an offer of representation from one of my top choices of agents."

He finished his food and stretched out his neck, inching closer to me as if he understood my news was important. I reached out once again but he darted toward the steps, and then turned back to look at me. It was ridiculous to talk to a cat, so I stood and brushed off my exercise pants. "Never mind. I just wanted to tell someone." He scooted off as I passed by him to head downstairs but then he decided to follow me from a distance.

Amazing how the fog had lifted and the setting sun peeked through a band of clouds. Earlier, I had been engulfed in a layer of misty fog. Weather on the coast was so unpredictable.

Tucker followed me to the edge of the parking lot, still too cautious to venture close to me, but following nonetheless. I was learning to accept the fact he might never allow me to touch him, unlike Keith.

I went for a power walk to burn off the tension and excitement but quickly realized no matter how fast I walked, the fiery energy remained. I clearly needed to talk to someone about everything happening.

As I walked past the ferry, I glanced toward the quiet dock. It was late enough the last ride had already returned, and no one was around. The clouds near the horizon were turning their usual neon shade of orange and peach, casting a stunning glow across the dark water. I pulled out my cell phone and took several pictures of the boats bobbing in their slips with the sunset as a backdrop. I needed more photographs hanging on the bare walls of my apartment. Maybe I'd blow up my favorite and frame it to hang in the hallway, or next to the one I had bought from Claire.

When I strode in the direction of Coffee Break, I made the decision to interrupt my exercise routine to visit Jenni. As I entered the cozy shop the little bell dinged above the door.

There were only a few patrons sitting randomly throughout, chatting and drinking from mugs. Jenni was wiping down windows and looked up as I entered.

She flashed a half wave. "Hi there. It's good to see you."

"You too. How's Gran?" She had been on my mind lately.

Jenni rolled her eyes. "She's hardheaded but doing well. We hired a couple of high schoolers and Alex to help out."

"Smart idea."

Jenni sprayed another section of window and swiped a cloth over it, and then glanced up at me as she continued to work. "Thanks. She is actually letting them help her. I think she enjoys the company."

I smiled at the thought of Gran with the kids. "She loves socializing. I miss seeing her everyday but I'm glad she's home."

Jenni set the cleaning supplies down and turned to face me. "Keith has been wonderful. Because he isn't here to help, he pays for Gran to have groceries delivered, her house cleaned, and for a lady to drive her to doctor's appointments."

I knew he was a great man.

"I'm sure it takes a lot off your plate," I said, diverting my gaze from her at the mention of Keith.

"Call him, Emily. Be the bigger person." Jenni stared directly at me. "He's miserable."

I wanted to crawl and hide somewhere.

"It's obvious the two of you are meant to be together."

I shrugged. "Apparently it's not obvious. I understand he needs to work, but the thought of him moving away hurts."

"Go with him."

I turned away to hide a tear sliding down my face.

Jenni stepped forward and wrapped her arms around me.

"If it's meant to be, things will work out. That's how life is," I said, my voice rough.

"Sometimes you have to help love along the way." She stepped back to take in my appearance. "Why were you smiling as if you won the lottery when you first walked in?"

For a moment I had forgotten about my good news and the desire to share it with a human instead of a cat who mostly ignored me. My mood lightened. "I received an offer for representation from one of my top choices of agents." It took everything possible to refrain from jumping up and down near the front door of the coffee shop.

Jenni's face lit up. "For your writing?"

"Yes!" I had to breathe slower to keep my emotions in check.

Jenni thrust her hand in the air and met mine for a high five. "Awesome, girl! Are you going to accept?"

Never once had I thought about declining the offer. "Yes, I've done a lot of research on her and think we'll be a great fit." I was grateful to have someone to share the news with, and Jenni was fast becoming a close friend. Claire too.

"Not to change the subject back to my brother, but did you tell him? You know he'd want to know. He's miserable without you." Jenni's face dropped her smile.

I didn't know what to say. I wasn't feeling much better than Keith about the situation.

"Call him."

I shook my head. I wanted to, I really did, but I needed more time to sort out my thoughts. The fear of loss weighed heavily on my shoulders.

Chapter Thirty

"You're visiting Big Cat, for sure?" I asked my mother on the phone after I mentioned the literary agent's offer. She was excited for me and had known how long I had wanted this dream, and how hard I had worked to obtain an agent.

"Yes. I'm looking forward to attending the reveal party and meeting Clark's friends and family."

What about meeting my new friends and family?

Not only was my mother visiting Big Cat, a town I claimed as my own, but she was attending Jenni and Scott's party. Despite the possible pleasure of seeing her, I still didn't want to share the safe haven I called home. Not yet. On top of my obvious territorial feelings, I had changed my mind about looking forward to meeting her boyfriend. It was too soon and I didn't like him living in Big Cat. The past seemed to be colliding with my present life, and in general, I often resorted to my annoying tendency to naturally resist change.

I glanced around my small, one-bedroom apartment. "Do you want to stay here with me?" I felt obligated to offer her my bed.

"No thanks." My mom paused. "I have a place to stay."

A hotel, the boyfriend's house?

Mom hadn't dated in a long while and the thought was awkward for me, although truly, I was happy for her. I wanted to see her couple up, to grow older with someone. No one was meant to live life alone.

The thought drove a sharp knife into my heart as I couldn't help but think of Keith.

"How's the man you're dating?"

I drew in a long, deep breath. "Well ..."

"Trouble already?"

"Not really." How much did I want to explain? "He lost the ferry contract to service the island with the wild horses. In order to find work as an architect, which he went to college for, he had to move to Raleigh."

"I'm sorry, sweetheart."

My mother never called me pet names, so maybe dating the doctor was bringing out her nurturing side. "I'll survive." I excelled at surviving.

"Will you continue to date him?"

"Long-distance romances don't work for me," I explained as I folded my legs underneath me on the couch. "I want someone to stop by in the evenings for long walks, for ice cream, for random dinners."

"Do you trust him?"

"Of course." I did trust him.

"I understand. But remember one thing," she said. "If he's the right man, a couple hundred miles between you isn't a big deal. You will both find a way."

I had forgotten Mom was in the midst of a long-distance relationship, and apparently they were handling it well.

"Everything always works out for you," she said with encouragement.

At first I wanted to argue, thinking back to Frank. That hadn't worked out well. But then, as I pondered the words, I had to admit dating him had led me to Big Cat, to a new life with new friends, and to Keith. Mom's words brought me some degree of solace.

"By the way, Terri said to tell you hi. All she does is work at the hospital and sleep."

"Tell her hi too, and to relax some." Maybe my feelings were changing about my sister. I changed the subject back to Keith. "I'll figure things out with him and I appreciate your advice. By the way, Dad called and I finally confronted him about walking out on us."

Silence.

"I wasn't able to hold it inside me any longer. I needed the conversation, especially with all that's been going on," I explained, my hand shaking as I held the cell phone. "Anyway, what he did was wrong."

Mom sighed. "Emily, maybe it's possible he was doing the best he could at the time."

I gasped. "What? How can you say that?"

"Trust me, it took me years to heal from what he did. But now I have forgiven him, for my own benefit, not necessarily his. I can understand how being a young parent had overwhelmed him."

"He left us because he was overwhelmed? Why are you making excuses for him?" The anger boiled inside me and threatened to spill over.

"As you get older, you start to realize we are all human. We all have our reasons for behaving the way we do." She sighed as if to allow me a moment of reprieve. "We have no way of knowing what's going on inside someone else's mind."

"I don't care what was going on in his mind. What about mine and Terri's minds?" I drew in a sharp breath. "What about you?"

"I understand why you are hurt, but things work out for the best, even if you don't understand why they happen. Being resentful hurts you, not him. That's all I'm trying to say."

It took a few more minutes of challenging my mom to realize she was right. It was time to let go of the past, to have faith my life was working out the best way possible.

After we disconnected the phone, Jenni called to check on me, and then Claire, just as awesome friends did. Claire invited me to Pony Island for one of her photography shoots of the wild horses, and while I valued Claire's work, I wasn't ready to venture out to the island yet. Not only did it remind me of Keith, but I wasn't ready to board the *Sea Horse Ferry* anytime soon. Right now the ferry still serviced the island until the new system took place.

Both Claire and Jenni called several times over the week, trying to engage me in activities with them. Finally I agreed to participate in dinner and a movie at Jenni's house. I wasn't prepared for the framed photographs hanging on the walls of the hallway of Jenni and Keith's childhood, not having noticed them before. The numerous photographs consisted of them on their father's sailboat, family Christmases, and working at Stallings.

I marveled at what appeared as the picture-perfect childhood, but to hear Keith discuss the subject, he had less than positive memories to share.

I picked up my cell phone. How could I love him and then drop him like an unwanted adverb from a manuscript? What the heck was wrong with me if I couldn't set aside my abandonment and trust issues for a chance at a relationship with him?

The next move was mine to make.

Move to Raleigh, a voice whispered.

But I didn't want to leave all I had created here in such a short time.

The move is temporary.

What if it was permanent? If I moved, I had to consider it a long-term relocation in order to avoid any resentment down the road if we never returned to the coast.

Did it really matter where we lived? But we both loved Big Cat.

And therein was the irony.

Jenni grilled chicken on the deck, Scott was working late at the bank, and it was just us girls plus their friend Gabbi, Jenni's artsy friend from the last get-together. I was truly enjoying their company until they started prying for information about my current status with Keith.

"Will you still see each other?" Claire asked. Of course she wasn't being nosey as much as curious.

"Would you consider moving?" Jenni asked. "I know my brother loves you."

"If you moved, could you find work easily?" Gabbi asked.

Physical therapy jobs were easy to find and not the problem. I had always imagined living in a quaint cottage with large windows and a view of the marsh, so my dream house was at the coast, not Raleigh.

"I love it here," I said, as if the words were answer enough. I didn't want to explain my past or admit I was actually considering following Keith to the city. That would cause a plethora of more unwanted questions.

Each day my friends initiated phone calls and extended offers to partake in activities. While I appreciated their attention, their concern was a bit overwhelming. Small-town living had its pros and cons, for sure.

Jenni had said Keith had started his job as a consultant, with the understanding they would offer him a full-time position after the first of the year. They were busy working on a large project right now and needed immediate assistance until the full-time position became available.

Jenni also said he wasn't contacting me because of the way things ended and he was under the impression that was what I wanted. Confused, I still had no solid answers as to if I wanted to relocate.

By the end of the week, I was missing Keith even more. I wanted to hear his voice, to see him, to hold and kiss him, and the silence of my cell phone was deafening. My mom always called me stubborn but I was just slow to process decisions. In the meantime, I'd focus on my writing to help me ignore facing the truth.

○

Keith buried himself in work. Not only did he enjoy being an architect, he thrived on most aspects of the job and barely had time to miss the ferry service. Honestly, when he was on the water it was difficult to imagine working elsewhere, as the water filled his soul. Now, and to his surprise, it was difficult to remember the lifestyle, or living in a small town.

And Emily. With the long hours he chose to work, he managed to push her out of his mind. Almost.

He was beginning to believe he wasn't cut out for romantic relationships. Who needed to endure heartbreak more than once in a lifetime? He thought the first time was painful but it was nothing compared to now. He loved Emily with all his heart. And here he was, alone and hurt.

Didn't she understand he needed to work, to make a living? Heck, to have a career? The ferry business was about to change drastically. There was always enough work to keep Captain Bill busy running to the other islands during the summer months but not enough for them both. If Keith wanted to fill his soul with green marsh and blue saltwater, he could visit.

And Sam ... he missed the bird already.

But he missed Emily more than he cared to admit. She was everything he was looking for in a woman, and more. Meeting her had been a blessing.

He glanced around his office space, filled with cubicles and people working diligently. A pang of regret shot through his chest, so sharp he wondered if he would keel over and collapse on his desk. A break up with the woman he loved was difficult.

He would survive another heartache. This was where his stubborn side kicked in full force. In a perfect world, he could work and live in Big Cat, but in the non-perfect world, he only existed, and was lonely and sad. If Emily didn't understand his work situation, and apparently she didn't because she hadn't reached out to him, it was out of his hands.

He shrugged, then glanced around to make sure no one saw him or heard part of the conversation he had with himself, mumbling out loud. He was losing his mind.

Call her. Send her a text, anything.

His stubborn side kicked in harder. He had a job dilemma, and instead of deciding on a solution together, she rejected him. She wouldn't even give him a chance.

That hurt.

After work he went straight to the hotel. He hadn't wanted to rent an apartment until they hired him full-time, nor did he want to buy anything. One home was enough, even though it was at the coast. He still had to maintain the yard, the house, pay his mortgage, so he didn't want to add another financial burden or commitment onto his existing one. Right now a hotel suited him fine.

Except life in a hotel was dull.

He changed into his swimsuit and rode the elevator downstairs. The lobby was elegant, but if he allowed himself to indulge in self-pity, he had no one to enjoy the luxury with. When he reached the outdoor pool, there was a family of four playing in the shallow end. The two kids wore floaties on their arms and giggled as their parents twirled them in circles.

Keith wanted kids, a whole slew of them. But he wanted Emily as the mother of his children.

Let it go, dude.

Keith dove into the deep end of the pool and swam several laps, avoiding the family playing in the water. When he finished, he climbed out and sat on a lounge chair. This was his miserable existence. No Emily.

Chapter Thirty-One

Today was Jenni's reveal party and I had mixed feelings about attending. After all, Jenni was Keith's sister. All his family and friends would be at the party.

I enjoyed possibly seeing Gran again, not having the opportunity to visit her at home before Keith left, but now it was awkward to show up without him.

When my cell phone rang, I set down the tube of mascara and darted into the living room.

"Hi, Mom. You in town yet?" I sat on the arm rest of the couch to talk.

"Last night. I arrived too late to call you." She sounded young and vibrant, happy even. Love did that to a person, although I was in love and not experiencing romantic joy currently.

It was strange knowing my mother was in Big Cat while staying with her "boyfriend." But really, it wasn't my business.

We chatted briefly, and to my surprise there was a certain sense of security knowing she was nearby as opposed to Mexico, or even Raleigh. Strange, and I was unable to explain why, but the town felt fuller.

When we hung up the phone, there was still time enough to exercise before the party, but I wasn't in the mood to walk the usual trek downtown past the ferry. Unfortunately, Keith weighed heavily on my mind as if I could feel his presence.

I pulled on a pair of shorts and an exercise top. It was a short drive, maybe ten minutes, and I found a parking spot up front near the public access. That was the beauty of waking up early and hitting the beach before the crowd flocked to the ocean.

I had mixed feelings about walking on our sunset and stargazing beach again, but at least I was no longer crying when I thought about him. Somehow I found a way to love him from afar.

I walked for a couple of miles until the morning's heat pressed down on me with the promise of a hot day. When I turned around to return in the direction of my car, a four-wheeler with the license plate tagged "Turtle Watch" approached me. It stopped at a roped off area with yellow caution tape. The woman climbed off the vehicle and tagged the pole with a red flag, currently housing a "Do Not Disturb, Sea Turtle Nest" sign along with an already existing yellow flag.

Curious, I approached the woman. "How do you calculate when the turtles will hatch? Is it based on when you first noticed the nest?"

"Yes, and a few other signs as well." The lady wore a sleeveless, lightweight shirt with a turtle embossed on the left side. She had her curly hair pulled back in a clip and sported sunglasses. "I love your interest in the sea turtles." She pointed to the center of the roped-off section. "See the crab hole in the center? There is movement underneath and the crabs eat the eggs."

"Oh, no."

She nodded. "It won't be long now. We'll monitor the nest tonight, along with nest number nine and twenty-one. We had one hatch last night."

I loved the thought of seeing the sea turtles hatch. "Don't you need to use an infrared light to watch at night?" I had read about the turtles in an article online once.

"Yes, we do. If you're around tonight, watching the nest hatch is an unbelievable experience."

"I'll consider it." I wasn't sure I wanted to sit all night waiting for eggs to hatch, if they even hatched tonight, but I was intrigued. Just yesterday I had seen a reminder asking residents to turn off porch lights, so the turtles didn't mistake them as the moon and head the wrong direction. The notices also warned about not digging holes in the sand, and to fill them in if needed, so the baby turtles didn't fall into them.

I chatted casually with the lady before continuing toward the public access where my car waited. What a delightful way to start my day. A clear mindset before the reveal party with Keith's family was an added bonus.

Once I returned home, I showered, dressed in a cute pair of white shorts and a colorful-flowered top for the party, and then sat down to write before I had to leave. The scene in my book took shape as I wrote about the two main characters working out their differences by talking. The heroine was being stubborn until the couple realized they were both wanting the same thing but just saying it differently. She had to drop her own plans and compromise, realizing she felt better by working together instead of alone.

Maybe I needed to apply the same important lessons my characters had in order to have our own happily ever after. *Forgiveness.*

The timer buzzed on my phone, and I was glad I was in the habit of setting an alarm. Otherwise, I would continue to write well into the day without realizing I missed the party. I barely wanted to attend, other than seeing Gran again. Everyone would ask what happened with my relationship with Keith, if I had heard from him, if we were still dating now he moved.

With reluctance, I slid off the couch and sauntered into the bedroom to touch up my makeup to make myself presentable. I took my time, deciding to be fashionably late. My plan was to drift in, mingle as if I had been present all along, and then slip away without notice. No harm in showing up briefly to support my friend, to hear the gender of the babies, to talk to my mother and her new boyfriend. Then I could disappear back into the quiet world of my apartment.

I wasn't up to smiling and acting jovial, as if I didn't miss Keith.

When I left the apartment, Tucker was nowhere around, his food untouched once again. I shook my head, perplexed. What was up with him?

By the time I arrived at the party, it was in full swing and thankfully Keith's car wasn't parked out front. Talk about an awkward moment if he were there.

People spilled out of the house and onto the back porch, chatting and laughing. I approached a small group outside to blend in without making a grand entrance through the front door. If I were in a better mood, a party was a great place to meet new people, but I wasn't feeling sociable today.

I recognized a few nurses who worked at the rehab center, my dental hygienist, a few unknown but familiar faces. Standing just outside the open patio door, I saw my mother with a handsome man. A true natural at socializing, she was chatting to a woman while holding a small plate of appetizers and laughing.

As I approached, my mother smiled. Her new, beautiful implants brightened her face and she welcomed me with outstretched arms. A stranger would misunderstand our relationship for that of a close one. I hoped it was becoming that and returned the warm hug.

"Mom, you look wonderful," I said, referring to the teeth but not wanting to call her out on it.

Mom smiled again to show them off and thanked me for the compliment. I made eye contact with the man and the woman standing next to them and noted how familiar the lady looked but didn't think I had met her before.

"This is Ms. Stallings and Dr. Randolph, and this is my daughter, Emily." Mom's face lit up when she said her boyfriend's name.

And I swallowed hard when she mentioned Keith's mother's name. Of course she would be there, and I wasn't sure why I hadn't thought about seeing her before.

Ms. Stallings stared back at me too. "The Emily? As in Keith's girlfriend?"

Ex-girlfriend to be exact, but I despised how it sounded, so I didn't correct her. Speechless, I nodded.

To my surprise she reached out and pulled me into a warm hug. Never one to like physical touch from strangers—or well, even from my own family—her hug was a comforting, motherly embrace and made me feel like I had been away for years and had returned home.

When we finished hugging, Dr. Randolph stepped forward and extended his hand for a good old-fashioned shake, and then we chatted lightly. He was friendly, and I liked him immediately.

"Emily works at Waterway Skilled Nursing Center," my mom explained.

He raised his eyebrows. "I refer a lot of my patients there."

Before I could answer, my mother placed her hand on my back, unusual, and I reasoned Dr. Randolph was softening her. "Emily is a physical therapist."

His smile held approval. "They have the best therapy department within a 100-mile radius."

"Thank you," I said with pride, resisting the urge to glance around to make sure Keith wasn't in attendance, and I tried to focus on what he was saying to me. So far I approved of my mother's choice of a man. "I enjoy working there."

As we chitchatted, Gran passed by. She was navigating the grass with a cane quite well, and I credited the outpatient clinic for convincing her to use it.

"Excuse me for a moment," I said. I walked up to Gran and reached out to touch her arm. "Pardon me, ma'am," I said playfully.

Gran turned toward me and squealed. "If it isn't my

favorite physical therapist ever." Gran pulled me into a tight hug, and I was starting to get used to the ways of this small-town community. I was surrounded by new family, and original family, and my heart was full. Except a gaping hole that only Keith was able to fill.

Keith's mom turned to mingle with another group of people, and my mother and Dr. Randolph closed the distance between us and I introduced them to Gran.

"You must be proud to have such a caring, wonderful daughter," Gran said with affection. "She is the best."

"Oh, Gran." I blushed, certainly not used to such praise.

With the cane in hand, she wrapped her arm around me. "It's the truth, sweetheart." She turned toward my mom. "Like I said, I hope you're proud of her. She's like a granddaughter to me."

My mother wore an odd smile and I had to wonder if it was pride or jealousy. Interesting. "Thank you," she said politely. "You're right. She's a good girl."

The exchange was awkward, so I broke the ensuing silence.

"Let me pull up a chair for you." I didn't want Gran to feel as though she had to stand while talking to us, as she used to fatigue so easily.

"I'm not an old lady yet." Gran flashed the stern look I remembered all too well. "But I need to meander and visit. I love these events."

"I understand." Although I was disappointed at the short exchange between us, I made a mental note to seek her out later, so we had more of a chance to catch up.

Gran pointed her crooked finger at me. "I fully expect you to make amends with my grandson. He won't admit it to me, but he loves you."

I was taken aback for a moment by the direct order from Gran. I wasn't used to such a blunt, open family, where everyone knew each other's business and offered their opinions so easily. On some level I loved the meddling, but it also took getting used to.

My mom watched the exchange closely and I didn't enlighten her. Gran sauntered away, using the cane correctly half the time, and then joined another group of people.

"Remember, for the right man a long-distance relationship will work out," Mom said, looking up at Clark. He stared down at her, a loving expression passing between them, and I knew they loved each other. My mother broke the gaze and turned toward me, and I noticed the diamond ring.

"Mom?"

"I was planning to tell you when the timing was right." Mom glowed, grinning wide and leaning against her fiancé.

"How long?" I fought for composure while I resisted tears of elation.

"Last night." My mom allowed the news to sink in, realizing I needed a moment for my mind to absorb the information.

I inhaled a calming breath and then stepped forward to wrap her in a hug. "Congratulations." I hadn't predicted the engagement and wondered if my sister knew. When I finished hugging Mom, I reached out to shake Dr. Randolph's hand but then changed my mind and pulled him into a hug. This seemed to be the thing to do in Big Cat. When I stepped back, I couldn't help but smile at the happy couple. "Do you have a date yet?"

"Yes," they said in unison. Then my mother finished the statement. "Next weekend."

My mouth dropped open.

"I know it's soon but when you're our age, why wait?" My mom's face held an unfamiliar radiance.

"Wow," was all I was able to say. This was too much, too fast for me. My mom's diamond glinted in the sunlight and I wondered how I hadn't seen it earlier. I took hold of her hand and admired the ring. "It's gorgeous."

Once again, Keith popped into my mind and I had to fight a pang of sorrow. It wasn't right to let other people's happy moments cause me pain, and I despised my reaction. Yes, I wanted marriage and kids, but until then, I needed to celebrate other people's blessings.

"Where will you live?"

The couple smiled at each other.

"In Big Cat," Mom said. "I'll keep my house and we'll rent it out."

My mind swirled. I'd have the close family I wanted, at least in proximity, but on the other hand, I ran away to Big Cat for a reason and wasn't sure I wanted to share my newfound safe haven.

Claire walked up. "Hi, Emily. I didn't know you were here yet."

Busted for being late but at least someone knew I was missing.

"I wouldn't miss the party for the world," I explained, leaving out the part about not wanting to be here. Thank goodness for my meditative walk on the beach this morning.

I introduced Claire to my mother and Dr. Randolph.

"I'm glad you could make it to the party," Claire said to them, extending her hand. She was always sweet, the most genuine person I had met so far in Big Cat.

A little girl ran up and tugged on Claire's shirt. "Mom! I want a sandwich."

"In a minute, honey." Claire played with a long curl in her daughter's hair. "This is Beth, my bounding joy."

I bent down toward the precious girl. "I love your dress."

The girl slid behind her mother's leg but peeked out, smiling.

"If you want, I'll help you with the sandwich," I offered.

The little girl stepped out from her mother's side and slipped her hand into mine, and I swear my heart melted. We walked inside toward the buffet table, offering a plentiful selection of sandwiches, chips, vegetables and dip, and other various temptations that didn't bode well for my plan to tone up and lose a little weight.

Just as I scooped pretzels onto Beth's plate, a ruckus ensued near the front door. A group of people gathered around a man. I glanced up, although it was difficult to make out who he was with the crowd, but I recognized the back of his head.

My heart lurched and my emotions soared high for a moment only to land hard with the awful heartache I had come to know all too well.

When Keith turned, his gaze met mine.

We stared at each other while he hugged relatives. He pulled his gaze away from mine to hug his mother, who embraced him as though she hadn't seen him in years. Whatever issue they had in the past seemed to evaporate.

Jenni, Claire, and peaceful Gabbi had parked themselves next to me, although I didn't recall when they had walked up.

"Can I have my plate?" Beth asked me.

"Oh, I'm sorry." I leaned over to hand it to her and Beth said thanks while she flashed her precious smile, and then scurried off to eat outside with more family.

When I glanced up, Keith was watching me closely. I wanted to run away, wanted to hide, but my feet refused to budge.

Keith stepped toward me but Jeff and Scott intercepted him.

I turned to leave when Jenni placed her hand on my arm. "Don't," she said.

I paused, fighting off the urge to run outside.

"Give him a chance."

Jenni was right. I fingered the silver heart necklace with diamonds still hanging around my neck.

You have my heart, he had said.

Keith closed the gap between us, and without hesitation he pulled me into his arms and kissed me square on the mouth. I softened into him and thought I heard a few folks clapping but it was too hard to notice anything other than Keith. When he pulled his lips away, still holding me close, I swore the room was spinning.

"I've missed you," he said.

Unable to speak, I smiled and buried my face into his neck. Tears trickled down my cheeks.

"I love you." His voice was deep and sexy.

Thankfully, I found my shaky voice and was able to whisper, "I love you too." When I glanced up, the room blurred with people watching, but I noticed my mom studying us with interest and curiosity.

He took my hand, winked at his sister and Claire in possibly a silent thank you, and we walked from the house, across the yard, and to a bench under a large magnolia tree. The scent of the widespread white flowers was overpowering in a delicious way.

We sat next to each other on the bench, not speaking for a long while. I knew we missed each other, loved each other beyond belief, and wanted a future together.

Uncertain as to how the logistics would play out, I decided to believe in miracles and to allow the details to work out without my interference. As my mom had said, if he was the right man, a long-distance relationship would succeed. After all, driving to see each other was better than being without him.

His familiar, light scent of ocean breeze swirled around me as if I were enveloped in a safe cocoon. His masculinity was difficult to resist as his strong arm wrapped with casual ease around my shoulder. He made me feel feminine, beautiful, as we stared into each other's eyes, smiling like school kids with a crush.

The aching hole in my heart filled with joy by his mere presence.

"I never want to let you go again," Keith said.

I swallowed hard. "Me either. What made you come home?"

"My sister told me you missed me. That's all I needed to hear."

I stared up at him, grateful Jenni had intervened. "It was all my fault. When you left, it tapped into my abandonment issues and I'm sorry."

"It was both our faults. I'm sorry too, Em."

His touch felt like home.

"I love you." He didn't wait for my answer and pressed his lips against mine, lingering.

He tasted of sea salt, and it made me wonder if he stopped by the ferry this morning for a visit, or did he take a ride out to the island? The one time I avoided the ferry and drove to the beach, he was likely on his boat.

"You ... taste good," I said.

He kissed me deeper. We fit together perfectly.

We sat there, so absorbed in each other I almost forgot where we were. When I remembered Jenni, I pulled away, albeit reluctantly.

"The reveal party."

"I forgot. Nothing but you existed," Keith said, planting a quick kiss on my lips. "We need to return to the party." He stood first, holding out his hand to me.

My legs were wobbly as we walked back to the house, and I held onto him for support. When we entered through the sliding-glass door, I noticed my mom watching us. It was past time to introduce them.

I pulled Keith's hand to redirect him toward Mom. He raised his eyebrows in question but smiled when he noticed the older woman's attention on us.

We approached my mom and Dr. Randolph, a handsome older couple I thought, and Keith reached out to shake the doctor's hand. "Good to see you again."

"You too, son."

I spoke up. "Mom, this is Keith. Keith, my mom ... and you already know Dr. Randolph."

"Please call me Clark," he said to me.

"Nice to meet you, ma'am." Keith shook hands with my mom, who was still scrutinizing him but smiling. He seemed to want to pull her into a southern hug, as seemed the theme of this party, but he picked up on her reserved nature. The difference between our families was vast.

Keith straightened and Clark gave him a quick slap of affection on the shoulder. Keith returned the sentiment with a squeeze of Clark's elbow. "I've known Clark since I was a boy. He was good friends with my dad," Keith explained to me.

Clark sighed. "Sorry again about your father. He was a good man."

No one else other than me seemed to notice Keith glance away at the mention of his dad. The emotion was still difficult for him to hide but he recovered rather quickly.

Jenni dinged a spoon on a glass to attract everyone's attention. Scott, the soon-to-be proud father, grinned like a mischievous boy as he stood next to her.

"You all know why we're here," Jenni said, choking up as she spoke. She looked up with adoration at her husband.

People hushed, turning their attention to the couple.

Keith wrapped his arm around me as we listened.

"Cupcakes are being passed out," Jenni explained. "The inside has either pink or blue colored icing injected in the middle. The gender of the twins is the same. Don't eat the cupcake until everyone has one."

A little girl, likely one of the many nieces in the family, carried a small tray of cupcakes up to us. Keith took one, handing it to me, and then selected a cupcake for himself. My mom and Clark each chose one off the tray.

Once the cupcakes were passed out, Jenni counted to three. In unison the group peeled away the paper and took a bite.

Blue icing filled the cupcakes. Twin boys!

Keith glanced down at me and gave me the lightest little peck of a kiss. I was sure to have blue icing on my mouth but he didn't seem to mind. For some reason, announcing the baby's gender, being with Keith, realizing how much I loved him, emotionally touched me and I fantasized about someday announcing our own baby's gender to the same group. Overwhelming love for him filled my soul.

After the party was over, we went to a late lunch, or early dinner—depending how we looked at it—with my mom and Clark. My mom's light spirit and almost constant smile spoke volumes. It was nice to see her happy.

After we finished eating, Keith drove me back to my car still parked at the party.

"I've been meaning to ask how your writing is going," he said as I climbed out of the truck.

I had no idea how I had forgotten about my good news. A surge of excitement erupted from me and I said, "I got an offer of representation from an agent!" I wanted to do the happy dance once more but was able to contain my enthusiasm enough to appear happy but calm.

His face lit up. "Wow! Congrats, Em." He wrapped his arms around me, lifted me up, and spun me around twice. "I'm so proud of you."

We kissed once again. Making up was delicious.

"I need to run home to change clothes first," he said when he pulled away with utmost disappointment in his voice. "But do you want to meet up tonight for a stargazing walk on the beach to replay one of my favorite memories?"

How could I resist his offer? "There is a turtle nest ready to hatch soon. Interested?"

"Yes," Keith said with a tone so light my heart danced. "As long as I've lived here, I've never seen the turtles hatch."

I hoped it was our lucky night and we were blessed enough to see the endangered sea turtles endure their sandy path to the ocean to begin their courageous journey. My intuition said tonight would be a memory I wasn't likely to forget.

Chapter Thirty-Two

It was unbelievable Keith was here in Big Cat, and he'd be here any minute for our sunset walk on the beach to watch the sea turtles. I hurried to finish applying the last light swipe of blush onto my cheeks. When he rapped on the door, I was ready and more than eager to leave. As I stepped into the hallway, I noticed Tucker chowing away at his food.

I pointed to the cat as I locked the door behind me. "Incredible. He hasn't eaten a bite of food while you were away. How does he know you're back?"

Keith shrugged. "I hope to never disappear again." He kissed me, lingering against my lips, and I darn near was giddy from excitement. When he pulled back, staring straight into my eyes, he said, "Seriously. I plan never to leave you again."

I wanted to believe him, I really did.

"I can see the all-too-familiar frightened look in your eyes." Keith held me close and his embrace was steady, loving.

I shook my head, choosing to believe in him by forgiving the past. It was time to move forward with my life. "I've had nothing but time to think, and you're worth leaving this sweet town behind. Who cares where we live as long as we are together."

He arched his eyebrows. "Wait a minute. You're willing to move to Raleigh?"

I nodded and lifted my chin up high.

He planted a small kiss on the tip. "Sweetheart, you are amazing." He held me close and tucked a curl behind my ear. "But you don't need to move anywhere."

He kissed me until a furry object rubbed against my leg. Tucker! He was touching me.

I bent down, extended my hand toward him, but he was more concerned about rubbing against my leg. I used slow movements, and he allowed me to touch his back and then pet him.

"Wow, can you believe this?"

"What progress you've made with him while I was gone."

I shook my head. "Like I said, he hasn't been around."

"It's a good sign then that things are meant to be with us." He placed his hands on my arms. "Em, I'm moving back home."

"Home?" I repeated, barely able to comprehend what he was saying.

"I'm moving back to Big Cat, honey."

"Really?" I folded myself into him. He was so warm, so strong, so … *mine*. "Where will you work?"

"Do you remember Jeff?" He pulled away from me, took my hand, and we walked downstairs toward the truck, Tucker following us.

We crossed the parking lot hand in hand, birds singing a melodious song nearby. "Of course, I remember him." He was Claire's husband, the wildlife biologist on Pony Island

"His cousin owns a construction company and knows a lot of people." Before he opened the door for me he took hold of both my hands. "Turns out, he knows someone in a small company one town over. They are hiring an architect for a new construction project. It is a huge job and will be ongoing."

"They hired you?"

He nodded. "They sure did, babe." He squeezed me into a loving embrace.

My mind swirled in circles and I was almost dizzy with love.

"Can you trust me once more?" he asked.

I had to catch my breath before I could speak. "Absolutely." I spoke the honest truth, and I smiled as he exhaled a long silent sigh.

The drive was as good a time as any to tell him about my father. As we headed down the road toward the beach, I said, "I need to tell you something." He visibly braced from what I might say.

"Did you date someone else?" His brow creased with unnecessary worry.

I tapped him on the arm. "No!"

"What a relief."

I shook my head at him, shocked he would think I could date someone else already. We climbed from the truck and headed in the direction of the beach.

"While I was writing, a disturbing scene unfolded all too easily, and I remembered the painful moment my dad left us. I was in the third grade and my sister in the second." I swallowed hard, finding it difficult to get the words out. "Keith, after all these years I remembered him leaving us." I paused for a moment to shake off a wave of emotion and he squeezed my hand tight.

When I could speak again, I said, "He called me the other day and I demanded answers but he wouldn't talk about it." I spoke so fast I hoped he understood the intensity of the situation. "I was so angry at him until I talked to my mom."

He stopped walking and we stopped in the middle of the sidewalk, and a handful of people had to navigate around us. "And I did the same thing to you. I promise I will never leave you again, and I mean it, sweetheart."

I glanced up at him and held his hand tighter. "And I'm not going to let you get away, either. We're in this together." Our conversation was better than any scene I wrote in my manuscript. "You know, things unfolded the way they were meant to. As everything came to a head, I had the chance to heal from my past, from my father leaving us."

"We both did a lot of growing." We started walking again and turned down a side street to the public access. "Just curious. Why did he leave in the first place? Did someone abandon your father when he was young?"

I stopped dead in my tracks. "His father died when he was young."

"How old was he?"

"I don't know. I think he was eight or nine."

His eyes widened, eyebrows raised. "Third grade? The same age he left you and your sister?"

I gasped.

I had an epiphany and realized my father was also suffering from abandonment issues. He had his own set of scars to work through.

"I think you hit on something powerful," I said, my voice thin and shaky. Years of stress poured from me like a thick layer of fog rolling out to sea. The setting sun filled me with a thawing warmth.

My father was as wounded as I was.

We stepped off the wooden walkway and onto the beach. I kicked off my flip-flops near a tussle of sea oats and took hold of Keith's hand. We strolled down the beach and the turtle nest was much farther than I remembered. Just this morning I had been lost in thought, daydreaming about Keith, missing him, but a few hours later here he was, walking next to me as a couple.

The sun ball was sinking fast, casting a fiery glow across everything its rays touched. A jagged, bluish purple tint painted the horizon line, almost resembling distant mountains. Just above, an array of orange hues streaked the sky in dramatic effect with flattened white clouds to top it off like whipped cream. The wake of vibrant colors was one of the best sunsets I had yet seen.

Keith stopped, ankle deep in the water, and pulled me into

a romantic embrace.

"I love you and never want to be without you again," he said, pulling my attention to him as he dropped to one knee.

I was unsure why he was kneeling in the water with the waves splashing into him.

He held my hand tight, and with his free hand he pulled from his pocket a ring, the diamond glistening in the hue of the sun.

"Will you marry me? Will you spend the rest of your life with me?" Keith asked, looking as if he might break into tears.

I stood there, a wave crashing into us and splashing my shorts and legs. It took a moment before I understood he was proposing to me.

He didn't appear to mind getting wet as he waited for my answer. "Will you marry me, Em?"

"Yes. Yes!" I wrapped my arms around his neck and had to fight off my own tears.

He stood, scooping me into his arms, planting the longest, most delicious kiss of my life on my mouth. He tasted of saltwater and was damp and sandy, but I didn't mind. This man was perfect for me in all ways. I squealed as he placed the ring on my finger.

I stared at the diamond, tears of delight running down my face and mixing with the salt water. "It's gorgeous." In awe, I pressed my lips to his again.

The sun had long disappeared. I barely noticed how fast our surroundings grew dark, as if someone had dimmed a light switch.

"I love you, Emily. My fiancée," he said as if trying the words out for size.

My heart about jumped in my throat. "I love the way that sounds, and I love you."

Hand in hand, we continued to walk in the surf toward the nearby turtle nest. It seemed like eons ago I was sad, lonely, and upset. Amazing how fast life changed in just a few hours.

It was dark when we reached the turtle nest. Several people were sitting on the beach, waiting for the possibility of watching baby sea turtles hatch.

Together we sat for hours, not that I minded one bit, as we snuggled into each other to keep warm from the chill. I was more than comfortable sitting between his legs and leaning against his chest as we stared up at the stars once again.

"Venus," he mentioned, pointing at a bright planet in the dark sky. "I did my research this time."

His ring on my hand filled my heart with love, hope, dreams.

Marriage. Keith.

"What time frame are we looking at?" he asked, his low voice vibrating against my cheek.

The thought was so new to me I hadn't thought about it. "I don't know. As soon as possible, a year, now." I fought off a giddy laugh.

"Look!" a woman said with excitement. "The sand is moving!"

We jumped up and brushed the sand from our legs and shorts. We moved closer to the nest and pressed our arms into each other as we stood near the roped-off section. The moon lit up the nest, and several of the volunteers had infrared lights to highlight the quaking middle section of the sand.

One, two, three minutes ticked away in slow motion. Finally, a tiny sea turtle emerged, followed by several of the cutest little critters. More followed until a stream of squiggly reptiles erupted and scrambled atop each other, the volunteer calling it a nest boil.

Thankfully, the nearby houses perched along the edge of the beach had their porch lights off and the full moon illuminated a glowing path to the shore. More turtles climbed from the nest. To give them a fighting chance from predators, in unison they made their way across the sand to the water as the crowd watched in awed silence. A few of the turtles tumbled into deep footsteps in the sand and had to scramble to climb their way out, but once they did, they made their way toward freedom.

Chills covered my arms as I watched the most amazing scene unfolding in front of us.

A small handful of turtles headed in the wrong direction. Not allowed to assist them physically, one of the main volunteers of the local turtle group used her sneaker to flatten a path in the sand to help redirect them. All but one rebel turned toward the path to the water.

The woman hurried in front of the turtle and built up a sandy mound and dug a rut with her shoe to redirect the sweet little baby. We silently cheered when the turtle followed the track and headed in the correct direction.

With their legs made to paddle the water, awkwardly they bounded their way across the beach to the surf, leaving tiny prints behind in the sand. A wave rolled in and swept them out to sea.

A tear slid down my cheek as I bid them goodbye. "Have a safe journey," I whispered.

When the last turtle made its way to the surf, the crowd cheered. They high-fived each other, made promises to get together for a celebratory dinner one night next week, and then we dispersed into the night with flashlights.

I was lost in thought about the events of today, and quiet on the ride home.

"Everything okay?" Keith asked.

"Yes," I mumbled. "I didn't expect the sea turtle event to touch me so emotionally."

"Me either," he said as he pulled into the parking lot of my apartment. He held my hand as we walked upstairs, where Tucker was waiting, curled up on my doormat.

"We'll have to take him with us," Keith said as I reached over Tucker to unlock the door. "I imagine we'll live in my house."

"At least I haven't unpacked most of my boxes yet." I turned around into his arms and looked up.

He kissed me instead. When he finished, he asked, "What kind of wedding do you want?"

I hadn't thought much about weddings lately. Frank and I had planned to have a large wedding to accommodate his big family and many friends. "Nothing big. Something simple, romantic, and small," I said.

He chuckled. "There is nothing small in this town when it comes to weddings. We are all one big family."

I loved the sound of having an extended family. It was the reason I moved here. My circle was growing even larger with my mother moving to town and marrying Clark.

"Just an idea," he said, his eyes gleaming. "We could have the small wedding you want, maybe on my ferry boat. And then the reception could be big."

"Wonderful idea. What will happen to the ferry service now?" Here we were, talking about *our* wedding.

"I will continue to have Captain Bill service the smaller islands. It will allow me to help out whenever I want, but I'll have the stability of a better paying job to support our family."

Our family. I just about grew dizzy thinking about it.

My life had changed from my father abandoning us, my past relationship crumbling, moving to Big Cat, to meeting my soul mate, signing on with a literary agent, getting engaged to the love of my life. What more could I want?

The biggest lesson I learned was it was far better to open up emotionally and to share my life with someone I trusted. Good communication was key, just like the main characters in my manuscript. And this time the happily ever after was *ours*. Life was one big blessing.

Epilogue

My mother's smile lit up her face as she secured my veil. The past year housed a lot of changes for us all. Mom was happily married and loved living in Big Cat. My sister and I started to talk more and she visited Mom often. Our sibling rivalry wasn't abolished completely, but we were making progress. I was also glad she still lived in Raleigh, so the distance between us helped. One step at a time was how I chose to accept our relationship. At least she was here for my wedding and helping me.

And Frank ... I had received one text from him a few months after his impromptu visit to Big Cat. Actually, he apologized to me and said he planned to no longer bother me. He was admitting himself to an inpatient rehab to overcome drug and alcohol addiction. The drugs were a surprise to me. And just like that, I never heard from him again.

I glanced around at my friends and family. We stood in a small room at the back of the bookstore across the street from Keith's ferry. In less than a half hour, I would be the proud wife of Keith Stallings.

I swear every nerve ending in my body was on fire and jittery.

All of my favorite females surrounded me to make sure I was dressed to perfection. My mother fussed and shifted my veil once more, and my sister, Terri, shook her head in disapproval, wanting it to look just right. Keith's mom, who

I had practically adopted as my second mother, messed with a stray curl running down my shoulder. Claire and Jenni knew the bookstore owner well, and the kindhearted woman agreed to allow us to convert her backroom into a dressing room for the wedding. My best friend, Kelly, and the free-spirited Gabbi, who I had come to know much better from more girls' nights, finished dressing. The only female I adored that was missing today was Gran, but she planned to show up for the celebratory dinner afterward.

A tear sprung to my eye when I realized I was about to inherit my very own grandmother. I needed to stop being so emotional, so I didn't ruin my makeup.

After the approval from my sister about the veil, my mother flattened my off-white dress with her hand once more.

"Mom, if you keep touching her dress, the oils from your hand will stain it," Terri complained, becoming unusually protective over me.

Mom sniffled. "Hardly. Doesn't she look like a princess?"

Princess. The name reminded me of my father and I wondered if he would show up to my wedding. It had taken close to a year to process my feelings toward him, and we had just started talking again.

"A successful author princess," Terri said. "Not only do I want the first copy of her book when it's released, but she has two more on the way. And she's getting married to the most handsome man in Big Cat."

"Hey there," Jenni protested as she picked up a baby and handed him to Gabbi's outstretched arms, and then she gathered the other baby and held him close. No way could I tell the difference between the two boys. "For the record, I consider my husband the best-looking man in Big Cat."

"And mine," Claire said.

"They are all nice looking," I said to make peace, although hands down Keith was the most attractive man in this town, if not the world.

"Let's get this wedding moving," Terri said when the horn from the ferry signaled the men were ready.

Chills ran up and down my arms. I had goose bumps because the man I was about to marry was my lifelong dream, the answer to my prayers.

Taking ownership, my mom scooped the train of my dress into her arms and carried it as we strolled across the heart-pine floor of the bookstore. Here I was, about to be married.

"Congratulations," the owner called out to me.

I smiled so wide my face hurt. "Thank you again!" I held up my flowers and waved.

We crossed the street, my mother passing off the train to my sister. "It's heavier than it looks," Terri said.

Jenni laughed, juggling a baby in her arms. "Good thing she didn't buy the other dress she tried on. It would have taken two of us to carry the train."

The women laughed but their voices were a blur to me. The moment was surreal.

There, standing on the *Sea Horse Ferry*, were the men. Even Keith's pelican, Sam, was waiting on the piling to greet us. We strolled down the dock toward the boat, toward Keith. As I neared, our eyes locked and I knew the real meaning of love. Love was a man I wanted to spend the rest of my life with, a man who was kind, thoughtful, spiritual, loyal, a man who loved me as much as I loved him.

The wedding march played from a speaker and filled the salty air, and I swallowed a lump forming in my throat.

I glanced around for my father. He was there, standing next to Jeff and Scott, laughing as if nothing had transpired between us. He glanced up, smiled, and mouthed, *I love you, Princess*.

Jeff reached out his hand and helped me on board. My sister set down the gown's train, allowing it to sweep across the boat's deck. I made my way to Keith, who stood at the helm with Pastor Dave and one of Keith's cousins, Matt, who was a local policeman. I noticed Terri exchanging warm looks and a flirtatious smile with Matt. Interesting.

Captain Bill winked at me and started the boat. We coasted over the water, and Keith chose a cove just off Pony Island for the exchange of our vows. I held his hands, lost in his gaze, and the ceremony was a blur. I barely remembered the words we said, repeating the vows we had practiced last night. The two of us stared at each other with love and affection as we exchanged rings and our first kiss as husband and wife.

~~The End~~

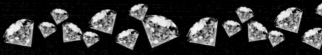